Forever, Darling

Linda Fausnet

My books contain steamy sex, bad words, and human beings of all sorts, include gay people. If you're not a fan of those things, you may want to stop reading now. If you're cool with that stuff, come take my hand and join me on this journey...

Published by Wannabe Pride 2016

Editing by Katriena Knights

Cover Design by Chuck DeKett

Formatting by Polgarus Studio

FIRST EDITION.

Library of Congress Control Number: 2016915780
ISBN: 978-1-944043-08-7

To my husband, Bill Fausnet.

You are forever my darling.

Books by Linda Fausnet

Romance

The Gettysburg Ghost Series

Somebody's Darling
Darling Soldiers
Forever, Darling

Women's Fiction / Chick Lit

Singles Vs. Bridezillas

LGBT Fiction

Queen Henry (**All proceeds from this book go to the Harvey
Milk Foundation**)

Middle-Grade Fiction

The Joyville Sweat Sox

Chapter 1

"I had no way of knowin' that I only had one hour to live."

Confederate reenactor and tour guide Jesse Spenser held the rapt attention of the tourists as he told the harrowing tale of the death of a soldier from the First Texas Infantry. Standing among the huge rock formations in the famous battleground of Devil's Den, Jesse certainly looked like a poor soldier from Texas. He wore gray wool pants, a white cotton shirt with suspenders, and a brown slouch hat. He also sounded like a real Southerner as he spoke with a thick, Texas drawl. The tourists were spellbound by Jesse's dramatic tale, but none more than the female tourists, who particularly enjoyed his tall, broad-shouldered build, sweet blue-gray eyes, and, of course, that *accent.*

"There was bullets whizzin' from all around, everywhere I turned!" Jesse exclaimed, his eyes flashing with excitement. "Then, outta nowhere, a bullet slammed into my right shoulder." Jesse grabbed his shoulder dramatically and grimaced like he'd been shot. "But I was okay! Oh, it hurt somethin' awful, but it wasn't no mortal wound. But then," He paused for dramatic effect. "Then another bullet came flyin' at me and hit me. Right here." He slowly raised his forefinger and pointed to his left temple.

A hush fell over the group as they waited for him to continue his story. Enraptured as they were, none of them could have guessed his secret.

Jesse Spenser had been a real soldier in the Civil War, more than one hundred and fifty years ago, and he was telling the story of his own death.

Thousands of tourists visited Gettysburg every year, but few were aware that some of the "reenactors" they saw were actually the restless spirits of real Confederate and Union soldiers still wandering the earth. Jesse had been one of them, having been trapped in ghost form for a century and half. Then he had fallen helplessly in love with a living woman named Lucy Westbrook. After recovering from the shock of learning Jesse was dead, Lucy fell in love with him, too. Instead of crossing over to heaven, Jesse was given the precious gift of life again. Now he was employed in the only job he was qualified for: Civil War reenactor. No one knew more about the town of Gettysburg than he did. He knew everything that had happened in the small town since he died in 1863.

Jesse groaned as if he'd been shot, then staggered backwards. He closed his eyes and fell to the ground. He lay there for a long time. Long enough for people to wonder if he'd really passed out or something. Jesse heard his co-worker, Remy Waters, giggle softly. She was used to his theatrics, yet she still found him entertaining.

Jesse suddenly jumped to his feet. "Okay! Now let's head on up to Little Round Top!"

The tourists laughed and started heading toward the tour bus.

As always, Jesse had sanitized the story of his death just a smidge. He had been shot in the shoulder and in the head, but unfortunately, that wasn't what had killed him. Moments before his death, Jesse had killed a Union soldier with his bayonet. He hadn't wanted to, but this was war, and he had feared for his life. The flag bearer of the

124th New York infantry, Joel Casey, was that soldier's best friend. In a fit of grief and rage, Joel shot Jesse in the head and then had stabbed what he thought was Jesse's corpse with the flagpole. But Jesse had still been alive. The flagpole being shoved through his stomach was what killed him. However, there was no reason for Jesse to horrify innocent tourists with such a gruesome tale. His being shot twice was all they needed to know.

"Oscar-worthy, Jesse," Remy said dryly, her pretty blue eyes sparkling with amusement. She pushed her shoulder-length brown hair out of her face as she smiled at him. She, too, wore a period costume: a simple, long-sleeved blue cotton dress with a floral pattern. She was dressed in character as Jennie Wade, a civilian who had been killed during the war as she stood in her kitchen baking bread for the soldiers. A stray bullet had struck her in the back, killing her. Jennie, not Remy. Unlike Jesse, Remy was flesh and blood and always had been.

"Okay, guys, let's get back on the bus and head on up the hill," Remy called cheerfully. An older man stopped to ask her a question, and she smiled warmly as she spoke to him.

Remy was a wonderful tour guide. She was smart, and she loved talking with people. Warm and friendly, she had a way of making people comfortable within seconds of meeting her. Jesse would never forget how kind she'd been to him on his first day of the job. She had no idea that working for the Blue and Gray Touring Company was Jesse's first real job *ever*. He had been terrified of screwing it all up, and she'd put him at ease right away.

Jesse and Remy rounded up the tourists and boarded the bus. Jesse took a seat at the front, while Remy stood up so she could address the group. She held on tight to the metal pole as the bus lurched forward.

"Okay, now we're headed up to Little Round Top. You might

want to get your cameras ready, because you're in for an incredible view of the battlefields from up there. So, how many of you have seen the movie Gettysburg?"

Some nods from the group, and Jesse raised his hand and said "I have!"

Remy laughed and so did some of the other tourists.

Not only had Jesse seen the movie, he remembered when they had filmed it on location here back in the early 1990s. He'd been in spirit form then, and watching them make the movie had provided him with hours of entertainment. As a ghost, he could be invisible whenever he wished and could go whenever he pleased. He even chose to be visible now and again, and often wondered if perhaps he'd made it into the final film somewhere, mixed in with all the reenactors.

"Little Round Top is the site of the famous, brave fight of the 20th Maine. If you saw the movie, Jeff Daniels played Lt. Col. Joshua Chamberlain, who led the charge."

Remy continued with the history lesson during the short drive to the large hill. When they reached the top, she announced, "Okay, we're gonna stop here for about twenty minutes. That should give you enough time to look around at the view and take some pictures if you like. Jesse and I will be available for questions, but other than that you're on your own to wander for a bit. There are several monuments here, including one where you can climb to the top and see for miles."

Remy and Jesse helped the tourists step down the steep stairs of the bus, taking special care with elderly and children guests.

Once everyone was safely off the bus, Jesse wandered over to find his new friend, Avery O'Rorke. Jesse always went out of his way to chat with Avery as often as he could, because he knew how lonely the man was.

Because he was dead.

Avery had died right here at Little Round Top on July 2, 1863. In fact, he'd been a part of the famous battle that Remy had just described on the bus. The charge of the 20th Maine. Except Avery had been on the losing side—he'd fought with the 15th Alabama Infantry.

Jesse found him sitting, or at least appearing to be sitting, on a huge rock near the 44th New York Infantry monument. Since he was in ghost form, he couldn't actually touch anyone or anything. He could choose to be visible when he wanted, so to tourists he just looked like another reenactor. If a ghost did choose to be visible, he'd better act like he was alive, lest he terrorize unsuspecting, breathing guests at Gettysburg. Thus, he chose to appear to be sitting.

"Avery, my man!" Jesse called.

Avery turned to him and smiled. He perpetually sported a gray button-down frock coat and gray trousers. He had brown hair and gentle gray eyes that lit up when he saw Jesse approaching. Jesse understood how lonely it was to be a ghost. Other than the occasional greeting or smile from a tourist, no one spoke to you. It was dangerous to get too close to the living, because it wouldn't be long before they discovered your secret.

"Jesse! How are ye?" Avery called out to him. Though he lived in Alabama while he was alive, he was originally from Ireland and spoke with a strong Irish brogue rather than a Southern accent. He had been part of an entire company in the 15th Alabama who were Irish, called Oate's Zouaves.

"I'm doin' well," Jesse responded. He glanced at the tourists milling around, keeping an eye on the ones wearing bright orange stickers indicating they were with his tour group. Everybody seemed okay at the moment, wandering around and taking in the sights, so Jesse sat down on the rock next to Avery.

Avery looked over at Remy, who was happily chatting with tourists. He stared at her, watching her brush her hair out of her face. She looked lovely as always, the color of her dress bringing out the blue in her eyes.

"How is she?" Avery asked.

Jesse smiled. Avery never actually came out and said it, but Jesse knew he was in love with Remy.

Though Avery had died in 1863 just as Jesse had, he had vanished for most of that time. Vanishing was different than simply being invisible. Being invisible meant you were still hanging around, but only other dead people could see you. Vanishing meant you weren't really conscious; you were still an earthbound spirit, but it was like being asleep. You could vanish for months, years, even centuries. But when you came back, your problems were still there. You couldn't cross over until you came to terms with whatever was holding you back. Avery had been gone for most of the time since he'd died, and had returned to consciousness just a few months ago.

The poor guy had been completely overwhelmed. It was like falling asleep in a time machine and waking up more than a century and a half later. What had been a horrific, bloody battleground was now filled with restaurants, shops, tour buses, and, most confusing, Civil War reenactors. Avery had been lost and terrified upon his return. Remy seemed to have radar for lost souls, usually tourists, and she had approached him with concern. She was the first person to speak to him in more than one hundred and fifty years. He'd stumbled out some story about meeting friends at a restaurant, and she'd cheerfully given him directions.

Avery hadn't been able to take his eyes off her since then. Not that Jesse could blame him. Remy was a lovely girl.

"She's doin' much better," Jesse reassured Avery. Remy had been sick recently. It was nothing major, just a bad cold, but she had lost her voice and had to miss a few days of work. Avery had been worried about her.

"Good, good," Avery said.

Jesse regarded Avery as he watched Remy. His heart went out to him. Jesse understood exactly how it felt to be in love with a woman who didn't even know you existed. Unlike Avery, Jesse had been conscious for much of the time since his death in 1863. He'd witnessed the changing times over the course of decades, but he had never known a girl as incredible as Lucy. He used to watch her work as a waitress in a local tavern. He would sit in the restaurant for hours, invisibly, falling more in love every day.

Remy walked past where Jesse and Avery were sitting. She smiled at them as she led the tourists over to the memorial of the 44th New York Infantry, which was a huge stone structure that resembled a small castle. Tourists liked to climb up to the top and look out over the battlefields. Remy obviously didn't remember speaking to Avery that one time, but then again she spoke to hundreds of tourists every week.

"Follow me. The staircase is in the back. You won't believe the view from up there!" Remy told her guests.

Avery watched longingly as Remy disappeared around the back of the monument. He looked up when he heard her voice coming from above. Remy stood at the top of the stone monument with several of the tourists from her group.

"Isn't it just breathtaking?" Remy said, as she looked out at the expansive view of blue sky and open fields all around.

Avery looked up at her and murmured, "My thoughts exactly."

Jesse chuckled softly. "She is beautiful."

Remy was a wonderful girl, generous and kind. Jesse considered her one of his closest friends, and he understood why Avery had fallen in love with her.

Avery continued looking up at her. "I feel like I'm lookin' at Juliet up in her balcony."

Jesse laughed again. "When are you at least gonna let me introduce her to you?"

"What would be the point?" Avery asked sadly.

"I dunno. Would be nice if you could at least talk to her. What's the harm in that?" Jesse asked. When Jesse was dead, he never thought he would get the chance to even speak with Lucy, yet here he was. Alive. And Lucy was in love with him.

"She might try to touch me," Avery said.

Jesse nodded. Avery knew all about Lucy and how she had come to know Jesse while he was still dead. His rival, the Union soldier who had killed him with the flagpole, had made a bet with Jesse that any random tourist woman would pick him if given a choice between the two. Joel Casey was dashingly handsome, and Jesse wasn't at all confident that he could win the bet, but he seized the opportunity to talk to his beloved Lucy. She became friends with them, but it hadn't gone over too well when she discovered the two were no longer alive. She'd accidentally touched Jesse, and her hand went right through his ghostly form. Terrified, she'd fainted.

"I can't stand the idea of frightenin' her," Avery said.

"I know," Jesse said. "Lucy was scared to death of me for a while, and it broke my heart. But she got over it."

Avery laughed. "Aye, that she did."

"Lucy was already terrified of ghosts when she met me. Believe me, that made it worse for her."

Avery nodded. "Yes, I suppose that's true."

They both knew Remy wasn't afraid of ghosts because she didn't believe in them. In addition to daytime tours, she moonlighted by giving ghost tours. She humored her guests when they claimed to see, feel, or smell something strange. She knew many of them were eager for ghost encounters, so she encouraged their stories and told many of her own. She didn't believe any of them, but she was happy to pretend she did.

"It would be wonderful to be her friend," Avery said. "I worry that's she lonely. She's got no family around here. I'm so glad you and Lucy are such good friends to her."

"I think it would be great if you and Remy could get to know each other. But, I gotta tell ya, Lucy doesn't want me to introduce Remy to you."

"Really? Why is that?" Avery asked, surprised.

"She adores Remy, and she worries about her. I know what it's like to be a lonely ghost, but Lucy knows what it feels like to be in love with one. She remembers how much it hurt when she couldn't touch me and how hard it was knowin' I could cross over any time and be gone forever. It was a miracle when I came back, but it ain't too likely that would happen again. Lucy doesn't want Remy goin' through all that."

Avery nodded, understanding. "That's awfully kind of her to be lookin' after Remy like that."

Jesse nodded and smiled. "Yeah. That's my Lucy."

"But, Jaysus, it's not like Remy's gonna fall in love with me. She doesn't even know me!"

Remy suddenly appeared from around the corner of the monument. Avery looked horrified. If he had breath, he would have been holding it. Remy was still talking with her tourists and walked right past Jesse and Avery.

"That was close," Avery said.

Jesse let out the breath that he *had* been holding and nodded.

"Is that Devil's Den down there?" a guest in his forties asked Remy.

"Yes!" Remy responded. "Exactly, that's where we just came from.

Where poor Jesse died." Remy gestured toward Jesse and laughed.

Avery and Jesse exchanged amused looks. They had discussed their deaths at length, swapping war stories, and had realized it was likely they had died around the same time on the second day of battle.

Remy walked off with her guests in tow, and Avery watched her every move. Jesse knew his longing for her was growing stronger every day.

"Maybe she and I could be friends some day. Maybe soon I'll be ready to try to talk with her," Avery said.

"You just name the time, Avery, and I'll make it happen. You know, provided I can get permission from my girlfriend," Jesse said with a grin.

Chapter 2

Ever since Jesse had joined the Blue and Gray Touring Company, it seemed Remy's circle of friends had widened considerably. She smiled as she sat at a table with Jesse, Lucy, and Lucy's best friend, Theresa, at a local pub in Lincoln Square.

"You weren't kidding about this place. This burger is delicious!" The huge sandwich tasted especially good since Remy hadn't had anything to eat since breakfast. Money was tight, and sometimes she had to skip meals to make ends meet. She'd graduated from Penn State last year with a degree in Recreation, Park, and Tourism Management and, between school loans and paying rent, she was pretty broke. She was worried about how much this dinner out would cost, but she was lonely and couldn't bear turning down the invitation to be with her friends.

"Is Sean still on base?" Remy asked Theresa, who nodded as she bit into her own sizable burger.

Theresa's boyfriend, Sean Stone, was a sergeant in the Air Force and was stationed at Joint Base Andrews in Maryland. Remy hadn't met him yet, but had heard good things about him not only from Theresa, but also from Lucy and Jesse.

"Let him stay on base!" Jesse declared. "I like being the only guy around you beautiful ladies."

Remy smiled at him. *He's so sweet*, she thought. He was handsome and chivalrous, and Remy had developed a huge crush on him when he came to work with her. Then she discovered he had a girlfriend whom he was madly in love with. Remy had been disappointed at first, but soon became quite fond of Lucy. Jesse had told Remy his girlfriend was painfully shy when first getting to know strangers, so Remy had been especially gentle with Lucy when they first met. Now they were close friends.

"Sean'll be back this weekend," Theresa told her. "Then maybe you can finally meet him."

"That would be nice," Remy said.

"Yeah, you gotta meet him. He's so nice," Lucy said. "And he's gorgeous."

Jesse frowned at Lucy, but then shrugged. "Yeah. I can't even argue. The guy is, as you ladies would say, '*hawt*,'" he said, making air quotes as he spoke.

All three women laughed.

"Seriously, he's really big and really cute, and I was afraid to talk to him at first. I know you're shocked," Lucy said. "But he's such a sweetheart."

"He is. And he's great in the sack," Theresa said.

Remy and Lucy giggled. Remy suspected had anyone else said that, Lucy would have blushed fiercely. She seemed to be used to Theresa's outspokenness by now.

Sean wasn't the only one Lucy had been afraid to speak to at first. Lucy had confessed to Remy that she'd been terrified of Theresa when she'd first been paired with her as her roommate at Gettysburg College. However, Theresa was as kind as she was bold, and she had helped draw Lucy out of her shell. They'd been the best of friends ever since.

Remy checked the time on her cell phone. "Oh, man. I gotta get going. I got two back-to-back ghost tours tonight." Though she enjoyed the ghost tours because she had fun with the tourists, she was already exhausted after being on her feet all day doing battlefield tours.

"You work too much," Jesse observed, worry in his voice.

"I work or I don't eat," Remy said simply. Things had been especially rough lately, as she'd had to miss a few days of work because she'd been sick.

"Speaking of which, I got this, hon," Theresa said as she picked up Remy's dinner bill.

"No way. I can't let you do that," Remy said, reaching for the tab.

Theresa triumphantly held the bill above her head. "Ha-ha, I'm taller than you! I'm paying it so quit arguing."

"Thanks, Theresa. I really appreciate it," Remy said, relief flooding through her. Theresa picking up the tab was a huge help, and they both knew it. Remy hated being dependent on people, but Theresa came from a wealthy family, and it wouldn't be a hardship for her to pay for Remy's meal.

"See you guys later," Remy said as she got up from the table.

"Don't let them ghosts getcha!" Jesse called out to her.

Remy giggled and rolled her eyes. "Yeah, okay, Jess."

*****

Lucy, Jesse, and Theresa found it amusing that Remy didn't believe in ghosts. She had just shared a meal with a former one, not to mention there was a certain dead Confederate soldier who was utterly enamored with her.

"Remy's such a sweet girl," Theresa said. "Can't help but think she deserves to know how that guy feels about her."

"Oh, now, don't you start," Lucy said.

"Well, it's true! She works herself to death, and I know she's lonely sometimes, and here she's got this man who's totally crazy about her and she has no idea."

Lucy nodded, but still felt torn. Theresa was well aware that Avery was dead and understood Lucy's reasons for not wanting Remy to know about him. Theresa had stood by Lucy during her whole relationship with Jesse, and no one had been happier for her than Theresa when Jesse had been able to come back to life. At the same time, Jesse's enemy-turned-friend, Joel, had crossed over to finally reunite with his wife and children. In fact, Theresa had been so inspired by what happened that she'd starting putting her psychology schooling to good use and ran a counseling group for some of Gettysburg's dead soldiers. And, since her boyfriend Sean suffered from Post Traumatic Stress Syndrome, she held a special place in her heart for soldiers who were suffering.

"I know Avery is lonely, too," Jesse said.

Lucy sighed deeply. From everything Jesse had told her, Avery sounded like a wonderful man. She knew he was lonely, and that made her sad. But Lucy couldn't help feeling protective of Remy. She was such a sweet girl, and Lucy didn't want her going through what she had gone through with Jesse. They'd talked to spirits who had been around since the great battle, and none of them had ever seen anyone else come back like Jesse did. Lucy didn't want Remy getting attached to this man, only to have him cross over and leave her behind.

"I know he is," Lucy said. "But I just can't stand the thought of Remy getting hurt. She has enough going on."

Remy was estranged from her family. Her parents had divorced a long time ago, and her mother was an abusive alcoholic who said terrible things to Remy, often calling her worthless. She'd even called her a mistake. A *mistake*. How could any mother say such a thing to her child?

"She sure does," Jesse said. "So don't you think she could use another friend?"

Lucy fell silent for a moment.

"I just remember how it feels to be like he is. You can't touch anybody, and people don't talk to you much." Jesse took Lucy's hand in his. "I was so lonely, and I was so much in love with you. I would have given anything just to talk with you, to hear you say my name."

Lucy squeezed his hand and smiled at him. She couldn't imagine what it must be like to exist as a ghost. She felt badly for Avery, all alone and pining for Remy. But Lucy remembered all too well that day when Joel crossed over and Jesse nearly followed him. Lucy wanted Jesse to be at peace, and had done her best to put his happiness above her own. When Jesse disappeared into the portal before his last-minute reprieve, Lucy felt like her heart had been torn from her chest. Had he gone, she would have grieved for him for the rest of her life.

"Do you think he's in love with her?" Lucy asked.

"Yeah. I really do," Jesse said.

Lucy sighed again. She let go of Jesse's hand so she could take a sip of her Diet Coke.

"You know that big memorial thing up on Little Round Top?" Jesse asked. "The one that looks like a castle?"

Lucy nodded as she drank her soda.

"Remy went up there today, and Avery said he felt like he was Romeo lookin' up at Juliet in her balcony."

"Oh, my God," Lucy moaned, putting a hand over her heart. Lucy was a hopeless romantic, and Jesse damn well knew it.

Theresa cackled. "You're wicked, Jesse. *Wicked.*"

Jesse grinned slyly. "Yeah, I knew that'd do it."

"He really said that?" Lucy asked.

"Yes, my lovely rose. He sure did." Jesse called her *rose* because he always said that, though she was a Yankee, she was his honorary yellow rose of Texas.

Lucy moaned again, and Jesse looked into her eyes.

"Darlin', they'll probably just be friends if I introduce them, and there'll be nothin' to worry about. I won't do it if you don't want me to, but I really want Avery to have a chance to talk with her."

"Really, Jess? The sad eyes?" Theresa asked. "Go ahead, Luce. Say no. I dare you."

Lucy slumped back in her chair, resigned to her fate. "I can't."

Theresa chuckled as she polished off the rest of her French fries.

Jesse grinned. "Thank you, darlin'! Everything is gonna be jus' fine. You'll see."

"Yeah, yeah," Lucy said, still unable to look away from that handsome face she loved so dearly. She sat up, gently touched his cheek, and smiled.

Chapter 3

Jesse sat on the steps of one of the historic buildings on Steinwehr Avenue in the main part of town. When he was dead, this spot had been one of his regular hangouts. It still was, since he was close with many of the spirits in town and it was impossible for anyone who had died in Gettysburg to go beyond the town limits. If they attempted to go any farther, they simply vanished and had to turn back.

"I told Avery to meet us here, Second Mama," Jesse said to his favorite spirit, a lady named Fillis who had died in her late fifties. She'd been a slave in life, and had made it as far north as Gettysburg after the master of the house discovered that Fillis had been having an affair with his wife. Fillis had fallen ill and died just before the great battle, and had witnessed firsthand the horrors of war. She was a motherly figure to many of the lost souls who'd died in battle.

"Good. He's such a sweet boy," Fillis said with a smile.

Like Remy, Fillis was always looking out for people who looked lost, only she focused on the dead. Fillis rarely vanished, and had seen most of the history of Gettysburg since she died in 1863. And, like Remy, she'd spotted Avery right away upon his return to consciousness. She had heard about him from some of the other ghostly soldiers, and when she first spotted him, he'd looked terrified.

She carefully introduced herself and had taken good care of him ever since. She loved being called "Second Mama" by her boys because she loved nurturing them but didn't want to take anything away from their real mothers. She considered herself a surrogate mama until her soldiers crossed over to be with their original families again.

Avery spotted them from a short distance away, and Jesse could see the relief in his smile. Though he'd died more than fifteen decades ago, he was still fairly new to the ghost life since he'd chosen to vanish for so long. He was nervous about being around the living for fear they would discover his secret. Jesse knew he felt safe hanging out with him and Fillis.

"Hello there, Jesse, Second Mama." Avery smiled and nodded his greeting.

"Hey, baby. How ya doin'?" Fillis asked with tremendous warmth and affection in her voice.

"Quite well. And yerself?" Avery asked.

"Jus' fine, honey," she answered.

"I got some good news for ya," Jesse said with a grin. "Lucy said it's okay for me to introduce you to Remy."

A panicked look crossed Avery's face, and Jesse couldn't help but laugh.

"Come on, man. It'll be fine. You're not proposin' marriage—you're just gonna say hello. Then she'll at least know who you are, and mebbe you can visit with her when we make our tour stops at Little Round Top."

"I don't know," Avery said, looking doubtful.

"Wouldn't it be nice if you could talk to her every day?" Jesse prompted.

Jesse saw the hopeful look on Avery's face and understood exactly how he felt. The highlight of Jesse's existence as a ghost had been those days when Lucy was working at the tavern and he could sit and watch her all day. He'd never been happier than the day he finally made his presence known to her and they were able to have an actual conversation.

"All right. I'm willin' to give it a chance," Avery said. "But I don't have any idea what I'm gonna say to her!"

"I know. That's what you got me for. We're gonna sit here and figure out what you're gonna say, all right?"

Avery glanced around at the tourists. "Are you sure it's safe, you know, for people like us?" He gestured at himself and Fillis.

"Trust me," Jesse said, lowering his voice. "Strangers don't usually reach out and touch us. Sittin' here you can say hello to folks and not feel so alone, but nobody's gonna figure out…you know."

Avery nodded uncertainly. Sure, there had been a handful of times over the years when a tourist had accidentally brushed up against Jesse, only to find he wasn't in solid form. Jesse hated frightening people, and he was especially heartbroken when he accidentally scared a child. Still, he usually took the risk to appear visible so he could interact with the living. It was wonderful to be alive again, but he knew he would never forget the loneliness, the isolation of being a spirit. That was why he was so eager to help Avery.

Avery looked around cautiously, then carefully sat down next to Fillis.

"You're fine here with us, honey. You'll see," she told him.

"Okay, Avery. Here's the plan. The next time our tour bus stops at Little Round Top, I'll just casually introduce Remy to you. I'm sure she's seen me sittin' with you sometimes, so she probably knows we're friends."

Avery nodded nervously.

"Now we just need to figure out how you're gonna answer any questions she'll have for you. You know, the usual polite stuff people ask when they first meet somebody. Easy questions for the livin' to answer, but a bit harder for you. Ugh, I made complete fool out of myself the first time I spoke to Lucy."

Avery groaned. "That's just what I'm fearin'!"

"That's not gonna happen with you, Avery." *Not on my watch,* Jesse thought. "My problem was I never thought I'd get the chance to talk to her, so I never thought about what I was gonna say! Of course, she looked at my soldier outfit and asked where I worked, and like an idiot, I didn't have an answer."

"Well, neither do I!" Avery cried.

"I know. So let's think one up."

"God, I hate lyin' to her."

"I know," Jesse said. "But you got to. Okay, so she's gonna see your Confederate uniform and she'll probably ask where you work. Joel and I told Lucy that we worked over there."

Jesse jerked his thumb at a nearby reenactor store that sold clothing and accessories. It was called the Regimental Quartermaster.

"That was all fine and dandy, until one day Lucy's friend, Theresa, went in there askin' about us."

"That's a fret!" Avery said, looking more scared than ever.

"I know. So we're gonna make up a tour company, so there's no way she'll know anybody who works there and she can't ask about ya. We'll tell her it's a new company."

"All right. Makes sense. What'll we call it?"

Jesse thought for a moment. There were all sorts of tours available in Gettysburg. Tour buses, trolleys, horse-drawn carriages, and even those motorized Segways.

"Tell her you're part of a walking tour. That way she won't be expecting to see you get on a bus or nothin'."

"Good, good. What'll we call the company?" Avery asked.

Jesse's eyes lit up. "Four Score Walking Tour!"

Fillis and Avery laughed.

"Clever, Jesse," Fillis said. "I like it."

"Me, too. I just hope I can get away with it without lookin' like a damned fool," Avery said.

"This girl must be very special to you, Avery," Fillis said.

"Aye, that she is," he said. "She's a wonderful gal, and that's puttin' it simply."

"You'd love her, Fillis," Jesse said. "She's real sweet. And if anyone needs a mama."

"Really?" Fillis asked with concern.

Jesse nodded sadly. "Well, she *has* one, but, you know…"

"Not a good one," Fillis said.

"'Zactly," Jesse agreed.

"Well, if this girl is as sweet as you say, she'll want to shake his hand. What then?" Fillis asked.

"Good point," Jesse responded. "Lucy was so shy that I knew it'd be a while before she tried to touch me or Joel. Remy's more outgoing."

"What do I do? I can't bear the thought of frightenin' her!"

Jesse nodded, remembering all too well when Lucy had been afraid of him. It had been unbearable. He suddenly snapped his fingers.

"I got it. Tell her you've been sick and you don't want to spread your germs."

"Germs? What are germs?"

"Damn, you have been gone a long time," Jesse said with wonder. "It's how sickness is spread. Tiny little bugs that you cain't even see. That's what makes you sick, and you can make other people sick if you shake hands and kiss and whatnot."

"Tiny bugs?" Avery asked, looked disgusted and little worried.

"Yep," Jesse said. "Not as bad as it sounds. Least we know more now 'bout how to keep from gettin' sick."

"I suppose." Avery looked a tad overwhelmed. "Jesse, I'm so nervous about talkin' to her!"

"It's gonna be just fine, Avery. I promise. You know how Remy is. She's the easiest person in the world to talk to," Jesse reassured him.

Avery smiled fondly. "Now that's the truth."

Fillis smiled as she watched Avery speak fondly of Remy.

"She has such a way with people, don't she?" Avery asked.

Jesse smiled. "Yeah, she sure does."

Remy knew how to read people, and she always seemed to know how to speak to everyone on their own level. She could put people at ease and make them comfortable in any situation. She exuded kindness and warmth, and people were drawn to her sweetness, not to mention her soft beauty.

"Well, I guess I'm as ready as I'm ever going to be. Except..." Avery looked over at Jesse, eyes full of worry.

"What?" Jesse asked.

"I know what I'm supposed to say to her, but what about the way I talk? I don't want to sound stupid to her."

"You mean your accent?"

"O' course!"

"Are you serious?" Jesse asked, incredulous. "Women go nuts over a guy with an accent. Lucy is crazy about my Texas twang for some reason, but you've got an *Irish* accent. Women fall all over themselves for a man who talks like you!"

"You got to be kiddin' me!" Avery said.

"You'll see. Believe me, you got nuthin' to worry about."

"Second Mama," Avery said to Fillis. "What about you? Would you go fer a man with an accent like mine?"

"Well, I prefer a woman with an accent," Fillis told him.

Both Jesse and Fillis watched Avery for his reaction.

"Oh? Ohhhhh," Avery said, understanding. "I see."

Avery chuckled softly and smiled at Fillis. Jesse was happy to see that Avery had no problem that Fillis was gay. He was from a different time, after all. So was Jesse, but since he'd been around so long, he felt like he was from the nineteenth, twentieth, *and* the twenty-first century. He'd pretty much seen it all through the years.

"I do agree with Jesse, honey," Fillis said. "I think your accent is lovely to listen to, and I know Remy will be right charmed by it."

"Thanks," Avery said, appearing slightly hopeful but not exactly convinced.

"Tomorrow, Avery," Jesse said. "First tour in the morning. I'll bring Remy over and just introduce her to my friend. It's gonna be great."

"I hope so, Jesse. I truly do."

Avery looked afraid.

*****

Avery had been a nervous wreck all morning. He was far too restless to sit still, so he paced back and forth on the high hill of Little Round Top.

Jaysus, he thought. *I haven't been this scared up here since I fought and died!*

He calmed down a bit whenever he pictured Remy's beautiful face, with her soft brown hair and bright, friendly blue eyes. He kept reminding himself that she was nothing to be afraid of. She was one of the kindest women he'd ever known, and she would be sweet to him even if he sounded like a bumbling idiot to her.

Avery's anxiety level shot up again at the thought of sounding dumb to her. He wanted so much to make a good impression. Other than speaking to Remy once and talking to Fillis, he hadn't spoken to a woman in decades!

To make matters worse, Avery had no way of knowing what time it was, so he wasn't exactly sure when the Blue and Gray tour bus would arrive at Little Round Top. The tour buses arrived on a winding road at the top of the hill that was covered with trees, so he couldn't see when the bus got here.

A surge of terror rippled through Avery's ghostly body when he finally saw Jesse walking toward him. Avery didn't understand how it felt like his heart was pounding in his chest when he no longer had a physical heart or blood to pump through it. Emotions were just as strong in death as in life; that much was for sure.

Remy was off in the distance, giving tourists directions about the monuments up here on Little Round Top. Avery was grateful to have a quick moment with Jesse before the big event. He needed a pep talk.

"How ya doin'?" Jesse asked with a grin.

"I'm so nervous, Jesse!" Avery answered honestly.

"I know you are," Jesse said with tremendous empathy. "I was scared to death, you know, so to speak, the first time I spoke to Lucy. But as soon as I started talkin', I felt better. You'll feel the same way with her. I mean, it's *Remy*. She's a darlin' girl and she's nothin' to be scared of."

Avery nodded. "I know. You're right."

Remy was headed in their direction, still chatting with tourists. Once the crowd had dispersed a little and people went off on their own to enjoy the view, Jesse called Remy over.

"Remy! Come 'ere a minute."

Remy walked over to where Jesse and Avery were standing. Avery's ghost heart hammered wildly.

"Hey!" Remy said warmly. "What's up?"

"Remy, I want you to meet my friend, Avery O'Rorke."

"Hi!" she chirped. "Nice to meet you."

With that, she held out her hand to shake his.

Avery held up his hands. "Oh, I'd better not. I just got over gettin' sick, and I don't want to give you my germs."

Jesse nodded proudly.

Remy dropped her hand and nodded. "Ugh, I know how you feel. I just got over being sick myself."

Avery stopped himself before he said *I know.* Then he didn't seem sure of what to say next.

"So," Remy began, looking down at Avery's gray Confederate uniform. "What tour company are you with?"

"Ah…I'm with one of the walkin' tours. Four Score Walking Tours."

Remy laughed softly. "Clever name. It's such a nice day for a tour." She took in a deep breath. "It's great to have a job where you get to be outside, isn't it?"

Avery nodded. "Indeed it is."

Avery was still quite nervous, and Remy had noticed. He was sure of it. Avery had watched her interact with people for hours on end. If someone was friendly and outgoing, she freely joked and laughed with him. If a person was shy or even afraid, like on a ghost tour, she switched to gentle mode to make the person more comfortable. She might not know why, but she obviously realized Avery was nervous because she spoke softly and her smile was especially warm.

"What regiment are you supposed to be from?" Remy also knew how to keep a conversation going when the other person was having trouble knowing what to say.

"The 15th Alabama Infantry," Avery stated confidently, grateful for a question he could finally answer honestly.

"Hmmm. You don't sound like you're from Alla-baaama," Remy said with an exaggerated Southern accent. "Thought you'd sound more like my man here." With that, she jerked a thumb at Jesse.

"Ah, but there were a number of us in the 15th Alabama who were originally from Ireland. A whole company of us. Oate's Zouaves."

"Interesting," Remy said, her pretty blue eyes sparkling. She actually did look interested, rather than just being polite. "Are you really Irish, or are you just good at accents?"

Avery laughed, feeling more comfortable by the moment. He'd seen her put tourists at ease all the time with her sweet, friendly manner, but this was the first time he'd been on the receiving end. She made him feel warm all over, which was no easy feat when you were a ghost.

"I am indeed from Ireland," Avery told her.

"Really?" Remy said, looking more intrigued by the moment. "Do you speak…what is it…Gaelic? Irish?"

"Aye, certainly I speak Irish," he said with a smile.

"Cool! Can you say something in Irish? I would love to hear it!"

A thrill went through Avery. This was going far better than he had imagined. He glanced over at Jesse, who smiled at him and nodded encouragingly. He was there to step in in case Avery needed him, but was content to keep quiet and let them talk.

"Of course! Okay, let me see now," Avery said, as he tried to think of something good to say. "*Tá tú go h-álainn*, Remy."

Remy's eyes flashed with pleasure upon hearing her name. She looked at Avery eagerly, waiting for the translation.

"It means 'you're beautiful, Remy,'" Avery said softly, looking into her eyes.

Remy let out a soft sigh. "That's lovely." She was clearly quite touched by his words.

"And so are you," Avery said.

Avery glanced over at Jesse. Jesse opened his eyes wide and nodded slightly as if to say, *You're on a roll. Keep it up!*

Remy turned to look at Jesse and said, "Jesse, where have you been hiding this guy?"

Jesse laughed. "In plain sight, my dear. His walking tour stops here 'round the same time our bus does, so I usually stop and chat with him."

Remy turned back to look at Avery. "I see." She looked into his eyes for a moment. "I swear, I could listen to you talk all day."

Avery laughed. "Well, then I best keep talkin' to ya! How is your tour going?"

"Great! We have a good group today. They're asking lots of questions, which is nice."

"Remy also does ghost tours," Jesse said.

"'Zat right?" Avery asked, looking amused. Of course, he already knew that. He'd followed Remy around on many of her tours while he was invisible. He'd watched Remy guide her group around Gettysburg after dark while the tourists eagerly hunted for ghosts, completely unaware that there was one in their midst.

"Yeah, but don't hold it against me. I know lots of, you know, legit tour guides like us don't like ghost tours, but they can be fun."

Avery nodded. Many historians in the area hated the ghost tours because they felt they detracted from the seriousness of the battle and its history, but the truth was the immensely popular ghost tours brought in thousands more tourists every year. There was really no reason the historical tours and the paranormal ones couldn't co-exist. Nobody did historical battleground tours at night, so they might as well let the ghost folks take over after sunset.

"I mean, of course there's no such thing as ghosts, but the guests love that kind of stuff, so why not do it? Brings lots of people to Gettysburg," Remy said.

"That it does. Ghosts are a big deal 'round here," Avery said.

"Well, ghost *stories* are," she said.

"You don't believe in ghosts?" he asked with amusement.

"No. Do you?"

"Yes," Avery said firmly, and Remy laughed good-naturedly.

Several tourists wearing orange stickers approached them. It was a group of parents who had come on the tour with their kids. One of the mothers gestured up at the monument to the 44th New York Infantry.

"Is that the one you can climb up in?" she asked Remy.

"Yes! Here I'll show you how to go up there," she said. Then she looked at Avery. "Sorry, gotta go for now."

Avery nodded, and Remy headed toward the monument with the parents and kids following her like baby ducklings. Jesse went with her to help herd the group up the narrow staircase around the back of the monument.

The moment Remy was far enough ahead to be out of earshot, Jesse turned around and whispered to Avery, "You did great! Even *I* was 'bout to swoon!"

Avery laughed and nodded as an intense feeling of relief washed over him. After a shaky start, he felt good about his first real encounter with Remy. Despite what Jesse and Fillis had told him, he hadn't expected Remy to be so enthralled with his Irish heritage. Where, or *when* he came from, Irish immigrants were looked down upon, and he'd genuinely feared she might think less of him for it. Of course, he should have known better. Remy didn't look down on anyone.

Avery looked up at the monument where Remy and Jesse had disappeared with their group. He could hear the excitement of the kids as they rushed to the edge of the huge monument and peered out at the view. Little girls particularly loved climbing up there because the ridges on the corner really did make it look like a big stone castle. As always, Avery was hoping to catch a glimpse of Remy. She always looked so beautiful up there in her Jennie Wade dress when she stood and looked out at the expansive view of the battlefields.

Avery's ghost heart skipped a phantom beat when he saw her appear at the top. This time, Remy leaned down and looked right at where Avery was standing. As if she was looking for him.

Avery locked eyes with her, and for a moment she seemed embarrassed to be caught searching for him. Now it was his turn to put her at ease. He smiled warmly at her and waved. She smiled, too, and waved back.

"*Tá tú go h-álainn*, Remy!" he called up to her. Though there were many other things he could have said to her, he repeated this phrase because now she knew what it meant.

Remy's lovely smile widened, and she tucked her hair behind her ear as she looked at him. Avery hardly considered himself an expert on women, but even he recognized the move as a flirtatious gesture. She obviously found him charming, which thrilled him.

She reluctantly turned away so she could tend to her guests. Avery continued watching her as she gestured toward Devil's Den and explained other points of interest in view. He didn't even care if Remy caught him staring. He wanted her to know he adored her.

Remy never did look back down, as she was busy with her group. Avery waited patiently at the bottom for her to return, but he knew it would soon be time for her group to move on to the next stop.

Finally, Remy and Jesse came back down and headed toward Avery. Remy smiled at him as she guided her group.

"It was so nice meeting you, Avery," she said.

Oh, how he loved hearing her say his name!

"And you as well," he said.

Remy held his gaze just a bit longer than necessary, then she headed toward the bus with her group. Jesse walked with her a little ways, then dashed back to Avery.

"She said you were *really cute* and she loves your *dreamy accent,*" Jesse said, grinning at Avery.

Avery gazed into Jesse's eyes with intense gratitude and said quietly, "Thank ye, Jesse. For everything."

Jesse nodded, still grinning, then he bounded off to join his group.

Avery sat back down on his usual rock, feeling a sense of happiness and relief. It had been wonderful finally talking to Remy, and he never could have done it without Jesse's help.

Avery hadn't thought it possible, but now that he was able to speak to her and look into her eyes, he was more in love with Remy than ever before.

Chapter 4

It was after eleven pm, and Lucy was outside on the patio of Meade's Tavern closing up the restaurant for the night. She was wiping down tables and shutting the huge umbrellas above the tables when Avery came walking toward her.

Lucy looked up and gasped slightly when she saw him standing just outside the railing that separated the restaurant tables from the street. She glanced at his Confederate uniform, and Avery figured she was trying to determine if he was dead or alive. He knew from Jesse that Lucy used to be terrified of ghosts, but now she was quite comfortable with them. Avery realized she would probably be more afraid of a living, breathing strange man standing here watching her late at night than a spirit. Lucy looked frightened, and he felt awful for scaring her.

"Hello. I-I'm Avery O'Rorke. I—"

"Avery!" Lucy cried with delight, her brown eyes lighting up with recognition. She dropped what she was doing and walked over to greet him. "It's so wonderful to finally meet you!"

Avery smiled at Lucy. She was just as Jesse had described—long, flowing brown hair and gentle brown eyes. She had such a sweet, friendly smile, and it was easy to picture her with Jesse.

"I should have realized it was you. Jesse's told me so much about you that I feel like I know you," Lucy said.

"I can say the same about you. He talks about you all the time. I must say, you're every bit as beautiful as he described."

Lucy blushed and looked down shyly. "Thank you. That's very sweet of you."

Avery chuckled softly. "He also said how lovely you are when you blush."

Lucy let out a short sigh. She tried to look irritated with Jesse, but Avery could see the love in her eyes.

"I don't want to disturb you here at work. It's late, and I'm sure you'll be wantin' to get home, but I just wanted to stop by and say hello."

"Oh, I'm so glad you did, Avery!" Lucy said with a smile.

Jesse had told him Lucy was usually quite shy around new people, but she seemed to be at ease with him. She probably did feel like she knew him already from all Jesse had told her about him.

"And Lucy, I know you didn't really want me meetin' up with Remy, but—"

"Oh, Avery, I didn't mean anything by that," Lucy said, blushing deeply. Now she did look uncomfortable with him, which was the last thing he wanted. "It was nothing personal."

"No, I know that," Avery said gently. "I just wanted to tell ye I think it's so nice of ye to be worryin' about her and lookin' after her. Makes me feel so much better knowin' she's got such good friends around her. But I want you to know I would never do anything to hurt her."

"I know you wouldn't," Lucy said. "I just can't help but worry about her. I know what it feels like to care for someone you can't even touch. It's very painful."

"I know," Avery said softly.

"Of course you do," Lucy said with a sad smile.

"I just wanted a chance to talk with her, and I'm so happy I did."

"I don't blame you. She's such a sweet girl, and I understand what you see in her. From what Jesse says, Remy was quite taken with you."

Lucy smiled, but Avery could see the worry in her eyes.

"Oh, I don't know about that," Avery said. "I'm hopin' we can at least be friends. I could use all the friends I can get."

"I know. Well, you have Jesse. And you have me."

"Thank ye, Lucy. I guess I'd better let you get back to work. I don't like you being out here after dark."

Lucy laughed. "You sound like Jesse. Take care, Avery. I'll see you soon."

"I hope so!"

*****

Lucy watched Avery walk a short way down the street then disappear. She wondered if he was planning to vanish for the night and then come back the next day when he could see Remy again.

Lucy finished up her work outside and then headed back into the tavern. The manager was in her office tallying up the day's receipts while the cooks and busboys were finishing up in the kitchen. That left Lucy alone to clean up the two dining rooms and prepare them for the next day. She thought about Avery as she worked.

He was handsome and broad shouldered, and had kind, gentle gray eyes. She loved hearing him speak, and it wasn't just the accent. Avery had a deep, masculine voice that was pleasant to listen to. Lucy had felt at ease with him rather quickly, which was unusual for her. Jesse had told her all about him and what a good guy he was. Now that she'd met him, she had a good feeling about him as well. Lucy could see the passion in Avery's eyes when he spoke about Remy.

Though Lucy was happy to have met Avery, she was more worried than ever that Remy might get hurt. Avery was a kind, handsome, and passionate man with pretty eyes and a sexy accent. How could Remy *not* fall for him?

Lucy was lost in thought for a few moments when she suddenly felt a presence, like someone was watching her.

The feeling of being watched wasn't unusual for her. She had always been quite sensitive to the paranormal and frequently sensed when there was a presence nearby. That sensation used to terrify her, but that was before she met and fell in love with Jesse. Now she had lots of ghost friends, and she wasn't afraid anymore.

Lucy looked around and didn't see anyone, but she knew someone was there.

"Hello?" Lucy called out. "It's okay to let me see you. I'm not afraid."

And she wasn't afraid. At least, she wasn't at first. A sudden chill ran through her, and a strange feeling of dread washed over her.

Lucy knew she was being watched, and it felt like whoever was watching was someone to be feared.

"Who's there?" Lucy asked, her voice shaky. She realized she was trembling. It had been a long time since she had been afraid around spirits. Jesse and Joel had been careful with her once she discovered their secret, and went to great lengths to keep her from being frightened. They initially kept their distance and eased her into a comfortable friendship with them. It wasn't until later that Lucy realized Jesse had been in love with her the whole time.

"I said, *who's there?*" she called out again, trying to sound more confident.

There was no response, but now she felt like the presence was standing right beside her. She slowly turned to look where she was almost certain someone was standing, even though she couldn't see him or her.

Lucy froze for a moment. There was complete silence in the dining room area. She was far enough away from the kitchen and the manager's office that she couldn't hear the sound of her co-workers finishing up their tasks. She felt utterly alone. Suddenly, all her old fears of ghosts came crashing down on her. She used to be terrified during this time of day when it was silent and she was alone. She had found it creepy to be alone at night so close to the battlefields where thousands of people had died. After meeting and falling in love with Jesse, Lucy had thought she would never be afraid of ghosts again.

Lucy still felt the presence, but whoever it was obviously had no plans to become visible. She tried to distract herself by wiping down the table in front of her, rushing her work so she could finish and get out of there.

Then she felt an unseen hand drag right across her breasts.

Lucy gasped and hugged her arms around her chest. After a moment of sheer fright, she managed to pull herself together enough to run out of the dining room. When she got to the door, she turned around for one last look.

Finally, she saw a flash of the spirit who had been torturing her. He turned visible just long enough for her to catch a glimpse of him. He was a Union soldier. He wore a blue uniform and a large black hat. He had a beard and a mustache, and had cruel, dark eyes. He sneered at her, then disappeared.

Lucy stared after him before running off to be among the living again.

Chapter 5

Jesse was almost always asleep by the time Lucy got home from working the late shift at the restaurant. However, when she climbed into bed next to him, he usually woke up enough to murmur that he loved her and to wrap his arms around her before falling back asleep. That was what Lucy needed more than anything right now.

Lucy was surprised—and grateful—to find that Jesse was still awake when she got home.

"What are you still doing up?" Lucy asked him when she found him in their bed watching TV.

Jesse gestured toward the television. "I'm… What is it you young kids call it these days…binge watching *Game of Thrones*," he said with a smile.

Lucy laughed. Jesse often commented about "kids" and "young-uns." He was so handsome and youthful-looking that she often forgot he was technically well over two hundred years old. He was still a kid at heart, though, and she hoped he would never grow up.

"You all right?" Jesse asked, his smile fading. He picked up on her mood immediately, as she'd known he would.

"Not really." Lucy went over to the bed and sat down. "Something happened to me at the restaurant tonight."

Jesse jumped up and was next to her in a flash. "What happened? Are you all right?"

"Yes, I'm okay," Lucy said. "It's okay."

Jesse wrapped his arm around her, his blue-gray eyes full of worry.

"It was so strange. I was cleaning up at the restaurant like always, and I felt this presence. I knew for sure there was someone in the room with me."

Jesse nodded. He knew how sensitive Lucy was and wasn't surprised at her words.

"Ever since I met you and Joel and I figured out, you know, what was going on with you guys, I haven't been afraid of ghosts. I know so many now and they're all my friends, but this felt different somehow."

"What do you mean, darlin'?"

"It was scary. Like I felt like whoever was there might try to hurt me."

"Oh, Lucy," Jesse said, pulling her close. "I hate that you're there all by yourself at night. Wasn't Craig or anybody around?"

"Yeah, I mean Craig and Mandy were around but not close by." Lucy glanced at Jesse, knowing how angry he was going to get when she told him the rest. "You have to promise not to flip out."

Jesse's eyes opened wide. "Whut?"

Lucy sighed. He was already starting to flip out. She could feel his muscles tighten as he held onto her.

"He...whoever he is...he managed to touch me." Lucy looked away, not wanting to tell him the rest but she knew she had to. He was going to get angry and want to defend her honor, but there was nothing he could possibly do.

"*Where?*" he asked, his voice hard.

Lucy swallowed, then gestured at her chest.

"I will *kill* him!" Jesse roared.

Lucy laughed ruefully and threw up her hands. "He's already dead! There's nothing we can do."

Jesse's eyes flashed with fury. Lucy winced, and Jesse realized he had tightened his grip on her and was hurting her. He released his grip, then gently rubbed her arm where he had been squeezing her too tight.

"Honey, I know you're upset, but there's nothing we can do. It's not like you can beat him up or anything," Lucy said.

"Did you ever see him?" Jesse asked, his teeth clenched.

"Yes! He was a Union soldier and wore a big black hat. He had a beard and mustache and creepy dark eyes. I've never seen him before. You?"

Jesse shook his head. "Don't think so." Lucy could see the wheels turning in Jesse's head. He was trying to figure out who this creep was and how he could manage to kick his dead ass.

"I'm all right, Jesse. I didn't want to worry you, but I figured I'd better tell you what happened."

"I'm glad you did, darlin'."

Jesse pulled her into a tender embrace, and she let out a sigh of relief. She felt safe in his arms.

"Oh! And at least something good did happen tonight," Lucy said to Jesse's back as he was holding her. He released her so he could face her as she spoke. "Someone else came to visit me earlier. When I was outside closing up."

"Who?"

"Avery," Lucy said with a smile.

"Really?" Jesse said, finally brightening a bit. "He's been sayin' he's been wantin' to meet you."

"He's so sweet, Jesse."

"Told ya."

"He's sweet and he's handsome and my God, that voice," Lucy

said, putting a hand over her heart.

"You always were a sucker for accents, my rose," Jesse said, kissing her on the cheek. "Thank God."

"Well, yours is my favorite," Lucy said, stroking his face. She sighed. "Remy's gonna love him."

Jesse didn't seem too sure of what to say to that. Lucy kissed his lips, then she sighed again. "He did look lonely."

Jesse nodded, and seemed grateful that Lucy understood his reasons for trying to get Remy and Avery together.

"I'm gonna get ready for bed," Lucy said.

After washing her face and brushing her teeth, she put on her nightgown and slid into bed beside Jesse. He put his strong arms around her, and she felt comforted and safe. Still, his muscles felt rigid and tense.

"I'm gonna found out who that asshole is, darlin'" Jesse said.

Wow. Jesse only cursed around her when he was *extremely* pissed off. It was rare.

"And I'm not lettin' him get away with hurtin' you."

*****

The next day at Little Round Top, Jesse jogged up to Avery, who looked up with surprise to see him in such a hurry.

"Avery!" Jesse called, slightly out of breath.

"Hey there, Jesse!" Avery said. "Everything all right?"

"Yeah. Yeah, kind of. Listen, I need your help."

"Of course," Avery said. "Anything I can do, just name it."

Jesse had been such a wonderful friend to Avery and he felt a strong sense of loyalty to him. Avery was willing to help out in any way he could, but he couldn't fathom what he could possibly do. It was hard to be of much use to anyone when you couldn't touch anything.

Jesse looked around, then lowered his voice. "There was some strange ghost harassing Lucy at work last night."

Avery's eyes opened wide. "She said that? Jesse, last night *I* came to see—"

"No, no, no," Jesse said, laughing and waving him off. "Lucy told me you came to visit her and you had a nice talk. That was real nice of you to go and see her. No, this was somebody else. It must have happened after you left. She was cleanin' up the dining room all by herself when she felt a presence."

"That's strange," Avery said.

"Not for her, it's not. She's real sensitive to that kind of thing. Always has been. She usually knows when spirits are nearby even when she can't see 'em. She used to be real scared of ghosts but, you know, not anymore."

Avery smiled. "No, I suppose you cured her of that."

"Yeah, 'zactly. Well, 'til now. Usually ghosts don't bother her, but this time she was scared. She said it felt different. Creepy." Jesse's expression darkened. "He touched her."

"He did? How is that possible?" Avery had never been able to touch anything since he'd died.

"It's not easy, but you can do it. Ya gotta concentrate real hard. Some ghosts like to play around with folks on the ghost tours, ya know? Grab their arms or ankles or whatnot. Some ghosts are better at it than others. Lotta times if you're feelin' real strong emotions, like fear or anger, then you can do it."

"Ah. I didn't know that," Avery said. He wondered if he just concentrated enough, could he ever touch Remy? He realized that was far too much of a risk. If it didn't work, his hand would pass right through her body. He couldn't bear the thought of her terrified screams.

Gritting his teeth with fury, Jesse said, "He touched her breasts."

"Oh, my God!" Avery said with disgust. His anger flared on Jesse's behalf, knowing how much he loved Lucy and how upset he must be. Avery pictured Lucy the way he saw her last night, those gentle brown eyes and tender smile. The idea of anyone molesting that sweet girl like that was unbearable.

"Lucy said he was a Union guy with a beard and a mustache and had a big, black hat. You know him?"

Avery thought for a moment. "No. No, I don't believe I've seen him around."

"Okay. Well, can you keep an eye out, let me know if you see him? Or mebbe you can find out somethin' about him by askin' around?"

"Aye, indeed I will." Avery had become friendly with several other ghosts since he'd returned from vanishing. He figured somebody around here must know something about this guy. "I'll see what I can find out."

"Thank you, Avery," Jesse said, his eyes still full of anger. "I don't know what I'm gonna do when I find him. Not like I can punch his lights out."

"Yeah. Too bad. I'd be right behind ya, fists raised, if it were possible for me to knock him out."

"Thanks," Jesse said. "Really appreciate that."

Avery nodded, then glanced up toward where the buses had parked. His ghost heart lurched as he saw a smiling Remy walking toward them. Panic shot through him. He was excited to see her, but hadn't thought about what to say. He didn't feel ready!

"Avery!" Remy called warmly to him. "Top of the mornin' to ye!"

"And the rest of the day to yerself," he responded reflexively.

Remy laughed as she walked up to them. She stood next to Jesse but looked at Avery. "I *like* that! I'll have to remember that one. How are you?"

Avery smiled at her and calmed down a bit. "I'm doing well. It's lovely to see you again."

"You too," Remy said, tucking her soft brown hair behind her ear. *Hair tuck again. That's a good sign, right?*

"And how are the ghosts treatin' ya these days?" he asked.

"Quiet. They're very quiet," Remy responded with a wry smile.

Good thing, he thought. He was angry enough about that awful spirit mistreating Lucy. He didn't know what he would do if anyone dared to touch Remy like that.

"So you do these tours here all day and then work again at night?" Avery asked.

Remy nodded.

"Don't you get tired from working so much?" Avery could hear the sadness and concern in his voice that he couldn't hide.

"Yes, but I gotta do it. I have lots of bills to pay. Rent, food, car insurance, not to mention my college loan. It won't be forever. I just need to pay off school and try to save up for the future."

Remy smiled as she spoke, but she looked sad. Empathy tugged at Avery's heart. He knew Remy's family was no help to her, and she was all alone in handling all those bills.

"And just what are you plannin' for the future?" Avery asked.

"You really want to know?"

"More than anything in the whole world."

Remy laughed softly and looked enchanted with him. Her eyes lit up when she spoke about her plans. "I want to travel all over. All over the country and the world. And for my work, I want to work with people, tourists, you know. Kinda like I do now. Maybe at a resort somewhere. I love talking to people, answering their questions. It's nice being a part of their vacations, their memories."

"That's lovely, Remy," Avery told her. "You're wonderful with the tourists."

She laughed and waved him off, dismissing his compliment.

"I mean it! You have this way of talkin' to people. Makin' 'em feel good by the way you talk to them, look at 'em. Especially me."

Remy looked at him curiously. She seemed surprised, yet pleased, at his words.

"I was so nervous the first time I spoke to you. You're so pretty," Avery said with a nervous laugh.

"I'm nothing to be afraid of," she said warmly.

Avery smiled at her fondly. "You remind me of Jesse's girlfriend. She's pretty, too, and doesn't know it."

"Oh, you're so right about Lucy!" Remy exclaimed. He could hear the fondness in her voice. "She's so sweet, and she has no idea how beautiful she is. She's such a great friend. I'm so glad I know her and Jesse. I didn't know a lot of people around here 'til I met them."

"Well, I hope you consider me your friend, too."

"Yes," Remy said. Avery could also hear the loneliness in her voice, and it pained him. "Yes, I'd like that, Avery."

Avery nodded, relieved that thus far he hadn't made a fool of himself in talking to her. She seemed to like him.

"I feel awful. All I've done is talk about myself! I'm sorry," Remy said.

"Don't be sorry. I like talking about you. You're one of my favorite topics of conversation."

Remy looked into his eyes, which gave him a huge thrill. Her pretty blue eyes sparkled. "Thanks, Avery. You're so nice."

Remy looked at the tourists milling around. It would soon be time to get back on the bus.

"Well, I guess I better start herding everyone together," she said.

Was that reluctance he heard in her voice? Like maybe she'd have preferred to stay here and talk with him?

"Yes, I b'lieve I best go find all my folks as well," Avery said. He figured he needed to start acting the part of a tour guide, lest she get suspicious.

Remy nodded. "Maybe we'll talk again soon?"

"I'll think of nothing else 'til then."

Remy giggled. *Hair tuck.*

*****

Remy's legs trembled as she walked away. She was acutely aware that Avery was watching her, so she took careful steps over the rocky terrain on the hill. The last thing she wanted was to trip and fall flat on her face in front of him. He was just so damned *cute*. And that voice of his! Deep, sexy, and with that accent. He should be on the radio or do audiobooks or something.

Jesse and Remy got the guests back onto the tour bus as they prepared to head to the next stop on the tour.

Remy looked at Jesse curiously. She was debating about whether or not to ask him if Avery was seeing anyone. Avery certainly seemed to be interested in her, but she would be so embarrassed if she turned out to be wrong. She'd barely dated anyone in high school, mostly because of the turmoil at home in dealing with an alcoholic mother. Throughout college, Remy had had to work a lot between school and holding down part-time jobs to pay for her classes, so she never had time to date. Not that anyone had asked her anyway. Avery was really the first man who took an interest in her. He seemed to look at her with a sense of admiration. It was strange and exciting.

She kept staring at Jesse, lost in her thoughts. What if Jesse asked Avery about her and it turned out he wasn't interested in her after all? Then she would have to face him every day on tour with him knowing she liked him. It would be horrible.

"You okay?" Jesse asked with concern.

Yeah. There was no way she was gonna tell Jesse she liked his friend.

Remy shook her head to clear her thoughts. She nodded. "Yeah. I'm fine."

Chapter 6

Lucy was glad Remy didn't have a ghost tour to work tonight, so she could join her and Jesse at an outdoor beer garden in town for drinks and dinner. Well, Jesse and Lucy were drinking. Remy never drank alcohol due to her family history, so she had an iced tea and a small appetizer for dinner. Lucy knew Remy must be worried about spending money she really didn't have on luxuries like restaurant food, but she loved spending time with her friends. Though she would occasionally allow Theresa to treat her to dinner, it was only because Theresa's family was quite wealthy. Despite Lucy's best efforts, Remy refused to take any money from her or Jesse.

Jesse had just gotten up to get in the beer line. Remy waited until he was out of earshot, then she asked Lucy, "So, do you know Jesse's friend Avery O'Rorke?"

Lucy was startled by the question, but struggled to keep her expression even.

"Yeah. The Irish guy. He's nice."

"He's more than nice," Remy insisted. "He's *gorgeous*. And he's so sweet. And my God, that accent. That *voice*." Remy put her hand over her heart like she was about to swoon. "I swear, I could listen to him call out Bingo numbers and it would be sexy."

Lucy chuckled. She pictured Avery's kind, hopeful face. She couldn't help but imagine his expression if he knew the way Remy was talking about him. He would be so happy.

"So, do you know if he's seeing anyone?" Remy asked hopefully.

A sense of dread settled in Lucy's stomach. *So it begins. Oh, Remy. You'll get hurt if you fall for him.* Lucy's heart ached as she looked at her friend. Remy, who had no real family to count on, and who struggled so hard to make ends meet. Remy, who was kind and loving and deserved a man as wonderful as Avery, but also deserved a man who was *alive.* Someone who could love her and hold her in his arms.

"Umm, I'm not sure," Lucy said.

"I'm scared to ask Jesse."

"Why?" Lucy asked.

"Because what if Avery is seeing someone? Or he's just not interested? If Jesse tells him that I asked about him, then he'll know I like him."

Lucy was about to answer when Jesse came back with two beers. He handed one to Lucy and then sat down next to her and across from Remy. Lucy desperately hoped Remy would drop the subject of Avery.

"So Jesse. What is Avery's, you know, deal?"

Jesse looked perplexed. "What do you mean, his *deal?*"

"You know what I mean, ya hick," Remy said.

Lucy giggled. Remy loved to tease Jesse about his accent. Lucy realized Jesse probably didn't know what she meant. He was pretty savvy, but he still wasn't completely up on all the slang from the *young kids these days,* as he would say.

"She wants to know if Avery is dating anyone," Lucy said evenly.

"Oh. Uh, no. He doesn't have a girlfriend or anything," Jesse said.

"Do you think, well, do you think he might be, you know, interested in me?" Remy asked tentatively.

Lucy could see the compassion in Jesse's eyes. Remy was usually so outgoing, but right now she seemed so vulnerable.

"Maybe you could, I don't know, ask him if— No. No, don't say anything to him. Forget I said anything. Please don't—"

"He's very fond of you, Remy," Jesse said with a gentle smile.

Jesse glanced at Lucy, who nodded her approval. Though she didn't want to encourage this doomed relationship, Remy obviously liked Avery and would be heartbroken if she thought he didn't feel the same way. It would be cruel to let her think he didn't care.

Remy's eyes filled with excitement and hope. "Really? You're not just saying that?"

"No. He likes you, Remy. A lot," Jesse told her.

"He does? Oh, I'm so glad," Remy gushed. "I love talking to him. It's like the highlight of my day."

Remy looked so happy, so excited about a future with Avery that would never happen. Of course, Lucy had never dared dream that she and Jesse could ever be together, but his return to life was a rare and wonderful miracle. The odds were not good that such a thing would happen again. Lucy's heart sank when she thought of what would happen if Remy got involved with Avery and he crossed over.

"What's the matter, Lucy?" Remy asked upon seeing her expression. "Don't you like Avery?"

"Oh, of course I do! He's a wonderful guy and a great friend."

Remy nodded enthusiastically. "I hope he asks me out. Every time I talk to him, I keep hoping he will. I'd love to go out with him and spend time with him outside of work. A few minutes with him just isn't enough."

Oh, Remy. It'll never be enough, Lucy thought. *Soon you'll want to touch him, to hold him, and you won't be able to. And it will hurt. It will hurt so much.*

Jesse exchanged a brief, worried glance with Lucy. Avery wouldn't be asking Remy to dinner anytime soon, that much was for sure.

Remy sighed. "He's so wonderful, Lucy. He's always so sweet to me." She added in a soft voice, "He called me beautiful. In *Irish*. No one's ever called me beautiful before."

Lucy felt a prickle of anger at Jesse for not heeding her warning. *This* was exactly why she hadn't wanted Avery and Remy to meet in the first place! Though Lucy empathized with Avery's lonely plight of pining for Remy, it would be Remy who suffered the most. Lucy was also angry at the whole situation. It was so damned unfair that the two of them couldn't be together.

"I hope I get to see him tomorrow," Remy said.

"He'll be there," Jesse said, glancing at Lucy. "I'm sure of it."

*****

Remy hopped off the bus at Little Round Top, nervousness tingling in her stomach. It was excruciating to give the tourists the usual instructions on where to go and when to be back for the bus when all she wanted to do was rush off to see Avery. Thank goodness there weren't too many questions from her group today.

She tried to walk casually over to the spot near the 44th New York Infantry monument where she usually found Avery, but she wanted to run over there.

Her heart sank. *He's not here.* Remy had wanted to so much to see his smile and hear that deep, masculine voice of his. She found herself craving the attention he gave her. *Better watch it, girl,* she warned herself. Remy had been on her own for a long time and was a strong woman. She'd never needed a man's approval, and she wasn't about to start now.

Still. She loved the tender way he looked at her, and he said the sweetest, most wonderful things. No one had ever made her feel the way he did with just a simple look and a kind word.

Finally, she spotted Avery in the distance. She drew in a nervous breath as she watched him looking purposefully around. He was probably checking on his tour members, making sure nobody had any questions or concerns. At last, he turned and spotted her. His face broke into a broad, handsome smile, and Remy felt her knees go weak.

"Hi, Avery," Remy called to him as he walked over to her.

"Hello, Remy! How are you? Still working too hard?" Avery asked. He actually looked like he was worried about her, which she found touching.

"Well, I did have the night off last night, so I guess that's something."

Please, Avery. Ask me out on a date.

"What have you been up to?" Remy asked him.

"Same old boring stuff. Best part of my day is talkin' to you," Avery said with a wink.

He's going to do it. He's going to ask me out.

Remy waited a moment to give him a chance. She knew she should act like the modern woman she was and just ask him out, but she couldn't bring herself to do it. If Avery wanted to date her, he would ask.

He didn't.

Maybe she had misinterpreted Jesse's words. He said Avery liked her a lot, but maybe he just wanted to be friends.

The silence was long enough to be unbearable, so Remy finally broke it.

"Well, I guess I better go check on my group," she said.

"Yeah." Avery nodded. He looked like he wanted to say something more, but Remy could be wrong. She felt like she was wrong about everything else about him.

Remy stifled a sad sigh, then turned to leave.

"Remy!" Avery said.

"Yes?" she said, turning back hopefully.

"I, uh, have a good day."

"You, too," she said with a forced smile.

I was so stupid to think a wonderful, handsome man like Avery O'Rorke would be interested in me. He's way out of my league.

*****

Jesse noticed that Remy looked upset as she walked past him. He also saw that Avery looked equally sad. Guilt stabbed at him for not listening to Lucy. She was right when she said it would only cause pain if Avery and Remy met. Still, it wasn't Lucy who had to look into Avery's eyes every day when he talked about Remy.

Jesse was planning to ask Avery what had happened, but he didn't get the chance.

"Jesse! I got some news for ye," Avery said.

"Yeah?" Jesse looked at him curiously.

"I know who it is that was botherin' Lucy."

"You do?" Jesse's eyes flashed with anger when he thought of how that creep had touched his beloved Lucy.

"I asked some other, you know, *guys*," Avery said, not saying the word "ghosts" out loud. "Some people have seen him skulking around. Name's Private Ellis George of the 6th Wisconsin."

"I see," Jesse said. "Good to know."

It was damned frustrating that the guy was dead. There wasn't much Jesse could do to punish him for hurting Lucy, and there wasn't much he could do to stop him from doing it again.

"Any idea why the hell he was bothering her?" Jesse asked.

"Yes, actually," Avery said, eyes wide. "Seems he hates women. He's known for harassing ladies on ghost tours, grabbin' 'em and stuff like that. Tryin' to scare 'em."

"Ugh," Jesse said with disgust. Born in 1839, Jesse had an old-fashioned reverence for women. He felt it his duty as a man to be protective of them, and none more than the one he loved.

Avery took in Jesse's devastated, worried expression for a moment, then added, "I'm sorry, Jesse."

"Well, at least I have some idea of what I'm dealing with here," Jesse said. "So far Lucy hasn't seen him since that night. If we're lucky, he'll just go vanish and leave everybody alone."

"I hope so. I really do," Avery said. "Let me know if there's anything else I can do."

Jesse smiled gratefully. "Thanks, Avery." He had to fight the natural, friendly urge to clap his friend on the back. Even as a former ghost himself, it was easy to forget the rules. "I really appreciate all your help. Well, I better get back. See ya soon."

Avery nodded. Jesse followed his gaze as Avery watched Remy in the distance as she guided her tourists onto the bus. He stared at her with an agonized look of longing.

I know, man, Jesse thought as he walked away. *I know exactly how you feel.*

Jesse climbed aboard the bus and looked at Remy. She sat in the front seat staring out the window.

"Remy? You all right?"

Remy glanced up at Jesse. He could swear she was close to tears.

"I don't think Avery's interested in me after all." She shrugged, pretending it was no big deal. He could see the pain and disappointment in her eyes.

Oh Remy, I'm so sorry, Jesse thought. *This is all my fault.*

So much for protecting the women in his life.

*****

Avery waited until no one was looking, and then went invisible. He knew he had completely blown his talk with Remy today, and he wanted to sulk in private. He sat down in front of the big, stone monument where he usually spoke with her and looked out across the battlefield.

Remy.

Avery pictured her sweet smile and bright blue eyes. Though he loved talking with her, those brief moments during the day only seemed to increase his desire for her. He wanted to spend as much time with her as he could, but he was running out of things to say.

He was angry at himself for being so awkward and tongue-tied today. He was nothing like the man Remy met that first time, when he'd managed to charm her with sweet words in Irish. There was so much he wanted to say, but his entire past was off limits. She had no idea who he really was, so he couldn't talk about his family, the war, or anything else that happened before he met her. He couldn't talk about his current life, because he wasn't even *alive.* He wasn't employed as a tour guide like she thought he was, and a ghost hardly has any hobbies to discuss.

Avery was at a loss. He didn't know what to say to Remy, but he couldn't bear to leave things the way he had this afternoon. He needed to see her again. And he wasn't about to wait until tomorrow's tour.

*****

Though Remy normally enjoyed giving ghost tours, tonight her heart wasn't in it. She smiled and put on a brave face as she stood before her excited tourists, determined to show them a good time. She knew it wouldn't be easy.

She was tired after being on her feet all day with the daytime tours, but that was nothing new. Now she was also emotionally exhausted. She couldn't help but be angry at Avery for leading her on. He had been so sweet and charming when she first met him, and he seemed to show genuine interest in her. Now Remy felt like a fool for fantasizing that he might be her first real boyfriend. Sure, he seemed to go out of his way to talk to her, but he never took it further than casually chatting.

Remy was angry at him, but she still wanted to be with him. She couldn't help it.

Well, he doesn't want me. At least not in that way. We're friends, and that's that.

"Welcome, everyone! Let's go ahead and get started."

Remy's smile became less forced and more genuine when she looked out at the enthusiastic faces before her. She really did want her group to have a good time. She enjoyed her work as a tour guide, and she realized that working tonight would be a welcome distraction.

As per her routine, she scrutinized her group. She needed to size them up in order to determine which type of tour to give them. A crowd of teenagers would get the scarier tour, whereas a group of younger kids would get the toned-down version. There was a fairly even mix tonight.

"Okay! So here we are standing in front of the legendary Farnsworth House Inn." With that, Remy gestured toward the house just behind them. The small, brick building now served as an inn with a restaurant attached next door. "The house was built in 1810 and is now notorious for being one of the most haunted inns in America!"

People turned around to look, some taking pictures.

"The attic upstairs housed Confederate sharpshooters during the battle," Remy continued. "And it is believed that the bullet that killed Jennie Wade, the civilian woman who was shot in her kitchen while baking bread for the soldiers, came from that very attic."

Remy always felt a kinship with Jennie, mainly because she spent so much time dressed as her during the bus tours. She always felt bad for Jennie, who was only twenty when she died. Remy was only twenty-two, and she couldn't imagine the tragedy of such a short life.

"There are at least twelve ghosts that are known to inhabit the Farnsworth grounds," Remy informed her group. "Two of the most beloved are Mary and Jeremy. Mary is a motherly type who likes to care for the guests staying at the inn whether they want her to or not!"

Gentle laughter came up from the crowd. It was a good group tonight. They seemed engaged, listening, rather than being distracted by their cell phones or talking among themselves.

"When you smell the scent of roses, you know that Mary is near."

Remy stifled a giggle when she saw most of the group members drawing in deep breaths, hoping to catch a whiff of Mary's floral scent. There was something to the power of suggestion. It amazed Remy how frequently guests claimed to smell roses, pipe smoke, or even the stench of rotting bodies left over from the war. People also cried out in surprise, terror even, claiming that someone or some*thing* had touched them in the dark. Though Remy didn't believe for one moment that any of these things had really occurred, she knew that her *guests* believed. And, since this was a ghost tour, after all, Remy encouraged such experiences.

"Mary has been known to put a cool, soothing hand on the foreheads of guests at the inn who are feeling ill. She has even pulled up the covers over shivering people in their beds!"

Remy usually got lots of smiles on that story. Oh, yes. People wanted to believe.

"As for Jeremy, he's a lovable little scamp! He's a little boy who was killed in a tragic carriage accident in the 1860s."

Remy felt a twinge of sorrow every time she told that story. It didn't matter how long ago the boy had died. It was still terribly sad. Legend was that Jeremy's father also haunted the house. Naturally,

Remy didn't believe a word of that. The real, historical story alleged that his father was so heartbroken that Jeremy's body had to be forcibly taken from him because he couldn't bear to let go. It brought tears to Remy's eyes whenever she thought about it.

"Jeremy loves to play with visitors, and many guests of the inn leave toys for him. There's even a special drawer in the house where we keep his toys. They rarely stay in the same place for long. Jeremy frequently moves his things around during the night."

Remy enjoyed the nods and wide-eyed looks for a moment, then turned on her heel. "Okay, the next stop is the Grove, which is just behind Gettysburg Middle School. This way," she said as she led her group forward.

She began walking, then gasped when she saw Avery. Remy wondered how long he had been standing there, watching. She had to keep walking because the group was following her, but Avery fell into step with her.

"D'ya mind terribly if I join your group for a bit? I don't have a ticket," Avery said with a grin.

Remy glanced back at the ghost tour headquarters building. As long as her boss wasn't around it was okay.

"Of course!" Remy said, a ripple of excitement going through her. She couldn't believe Avery was here. Just when she had given up on him.

Avery glanced at the black, knee-length dress she always wore on ghost tours. "You look different without your clothes. I-I mean, I didn't mean…."

Remy laughed softly. He was *adorable* when he was nervous. "I know what you mean," she said kindly, doing her best to put him at ease. "You mean you've never seen me dressed as Remy Waters as opposed to Jennie Wade."

"Yes. 'Zactly," he said.

Remy glanced at Avery's Confederate uniform. "So did you not have time to change after work, or do you just like being dressed like that?"

"A bit of both, I suppose!" Avery said.

Remy glanced back and did a quick head count, making sure she had everyone with her.

"You ever been on one of these ghost tours?" she asked him.

"Nope. Seen them around, but I've never officially been on one. Woulda joined one much sooner if I'd known they had such lovely guides," Avery said.

Remy smiled. "Each tour varies depending on the tourists. I have different stories I tell based on who's in my group." She glanced back at the group and said quietly, "Okay, see that blonde lady all the way on the left?"

Avery nodded.

"She's afraid. I figure that guy with her dragged her on the tour, but I don't think she wants to be here. Plus, I have some younger kids here tonight. So I'll give this group the more family-friendly version."

"That's very kind of you, Remy," Avery said.

She shrugged, but she was thrilled with his compliment.

"Okay!" Remy said, addressing the group as she walked backward for a few paces. "We're almost at the haunted grove. Now you'll want to keep your eye out for anything *unusual* during the tour. You just might see, hear, or even smell something otherworldly while we're out here. If you do, be sure to speak up! Spirits have been known to touch tourists, and we have quite a few soldiers who seem to be particularly fond of women."

Remy directed that comment to a group of girls in their twenties who seemed excited to be on the tour and were probably hopeful for a ghost encounter.

"Some people have noticed strange smells as they walk through the streets of Gettysburg at night—the scent of pipe or campfire smoke or even the smell of gunpowder."

Remy leaned in toward Avery and added, "Some people have also claimed to smell blood and even rotting bodies, but that tidbit is for the scarier tour."

Avery nodded, smiling.

Remy stopped walking and stood under a huge tree near the middle school. Avery stepped off to the side so she could address her group.

"This area here, known as the Grove, was the site of deadly hand-to-hand combat. There's no telling how many men died right here on this spot. You may want to take some pictures around here, because a lot of guests have reported eerie images in their photos they couldn't see with their naked eyes."

Many guests pulled out their cellphones and took pictures in the dark, wooded area.

"There were lots of quick and violent deaths right on this spot and many bodies were hurriedly buried here. It's no surprise that this is a heavily haunted area. Feel free to wander around and take a few more photos before we move on."

Some of the hardier souls wandered into the dark, taking photos and looking for spirits. The poor lady in the back clung to her boyfriend. He seemed to be having a good time even if she wasn't.

"You know," Remy said softly to Avery as she looked around at the wooded area. "It's still sad, no matter how much time has passed. So many lives lost."

"Indeed," Avery nodded somberly. He brightened a little and asked, "So do you think they'll catch any ghosties on their cameras?"

Remy laughed, then said, "I *highly* doubt it. People do get weird images here all the time though. Orbs and whatnot. It's a trick of light, dust on the lens, whatever. I hope people do get something, though, because they really love that kind of thing."

Avery regarded her with amusement. "You really don't believe any of this stuff, do ye?"

"Of course not," Remy said with a laugh.

"You're a good liar, then."

"Oh, I hate to think of it as lying. The idea of ghosts gets people intrigued, excited, and that makes me happy, too." Remy looked at the amateur ghost hunters in her group with fondness. "If they think they see or feel something, it gives them a thrill and a fun story to tell for the rest of their lives. I like that I'm a part of that."

Avery smiled at her with such tenderness and affection that her heart flipped inside her chest. *Maybe he does like me after all.* Remy spent so much of her time alone, and it felt good to have someone there with her tonight. Someone who wasn't paying for entertainment, but who was actually there to visit *her.* And she was in her element when she was leading a tour. She was confident in her knowledge, both of Gettysburg history and ghost tales, and in her ability to interact well with her group. Remy was proud of her work as a tour guide, and it felt good to have the man she adored here to watch her do what she did best.

"Okay guys, let's move on to our next stop—the Jennie Wade House!" Remy led her group back out onto the main streets of Gettysburg.

"Ahh, your home," Avery said with a twinkle in his eye. "At least durin' the day."

"Well, technically, it wasn't Jennie's home. It belonged to—"

"Jennie's sister, Georgia McClellan,'" Avery finished for her with a grin.

Remy laughed heartily again. "Of course! Sometimes I forget you're a tour guide, too. You probably know as much as I do, if not more."

"Nonsense. I'm learning a lot tonight about ghosts."

Remy smiled and looked into those handsome gray eyes of his for as long as she could before tearing her gaze away. She loved talking with him, being with him. And she couldn't help but wonder what it would feel like to touch him. Avery had an impressive build, tall and broad-shouldered. *He must be so strong.* For a brief moment, she allowed herself to fantasize about Avery gathering her into those strong arms and carrying her to bed. She let out an audible sigh just thinking about it.

"You all right?" Avery asked.

Oh, don't mind me. I'm just having sexual fantasies about you, you gorgeous Irishman.

"Yes. Just a little tired," Remy said, forcing herself back to reality. She faced her group and told the Jennie Wade story pretty much the same way she told it during the daytime tour; at least the first part. She could feel Avery watching her as she led the group inside the house, though he kept a careful distance from her. She figured he didn't want to get her in trouble for talking too much to a personal friend while she was working.

Remy led her group down to the basement, which was a rather creepy place even in the daytime. It was dingy and dark, with cool yet humid air. Jennie's family had carried her corpse down here while they hid from bullets still flying as the battle raged just outside their door. There was a fake dead body lying on a table in the corner of the small basement room, an arm hanging out from under the blanket. Most tour guests found it creepy and cool. She checked on the scared blonde lady, who looked tense and a little pale. Remy smiled warmly at her, and the woman smiled gratefully back.

Remy hated scaring sensitive people who were genuinely upset, but she owed it to her group to give them a spooky tour. She waited until all was quiet before she spoke.

"It's not uncommon to hear strange noises down here, especially late at night. Jennie herself has been spotted on many occasions, just drifting aimlessly through the house."

Her audience was captivated. Several guests looked nervously around, as if expecting to see the ghost of Jennie Wade at any moment. Avery looked fascinated as he watched Remy speak, and a tingly thrill went up her spine. *He's so damned cute,* she thought. She found herself longing to be alone with him. To stare into those kind, gray eyes of his and listen to that masculine, accented voice as he told her everything she wanted to know about him. Remy imagined how it would feel to have his hand holding hers, or what it would be like to have his strong arm wrapped around her waist. She thought about how Avery would look as he dipped his head down to kiss her. His lips gently touching hers as he ran his fingers through her hair. It all seemed too much to hope for.

Remy fell silent for a moment. She was lost in her fantasies about Avery, but the moment of silence worked well on the ghost tour as it gave people a chance to revel in the eerie quiet.

"Okay," Remy said in a quiet, spooky voice. "Now we head to our final stop. The haunted orphanage."

Remy led her group out the door and headed across the street.

"Great job in there," Avery said. "I'm good and scared!"

She laughed. "Don't worry, Avery. I'll protect you from the ghosts."

Avery laughed harder then she would have expected at that. He had a deep, sexy laugh, which made her wish she were funnier so she could hear it again.

"What is now a Civil War museum was once the site of a children's orphanage," Remy explained. "Late at night, you can still hear the sounds of children laughing and playing. Some of the little ones have even been spotted across the street over at the Jennie Wade house. Like at the Farnsworth House with Jeremy, guests sometimes leave toys inside for the children to play with. There have even been reports of a rubber ball moving by itself inside."

Remy paused for a moment, allowing her guests the chance to peer inside the windows of the museum and mill around a bit.

Avery leaned in close to her and said gently, "I see you left out the part about how the owners used to keep the orphans locked up in the cellar."

Remy looked into Avery's sweet, sad eyes, and her heart melted. It didn't matter that the tragedy happened over 150 years ago. Avery clearly found the story as sorrowful as she still did.

"Yeah, I leave that part out when I have little ones on my tour."

Avery nodded and smiled at her.

"Okay!" Remy announced cheerfully. "Time to head back to where we started. I hope you all enjoyed the tour, and please feel free to ask me any questions you might have."

A few of the tourists walked toward her to take her up on her offer.

"Well, I better go and let you finish up your tour," Avery said.

Remy's heart sank. She hated to see him go, and she berated herself for not asking him to go out for a drink or something. Never mind the fact that she didn't drink.

"Oh, okay. Maybe I'll see you on tour at Little Round Top?" she asked hopefully.

Avery smiled fondly at her. "I certainly hope so."

Remy smiled as he walked away.

"He's cute," said an older lady, who smiled knowingly at Remy. "I think he likes you."

Remy giggled. "Maybe."

I hope so.

Chapter 7

Lucy felt the man's presence again. Not only did she know someone was in the room with her; she knew it was the ghost who had harassed her before. When Jesse was still a ghost, she always knew when he was near even when he was invisible. She could feel his warmth and love when he was close by.

Now she felt a heavy sense of dread.

"I know you're here," Lucy said as she continued filling the salt and pepper shakers in the empty dining room of the restaurant. "And I know who you are, Ellis."

Lucy jumped as Ellis faded into view. His black hat was so large that it obscured his face when he looked down. He lifted his head and peered at her with those creepy dark eyes of his.

"What I don't know is why you're bothering me and why you felt the need to touch me like you did," she said, her anger flaring when she remembered how he had put his hands on her breasts. She was shy and protective of her body. No one but Jesse had permission to touch her there.

"Women are nothin' but cheap whores. You all deserve to be grabbed like that. That's all you're good for," Ellis said gruffly.

Lucy rolled her eyes, doing her best to not to show that he was getting to her. She pictured Jesse's gentle face and was grateful that her boyfriend was kind and respectful of women.

"You don't think you're a slut?" he asked.

Hardly. She'd only been with two men, which was beside the point. It didn't matter if she'd been with dozens of men. Who was this guy to pass judgment on how she lived her life? Lucy kept her expression steady and refused to answer him.

"I know what a whore you are. I saw you that night on top of the bar downstairs."

Lucy froze.

When he was still a ghost, Jesse had fallen in love with her as he watched her work in the tavern day after day. He once confessed his private fantasy of having sex with her on the bartop. When he was alive again, she had taken him to the restaurant after hours and they'd made love on top of the bar just as he had fantasized. It been the most exciting, satisfying sexual experience she had ever had. It was a special memory she held in her heart, and she thought of Jesse every time she passed by that bartop when she was at work.

Ellis must have been there that night. Invisible. Watching.

A wave of humiliation and revulsion crashed over Lucy. Jesse had insisted that she keep her clothes on the whole time, just in case anyone walked in on them. Ellis might not have seen her naked, but he had watched her during one of the most intimate moments of her life.

Lucy tentatively glanced at him, and he laughed derisively.

"Thought you two were alone, now, didn't ya? Didn't feel my presence then, did ya? You were too busy feeling Jesse's cock in your—"

"Stop it!" Lucy cried. "Why are you saying these horrible things?"

"Because you're a cheap slut just like every other woman I've ever known. 'Cept you're worse because you think you're so sweet and pure.

You're not." Ellis laughed again, an awful, scornful sound. He drifted closer to her and leaned in. "I saw you, Lucy. I saw you spread your legs for him. I heard you scream his name when he made you—"

"Stop it!"

"Well at least your cowboy's a good lover, judgin' by the way you kept hollerin' his name. Hope that made it worth what happened to you at Devil's Den. You screamed a lot that day I hear, but I don't think you was havin' much fun that time."

"How do you know about that?" Lucy asked, horrified. Her natural sensitivity to the paranormal came at a price, and she had suffered a rare phenomenon at Devil's Den. If she stood on a battlefield where a soldier had died, someone she had some connection to, she would feel their mortal wounds. She had experienced the agony of Jesse's excruciating death that day, when he was still a spirit and could do nothing to save her. It wasn't Jesse's fault, but he still blamed himself for what happened to her.

"I hang around. I hear things. Everybody knows what happened to you. And now you know how bad it hurt when Jesse died. Lord, how he must've suffered. Prob'ly still has nightmares about it. Goddamn Reb. He deserved to suffer. I'd'a killed him myself if I'd had the chance."

Tears spilled from Lucy's eyes as she let out a choked sob. She was about to run downstairs to reach the safety of her coworkers, but Ellis let out another taunting laugh and then floated out of the room.

Lucy let out a deep but shaky sigh. She looked around the room and she could feel he wasn't just invisible; he was gone.

Lucy covered her eyes and wept harder.

*****

Avery floated down the street, invisible, and in a happy daze. Being with Remy had lifted his spirits so high that he didn't think he'd ever felt more alive, even when he was still living. He had loved watching her give her tour presentation. She was masterful, knowledgeable, yet sweet and approachable. Remy was like a movie star, and he had been dazzled by her dynamic, commanding presence. Any man would be lucky just to have her look his way. And, if he wasn't mistaken, she seemed to enjoy looking at him. Being with him.

Avery continued meandering down the street with no real destination in mind. He typically vanished during the night due to sheer boredom, but now he was so happy that he didn't want the feeling to end.

His eyes narrowed as he caught a glimpse of a familiar yet unwelcome sight. It was that awful black-hatted man. Avery saw Ellis float out of Meade's Tavern and disappear down a side street. Anxiety prickled in his ghostly stomach.

Lucy.

Avery rushed down the street, still invisible, and floated into the tavern. He drifted into the main dining room, where he saw a busboy clearing off some tables.

Maybe she's not working tonight, he thought hopefully. Maybe Ellis came to bother her but she wasn't here.

Avery rushed up the stairs and found Lucy in the upper dining room sitting by herself. Crying.

A rush of tenderness flooded through Avery when he saw her.

Lucy lifted her head and looked around fearfully. "Who's there?"

Avery carefully faded in, not wanting to scare her.

"Oh, Lucy, darlin'" Avery said softly. "I saw Ellis out on the street."

Lucy looked relieved as she looked into Avery's sad, worried eyes. "He was here," she managed in a shaky voice.

"Oh, dear God, did he hurt you?" Avery said, rushing to her side.

"No," Lucy said, wiping her eyes. "Not physically, anyway. He said some horrible things to me. I know it's stupid to be upset over it. It's just words."

There was a chair next to her that was already pulled out, so Avery sat in it. Or at least he appeared to sit. He gazed into her eyes.

"No, it's not stupid, Lucy. Not't'all."

Lucy smiled gratefully at him. Avery wished with all his heart that he had the physical strength to go after that horrid man. If nothing else, he was thankful that he could be here to comfort Lucy. He knew Jesse would be heartbroken if he knew how distraught she was. At least Avery could take care of her until she could get home to him.

"He said awful things like he wished he had been the one to kill Jesse." Lucy stifled a sob and dabbed at her eyes again.

"Oh, darlin'. I'm so sorry. It's all right. He's gone now. I won't let him hurt you anymore." Avery might not be able to physically stop him from coming into the restaurant, but maybe he could chase him away. Even if Ellis stayed to taunt her, she wouldn't be alone.

"Thank you. That makes me feel a lot better." Lucy drew in a deep breath and let it out. She seemed a bit calmer. She looked around at the dining room. "I better finish up so I can get out of here."

Lucy stood up. She looked a little shaky, but all right otherwise.

"Would you like me to stay with you?" Avery asked.

"That would be wonderful, Avery. Thank you so much," Lucy said with a sweet smile.

She sounded relieved, and Avery was grateful that he could make her feel better. It wasn't often that he felt useful to anyone anymore.

Avery smiled at her as he watched her straighten up the tables. "Happy to do it. I just wish I could help you with your work!"

Lucy laughed softly. "Jesse used to say the same thing. You know, when he was like you."

"Jesse's a good man."

"Yes, he sure is," Lucy said.

"Sooo," Avery began, figuring it might help if he distracted Lucy with a bit of conversation. "I don't know if you'll approve of this or not, but I just came from joining Remy on her ghost tour."

"Is that so? Did she *know* you joined her?" Lucy asked dryly.

"Yes, she surely did," Avery said with a laugh. "I know Jesse got himself into a bit of hot water with you over that kind of thing. I confess I have watched her without her knowing. Only in public, you know! I am a gentleman, after all."

"I know you are," Lucy said with fondness.

"Remy knew I was there, and we had a nice talk. She's a wonderful tour guide, ya know? She's got such a way with people."

"Well, she has you wrapped around her little finger, that's for sure," Lucy said as she placed silverware on each table.

"Aye, that she does!" Avery said with a laugh.

Lucy scanned the room to make sure she had taken care of everything. "Well, I guess I'm about done. I just need to wrap up a few things downstairs and clock out."

"Where did you park?" Avery asked.

"Just a few blocks away."

"May I walk you to your car?"

Lucy's grateful smile filled him with warmth. It made him happy that he could help her, and therefore help Jesse indirectly. Avery knew Jesse would want him to protect her in his absence.

"That would be lovely, Avery. Thank you."

*****

The next morning, Avery was happy to see Jesse and Remy walking toward him at Little Round Top. As always, he was eager to talk to Remy, but he also wanted to find out how Lucy was doing. Sorrow tugged at his heart every time he pictured her sitting there in the restaurant dining room, crying all alone.

"Hello, beautiful!" Avery called to Remy when she got near.

"Good morning, Avery," Remy said with smile. Avery found it hard to tear his gaze away from those pretty blue eyes of hers, but he turned to Jesse.

"Jesse," he said worriedly. "How's Lucy? Is she all right?"

Jesse nodded grimly, his expression hardening. "She's doing a little better. She was really upset last night."

"What happened to Lucy?" Remy asked, her eyes wide.

"Some horrible man was harassing her in the restaurant last night," Jesse said. "And it's not the first time he's bothered her."

"I stopped in to say hello last night after I was with you," Avery told Remy. "And I'm so glad I did. She was all upset and cryin'."

"Oh, no," Remy said, looking distressed.

"Avery, I can't thank you enough for takin' care of her. She said you stayed with her and walked her to her car." Jesse's eyes were filled with relief and gratitude.

"I'm glad I could help. And I'll be happy to check on her at night when she's workin' late," Avery said.

"That would be great," Jesse said. "I really appreciate it. I can't wait 'til she graduates and starts teachin' during the day so she don't have to work late no more."

"Indeed," Avery agreed.

"Well, I'm gonna go check and make sure my tourists are okay," Jesse said, giving Avery a knowing smile. He walked away, leaving Remy and Avery alone for a few moments.

"That's awful about Lucy," Remy said with concern. "Do you think that guy's dangerous?"

"I don't know," Avery said, wishing he could reassure Remy by telling her that the guy barely had the strength to touch Lucy, and there wasn't much he could do to physically harm her. "But he must have said some awful things to her. Don't know what he said 'zactly. I didn't want to worry her more by pressin' for details, but she was really upset."

"Poor Lucy," Remy said. "I'll call her later and make sure she's all right."

"That's kind of you, Remy," Avery said.

"Hope you got some rest last night," Remy said. "You were out late."

"Surely was. But worth losin' rest if it means I get to be with you," Avery said.

Remy smiled, and Avery could swear he saw hope in her eyes. Was she wishing for a future with him? He knew he should feel guilty for getting her hopes up, but right now all he felt was sheer joy. She looked at him like she truly cared for him, and he couldn't help but be happy.

"Do you think maybe sometime we could..." Remy trailed off, uncertain.

Avery stood there, frozen. If she asked to go out with him, what should he say? He realized he should have rehearsed this possibility with Jesse before it came up.

Remy seemed embarrassed by his silence, and Avery hated himself for making her uncomfortable. It was horrible of him to enjoy her affection for him while he knew all along it could only result in heartbreak.

"Never mind. I better go help Jesse," Remy said, avoiding his gaze.

"Remy, please don't—" Avery began.

She kept walking as if she didn't hear him.

Chapter 8

Remy knew she needed to get over Avery O'Rorke. She'd known the man for over a month, and all they ever did was talk. As *friends*. Every time she thought Avery was going to take their relationship a step further—ask her to dinner or just to hang out after work instead of during her shift—he pulled back.

Avery was the most wonderful man Remy had ever known. She adored his soft, compassionate gray eyes, his sense of humor, and his sexy Irish brogue. For a time, she had dared to believe he might be interested in her. Now, she was forced to face the harsh facts. The man had had ample opportunity to pursue her, and he just plain wasn't interested. Remy was heartsick and exhausted. Tired of the games and the constant, crushing disappointment. She wasn't just hurt, she was angry. Angry at Avery for leading her on and breaking her heart.

Remy sat in the break room at work, grateful that no one else was in there eating lunch. She picked up her cell phone and dialed.

"Lucy? It's Remy. Got a minute?"

"Of course!" Lucy chirped in her usual friendly voice. Remy felt better already.

"Well, it might take more than a minute. Do you have the time and the energy to listen to me vent?"

"Of course I have time for you, Remy. It's actually a good time. I'm at home just hanging out. I don't have to go into work for a few hours."

"Cool," Remy said. She sighed heavily. "But before I start whining about my problems, are you all right? Jesse says some creep was bothering you last night at work?"

Lucy let out a sigh. "Yeah, it was pretty awful. Avery happened to stop by and cheer me up, though, and Jesse took good care of me when I got home. I'm okay, Rem. Really. Now tell me what's going on, sweetie."

"It's Avery. Ugh, it's so stupid. I'm all upset about him, and I hate myself for it. I've been on my own for so long, ya know? I can take care of myself. I've been doing it long enough."

"I know you have, and I really admire you for it. You have zero support from your family, but you made it all the way through school, and you work so hard. I'm proud of you, even if your awful family isn't."

"Thanks, Lucy. I really appreciate it," Remy said. "That's why I hate myself for getting all worked up over some stupid guy. I don't *need* a man in my life!"

"Of course you don't, but you need to stop being so hard on yourself. Needing a man and wanting to have a really nice guy in your life are not the same thing. You're not one of those needy girls who's always on a manhunt because they don't know how to live without a guy."

"That's true," Remy grumbled. "I never want to be like that."

"Don't be mad at yourself for liking Avery. That's silly."

"I guess," Remy said with a sigh. "I'm starting to be mad at him, though. I just don't understand him! He acts like he really likes me, you know? I let myself hope that he might want to be with me, and then," Remy choked back tears. "And then he rejects me every time. Just when I think he's gonna ask me out or something, he doesn't. He might have a girlfriend or something, and maybe he doesn't mention it because he doesn't want to hurt my feelings."

Lucy sighed, but said nothing.

"God, I feel like such an idiot! I go and talk to him every day, and he probably thinks I'm like some dumb, annoying girl who likes him and won't leave him alone."

"Remy," Lucy said firmly. "I'm sure that's not true."

"I just don't know what to do anymore." Remy finally let her tears fall. She took a moment to compose herself before speaking again. "All I know is I don't wanna feel like this anymore. I think I just need to start avoiding him from now on. I'm tired of these games. I just need to accept that he's not interested in me, and I just need to move on."

"I know it's hard to understand what's going on with him. You never know, there might be some kind of reason that he's holding back. I've seen the way he looks at you, Remy. I think he genuinely likes you. More than you know," Lucy said.

"I want to believe that. I used to believe that. But for my own sanity, I have to just let him go." Remy wiped her eyes again and silently resolved to be cordial to Avery the next time she happened to see him, but offer nothing more. She was done making a fool of herself for him. "The next time I go to Little Round Top, I'm not gonna go over and talk to him. I'm done. I'm so done."

*****

Lucy wrapped up her work at the restaurant at 5:30 pm and headed straight to the spot on Steinwehr Avenue where she knew Jesse and Avery would be chatting with Fillis. She was glad the two guys were there, because she had something important to discuss with them.

Jesse smiled warmly as she walked up to them, and Lucy knew she had to stay strong in her resolve. It was all too easy for her to be swayed by that sweet face of his.

"Hi," Lucy said as she looked down at Fillis and the boys as they sat on the steps.

"Uh-oh," Jesse said with that boyish grin that made Lucy weak. "Are we in trouble or somethin'?"

"Not yet," Lucy said kindly but firmly. "Guys, we need to tell Remy the truth about Avery."

Avery's face fell. Empathy twisted up in Lucy's stomach, but she knew this was best for Remy.

"I know it's hard, but we have to do it. She's falling hard for you, Avery."

Avery perked up, his eyes wide. He looked so delighted that Lucy couldn't suppress a giggle.

"I know that's good news for you, but she's really hurting right now. She feels rejected. She thinks you don't like her."

"Oh, God," Avery moaned. "How could she think I don't *like* her! I *love* her!"

Lucy let out a soft, sad sigh. It was the first time she'd ever heard Avery say that out loud.

"I know you do," Lucy said with compassion. "But she doesn't understand why you seem interested in her one minute and the next minute you're telling her goodbye. She has no way of understanding why you never ask her on a date. She's starting to think you have a girlfriend or that you just don't care about her. We need to tell her the truth about you so she knows why you can't ask her out on a normal date."

Avery paused, considering her words. Lucy's chest ached when she looked at him, and her anxiety worsened when she looked at Jesse's worried face.

Lucy sat down next to Avery, wishing she could take his hand in hers. "She's going to find out eventually. At least this way we can break the news to her as gently as we can. Otherwise, she's going to find out the hard way."

"Lucy's absolutely right," Fillis said confidently. She turned to Jesse. "Boy, you was a mess when Lucy found out about you, 'member? 'Cause I sure do!"

"Yeah," Jesse said sadly. He looked over at Avery. "She sure did find out the hard way. I scared the hell out of her, and that was the last thing I wanted."

"She needs to know all the facts, honey," Fillis said gently to Avery. "From what you all told me 'bout that poor girl, she ain't had anybody in her life care for her 'til now. Her own family treated her bad, and the last thing she needs is to think you're rejectin' her, too."

Avery nodded, his expression pained. Lucy knew he hated the idea of hurting Remy.

"Aye, that's true. She deserves so much better," Avery said.

"Well, they don't come much better than you, boy. It'll be good for her to know there's somebody out there in the world who loves her. No feelin' like it in the world." Fillis fell silent for a moment, and seemed to be lost in thought.

Lucy looked at her curiously. "Have you ever been in love, Fillis?"

"Yes," Fillis said simply. She sounded tired.

"You were in love with Helene, weren't you? The master's wife?" Lucy asked. Fillis often joked about her sexual relationship with the woman, brushing it off as if it were just physical, but Lucy had long suspected there was more to it.

Fillis hesitated in responding, and Lucy regretted asking her something so personal.

"I'm sorry, Fillis," Lucy said, blushing deeply and looking down. "I shouldn't have asked. It's none of my business."

"Oh, honey, don't be sorry," Fillis said in her usual motherly tone. "It ain't that I *was* in love with Helene. I still *am* in love with her. Even after all this time. When her husband found out, I hadda go or he'd have killed us both." Fillis closed her eyes and said quietly, "He mighta killed her anyway. I don't have no way of knowin.'" Fillis opened her eyes again and smiled sadly at Lucy.

Jesse's eyes opened wide. "You ain't never told me none of that!"

"You ain't never asked!" Fillis said with a laugh.

Jesse stared at her, his gentle eyes full of sorrow. He said softly, "You're right. I'm always so busy runnin' to you with my own problems that I don't ever listen to you. I'm real sorry, Second Mama."

"Don't you be sorry, honey. I much rather talk about you than me, boy."

"Do you miss her?" Lucy asked.

"Every single day," Fillis told her.

"What was she like?" Lucy asked.

Fillis looked surprised at the question, then she smiled. "She had pretty brown hair like yours, only lighter. And she had nice gray eyes kinda like yours," she said to Avery. She laughed. "At first, I thought she was a terrible snob, just like her husband. All high and mighty like him. Come to find out she was only like that 'round him because that's what he wanted. Found out he hit her when she didn't act right."

Lucy put her hand over her heart. She could hear the love in Fillis's voice when she spoke about Helene. She sounded just like Avery did when he talked about Remy.

"But when he was gone outta town? Oh, that's when we got to see the real Helene. She'd come down to the slave quarters and play with us. Especially the chillren. Oh, she loved our chillren. And I loved hers."

Fillis paused for a moment, gathering her emotional strength before she could continue.

No one made a sound as they waited for her to go on. Jesse had known this woman for more than one hundred and fifty years, yet Lucy had the feeling he'd never heard her talk like this.

"She had two little boys and a girl. Loved them like my own. Lost 'em all when I had to run away."

Lucy wiped a tear from her eye. Fillis mothered all the soldiers around her, but who was mothering her?

"I lived for those times when her husband was away. She'd come down to visit us, laugh with us. Was easy to forget our differences durin' those times. I fell in love with her when we were both young women. Happiest day o' my life was one day when we's working the fields and she told me she needed my help up at the house. After she shooed away all the house servants, she took me aside and told me she loved me." Fillis laughed softly. "Biggest shock I ever had! I told her I loved her, too. She and I were secret lovers for more than thirty years 'fore her idiot husband found out."

Jesse, Lucy, and Avery were spellbound by her tale.

"The place we lived in was called Bellflower Plantation 'cause of the beautiful gardens we had all around. Huge, colorful flower gardens all around the place. They was her pride and joy. Oh, how she loved them flowers. My favorite memory is her standing there in the middle of them flowers. She was just as pretty as they were. That's the way I like to remember her."

Lucy drew in a shaky breath and wiped her tears.

"Oh, honey, now don't go gettin' all upset," Fillis told her warmly.

"Maybe we can help you get back to her, Fillis. Theresa and I, we've helped so many others cross over. Theresa could counsel you and figure out why you—"

"No, no. I'll hear none of that!" Fillis said kindly but firmly. "Right now, we need to focus on Avery's troubles." Fillis got up and looked around at all the tourists on the busy street. "Now, let's go somewhere quiet where we can talk so's we can figure out how you all are goin' tell Remy the truth without upsettin' her too much."

There was so much more Lucy wanted to say to Fillis, but the older woman had made it clear that the conversation was over.

"It's goin' be all right, Avery," Fillis told him. "We'll sit down and figger out what you're goin' say, and it's gonna be just fine."

Avery smiled gratefully and followed Fillis's lead down the street.

Jesse and Lucy exchanged a wide-eyed look, stunned at Fillis's story. Like most children, they mostly thought of Fillis as a mom, not as a real woman with a life outside of them. Lucy's heart ached for Fillis, and she was determined to do her best to reunite her with Helene. Fillis was every bit as stubborn as some of her soldier boys, but Lucy wasn't going to give up until she helped her cross over to be with her family.

Chapter 9

Avery was a nervous wreck. He knew he had to tell Remy he was dead, but he couldn't bear the thought of her thinking of him as some kind of ghoul.

Jesse and Lucy watched him as he paced back and forth across the floor of the break room of the Blue and Gray Touring Company. The daytime tours were done, and Remy had the night off from her ghost tours, so this was as good a time as any. Since Remy was an assistant manager of the company where she and Jesse worked, she would be able to close the place and lock up when they were done. Right now, Remy was closing out the register in the main room and gift shop. Jesse had texted her and asked her to come to the break room when she was done.

Finally, the door swung open.

"Hey," Remy said, looking at Avery and Lucy. "What are you guys doing here?"

Avery froze when he saw her. He had thought he was ready, but when he gazed into her lovely but confused blue eyes, he wasn't sure he could go through with it. Jesse had warned him that there was really no way to prepare yourself for what it feels like to have the woman you love be afraid of you.

"Uh, Remy, there's…there's something we need to talk to you about. Something we need to tell you," Avery cautiously began.

"Oh," Remy said, looking terrified already.

Remy looked at Avery, then at Jesse, then at Lucy. No one spoke. Remy waited.

"Will somebody please say something? You're scaring me!" Remy said, looking at Avery pleadingly.

"Uh, well, uh…"Avery faltered. There was so much he wanted to say to her. He desperately wished he could start by saying how much he loved her, but he knew that would be all wrong. Way too much too soon, and that might frighten her off as much as his being dead would.

Lucy looked at Avery pleadingly, willing him to say something, anything, to help put Remy at ease. Finally, Lucy couldn't stand it anymore.

"Well, the good news is that Avery is absolutely crazy about you," Lucy said.

Remy looked over at Avery. She seemed shocked at first, but then smiled with relief. She glanced over at Jesse and Lucy, no doubt wondering why there was an audience for such a private conversation.

"Well, then, why doesn't he just say so himself?" Remy said, looking over at Avery.

"I'm absolutely crazy about you," Avery repeated Lucy's words, finally finding his voice. "Remy, I *adore* you, and I'm so sorry if I didn't make that clear sooner."

Remy let out a breath. She looked into his eyes, and his heart melted. He was finally able to stop putting up a front and gazed at her with all the love and affection he felt for her.

"Avery," she said softly. "I feel the same way about you."

Remy took a step toward him, but Lucy put a hand on her shoulder to stop her. "There's more," Lucy said. "A lot more."

Remy looked at her, then at Avery.

"Avery," Lucy said. "I know how hard this is, but I think this news really needs to come from you."

"I know," Avery said nervously. "You're right o' course. Remy…"

Remy met his gaze fearfully. "It's something terrible, isn't it? You're not dying, are you?"

Avery laughed ruefully. "No. Not exactly. Okay. Here's what's going to happen. I'm going to tell you something about myself, you're not going to believe it, and then Lucy is going to help me prove it to you."

Avery glanced over at Lucy, who nodded, ready to go forward with the plan the way they had rehearsed.

"Okay," Remy said, still looking terrified.

"Remy, me darlin'," Avery began cautiously, "I'm not really a Civil War reenactor or a tour guide." He gestured toward his gray Confederate uniform. "This isn't a costume. They're me real clothes. I really did fight with the 15th Alabama durin' the war. I fought…and I died. I'm just a spirit now." He gazed deeply into her eyes and whispered, "A ghost."

Remy let out a deep, weary sigh. She gathered her thoughts a moment before speaking. "I just…I'm trying to figure out why in the hell you would say something like that to me."

She shook her head angrily.

"Aye, well, this is the part where you don't believe me," Avery said sadly.

Lucy turned to Remy, her eyes full of worry. "Remy, I know this seems absolutely crazy to you. Believe me, I understand. But what Avery is telling you is true. He fought in the war and died in the year 1863."

Remy let out another bitter sigh. She looked so defeated. Avery's heart ached as he could only imagine what was going through her mind. She must think they were all crazy, or that the people who she thought were her friends were messing with her head for some reason.

"Now Avery and I are going to prove to you that what we're telling you is true." Lucy took Remy's hand and squeezed it, and she was sure to look her in the eye. She said kindly but firmly, "Remy. I'm going to try to touch Avery now, and you need to understand that when I do, *my hand will go right through his.* Because when you see Avery, you're seeing his spirit. His wonderful, kind, loving spirit. But he doesn't have a physical body anymore. Because he died long ago."

Remy studied Lucy's serious expression, looking more confused than ever.

Lucy let go of Remy's hand and walked over to Avery. She gazed into his eyes and smiled warmly. Avery was grateful to have such a sweet, gentle friend like Lucy to help him through this. She seemed every bit as worried about him as she was about Remy.

"It's okay," Lucy whispered to Avery.

Lucy held up her hand, and Avery held up his. She smiled again, still looking reassuringly into his eyes as she pushed her hand all the way through his. They both waited a moment, afraid to look to see how Remy would react.

Lucy turned around and gasped. "Jesse, catch her!"

Remy looked frighteningly pale and was wobbly on her feet.

Jesse rushed to Remy's side and put his arm around her. "It's okay, darlin'." He carefully sat her down in a chair and crouched beside her. "Don't be afraid, Remy. Avery is still the same guy he always was. It's not his fault, he's, you know…"

Jesse must have figured it was wise to avoid using the word "dead" until Remy had a chance to get used to the idea.

Remy lifted her gaze from Jesse to look over at Avery.

"Wh-what is that? Some kind of hologram or something?"

Bewildered, she looked at Jesse and then at Lucy. "Wh-why would you do something like this to me?"

"That's just it, Remy," Lucy said softly, walking over to her and putting a comforting hand on her shoulder. "We wouldn't."

Remy looked into Lucy's worried face, then turned to see Jesse gazing at her with equal concern. Avery watched as the realization dawned on her.

"No," Remy whispered. "No, you wouldn't do a thing like that to me." She looked over at Avery, who was still standing a safe distance away from her. "I-I don't understand."

"I know it seems impossible, Remy," Avery said. "Most of the men and women you see 'round here are indeed reenactors or guides and such, but some of us...some of us are the real deal. We died long ago, and yet, we're still here."

Remy covered her face with her hands and drew in a deep breath. Avery had never felt so damned helpless in his long, lonely existence. The woman he loved more than anything in the world was upset and terrified, and there wasn't a damn thing he could do about it. Worse, he knew it was his fault she was feeling this way.

Jesse and Lucy put their arms around her and murmured words of comfort to her.

"I'm the same man you've known all this time, Remy," Avery said plaintively, aching to find some way to make her understand. A way to make her go back to looking at him with affection like she used to. "*Tá tú go h-álainn*, my darling Remy."

Remy glanced up in recognition of the phrase.

"*Tá tú go h-álainn*," Avery repeated. "*Adhraím thú*, Remy. That means I adore you."

Remy finally looked into his eyes from across the room. It was only for the briefest of moments, then she tore her gaze away and let out a shaky breath.

"*Táim i ngrá leat*," Avery whispered to her. He didn't translate that phrase, but from the sorrowful way that Jesse and Lucy looked at him, he figured they could guess what it meant. *I'm in love with you.*

Remy carefully stood up, still looking pale. "I need…I think I need some air."

Jesse nodded, watching her carefully to make sure she was steady on her feet. Her hands trembling, Remy picked up the keys from the table and handed them to Jesse.

"Jesse, can you lock up and—"

"Of course, Remy. I'll take care of the shop here," Jesse reassured her.

"I'll walk out with you, Remy," Lucy said, putting her hand on Remy's back. She turned to Jesse and said gently, "I'll take care of her. You take care of Avery."

Jesse nodded sadly.

Remy looked fearfully toward the door where Avery was standing. She was visibly petrified to go near him.

Avery slowly walked away from the door to let her pass. Jesse was right. There was no way to prepare yourself for what it feels like to have the woman you love be afraid of you.

Lucy led Remy to the door.

"Remy!" Avery called after her. She turned, her expression one of fear and bewilderment that sent a sharp stab of pain right through his heart. "I'll understand if you don't want to be near me anymore. I know you need time to think. But if you want to see me again, you know where I'll be."

Remy nodded numbly, then turned to leave.

*****

Remy was dimly aware of Lucy's hand on her back as they made their way out of the Blue and Gray Touring Company gift shop and ticket office. She let Lucy lead her over to a picnic table outside the store and, as luck would have it, overlooking Gettysburg National Cemetery.

Good God, was Avery buried there?

Her mind cleared enough to register that it was unlikely since Avery fought for the Confederacy, and the cemetery was populated almost entirely by Union soldiers.

Avery fought for the Confederacy.

Remy's logical, rational mind tried to refute the whole crazy notion. That wasn't possible. Was it? Remy recalled seeing Lucy's hand go through Avery's, and she shivered.

"It's gonna be okay, Remy. Just try to take a few deep breaths and you'll feel better," Lucy said, squeezing Remy's hand from across the picnic table.

Remy did as she was told, and inhaled the fresh, warm air. It did help a little.

"I know you're feeling completely overwhelmed right now and you must have a million questions. Just take your time, and let me know what I can possibly do to make this easier on you," Lucy said gently.

Remy let go of Lucy's hand and covered her face for a moment. Then she said, "It just…it can't be true…can it?"

Lucy smiled. "I know it seems impossible. And believe me, I understand exactly what you're going through. I felt the same way when I found out that not all the uniformed people around here are reenactors. I was terrified and confused, too. But Remy, what we told you is true. Avery is a wonderful man and a loyal friend. But he's dead."

Remy gasped. Hearing it out loud like that was shocking.

"But he's the same sexy, sweet Irish guy we all know and adore, Remy."

Remy nodded.

"Oh, Remy," Lucy began. "There's so much I want to tell you, but I don't know if more information will help you or just overwhelm you more."

Remy drew in a sharp breath and let it out. "No, I think more information is good. I need to know exactly what the hell is going on. What else do you know that I don't?"

"Oh, my goodness, where to begin," Lucy said with a laugh. "Okay, just like you, I was friends with a guy—well, two guys actually—who I thought were reenactors, but it turned out they were real soldiers like Avery. I found out by accident when I went to touch one of them on the shoulder."

"Oh, no," Remy said, eyes wide.

"Remy, I had *never* been so scared in my life. I'd always been afraid of ghosts. I would be one of those tourists you had to tiptoe around on your ghost tours, you know? You'd be like, 'Oh, man that brown-haired lady is scared out of her mind. I better go easy on the spooky stories.'"

Remy laughed, feeling a little better. Lucy was such a dear friend, and it felt familiar and comfortable to talk with her, even about this insane topic. She was grateful for the sense of normalcy she felt with her friend.

"I was so scared that I passed out, so you took the news a lot better than I did!" Lucy said with a laugh. "Okay, so do you promise you'll believe what I say next? Do you believe we're all telling you the truth about Avery?"

Remy nodded slowly. She still wasn't sure, but her mind was struggling to come up with any other rational explanation for the day's events. Avery O'Rorke did not seem to have a physical body, and she trusted that Jesse and Lucy wouldn't play a horrific trick on her like that.

"The soldier I tried to touch when he was dead? It was Jesse."

"Jesse!" Remy practically shouted. "He can't be dead. I touch him all the time. I mean, I didn't mean…I just mean he teases me and I punch him on the shoulder and stuff. And I just handed him my keys in there and—"

"He *was* dead. He's not anymore." Lucy surveyed Remy's expression and pressed on. "I know, I know it's crazy. Okay, look…the way it works is, most people who die go on to heaven right away. I mean, thousands of soldiers died in the battle of Gettysburg, and most of them are, you know, *gone*. But there are some who have personal issues or whatever that keep them stuck here on earth. When they finally work through their emotional issues, you cross over to heaven. When it was time for Jesse to go, he was in love with me and I was alive. So God gave him a choice and let him stay with me instead of going to heaven."

Remy put her head down on the picnic table. She heard Lucy laugh softly.

"I know, Remy. It's a lot to process."

Remy lifted her head and said, "Avery's dead. Jesse used to be dead but he's not anymore. Anything else?"

"Nope!" Lucy said brightly as if they were discussing what to have for lunch. "That's about the gist of it."

Remy smiled weakly.

"But Remy, I want to warn you, it was a *miracle* that Jesse came back to life, but the chances of that happening again with Avery…well…just know that Jesse is the only instance we know of that happening around here. I know lots of people who are, you know, like Avery is now, and they've been around here for a long, long time. Nobody's come back to life before or since Jesse. When a spirit crosses over…" Lucy trailed off, not wanting to say the harsh facts out loud.

"They're gone for good," Remy said quietly.

"That's one of the reasons I knew we had to tell you the truth about Avery. You need to know what could happen. What probably will happen. Those two soldiers I mentioned? One was Jesse and the other one was a Union soldier named Joel."

Remy could hear the fondness in Lucy's voice as she spoke about this other soldier.

"Joel and Jesse *hated* each other. They'd been enemies for more than a century and a half before I met them."

"It's hard to imagine Jesse hating anyone!" Remy said with surprise.

"I know!" Lucy said with a laugh. "But they fought all the time. All they could do was yell at each other, and they would have punched the hell out of each other if it had been physically possible. Anyway, as usual, they were trying to best each other in any way they could, so they made a silly bet. They decided they would pick a random, living woman and ask which guy she would choose."

"And you were that woman," Remy said.

"Exactly. I didn't want to choose right away because I didn't want to hurt anybody's feelings. So we got to be friends, and then when I tried to touch Jesse and couldn't, I realized they were both real soldiers. Dead soldiers."

"Wow," Remy said.

"That's why we wanted to break the news to you as carefully as we could. We didn't want you to find out by accident."

Remy nodded, and found she was grateful that her friends were so considerate of her feelings. She adored Avery, and it was only a matter of time before she would have found some excuse to touch him.

"So I became close with Joel and Jesse—"

"*Especially* Jesse," Remy said with a knowing smile.

"Yes," Lucy said with tremendous affection. "I fell in love with him when he was still a ghost."

"And he fell for you, too."

"That's the really incredible thing," Lucy said, her eyes wide. "Turns out he was *already* in love with me. Joel didn't know it at the time, and I sure didn't either, but Jesse had been watching me work in the tavern. He was invisible so I didn't know he was there!"

"Whoa! So he was like creepin' on ya!" Remy said.

"Yeah, kinda," Lucy said. "I was upset at first. I liked him so much, and I hated the idea that he was watching me without me knowing. But he fell in love with me then, so I could hardly stay mad."

Remy smiled and nodded.

"So like I said, ghosts are still here because they have personal issues that are keeping them earthbound. Jesse was struggling because he loved his home and his family in the South, but he was coming to terms with how horrible slavery was and his role in fighting as a Confederate soldier. And Joel, well, he had some guilt over some problems in his marriage. He loved his wife so much, and I knew he needed to cross over to be with her. So I spent time with Joel and Jesse and helped them work out their issues so they could cross over."

"Did the other guy make it?" Remy asked, hardly believing her own ears. What Lucy was saying was certifiably *nuts,* but Lucy wasn't. She was a stable person, and Remy couldn't help but believe her story.

"Yes," Lucy said with a warm smile. "He made it home to his wife and children. I really miss him, and so does Theresa. She was pretty close with him, too."

"So Theresa knows about all this stuff, too?"

"Yes! Yes, as a matter of fact!" Lucy said excitedly. "So you can call her up, and she'll confirm everything I'm telling you. She probably knows more dead soldiers than I do. She's working on her degree in psychology, and she has a kind of ghost counseling group to help them deal with their issues and cross over."

Remy stared at Lucy.

"Sorry, I'm probably overwhelming you with too much ghost info," Lucy said.

"No, it's okay," Remy said uncertainly. On one hand, she wanted as much information on this strange new ghost world as possible. On the other hand, she was starting to feel like she was losing her mind.

"So yes, Joel made it. And Jesse almost went, too." Lucy fell silent for a moment, and Remy could see this was hard for her to talk about. "I figured there was no humanly possible way Jesse and I could be together, and I wanted him to be at peace. So I tried to help him cross over. When the time came, Joel disappeared into this big, bright portal. His wife was waiting for him. He was so happy."

Lucy seemed lost in her memories, and Remy was enraptured by her tale.

"And then Jesse…Jesse saw his mother in the portal. I'll never forget him saying…*Mama…*" Tears formed in her eyes. "I knew how much he missed his mother, and I was glad he saw her, but…but then he walked into the portal." Now Lucy spoke in a whisper. "I thought was he gone."

Remy reached across the table and took hold of Lucy's hand. Tears ran down Lucy's cheeks.

"I'm sorry," Lucy said, wiping her face with her free hand. "It's still hard to think of how close I came to losing him forever."

"Oh, Lucy. I can't imagine. You two are inseparable!"

Lucy nodded. She looked into Remy's eyes. "And that's why you need to be careful. I know you care about Avery and, well, I just don't want you to go through what I almost went through."

Remy nodded, carefully considering Lucy's words.

Lucy took her hand away from Remy's so she could dig in her purse for some tissues to wipe her eyes. "I know you're in shock now," Lucy continued. "But I loved Jesse even when he was dead. So before you get any more involved with Avery, I wanted you to understand what you're getting into."

"Okay," Remy said cautiously, still trying to comprehend the day's events.

"But even so," Lucy said, her eyes filled with compassion, "Avery's so lonely. And he cares so much for you. I know he would love to be able to spend time with you." Lucy glanced toward the Blue and Gray Tour building. "Do you want to go see him?"

Remy shook her head rapidly. "No. N-not now. I'm not ready. I…I just…"

"It's okay, Remy. You don't have to explain. I'm just glad it's all out in the open now. It was so weird being in the middle and not being able to tell you the truth! Here I've had you telling me how crazy you were for Avery, and Jesse's had Avery talking about how much he wanted to be with you."

"Really?" Remy asked hopefully. In all today's confusion, it was easy for her to forget the good news that Avery cared for her after all. She dimly recalled him saying a few Irish phrases to her earlier. She hadn't understood everything he said, but she knew they were all words of affection.

"Oh, yeah. You're all Avery talks about."

"That's so hard to imagine," Remy said softly. *To think that's he's cared about me all this time.*

"Believe it, Remy. I know it's hard to think of him as anything but a ghost right now, but he's so much more than that. He's a real man with real feelings. Feelings for you." Lucy smiled, her eyes lighting up. "Remember that day Jesse introduced him to you?"

"Of course!" Remy responded.

"That was no casual introduction. Not for them anyway. They had it all planned out ahead of time. They even practiced what they were going to say to you."

"No way!" Remy said incredulously.

"Oh, yeah. Avery was already quite smitten with you." Lucy winced a little before adding, "He kinda watched you a little like Jesse watched me."

"Really?" Remy asked.

"Yes, but only in public. I promise. He just watched you give your tours and stuff. I think he was even visible most of the time. You just didn't notice him."

"Awww," Remy said. How could she not have noticed the handsome, broad-shouldered Confederate soldier?

"Avery was a nervous wreck that day he spoke to you at Little Round Top," Lucy said, chuckling.

"Yes," Remy said with sudden realization. "He *was* really nervous. I didn't understand why. It was because of *me*?"

"Yes. He wanted so much to make a good impression."

"He did. Believe me," Remy said.

"I know. Jesse said he did great. They practiced what to do if you tried to shake his hand."

"Yes!" Remy said. "He said he was sick and didn't want to touch me."

Lucy nodded knowingly. "Yup. But all that Irish stuff he said? That was all Avery. He was so afraid he would sound stupid to you because of his accent. But it turned out you love it."

"Of course I love it! Every word that comes out of that man's mouth sounds sexy."

"I know," Lucy said, blushing slightly. "I love hearing him talk."

Remy giggled, and for a brief instant, Avery was no longer a dead guy. He was the sweet, charming Irishman who made her want to swoon when he looked into her eyes.

But he was dead. He was soldier who died in battle. In 1863.

He was a ghost.

Remy suddenly felt utterly exhausted. She was beyond grateful that she didn't have to give a tour tonight.

A ghost tour. Good God.

"I'm so tired," Remy said. "I think I need to go home and get some rest."

"Okay, sweetie," Lucy said, looking worried. "I was really upset when I first found out about Jesse. I mean, I don't think you're anywhere near as scared as I was, but still. I remember being alone in my apartment being terrified and crying myself to sleep that first night."

"It's okay, Lucy. I'm all right. Really."

"I hope so. But seriously, call me if you need anything or if you have more questions. I don't care if it's three a.m."

"Thanks, Lucy," Remy said, getting up from the table. She hugged Lucy warmly before heading to her car.

As she walked away, Lucy called after her, and Remy turned around.

"Remy? Your tour with Jesse stops in the Visitor's Center museum, right?"

"Yeah."

"Next time you go, take a good look at that big wall with all the black-and-white photos of the soldiers. Lower right side."

Remy nodded slowly, then got into her car.

When she got home, she microwaved a frozen dinner, then ate it without tasting it. She went to bed early, but lay awake for a long time, her mind reeling. She wasn't terrified like Lucy said she had been at first, but she wondered if maybe she should be.

Ghosts were real.

Remy had spent her whole life dismissing anything even remotely paranormal. She had humored her ghost tour guests whenever they claimed to see, smell, or touch something strange. Had they really been having ghost encounters?

She also had never believed in God. Now she knew there was an afterlife. A heaven. A God who was merciful enough to let Jesse live again so he could love and cherish Lucy.

Remy's thoughts were spinning wildly out of control, and she thought she would never be able to rest. Exhaustion finally won out, and she fell into a deep sleep.

Chapter 10

Remy arrived at work the next morning to find Jesse already inside, getting things ready for the day.

"Hi," Jesse said gently when Remy walked into the touring company gift shop. "I still had your keys. Hope you don't mind that I let myself in."

"No, it's fine."

Jesse walked out from behind the counter and handed her the work keys. He looked at her with concern. "How are you doing?"

"I'm okay, I guess."

Remy was grateful that none of the bus drivers or other employees had arrived yet, so they could talk freely. She looked at Jesse's outfit, as he was dressed in his usual Confederate soldier uniform.

Remy looked into his eyes and asked softly, "Did you really die at Devil's Den?"

"Yeah," Jesse replied. "Here, come sit with me a minute."

He led her over to the row of chairs by the wall where guests usually sat while waiting for the tour buses to arrive. Remy sat down, and Jesse took a seat next to her.

"So," Remy began, her mind still whirring from yesterday's events. So much had changed. She looked at him sorrowfully. "You were really shot in the shoulder and the head? Just like the story you tell on tour?"

"Well, yes." Jesse ran his fingers through his hair. "Except, well you know how you kinda tell cleaned-up versions of some of the more gruesome stories on certain ghost tours?"

"Oh, no," Remy said. "You mean your death was even worse than what you describe?"

"Yeah," Jesse said, looking at her tenderly. Remy could see that he wanted to be truthful with her, but he was also trying not to upset her. "Lucy told you all about Joel, right? How we was enemies?"

Remy nodded, remembering how affectionately Lucy had spoken about her friend.

"Well, we was enemies for so long because he killed me."

Remy nodded slowly, feeling confused. This Joel guy had killed the love of Lucy's life, and she was his friend?

"It was the heat of battle, ya know? Anyway, somebody else shot me in the shoulder. I didn't see who," Jesse continued. "It don't matter, I guess. But then there was this guy standin' right in front of me. I had half a second to decide what to do."

Jesse paused for a moment. Remy's heart caught in her throat, as she could see how difficult this was for him to talk about. It wasn't easy to hear, either. Jesse was one of her dearest friends, and she hated to think of him suffering.

"I shot him," Jesse said. He suddenly looked worried, like he was afraid Remy would judge him for shooting an enemy soldier in the middle of a war zone. "Turned out he'd dropped his musket. He might have been surrenderin', I don't know. If I'd have known he was unarmed, I never would have—"

"Of course you wouldn't, Jesse," Remy said reassuringly. "You'd never hurt anyone unless you felt you had no choice."

Remy saw relief in Jesse's eyes.

"Yeah, yeah, I really wouldn't! Anyway, I killed the man. Charles. His name was Charles. And it turns out he was Joel's best friend. They grew up together. And Joel had to see it happen 'fore his eyes. And he couldn't do nothin' to save him." Jesse paused for a moment, lost in that sorrowful memory from so long ago. "So Joel shot me in the head."

Remy grimaced and closed her eyes.

"I'm sorry, darlin'. I don't have to tell you all this if it'll upset you."

Remy opened her eyes. "It's okay. I want to know the truth. All of it."

Jesse looked uncertain, and Remy couldn't imagine what was coming next. What could be worse than being shot in the head?

"Well, Joel was angry and grievin' and well, I think he thought I was already dead. I'd been shot and was bleedin' and all, and well he'd been holding his regiment's flag, and in a rage he rammed the flagpole right through my stomach. He thought I was dead, but—"

Remy gasped in horror and covered her mouth.

"Yeah," Jesse said quietly. "Ain't no reason to upset the tourists with that kind of detail."

Remy slowly lowered her hands and stared at Jesse. She looked into his kind eyes and wanted to break into a sob.

"Jesse," Remy said, her voice shaking.

Jesse reached over and grasped her hand in both of his.

"It's all right, darlin'," Jesse said in a calm, reassuring voice. "As you can see, I've recovered quite nicely!"

Remy burst into laughter instead of tears. It was all so *absurd*.

Jesse laughed heartily, too.

"I feel so bad for all the times I joked about your death!" Remy exclaimed.

Jesse let go of her hand and waved his hand dismissively. "Think nothin' of that. If it's one thing we ghosts—or former ghosts—got goin', it's a good sense of humor 'bout our dyin'."

"Thank you for telling me, Jesse."

He nodded, then his expression darkened. "Oh, and there's somethin' I else I need to tell you. It's real important."

Remy nodded, a little worried at his suddenly serious tone.

"It's about Lucy. She's real sensitive to anything paranormal. Always has been. You know how some people on your ghost tours see and hear stuff, but others don't?"

Remy nodded slowly. "I always thought it was just their imagination."

"Well, probably is sometimes. But some people are just real attuned to ghost stuff. Don't know why. Sometimes it's kinda neat. When Avery comes to visit Lucy in the restaurant, she can feel that he's there. Even if he's invisible."

"Wow!"

Jesse nodded. "But it can be real dangerous for her. Sometimes... sometimes when somebody's super sensitive, they can feel other things. Bad things."

Remy was alarmed by Jesse's fearful expression.

"Like what?"

"Well, if somebody with Lucy's, you know, ability to sense stuff has some kinda connection to a soldier, like say they had some ancestor die in the war or in her case she's actually friends with lots of soldiers...well, if she goes on the battlefield around the time the guy died, she'll feel what happened to them. She'll physically *feel* the battle wounds that killed 'im."

He closed his eyes and drew in a deep breath. Anxiety prickled in Remy's stomach. Jesse seemed utterly distraught.

He opened his eyes and whispered, "It happened to Lucy. She felt my death."

"Oh, my God," Remy said.

"I was stupid. God, I was so *stupid*. It's just…it's so rare that it happens. I only seen it maybe five or six times in the last hundred years, and I just didn't *think*. But Lucy took us, me and Joel, to Devil's Den to try and work out our differences. It was around five p.m. when I died. Remy, she felt *everything*." The anguish in Jesse's eyes was almost more than she could bear.

Remy's heart ached for both Lucy and Jesse. She couldn't fathom the horror of it all.

"She just kept screamin' in pain, beggin' me to make it stop. But I was dead! I couldn't touch her. I couldn't stop it. I-I couldn't stop it—"

Remy put her hand on Jesse's back and rubbed gently. "It's all right, Jesse. She's all right now. Isn't she?"

Jesse nodded. "Yeah. It don't leave no lasting damage. The other tourists…when it happened, they had no idea what was happening. Poor folks probably thought they was dyin. When it's over, it's over. But it's so awful."

"Oh, Jesse I can't imagine."

"I'm jus' telling you all this so you'll know to help keep Lucy safe. She likes to help Theresa counsel the soldiers, and sometimes they go to where the guys died, but I can't let her do that. It's too dangerous!" Jesse looked at Remy pleadingly. "Avery died at Little Round Top, so Lucy can't ever go there again. Or she'll feel what happened to him."

Remy felt a sharp stab of pain in her chest at the thought of Avery dying.

"Avery…did he…did he suffer?" Remy said, feeling the threat of tears behind her eyes.

"Not for long, I don't believe," Jesse said gently. "Sweetie, he was shot near the heart and, no, darlin'. It didn't take long."

"Thank God for that," Remy said.

Jesse looked at her with concern. "Do you want to go see him today?"

Remy felt utterly overwhelmed at the prospect of talking to Avery. A ghost. It was all too much.

"I-I don't know. I don't think I'm ready."

"Okay," Jesse said, looking disappointed. "I don't want to pressure you. I just know how worried he is about you and how much he wants to see you."

Remy nodded. Her chest hurt when she pictured Avery sitting alone up on Little Round Top. *Where he had died.*

Jesse must have realized she was feeling overwhelmed, so he added, "It's okay, Remy. I know all this will take some time to get used to. And really, ghosts are nothing to be afraid of. You...you're not afraid of me now, are you?"

Remy looked at Jesse, who was one of the nicest guys she had ever met in her life. She couldn't imagine ever being afraid of him.

"Of course not!"

"Good, good," Jesse said with a laugh. "There are, you know, lots of dead people around here. And I'm friends with lots of 'em."

"That's so hard to imagine!" Remy said, shaking her head.

"Not as hard as you might think, my dear," Jesse said with a knowing twinkle in his eye. "You were friends with Avery without knowing.

"True."

"And I bet you know some other dead folks."

Remy looked at him dubiously.

"You ever see an older black lady hangin' out in town? Not far from where Lucy works? Near the Regimental Quartermaster?"

"Not sure," Remy said, thinking hard. She might have seen the woman around.

"That's Fillis. She looks like a slave reenactor, but she ain't. She was a real slave."

"Wow," Remy said sadly. She couldn't fathom what it must have been like to be owned by other people like some kind of animal. *That poor woman.*

"We all love her. Name's Fillis—with an F—but we call her Second Mama 'cause she's like a mother to us." Jesse thought for a moment, then suddenly snapped his fingers.

"What?"

"Okay, you know you told me 'bout that little boy who hangs out near where you do your nighttime tours? You're always worried about him 'cause nobody's really supervisin' him?"

"Yeah," Remy said, picturing the cute little boy with neglectful parents who didn't keep a good eye on him.

"You know how he tells you his mama works as one of the waitresses at that tavern there? He only says that so you don't worry 'bout him. Remy, that's *Jeremy.*"

Remy gasped. "Jeremy!"

Jesse chuckled at her reaction. "Yep."

Jeremy. The little boy she spoke of every night on her ghost tours. The one who was tragically killed in a carriage accident. Jeremy, for whom overnight guests left toys that they'd swear had been moved the next day. *Jeremy.*

The door swung open, and one of the other tour guides, dressed as a Union soldier, came in. He eyed Jesse and Remy curiously, probably wondering what they were doing sitting alone together. Everybody knew Jesse had a girlfriend.

"Everything okay?" Rick asked.

"Yes. I'm having personal issues, and Jesse is listening to me whine," Remy said.

"Okay, then. Better him than me!" Rick said, then added, "Hope you're okay, Rem."

"Thanks," Remy said, standing up. "Let's get to work!"

*****

Remy sat nervously on the tour bus, listening to Jesse talk about what had happened at Little Round Top as the bus headed to the battleground. She'd heard his speech a hundred times, but suddenly the information seemed brand new. Remy knew lots of facts about the battle, how the 20th Maine had heroically taken on the Confederates in the 15th Alabama and other regiments. But now she *knew* one of the Confederates who had died in that battle. It all was all too real now.

When they reached their destination, Remy and Jesse helped the tourists get off the bus and instructed them that they were free to wander. Once everyone had dispersed, Remy glanced over toward the area where she knew Avery was waiting. She couldn't see him because of the trees in the way, but she knew he was there.

"I can't, Jesse. I just can't. I need more time. Tell him...tell him...I don't know what to tell him!" Remy cried.

"It's okay, Remy. Try not to be upset. He wouldn't want that," Jesse told her.

Remy nodded. "Well, tell him I'm all right. And that I'm not mad at him! I'm just not ready to see him yet."

"Okay, darlin'," Jesse said with a smile.

Remy felt terribly guilty about not going to see Avery, and she was grateful that Jesse was there to help. He would be kind to Avery and make him feel better the way he had comforted her this morning.

Remy's emotions were running high, and she just couldn't face Avery yet. What could she possibly say? *How do you talk to a dead man?*

The last stop on the tour was the Gettysburg Visitor's Center, where guests could visit the museum and the gift shop. Like at the other stops, Jesse and Remy would be around to keep an eye on their tour members and be available to answer any questions, but otherwise the tourists were on their own to explore for a little bit.

Remy walked through the museum and scanned the exhibits. Though she had always found the displays of Civil War artifacts, uniforms, and weaponry interesting, today they seemed to take on a whole new meaning.

Out of the corner of her eye, she caught sight of the huge wall that was covered in black-and-white photographs of real Civil War soldiers. She had looked at the wall from time to time and couldn't help but wonder what had happened to those men. Many of them had died in the war for sure. Had they left behind wives and children? She pictured Lucy and how distraught she became when she spoke about nearly losing Jesse. The idea of a woman like her receiving news that her love had died in the war was unbearable.

Remy slowly turned and made her way over to the wall of photographs. She recalled Lucy's words—*"Look at that big wall with all the black-and-white photos of the soldiers. Lower right side."*

Remy scanned the wall of photos and gasped at the photograph of the Confederate soldier with those familiar, kind eyes.

Avery.

Her heart lurched. Since Lucy had told her to carefully look at the photographs, she'd known she should expect to find either Jesse or Avery there. Lucy had obviously been offering more proof that what they'd all been telling her was true. But to see it in black and white was still quite a shock.

Remy felt a bit faint, so she held on to the wall with her right hand as she stared at the picture. Avery looked so handsome in the photograph. So kind. Remy recalled Jesse's words about his death. *"He was shot near the heart. It didn't take long."* The shock began to wear off slightly, and, for the first time, Remy began to grieve for him. Avery was dead. He was still here in a different form, but he was dead.

Remy closed her eyes and pictured Avery as she knew him. The gentle soldier who joked with her and said beautiful things to her in Irish.

"Remy?" She heard Jesse's soft voice coming from right behind her. "Are you all right?"

Remy turned around and said quietly, "He's really dead, isn't he?"

Jesse nodded sadly. "Well, his body is. His spirit is still alive and always will be, no matter what. Not even death can stop that."

She nodded, then turned back to stare at the photograph again.

"He's still the same man, Remy."

"I know."

Remy managed to finish her morning tours, all the while consumed with thoughts of Avery. By the time she and Jesse got started on the afternoon tours, Remy could hardly stand it anymore. She needed to see Avery. The thought of him sitting at Little Round Top, alone and *dead,* probably hoping for her to come see him made her want to cry. She wanted to see him, but she knew it would be impossible for her to try to talk to him with all those tourists around. She couldn't imagine having a friendly chat with him like she used to, pretending nothing had changed.

When they arrived at Little Round Top with their afternoon group, Remy pulled Jesse aside once they got off the bus.

"Jesse, tell him I want to see him, but not now. I just...I can't with all these people around. Tell him I'll come see him after work and before my ghost tours start."

"Yes, ma'am!" Jesse said, his face lighting up. He seemed thrilled to have good news for Avery this time.

Remy couldn't help but laugh and feel flattered. If Jesse was this happy, she would love to see Avery's face when he told him. Avery really did care about her. *I adore you* were the words he used. It was hard for Remy to imagine being adored by anyone, never mind someone as handsome and wonderful as Avery O'Rorke.

Remy was a nervous wreck for the rest of the afternoon. She was sure she wanted to see Avery, but was second-guessing her request to be alone with him. She'd never been afraid of ghosts, no matter how many ghost stories she heard or how late at night she wandered the allegedly haunted streets of Gettysburg. She'd never been afraid because she'd never *believed* in ghosts. Now that she knew they were real, would she freak out when she was alone with Avery?

Remy knew it was best to meet with him privately. She needed to talk to him and ask him questions about things they couldn't talk about in public. Besides, she found the idea of being alone with him made her equally nervous and excited. It would be wonderful to finally have some private time with him.

Chapter 11

The drive to nearby Little Round Top seemed to take much longer than it did on the bus tour. Remy parked her car, then began walking on shaky legs through the trees to where Avery always sat. There was still a handful of tourists around, but it was dinnertime and the daytime tours were over, so the big crowds were gone.

Avery had his back to her when she first approached. A surge of nervous adrenaline coursed through her body. For a moment, she wasn't sure she could go through with this. Still, she kept walking.

Avery turned and saw her. He stood up slowly, carefully, as if not wanting to frighten her.

"Remy," he said softly. For the first time, Remy noticed the longing in his eyes. Was he just lonely, or was he really longing for her?

Remy walked up to him and stood just a few feet away.

"It's all right, darlin'," Avery said softly, and his familiar Irish lilt soothed her. He really was the same man she'd been so crazy for all this time.

Avery gestured for her to sit, and she sat down on a flat surface in the rocky terrain. He took a seat near her, but not too close.

"Are you all right?" he asked her.

Remy gazed into Avery's gentle, worried eyes and began to relax. "Yes, I'm all right, Avery."

He looked relieved. "I was afraid you'd never speak to me again. I'm sorry I didn't tell you sooner. I just didn't know how."

"I understand," Remy said. She imagined it must have been stressful for him all this time. Knowing he'd have to tell her eventually and worrying that she might find out by accident like Lucy did.

"Remy, I'm so sorry I dragged you into all this. It's me own damned selfishness. From the day I first met you, I haven't been able to stop thinkin' 'bout ye. Think I wore Jesse out 'til he finally said, '*Will ye just talk to her, for the love of Jaysus!*'"

Remy laughed and tucked her hair behind her ear. It was hard for her to fathom that this incredible man had become so enamored of her without her knowing. She was usually so busy working two jobs and just trying to get by that she didn't have much time for a social life.

"The last thing I wanted was to hurt you, Remy, but I know I have. First I get you thinkin' I don't care...and I do, Remy. You don't know how much. And then I go and scare you half to death. 'Twas selfish of me to try to woo you like I did, knowin' full well I could never be a proper suitor to ye." Avery leaned in close to her, and she felt her heart racing. If only he could touch her, he would kiss her. She was sure of it. "Ah, but if I could have. Oh, I'd have courted you relentlessly. I'd do whatever it took to win your heart, and I'd take on any man who dared stand in my way!"

Avery leaned back, laughing, but Remy got the feeling he meant every word he had said.

"I don't think it would have been all that difficult. In case you haven't noticed, I haven't been putting up much of a fight."

Remy relished the smile on Avery's face as she spoke. He'd been so open about his feelings for her, and she wanted to return the favor. She moved in closer to him and said, "Avery O'Rorke, you're the sexiest man I've ever met. You're so smart and so sweet, and you have the deepest, manliest voice I've ever had the pleasure of listening to. Everything you say in that accent of yours makes me want to swoon in your arms."

Avery blinked, taking in her words for a moment, then his eyes lit up with delight. "Never in my wildest dreams would I have expected you to say something like that to me. And here I was just hopin' you wouldn't hate me!"

"Of course I don't hate you," Remy said with great affection. "I think you're wonderful, dead or alive. You have a beautiful soul, and that's all that matters to me."

They looked into each other's eyes for a moment. Remy signed inwardly. *Yes,* she thought. *This is the moment where he would lean in and kiss me if he could.* She'd only been kissed a few times in her life, and never by anyone as handsome as Avery.

"Can I try to touch you?" Remy asked.

Avery glanced around at the tourists in the distance. "Sure. Just so long as nobody's watching. I can't stand scaring people."

Remy nodded, touched by his kindness. She slowly raised her right hand toward his face.

"It will feel very cold," Avery warned her.

Remy nodded. She gently placed her hand against his cheek. It felt like she'd dipped her hand in ice water. She let out a short gasp, both from the cold and from the sight of Avery's image wavering slightly.

"Can you feel anything when I do that?" Remy asked him.

Avery shook his head sadly. "I wish I could. I would give anything if I could feel your touch."

"Believe me, I would touch you a *lot* if I could," Remy said seductively.

Avery let out a low moan that sounded almost like a growl. "That would have been wonderful."

Remy felt her slumbering sex drive awaken. Her other needs had always had to take precedence, like earning enough money to buy groceries and to keep a roof over her head. When it came to sexual satisfaction, she'd always had to take care of her own needs. She usually touched herself quickly and efficiently when she felt the urge, but that was it.

With Avery sitting so close, Remy found herself indulging in the now-familiar fantasy of him picking her up and carrying her to the bedroom. A new and exciting tingle of desire stirred between her legs. She'd never been so attracted to a man in her life, and she could hardly believe the way he was looking at her. With actual *lust*. No man had ever desired her like that, and she'd never wanted a man as much as she wanted Avery.

"I'm so glad you're not afraid of me, Remy," Avery said.

"Not at all," she replied. It was so easy to forget that he was a spirit when she couldn't stop thinking of his solid form. His tall, broad-shouldered, muscular, solid form. She had the feeling he would have been amazing in bed. Too bad she'd never know. "I'm not afraid. It just takes some getting used to."

Avery nodded. "I'm just glad you gave me another chance. I know it's not easy being friends with the dead."

"It's not just that. I mean, knowing that there's an afterlife... It goes against everything I've ever believed." Remy looked at Avery cautiously. "I don't like telling people this because I don't like people judging me."

"I would never judge you, Remy," Avery said softly. "I want you to be able to confide in me."

Remy smiled at him. It was a relief to have someone like Avery in her life. She could never rely on her family, and it felt good having Avery to lean on.

"I've never believed in God. Lots of times people think you're some kind of monster if you're an atheist. Like I'm some kind of evil person who doesn't care about anybody but myself and that I—"

Avery laughed, and for a horrible moment Remy thought he was laughing at her.

"Sorry, me darlin'. It's just the idea that you're a bad person is ridiculous. You've got such a good heart," Avery said, smiling fondly at her.

"Thank you, Avery."

Avery looked at her curiously. "I bet you don't remember the first time you spoke to me."

"Of course I do! When Jesse introduced you I remember thinking *where has this sexy Irishman been all my life?*"

Avery laughed. "No, no me darlin'. That *wasn't* the first time we spoke."

Remy's eyes widened. "Really?"

Avery shook his head, his eyes dancing with amusement. "No, ma'am. You see, when you're dead, you have a wee bit of control over your existence. You can be visible, as I am now, or invisible. When you're invisible, you're still here, but only other dead people can see ye."

Remy nodded, fascinated.

"Then there's this other form of existence. We call it vanishing in ghost circles. When you vanish, you still exist in ghost form, but you're not conscious. You just disappear into a kind of limbo. You can do it for as long as you like. Many of us do it at night, since there's no tourists to watch and nothing to do 'til morning."

"So it's kind of like sleep?" Remy asked.

"Yes. You could say that. You can vanish for years if you want. That's what I did. I didn't like bein' a ghost," Avery said, sounding tired. "I didn't want to deal with it, I guess. So I vanished for a long time. Been gone most of the time since I died. I only checked in on the world every few decades or so," Avery told her.

"Wow," Remy said. It was hard to wrap her mind around how long Avery had existed.

"Some folks like to stay around all the time. That's what Jesse did. He didn't vanish much. He's watched the time roll by decade by decade."

"Incredible," Remy said. She couldn't imagine all that Jesse must have seen during that time!

"I'm ramblin' here. Sorry, me dear."

"Not at all," Remy said, eyes wide. "This is fascinating!"

Avery looked at her with amusement, enjoying her enthusiasm. "Well, anyways, I'd been gone a long time and I came back to this...well...the craziness that is modern-day Gettysburg. The crowds, the stores, and all these people dressed up like me. I didn't know what in the name of Janey Mac was going on!"

Remy smiled and nodded sympathetically. She couldn't begin to imagine how overwhelmed he must have felt. He must have felt so confused, disoriented.

"I was lookin' around, trying to figure out what in blazes was happenin' 'round here. And then," Avery smiled at her with such adoration that it made her tingle all over. "Up walks this beautiful young girl with the prettiest blue eyes I'd ever seen."

Remy stared at him, amazed. She racked her brains, but simply could not recall meeting him before Jesse introduced him. *How could I forget meeting this incredible man?*

"You walked right up to me and asked me if I needed help," Avery said, smiling at the memory. "You were the first person to speak to me in decades. I think you could see I was feelin' totally overwhelmed. You were so gentle and kind, and you were so pretty that I could hardly speak at first. I made up some story about looking to meet my friends at some tavern nearby. You gave me directions."

"I'm so sorry I don't remember!" Remy said.

"Oh, don't be sorry, darlin'. You speak to a hundred people every day! And I see how you are with everybody. You're so gentle, so kind. Point is, you don't have to believe in God to be a good person."

Remy smiled and said softly, "Thank you, Avery."

"I was smitten with you from the first moment I saw you. I knew right away that you were so much more than just a pretty face. You have a beautiful soul, too, Remy."

Remy gazed into his eyes. "I don't know what to say." No one had ever said anything so lovely to her before.

"You don't have to say a word, Remy. I'm just so happy you're here with me." Avery paused for a moment, then said, "It's strange. I used to be able to vanish whenever I wanted to for as long as I wanted, but now? Now it's getting harder all of a sudden. Like, I don't know, almost like God is tellin' me enough stalling. Enough hiding. You got to come out and face your troubles already."

Remy drew in a deep breath and tried to quell the anxiety that brewed in her stomach when she thought about Avery crossing over. "Do you know why you're still here? Lucy said that ghosts have some kind of unresolved issue that keeps them trapped here."

Avery nodded slowly. "Yes. Yes, Lucy's right about that. I do have things that I've left…unresolved."

Avery seemed sad as he spoke. She wondered what had happened to him to keep him trapped on earth for so long.

"Remy," he began gently. "You should know that when I was alive, I was married."

Remy was stunned by Avery's words. It had never occurred to her that he might have been married. Avery had been alive for more than a century before she was born, and of course he had a whole other life then. Still, the thought of Avery with another woman made her want to cry. Not just any other woman. His *bride*. A wife who had shared Avery's bed, his body, in a way that Remy never could.

"Oh, Remy, I'm sorry. Please don't be sad," Avery said, his eyes full of concern.

"Don't be sorry, Avery," Remy said. "I-I mean, of course I should have realized you would have been married. You were...how old where you when you died?"

"Thirty-one," Avery answered, still looking sorrowful. "And how old are you, Remy?"

"Twenty-two."

"Jaysus. I'm robbin' the cradle," Avery said, shaking his head.

"And I'm robbing the grave!"

Avery threw back his head and laughed heartily. It was a rich, sensual sound, and Remy was relieved to see that sad look gone from his face.

"Yes, I s'pose you are!"

Remy smiled warmly at him. She couldn't help but be devastated at the thought of Avery marrying someone else, but she knew he had no reason to feel bad about it. He had a right to live his life, and it wasn't as if he had lied to her about it. Until now, he'd been unable to talk about his past with her.

"Remy," Avery said softly, the sorrowful look returning to his face. "I don't want to tell you more than you want to hear, but I do want to be honest with you."

Remy nodded, her stomach clenching. She was nervous about what he was going to say next. *He's going to say that she was the love of his life, and that no one could ever replace her in his heart.*

"Me wife was a wonderful, God-fearin' woman and— Oh, Remy, I didn't mean anything by that. I understand you're not religious and—"

"It's okay, Avery. There's no need to apologize for anything. You shouldn't feel guilty."

"Of course I feel guilty. I'm Catholic!" Avery said with a grin. "I did love me wife, Nora. I loved her, but...this is going to sound terrible to you..."

He looked afraid to continue, like she would think less of him after hearing what he was going to say.

"No, it won't. I want you to be able to confide in me, too, you know," Remy said with compassion.

Avery nodded. "I loved her but, I felt, I don't know, trapped in my marriage. She was a wonderful woman, but it was like living with a friend, you know? A good friend, to be sure. But there was no..."

"Passion?"

"Yes!" Avery said, looking thrilled that she understood. "Yes, exactly! She didn't really like being touched all that much. We didn't...it wasn't often that we...you know..."

"You didn't have much of a sex life," Remy finished for him. She nodded with empathy.

"Right! I mean, it wasn't only that that made me so unhappy. But that was part of it. I had *needs* of course. The normal desires a man has. She would always let me be intimate with her when I wanted, but I always felt like I was botherin' her. I think she thought of it as her wifely duty."

Remy shook her head. How could anyone think of sex with a man like Avery as a *chore*? An awful thought suddenly occurred to Remy.

"Did you ever...since your wife didn't enjoy sex...were you ever with someone else while you were married?"

"No," Avery said, looking into her eyes as if to be sure Remy believed him. "No, I never did that. She was me wife, and I wanted to do right by her. But I was unhappy. I know it sounds awful, but I was bored. Bored with our everyday life, just going to work and coming home where nothing ever changed. I always wanted to see the world, Remy. To travel, to meet new people, to see new things and learn everything there is to learn!"

There was a delightful spark in Avery's eyes when he spoke of his hopes and dreams. The sad look was gone, and he was like an excited kid. Remy smiled fondly at him.

"I know it sounds so silly, so childish, but I wanted to go off on an adventure somewhere, anywhere!" Avery glanced at Remy, then suddenly looked embarrassed. "I know it's stupid."

"Avery! It's not stupid. I think it's wonderful! Who could blame you for wanting to do something exciting with your life? I feel exactly the same way!" Remy said, feeling like she had met a kindred spirit. "I would love to travel. And I'm gonna do it, too, if it kills me. Which it just might. I have to fight just to keep my apartment and keep milk in my fridge, but I'm gonna travel. Someday I'm gonna travel the world and I'm gonna have my own travel-business. Something to with tourism, like maybe I'll open a bed and breakfast and I can run my own tours. I'm gonna make my dreams come true. I'll leave my horrible family behind and make a real life for myself!"

"I know you will, Remy." She could hear the pride in his voice. She couldn't ever remember anyone being proud of her before. "You are an amazingly strong woman. Lucy and Jesse told me how your family has treated you," Avery said, his voice taking on a hard edge. "But you never let that stop you. Nothing stops you. You're incredible."

Remy gazed at him gratefully.

He pointed at her and said, "You said it just right about what was missing in my marriage. *Passion.* I didn't know what passion was until I met you."

Remy stared at Avery, scarcely believing what she was hearing. It seemed impossible that someone as alluring as Avery could feel that way about her.

"I feel the same way about you, Avery. I'm always so busy working that I didn't realize what I was missing out on by not having someone like you in my life." She looked into his eyes, then sighed. "If I could, I would drop everything and run off to see the world with you."

Avery's eyes opened wide, and he whispered, "Wouldn't that be tremendous?"

Remy nodded.

"I s'pose that's what I tried to do," Avery said, his face falling again as he continued his tale. "I wanted to escape. Then comes this call for young men to go off and see the country."

"The war," Remy said.

Avery nodded sadly. "It was utterly stupid of me, but that's why I went off to fight. I mean, I did want to help my country. I did! America was so good to me, offering an escape from the poverty we were sufferin' in Ireland. And I thought it right that I fought for the South because Alabama was my new home."

Avery looked at Remy pleadingly, needing her to understand his reasons for fighting for the Confederacy.

"I understand," Remy said quietly. As a student of history and an expert on the battle of Gettysburg, she understood that soldiers had a myriad of reasons for fighting in the war. Most of them weren't bad guys fighting to keep slavery. It was so much more complicated than that.

"Sounds so dumb now, but I saw joinin' up for battle as my chance to get away from my tedious life." Avery shook his head, and Remy could see that he was disgusted with himself.

"Darling, lots of men did that," Remy said reassuringly. "Many of them wanted to join up as fast as they could because they were afraid the war would end before they got the chance to enlist. They had no way of knowing how awful the war would be and how long it would drag on."

Avery smiled at her.

"What?" she asked.

"Can't help it. I love hearin' you call me *darling*," he said.

Remy laughed. "Really? That's all you got out of what I said?"

"No, no of course not. But that was my favorite part," Avery said with a grin. "I understand what you're sayin', it's just… You still don't know the whole story. I knew by joinin' the war effort, I'd get to meet new people, see new places. Wasn't exactly world travel, but at least I could get away from the same old town for a while. Thing was…there was another very special girl I left behind." Avery's eyes took on a mournful, faraway look. He said quietly, "Me daughter."

"You had a little girl?" Remy asked with wonder. She could easily imagine Avery as a doting father. She could see how much he loved his daughter. "Tell me about her."

Avery seemed surprised, then pleased by her question. "I haven't spoken about her in so long. The last time I saw her she was only six years old."

Remy's heart ached. She could practically feel Avery's pain.

Avery was silent for a moment, then his face brightened a bit. "She had my gray eyes. And my curiosity about the world. Oh, she wanted to know everything. 'Daddy, why is the sky blue? Daddy, how does the fruit get on the trees?'" Avery's eyes twinkled with amusement. "And one time she asked, Daddy, what on earth are those horses *doin*?"

Remy clapped her hands and laughed heartily. "She sounds delightful."

"Aye, that she was," Avery said with a fond smile. "She was my little walkin' companion. Whenever I went into town to get supplies, she came with me, chatterin' the whole way. I loved hearin' her talk. She was so excited about everything. She charmed everybody, that was for sure. Such a friendly little girl, smilin' at every person and every animal we saw along the way. Brightest spot of me life, that child."

"What was her name?"

"Charlotte," Avery replied, speaking her name with reverence. "And because I had to go roamin' all over the country, fightin' in that pointless war, she grew up without a father. And that's why I'm still here. You want to talk about Catholic guilt!" He laughed ruefully.

"Avery, it's not your fault you were killed!" Remy said.

"I never should have left my family in the first place. Nora. She deserved so much better. She shouldn't have had to be a single mother. And Charlotte, she was just a baby. I can't imagine how she took the news...when her mother had to tell her that her daddy..." Avery closed his eyes.

Tears spilled from Remy's eyes. She wished with all of her heart that she could pull Avery close and hold him.

Avery opened his eyes and saw how distraught Remy was. "Oh, me darlin', please don't cry."

"Don't worry about me. Avery, you can still be with your daughter. I'm sure she's waiting on you where she is."

Avery nodded. "I have no doubt that my little girl is in heaven. That's where she belongs."

So do you, Remy thought, beginning to feel the heartache that Lucy had warned her about. Maybe Avery would be able to come back like Jesse. Or maybe he would cross over and she would never see him again. Who knew if Avery would even want to come back to life? And who the hell was she to try to keep Avery from being with his daughter?

"Then you need to try to get home to her. Avery, I would miss you so much, but I want you to be at peace. You've suffered here on earth long enough. You know Lucy helped another soldier cross over, right? And do you know her friend Theresa? She has a whole counseling group for soldiers."

Avery nodded. "I've seen Theresa around, but we've not been

formally introduced. I know 'bout her work with the soldiers. She's a lovely woman for doin' that for them."

"She really is," Remy said with affection, recalling all the times Theresa had paid for her meals. She was a wonderful friend. "Maybe you'll let her help you? She can counsel you and help you deal with the regrets that are keeping you here."

"I don't know," Avery said. "Perhaps I'll think about it."

Remy looked out across the battlefield, her heart heavy. She couldn't help imagining what it would be like if Avery were still alive. They would be dating now. He would be her boyfriend. He would be able to kiss her and hold her. It'd been so long since anyone had touched her since she lived alone and her family was far away. Not that they were the touchy-feely-huggy type anyway. The only time she had physical contact with another human being was when she offered a hand to help a tourist down from the tour bus. That, and occasionally punching Jesse on the shoulder when he was teasing her.

"You all right?" Avery asked, sounding worried.

Remy sighed. The sun was beginning to set, and she knew she had to leave.

"I hate to leave you here alone, Avery, but I've got to get going. I have two ghost tours tonight."

"You must be so tired," Avery said. "And you must have come right from work. You probably haven't even eaten dinner yet!"

"No, it's okay. I'm not really that hungry," Remy said.

"Darling! You've got to eat something. You've been on your feet all day, and now you have to work more!"

Avery's concerned face made her want to cry. Though she didn't want to upset him, it felt good to have somebody worry over her.

"I can't." Remy sighed. "Tomorrow is payday. I get paid every two weeks and, well, sometimes after I pay my college loan and my rent and electricity and all…sometimes I can't afford to get groceries 'til my next paycheck hits."

"Remy!" Avery cried, sounding horrified. "You can't go hungry!"

"It's not like I'm starving to death. It's okay. I still have some cereal and a little milk left to tide me over until tomorrow."

Avery looked so sorrowful that Remy could hardly bear it. She regretted telling him the truth about her money situation. There wasn't a thing Avery could do to help her, and she'd upset him for no good reason. She would be heartbroken if the situation was reversed and there was nothing she could do to help him.

"I'll be okay, Avery. Please don't worry about me. I'm sorry, but I really have to get going." She stood up, and Avery stood, too. She felt a delicious ripple of attraction when she looked up at him. He was so tall, so *big*. If he were alive, he could easily have picked her up and carried her to bed just like in her fantasy.

"Avery," Remy said with a seductive smile. "Back at the tour company you said *I adore you* in Irish. Will you say it again?"

Avery's face broke into a wide grin. "*Adhraím thú*, Remy."

Remy smiled at him. "I know it doesn't sound anywhere near as romantic in English, but I adore you, too."

"Believe me, hearin' that is music to my ears."

Remy blew him a kiss, then headed to her car.

Chapter 12

Remy stood at the front of the tour bus, holding onto the silver rail while the bus was in motion.

"If you look out the window right over there," Remy said, gesturing, "you'll see what is now a railroad track."

The tourists peered out the window as instructed. "That spot there is the infamous Railroad Cut that was the site of intense fighting on the first day of the battle of Gettysburg. A deep hole had been dug there in preparation for that railroad track to eventually be installed. On July 1, 1863, many Confederate soldiers jumped down into that trench, finding it an excellent place to fire at the Union soldiers while being shielded from the return fire. That tactical decision would prove deadly as the day wore on."

Remy glanced out the window at the railroad tracks. As with everything else on her battle tour, the site of so many deaths affected her much more deeply now that she knew some Civil War soldiers personally.

"The Union attacked the Railroad Cut later that day. The men hiding in the deep trench were unable to get out, making them easy targets. It was like shooting fish in a barrel, with no hope for escape, except for surrender. Many Confederates were slaughtered in the cut, and many were taken prisoner."

Those poor men, Remy thought. The Railroad Cut was a sad story, but telling it several times a day certainly made it lose its emotional power after a while. Now that she had two dear friends who had been Confederate soldiers, it took on a whole new meaning.

"Our next stop is the McPherson Barn. We'll get out for a few minutes so you can take some pictures if you like. The fields around the house were the site of bloody fighting on the first day of the battle. The McPherson Barn is the only part of the original farm that still stands."

Once they arrived at the McPherson Barn, Jesse and Remy got everyone off the bus and told them they were free to wander around for a few moments. An attractive young woman was chatting Jesse up. *Don't bother*, Remy thought. *His heart belongs to somebody else.*

Remy strolled around the old farmhouse and looked out onto the fields. She thought of all the men who took their last breath here. At least most of them were at peace now.

"Awful lot of blood spilled right 'round here, huh?" came a gruff, angry-sounding voice right next to her.

Remy was startled by the strange man in the Union uniform with the black hat. He'd seemed to come from nowhere.

"Yeah," Remy said cautiously. She looked around and didn't see any other tours in the area, and they were in the middle of a huge field. *I know this guy wasn't on our tour.*

"That Railroad Cut was a real horror show," the man said. Then he let out an eerie laugh. "Well, for them Rebs it sure was."

A shiver went through Remy as the truth dawned on her. The guy had a good laugh at her frightened expression.

"That's right, sweetheart," the man said. He touched her arm, and she jumped back from the shock of the cold. "I was there that day. Yes, sirree."

Remy surveyed his large black hat and blue uniform. "You were with the 6th Wisconsin. They wore those big black hats."

"Yep. You were right 'bout those guys getting slaughtered like fish in a barrel."

"How-how did you know I said that?" Remy asked nervously.

"Oh, I'm a member of your tour! I was on the bus, even though you couldn't see me."

Remy remembered how Avery had told her that ghosts could be invisible when they wanted to be. It was beyond creepy to think this guy had been around all this time and she had no way of knowing.

"I like hearin' you tell that story. Brings back memories. I was havin' a real bad day that day. *Real* bad. And killin' folks has a way of makin' you feel better, ya know?"

No I don't know, you disgusting pig. Remy stared at him, keeping her face neutral. She didn't want this awful man to get a reaction out of her, which was obviously what he wanted.

"They was surrenderin' left and right. Throwing their guns down, their hands in the air. 'Don't shoot! Don't shoot!' they yelled." The man laughed again. "I let some of 'em go, captured 'em up, ya know. But I shot two of them. Just for fun. They had no weapon no more, so I just shot 'em. Boom boom. Dead."

Remy swallowed hard to hide her revulsion and heartache. In a matter of seconds, this horrible human being had probably made two widows. Maybe there were a bunch of kids that had to grow up fatherless because of this bastard. She thought of Avery's pained expression when he spoke of his daughter grieving his death.

Remy was about to try to turn and casually walk away, pretending she was indifferent to the monster's words, when Jesse suddenly came dashing up.

"You son of a bitch," Jesse growled. His hands were clenched and his eyes wild. He was clearly infuriated, but trying not to make a scene in front of the tourists. "You're the one who's been botherin' Lucy."

Remy's eyes lit up with recognition. She knew some guy had been harassing Lucy at the tavern. It had never occurred to her that it might have been a ghost who was taunting her.

Jesse looked at Remy with concern. "You all right?"

"Fine!" Remy said brightly, looking over at the hideous Union soldier. It was getting tougher by the second to act like the man wasn't upsetting her. Not only was he being horrible to her, but he had hurt Lucy as well.

"Ellis," Jesse said menacingly. The man looked surprised that Jesse knew his name. "Leave Remy alone. And quit botherin' Lucy."

Ellis scoffed. "What are you gonna do about it? You've been like I am now. You know how it works. I can be invisible and see anything I want. I can watch ladies get undressed, watch 'em in the shower, and they'll never know."

A sick feeling settled in Remy's stomach. Had he watched her before without her knowing?

Ellis leaned in and sneered at Jesse. "I'd love to take a good look at that pretty girl of yours without her clothes."

Jesse's hands shook with rage, but he managed to keep his voice steady. "First of all, you can't watch Lucy naked because you know damn well you can't follow her home. If you tried to go outside Gettysburg and where the battles were, you'd just vanish and have to go back. Second, Lucy always knows when you're around. She can sense your evil presence."

Relief and triumph coursed through Remy. Her own apartment was just outside of Gettysburg, so she would be safe from Ellis at home. She also felt a sense of satisfaction that Ellis didn't have an answer to Jesse's words at first. Jesse was right. Lucy was sensitive and always knew when a ghost was present.

Ellis cackled. "True. She always knows when I'm around. Except that one time when she and you were fu—"

"Shut your filthy mouth," Jesse said, his steady veneer beginning to crumble. Lucy was his weakness, and Ellis knew it. Threatening her was the best way to get a rise out of Jesse.

Ellis turned to Remy. "I'm so happy I shot those guys in the Railroad Cut as they were beggin' for their lives. I only wish I'd have been able to shoot more. I'd have killed that mick Irish guy of yours, too, if I could have. Woulda shot him right in the head."

Turned out he knew Remy's weakness as well.

She gathered every ounce of strength she had, looked Ellis straight in the eye, and smiled.

"All right, everyone!" Remy said in a cheerful voice. "Snap a few more pictures, and let's get moving to the next stop!"

With that, she turned on her heel and walked away.

Remy tried to put the awful man out of her head as they headed toward Little Round Top. She was looking forward to seeing Avery, but she had no intention of telling him that Ellis had been harassing her. There was nothing Avery could do to stop the man, so there was no sense in worrying him.

The Blue and Gray Tour bus arrived at Little Round Top, and the tourists scattered to take in the view.

"Excuse me, Miss?" said one of the moms on the tour. "I'm so sorry—I forgot your name?"

"Remy," she replied with a smile.

"Yes, Remy! Would you mind getting a picture of us?" the lady asked, holding up her phone and gesturing toward her kids.

"No, of course not!" Remy was eager to see Avery, but she genuinely liked making the tour enjoyable for her guests so she really didn't mind.

Jesse walked over to where Avery was waiting while Remy took care of her tourists.

"Here, why don't you guys go right over there and stand by those rocks? That way, I can get a great panoramic view of the battlefields behind you."

"Perfect!" the mom said as she pulled her kids close.

Remy took her time in lining up the perfect shot. It always pleased her to know that the pictures she took would be proudly displayed to people's friends and families when they got home from their trip.

Remy took a few pictures, then handed the cell phone back.

"Thanks!" the mom said, smiling as she reviewed the photos.

"My pleasure," Remy said. She looked around to see the other tourists seemed content for the moment. A ripple of excitement went through her as she went to visit her favorite guy.

Remy got close to where Jesse and Avery were standing, then she stopped in her tracks. Both men were glaring at her. They looked furious.

What in the world could I have done to make them mad at me?

"What?" Remy asked, alarmed.

"Has that horrible man been bothering you?" Avery asked, his eyes blazing.

"And what's this about you not eatin' supper?" Jesse demanded.

"Oh," Remy said with a sigh of relief. They weren't angry *at* her. They were angry on her *behalf.*

Avery walked over and stood close to her. She had to look up to meet his eyes because he was so tall.

"Darling, are you all right?"

"Yes, Avery. Really. I wasn't going to tell you about it because I didn't want you to worry."

"Remy," Jesse said softly. "I knew money was tight for you, but I didn't know it was that bad. I can't let you go hungry. You're welcome to come to our place and have dinner with Lucy and me anytime."

"Oh, Jesse, I'm fine," Remy said with a wave.

"But Remy—" Jesse started to argue.

"That's so sweet of you, Jesse. But really. I'm okay! My paycheck hit the bank, and I can get food now. It's usually not a problem—just sometimes when my college loan payment is due, things get a little tight."

Avery and Jesse exchanged worried looks, but Remy was determined to stay strong. She'd made it this long without having a man take care of her, and she wasn't about to lean on one now.

"Remy," Jesse said, a pleading note in his voice. Remy was touched by his kindness, but she stood firm.

"I'm fine," Remy said curtly, making it clear the discussion was over.

"Remy, sweetheart," Avery said, his voice sounding anguished. "Did Ellis hurt you?"

"No, he didn't hurt me. I promise. He doesn't scare me. He can't even touch me!" Remy said, deliberately leaving out the part where he put his hand right through her arm, chilling her to the bone.

"He touched Lucy," Jesse said gritting his teeth. His hands were balled into fists.

"Really?" Remy asked, incredulous. "How?"

"It's possible. If a spirit is really emotionally charged up, like in Ellis's case—he's an extremely angry person—you can concentrate real hard and make it happen. He grabbed her breasts."

Remy winced. "Oh, that's awful. He's such a bastard." She looked up at Avery and saw that he looked even more distraught. "He didn't do anything like that to me. Just said some mean stuff, but it's just words."

"Did Lucy tell you what he said to her?" Jesse asked. Remy shook her head. "Well, it was very personal, and she may not want to talk about it, but it was pretty awful."

Avery nodded grimly. "She was cryin' pretty hard when I found her."

Remy looked at Jesse's sorrowful expression, and she found herself clenching her fists just like he was. What a wretched human being Ellis was. Lucy was probably the sweetest person Remy had ever known, and she didn't deserve to be treated like that. Remy also knew how shy and private Lucy was, so she would be especially sensitive to Ellis's attack. She was a big-hearted person who cared about everybody and, unfortunately, was easily hurt. She was the perfect target for a monster like Ellis.

"I'm really sorry, Jesse," Remy said. She hated seeing that pained look on his face. She knew how desperately Jesse wanted to protect Lucy, but how could he keep her safe from a spirit who could come and go as he pleased and disappear at will?

"There's got to be a way to stop him," Avery said, his jaw set with determination. "And we're going to find it."

*****

Avery stood outside the Farnsworth House Inn, invisible, when Ellis showed up.

I knew it, Avery thought. The guy was probably planning on harassing Remy during her ghost tour, and then would go down the road to pick on Lucy. *Not on my watch, he won't.*

Ellis floated up to Avery, looked him up and down with derision, then said, "What're you doin' here, Paddy?"

It had been a long time since Avery had been called by that Irish slur. It annoyed him because he was proud of his heritage, but he was far more concerned about Remy.

"I'm here to make sure you quit harassin' the women around here."

Ellis snorted. "That so?"

"What's your problem with them, anyway? They've never done anything to you."

Ellis shrugged and said simply, "I'm bored. Gotta get my kicks somehow. It's fun seein' 'em get all riled up. That brown-haired girl...it's easy to make her cry. That blue-eyed slut, though, she's tougher. Gonna have to step up my game to get her to crack."

"Leave her alone," Avery said menacingly through gritted teeth. "Why don't you just vanish? Nobody wants you 'round here."

"Would love to," Ellis responded. He looked tired all of a sudden. "Seems I can't do that as easy as I used to. Used to be I could vanish for years. Now it seems I can't vanish for much more than a night."

Avery stared at him. "Me, too." It was strange. Avery had chosen to vanish for decades. He'd barely been conscious since he died more than one hundred and fifty years ago. Lately had found he could vanish overnight, but then by morning he would be conscious again whether he wanted to be or not. Nowadays, with lovely Remy around, he wanted to be here. Still, it was quite odd.

"You, too?" Ellis asked with surprise, dropping his cruel expression for once.

"Yeah. I don't know. I guess maybe God's thinkin' enough is enough. Time to go wherever you're supposed to go already."

It was so brief that Avery nearly missed it, but a look of sheer terror crossed Ellis's face. Then it was gone, and he was back to being his old, miserable self.

"Well, it ain't my idea of a good time to just hang 'round here all the time," Ellis said bitterly. "But since I got to, why should I be the only one to suffer?"

Ellis looked around, as if scanning the area for Remy or any other innocent women to torture.

"I'm stuck here, too, you know. You don't see me goin' round tormenting innocent women!" Avery practically shouted. Not that it mattered, as the two were both invisible and only other dead people could see and hear them.

"No, you're too busy flirting with that tour-guide girl."

Avery flinched at the mention of his beloved Remy. The idea of this horrible man getting anywhere near her was unbearable.

Ellis leaned in close to Avery. "You know you want to fuck her. You'd love to bang her so hard—"

"Don't you dare talk about her like that!" Avery roared.

Ellis laughed, pleased that he got the reaction he wanted. "What're you gonna do about it?"

"As long as I'm around, I won't let you bother her," Avery said, clenching his ghostly fists and wishing in the name of all things holy that he could give this guy the beating he so richly deserved. "And you can't go visible and cause a scene in front of everybody. You'd never be able to be visible on the streets of Gettysburg again. All those tourists screamin' at the sight of that hideous man in the black hat. And since you can't hardly vanish no more, all you could do was stay invisible, all by your lonesome, for eternity."

Avery was thrilled to see that, for once, Ellis didn't quite have an answer for that. Aside from gently teasing tourists on ghost tours, like grabbing their ankles or touching their backs, most ghosts preferred to hide what they were from the living. Most ghosts did not enjoy scaring people and wanted to be seen as the human beings they still were. Ellis surely wouldn't feel bad about scaring people, but his loss of privacy and his ability to come and go as he pleased was too big of a price to pay. He wouldn't cause a scene by appearing visible and harassing Remy on a public street.

Ellis glanced down the road toward Meade's Tavern.

"Don't even think about it," Avery said. "You try to go after Lucy and I'll be right behind you."

Ellis looked annoyed, his plans clearly foiled for the night.

"That's the thing, you dirty Paddy," Ellis said with a sneer. "You can't be everywhere."

A ripple of fear went through Avery's ghostly form. Ellis was right. It was nearly impossible to protect the women he cared about from this devil of man.

Chapter 13

Remy had finished her daytime tours and had a little time before her evening ghost tour shift started. Just as she was closing up shop at the Blue and Gray Touring Company, a young man had called and said he had dropped his wallet while on the tour. He thought he might have dropped it somewhere around Culp's Hill, so Remy told him she would go look for it.

For once, she had a few dollars in the bank, so she splurged on a value meal from McDonald's before driving out to Culp's Hill. She parked her car, got out, and looked around. Culp's Hill was a heavily wooded area that also had some big rocks, similar to but smaller than the boulders at Devil's Den. The battlefield's biggest attraction was the sixty-foot metal observation tower. Those tourists with the stamina to climbs the dozens of steps to the top were rewarded with an incredible 360-degree view of the area.

"A-ha!" Remy said as she spied a brown leather wallet around the base of the big metal structure. She happily dialed the guy's phone number and left him a message telling him that his wallet would be waiting for him at the tour company building in the morning. Losing your wallet was such an awful feeling, and Remy was glad she was able to set the man's mind at ease.

As she walked back to her car, she saw the familiar form of a man in a big black hat sitting among the rocks. Ellis had his back to her and didn't seem to know she was there. It had been a while since Ellis had bothered either her or Lucy, mainly because Avery did his best to stay one step ahead of him.

Remy paused for a moment and watched him. A prickle of sympathy jabbed at her heart. He looked lost and alone, much like Avery looked sometimes when he sat by himself at the peak of Little Round Top.

I bet Ellis died right here at Culp's Hill, she thought.

Remy felt only slightly anxious at Ellis's presence. She wasn't really afraid of him. Still, she couldn't help but wonder what he'd said to Lucy to make her cry.

She walked toward him. "Ellis!"

Ellis whipped his head around, startled. "What are you doing here? Shouldn't you be off strutting your stuff for that Irish soldier like the cheap slut you are?" he growled.

Remy rolled her eyes. He called all women sluts, whores, and harlots, so she didn't take it personally. Besides, he was way off base. She'd had sex exactly *once*, and it was years ago.

Ellis seemed quite surprised to see her walk right up to him, then plop herself down beside him.

"You sure do like calling women names, don't you? And you also like groping them, I hear," Remy said, recalling Jesse's fury when he told her how Ellis had touched Lucy's breasts.

Ellis glanced down at Remy's chest. "You don't have to worry 'bout me touching you. Your tits are too small."

Not that she would ever want Ellis's disgusting hands on her, but the criticism stung. She knew she was too thin, and she was sensitive about her chest size. Still, she would be damned if she would let him know he was getting to her.

"So!" she said brightly. "Do you wanna call me a slut a few more times and threaten my already dead boyfriend, or would you like to have an actual conversation?"

He eyed her curiously, as if not sure what to make of her.

"Why are you so mean?" Remy asked him bluntly.

Ellis laughed, clearly surprised at the question. "I'm bored. Gotta have something to do to keep me occupied."

"You could talk nicely to people like most dead folks around here do."

"But that would be *boring*." Ellis scanned the battlefield area. "I see you don't have your knight in shining armor here to protect you from me."

The thought of Avery as her white knight made her smile. "I don't need him to protect me. I'm not afraid of you."

Ellis sneered at her, but she could see he was slightly impressed that she refused to run away from him.

"Why do you hate women so much?" she asked him.

He looked away and said nothing.

"I bet somebody broke your heart," Remy said softly. Ellis narrowed his eyes, glaring at her. "I'm sorry if that happened to you."

Ellis studied her like she was a strange new specimen of insect. "Why are you being so nice to me?"

"Because I have a soft spot in my heart for lost souls," she told him. It had always been in her nature to comfort others and put them at ease. She understood that sometimes the most unlovable people were the ones who needed nurturing the most. Ellis seemed so vulnerable right now. So different from the man who had boasted that he'd killed those men in the Railroad Cut.

"Were you married?" Remy asked him.

"That is none of your business!" Ellis shouted.

"You're right," she said quietly, determined to stay calm. "I shouldn't ask you personal questions like that. It's just that I can see you're suffering, and I wish I could help. You know, my friend Theresa counsels soldiers around here. Maybe she could help you cross over."

Theresa Hetty was fiery and strong. If anyone could handle Ellis, she could.

"Oh, yeah. I know all about Theresa. She's that redheaded girl. The one that guy tried to take behind the Jennie Wade house."

Remy swallowed hard and tried to keep her voice steady. "No, not *take*. Rape. He tried to rape her."

Remy wondered how Ellis knew what had happened, then she realized he could flit around, invisible, and might have witnessed it. Theresa had been traumatized by the attempted sexual assault from her ex-boyfriend. She had told Remy how Lucy, Jesse, and Theresa's boyfriend, Sean, had supported her through that nightmare. Theresa had even confided to Remy that Sean had been especially gentle with her in bed at first because she found it somewhat frightening to have sex after being assaulted. Sean had been patient and kind, just as she was when supporting him with his struggles with PTSD. The two were fiercely loyal to each other and were very much in love.

"Talk about sluts," Ellis said. "She's a wild one. You just know she was asking for it."

Ellis looked at her, waiting for her to react. It took tremendous effort to swallow the rage that threatened to erupt from inside her. Remy took a few deep, cleansing breaths, knowing that a lecture on consent would be wasted on someone like Ellis. She wasn't even sure if he believed half the garbage that spewed from his mouth, or if he was just trying to piss her off. And he was. Pissing. Her. Off. But she somehow managed to keep her cool.

"Do you know why you're still here? Why you haven't crossed over?" Remy asked.

"Why? Trying to get rid of me?"

"You're changing the subject," she told him, looking him directly in the eye. Remy got the feeling that Ellis really did want to talk, to be able to confide in someone, but he had so much anger in him. And, if Remy wasn't mistaken, there was fear in his eyes. He was always trying to upset and scare everybody else, but what was *he* afraid of?

"Did you die here at Culp's Hill?"

Ellis shook his head. "Nope. Wish I had. Got wounded here, though. Died after they sawed off my leg. They didn't give you nothin' for pain back then. So I felt 'em cuttin' into me."

"I'm sorry that happened to you, Ellis."

"Save your pity for somebody who cares, ya whore."

Remy looked out at the battlefield and saw the sun sinking lower in the sky. She stood up.

"I have to go. Other ghosts are waiting," Remy said, looking down at Ellis with a smile. "Ellis, I may not understand why just yet, but I know you're angry and you're hurting. And I really do want to help you."

"You must be crazy," Ellis muttered.

Probably, she thought.

"I don't have a tour tomorrow night, so I'll be visiting with Avery all evening. But on Friday, I'll stop by here after my day tour and before my nighttime one. Be here if you want to talk."

Ellis laughed and shook his head.

Still, Remy had a strong feeling that the man was going to show up on Friday. He had a look in his eye that told her he didn't trust her. But he wanted to.

*****

The next evening, Remy took a few moments to touch up her makeup and brush her hair before getting out of the car at Little

Round Top. She wore blue jeans and a black button-down blouse. She loved this black blouse because it made the blue in her eyes stand out. She wanted to look pretty for Avery, and she liked when he could see her in something other than her Jennie Wade outfit.

Remy eagerly walked toward where she knew Avery was waiting. She loved that she didn't have to hide her feelings for him anymore. She could run toward him if she wanted to.

Her heart fluttered when Avery stood up as he saw her approach. She couldn't get over the way he looked at her. He had such sweet affection in his smile. Remy knew that part of his longing to see her was due to loneliness. It wasn't like there were that many people he could talk to. Still, his expression was different than the warm smile he gave to Lucy or Jesse when he saw them. It was like he had a special look reserved just for her.

Avery looked her up and down. "You look so beautiful, Remy." His gaze lingered on her eyes, which she knew were her best feature. "I only wish I could change my clothes. I would love to wear something nicer for you."

"Don't be silly. There's nothing sexier than a man in uniform," Remy said, looking him up and down as well. The gray of his Confederate uniform brought out the soft grayness of his eyes. He looked so handsome that she actually sighed out loud. "Do you want to go for a walk or something? No reason we have to stay here all the time."

"I would love it," Avery said.

Remy turned and started walking, and Avery fell into step next to her. She wished he could hold her hand as they walked down the street behind Little Round Top. Avery let Remy lead the way as they walked down a trail through the woods.

"Remy," Avery began. "I love when you visit with me, but I hope you know I'll understand if you have other things to do. I know you have a life to live even if I don't."

"Avery," she said softly, "there's no place I'd rather be than with you."

"I do love hearin' you say that! By the way, did you eat dinner?" he asked, his tone somewhat accusatory.

"Yes, I did. I got something to eat right after work," Remy told him. She had heated up one of those tasteless frozen dinners at her apartment before changing her clothes so she could look nice for him.

"Good!"

Remy took a deep breath of fresh air and looked around at the trees. It was nice to be able to walk and take time to enjoy the sights without being on tour. She rarely walked through this particular path through the forest since it was more for hikers and other tourists who liked to wander around on their own.

"So last time we spoke, we talked about my family. Why don't you tell me about yours?" Avery said.

Remy's heart sank. Her family was not among her favorite topics.

"I know you've had a hard time with them," Avery said gently.

Remy nodded. It was hard for her to talk about, but she knew she could tell Avery anything.

"Yes, you could say that," she said. Avery looked worried about her, and it felt good to know someone cared. She wasn't used to that. "Well, my parents got divorced when I was really young."

"Do you have any brothers and sisters?"

"No, which is probably a good thing. I don't think my parents even wanted me, let alone more kids. I'm pretty sure I was an accident."

"Oh, Remy!" Avery said, horrified. "You mustn't say that, darling. You weren't an accident—you were a blessing!"

Remy looked over at him gratefully, but said quietly, "Not to my parents, I wasn't."

"To me, you certainly are. You're a beautiful gift from God,"

Avery said with affection.

Remy fell silent for a moment. She was still getting used to the idea that there really was a God.

"Thank you, Avery. I'm pretty sure neither my mom nor my dad wanted me. My dad wasn't around much, and when he did bother to visit me he didn't seem interested in me at all. Like he couldn't wait to get rid of me. My mother had a bad problem with alcohol. She didn't take very good care of me, so I had to learn to take care of myself when I was pretty young. Had to get myself dressed for school, and I learned to tell time so I could be at the bus stop on time."

Avery looked devastated. She didn't like upsetting him, but it felt good to get this off her chest. So far, Lucy had been the only one she'd had confided in about all of this. Remy had told Lucy it was okay to tell Jesse and Theresa about it, so she knew they were aware of her background.

"And-and I know for sure that my parents hadn't planned on having me because…because…" She struggled to finish as the tears welled up in her eyes. "Because one time when my mother was really drunk she…she said I was a mistake."

Avery stopped walking, and so did Remy. She took a moment to compose herself, pulling a tissue from her pocket and wiping her eyes. She finally turned to look up at Avery, whose eyes were full of compassion.

Remy held his gaze and let out a shaky sigh of sorrow and relief. She hadn't realized how much she had needed to confide in him. She could see both empathy and helplessness in his eyes. Remy had never ached for someone's touch so much in her entire life, which had always consisted of physical and emotional neglect. She desperately wanted to run into Avery's arms and let him hold her until she stopped shaking.

"Oh, Remy, darling, I'm so sorry," Avery said. He lifted his hand

and gently touched her cheek. His touch was ice cold, but she still appreciated the gesture. It helped to know that he ached to hold her, too.

"I think I believed what she said for a long time. I thought I was a mistake." She felt the tears form behind her eyes, but then she recalled what Avery had said to her just moments ago. He had called her a beautiful gift from God. "I felt like I had no business being alive since nobody wanted me and I wasn't even supposed to be here. Now that I'm an adult, I can be a little more objective. I understand now that I was just a child, and I didn't do anything wrong. My mother resented me for being born, but that's not my fault. I've come to terms with all of it as best I can, but sometimes I still feel like a little girl who wants her parents to be proud of me. I know that'll never happen."

"I'm so very proud of you, Remy. It's remarkable…the brave, strong, kind woman you've become. But it doesn't matter what I think. What matters most is that ye be proud of yerself."

"I am," Remy said truthfully. She'd worked hard to put the past behind her so she could move on. She was proud that she'd become a responsible, hardworking adult who truly wanted to make the world a better place. "I always felt uncomfortable, afraid at home. I think that's why I like to put people at ease when I talk to them. Make them feel good."

"Well, you're a natural at doin' that, darling. That's the first thing I noticed about you. You have such a way with people. You know how to relate to a stranger just by lookin' at 'im. I don't know how you do it. You just instinctively know how to care for people."

Avery smiled fondly at her, and her feelings of despair over the harsh memories of her family began to fade away. The way Avery had described her was exactly how she wanted to be. A comforter to strangers, a friendly, knowledgeable guide not just on tours but on life in general. That was her way of trying to make the world a better place. It was hard for her to know if she was succeeding or not. You never knew how others perceive you, but Avery's kind words reassured her that she was doing just fine.

Remy thought of Ellis sitting all alone at Culp's Hill. Maybe she really could help him if she persevered.

As if reading her mind, Avery said, "You're always lookin' out for everybody else, but who's lookin' out for you?"

"No one, until recently," Remy said with a smile. She started walking again, and so did Avery. "I feel like everything changed for the better when Jesse started working with me. He's such a good friend to me, and Lucy is probably my best friend. Theresa has been wonderful, too." Remy laughed.

"What?" Avery asked, looking relieved to hear her laugh after being so upset.

"Okay," Remy said sternly. "You have to promise not to tell *anyone* if I tell you this."

"Of course I won't! Cross me heart," he said, making a crisscross motion across his chest.

"I had a huge crush on Jesse when he first started working with me."

"Really?" Avery said, looking slightly wounded.

"Yup. Until I met Lucy. When I saw the two of them together, I knew it was all over. The way he looks at her. Well, you just know there could never be anybody else for him."

Avery nodded, still looking sad. Remy stopped walking and looked up at him.

"Avery, it was just a silly crush. It was nothing compared to the way I feel about you. As soon as I met Lucy, I got over it. You, on the other hand…"

Avery looked intrigued about what she was going to say about him.

"I was completely heartbroken over you when I thought you weren't interested. If you don't believe me, ask Lucy. She had to put up with me pining for you. I called her one time, all upset because I was crazy about you and you never made a move on me. I was afraid you had a girlfriend or just weren't interested. I was all upset, and that's when Lucy decided enough was enough and insisted you guys tell me the truth." Remy looked at Avery and sighed. "I gave up easily when I knew Jesse wasn't available, but there was no getting over you."

Avery's smile reached all the way up to his eyes. "Thank you for telling me that, Remy."

"So because of Jesse, I have lots of friends now. And I have you."

"I know of someone else you should meet," Avery told her.

"And who's that?"

"Fillis."

Fillis. She knew that name, but she wasn't sure why.

"She's, you know, like me. Deceased. She's an older lady, maybe in her fifties and—"

"Yes! I know who you're talking about," Remy said, suddenly remembering. "I don't know her, but Jesse mentioned her. She used to be a slave."

"Right," Avery said with a sad nod of his head. "She's a terrific lady. She's a nurturer, just like you. Lots of soldiers call her Second Mama since our own mothers aren't around to take care of us anymore."

"She sounds really nice," Remy said. Avery spoke of Fillis in the same warm tone as Jesse had, and it made Remy happy to know there was someone looking out for Avery.

"Oh, she's gonna love you. Take you right under her motherly wing, she would. Once she hears what you've been through with your family, she'll want to adopt you like the rest of us."

"I don't know. I don't want to burden any more people with my problems. Bad enough I dump all my issues on you and Lucy. Ugh, I made it most of my life without telling people about my family drama, and now it seems like everybody knows."

Remy suddenly felt self-conscious. Exposed. She usually did her best to appear confident when she was talking with people and leading tours. Now she felt vulnerable, knowing all her new friends knew all her dark secrets.

"Remy," Avery said softly, immediately picking up on her discomfort. "I would never force you to do anything that makes you uncomfortable, but I would really love to at least introduce you to Fillis."

Remy looked into Avery's eyes, feeling her resolve weakening. "When you look at me like that, how am I supposed to resist? Say it in Irish, and I'll really be sunk."

Avery grinned, leaned over, and said, "*Beidh do thoil tú ag freastal ar mo chara, Fillis?*"

"Anything you say, Avery," Remy said in a dreamy voice.

His rich, sexy laugh made her tingle all over.

Chapter 14

Remy agreed to meet Fillis on Saturday since she had no tours scheduled on that day. Today was Friday, and she had day tours all day and then two ghost tours at night. It was also the day she had told Ellis to come to Culp's Hill in the early evening if he wanted to talk. Rehashing her past with Avery the other day had been exhausting yet liberating, and she hoped to be able to help Ellis in the same way. She had the feeling he'd had a tough life and probably desperately needed a friend.

She parked her car at Culp's Hill and got out. She smiled and bit her lip as she saw Ellis sitting among the rocks where he'd been last time. *I knew it. He needs me.* She took a deep breath and prepared for battle. She fully expected him to be defensive about his vulnerability, and she knew she should expect him to treat her with cruelty at first like he always did. She knew she had to be patient with him to earn his trust. Only then could she help him.

Ellis turned around and scowled at her. "You again? Oh, yeah. Forgot you said you were gonna show up here again to bother me."

They both knew damn well he hadn't forgotten what she'd said, but Remy was happy to allow him to save face by pretending to believe him.

"Well, as long as you're here, we might as well talk." She walked over and plopped down right beside him and smiled. A tingle of excitement rippled through her when she saw him hide his smile. She also saw relief in his eyes. Remy prided herself on being able to read people. He needed a friend, all right.

"Well, it ain't like I got anything better to do," Ellis grumbled.

Remy fanned herself with her hand. "Stop it! You're making me blush, kind sir!"

Ellis's laugh was more of a snort, but it was there. He actually *laughed*.

"What do you want with me, anyway?" he asked.

"I've been talking to a lot of ghosts lately. Well, ghosts and former ghosts."

"Jesse," Ellis said, shaking his head. "That was so weird. That he came back."

"He was in love, so God let him stay."

"Yeah, we'll see how long that relationship lasts. She'll find somebody better. Or he will." Ellis said gruffly.

Remy could hear the pain in his voice. Yes, some woman had definitely broken his heart somewhere along the way.

"Well, I understand how lonely it is to be a ghost. I'm lonely a lot, too," Remy said quietly, fully aware of how risky it was to confess such a thing to Ellis. He had no problem grabbing hold of your insecurities and throwing them back in your face. She had to be careful of how much she told him. Still, she knew it might be the only way to get him to open up.

"I don't need your pity."

"I know you don't. But I thought you might need a friend, and I could always use more."

"What, that Irish paddy ain't enough for you?"

Remy hated hearing Ellis talk that way about Avery, especially since she knew he had probably called him that and worse right to his face.

"I love being with him. That's true," she said.

"Oh, I bet you wish you could be with him. You'd spread your legs wide open for him if you could."

"You're damn right I would," Remy said, refusing to so much as blink at his crudeness. She didn't enjoy being spoken to with such disrespect, especially about something as sacred to her as making love with Avery, but she refused to let him bait her. "But we're not talking about me right now."

Ellis peered over at her, looking impressed. He had probably expected her to be more like Lucy. Tenderhearted and easy to crush. Remy felt her fury rise at the thought. She didn't care if Ellis hurt her feelings, but the thought of him torturing Lucy infuriated her.

"I just want you to know that I'm here if you want to talk," Remy said.

Ellis was quiet for a while. Remy had the feeling he wanted to say something, but he was afraid. She sat still and waited patiently.

"I can't…" Ellis began cautiously. "Do you know what vanishing is? For ghosts?"

"Yes. Avery explained it to me. It's like when you're not really conscious. Different than just being invisible."

Ellis nodded and seemed relieved that she understood. "I used to be able to vanish whenever I wanted, and now I can't. I don't understand what's happening to me." He refused to look at her as he spoke.

"That must be really scary," Remy said softly.

Ellis turned and glared at her. She steeled herself for an angry insult, but when he finally spoke, he said, "Yeah. It is scary."

"Well, maybe it's a good thing. Maybe it will be your time to cross over soon.

Remy eyed him carefully, but his expression remained neutral.

"You should join Theresa's counseling group. I'm sure she could you help you."

"That's the last thing I need. To be in some group with a bunch of pansies whining about their feelings."

"Well, maybe you could just come to a meeting and sit with them for a while. Just listen. A lot of soldiers are going through the same thing you are."

Ellis fell quiet again, and Remy hoped she was getting through to him. Though she believed the group might really help him, she was worried about the way he might treat the other soldiers. It would be just like him to call them pansies to their faces, and she could easily see him starting a fight. Theresa was compassionate and kind, yet she didn't take shit from anybody. Hopefully, she would be able to keep him in line.

"Who says I want to cross over?" Ellis asked angrily.

Remy looked at him curiously. It had never occurred to her that he wouldn't want to leave this lonely ghost existence.

"Jesse wanted to stay because he loves Lucy. What's keeping you here?" Remy asked as gently as possible.

Ellis shook his head and looked away, making it clear that he had no intention of telling her why he didn't want to leave the earth behind.

"I have to go," Ellis said, abruptly standing up.

They both knew damn well he had nowhere else to be, but Remy let him go without argument.

"Okay," Remy said. "I've got some tours to do anyway."

Her heart ached with empathy as she watched him start to walk away. He looked like such a sad, lonesome figure.

"Ellis!" she called after him.

He paused a moment, then turned to look at her.

"I can come back on Monday."

Ellis looked at her. For once, he wasn't sneering. He simply nodded, then turned and disappeared.

*****

Remy walked with Avery toward the Gettysburg College campus where they had agreed to meet with Fillis. Jesse, Lucy, and Theresa were also coming, so they needed a space big enough for all of them. Jesse had made it clear that under no circumstances would they meet on a battlefield. It was far too risky for Lucy, given her sensitivity to sympathy battle pains.

Remy hadn't thought much about the meeting with Fillis before, but now she was having second thoughts.

"I don't know about this, Avery," she said, hearing the nervousness in her voice.

"Why? What's the matter?" Avery asked.

"It just feels weird that everybody knows all about my family situation. I'm not sorry I told you, of course. And I'm comfortable talking with Lucy and Theresa sometimes. But…I told Lucy it was okay to tell Jesse, and now this Fillis woman knows… It's so awkward. Like this is some kind of counseling intervention or something. I've spent most of my life hiding my family secrets, and now I feel like everybody's just feeling sorry for me. Ugh."

She prided herself on being a strong woman, and she couldn't bear being pitied.

"Oh, darling, I promise you it won't be like that," Avery said, his expression softening with concern. "I think of Fillis as part of my family. She's a wonderful lady, and I know she wants to meet you. That's all. I promise."

Remy nodded, resolving to put on a brave face for Avery's sake. If this lady was important to Avery, then she was important to Remy.

She smiled at him uneasily, and the knot of anxiety grew as she saw the whole group waiting for them on the campus lawn.

Theresa rushed right up to Avery and looked him up and down. "So! You're the gorgeous Irishman I've heard so much about."

Avery chuckled, and Remy relaxed a bit. Leave it to Theresa to know how to break the ice.

"Well, I'm Irish. That much I'm sure about."

"Yeah, ya are!" Theresa said, her blue eyes flashing with amusement and mischief. "That is a fantastic accent. Say something in Irish!"

"He's not a trained dog, Theresa," Lucy said dryly.

"Shhh!" Theresa said, waving her off and looking at Avery expectantly.

Avery laughed again, and then said, *"Deas bualadh leat*, Theresa."

"Wow," Theresa said, then looked over at Remy. "It doesn't even matter what he's saying, does it? It all sounds sexy as hell."

Remy laughed warmly, feeling more comfortable by the moment. "Yes, it certainly does!"

"I'm very happy to meet you finally," Theresa said with a warm smile.

"Likewise," Avery said with a grin.

Fillis walked over to them, and Remy realized the woman did look vaguely familiar. She probably had seen her on Steinwehr Avenue from time to time, perpetually dressed in her blue cotton dress. She had a warm, motherly smile. Remy was still uncomfortable knowing that this woman, a stranger, already knew so much about her ugly past.

"Remy, it's so nice to finally meet you. Sit down! Sit down!" Fillis said as she sat on the grass and gestured for Remy to sit beside her.

Fillis seemed sweet, and it warmed Remy's heart to see the way both Avery and Jesse looked at her. They were like two kids with their mama, and she looked at them like they were her pride and joy.

That's the way real mothers are supposed to be, Remy thought.

Avery sat on the other side of Remy. Fillis looked at Avery, then over at Remy.

"Oh, it's so nice to see the two of you together. This guy's been so crazy over you for so long. You're all he ever wanted to talk about," Fillis said with a smile.

"That's really sweet," Remy said, smiling at Avery.

"And it was *killin'* us not to be able to tell you how he felt about you!" Theresa chimed in. "I felt so bad. You were so upset, and Luce and I wanted to scream, *Oh, my God, this guy is so nuts about you. You have no idea!*"

Remy laughed and tucked her hair behind her ear. It was still a little strange to be fussed over, but at least they were talking about her and Avery and not her wretched family.

"Well, I'm just so happy you two worked it all out," Fillis said. She turned to face Remy and spoke gently to her. "Now look, honey. I know you don't know me from Adam. Or Eve, as it were, and I sure don't want to get into your personal business…"

Remy felt her muscles tighten. She really didn't want to discuss her personal trauma in front of all these people.

"But I heard you ain't too close with your family. 'Round here, we kinda make our own family." Fillis glanced up at Jesse and Avery. "Now, I know it's hard to b'lieve given the strong family resemblance and all, but we ain't actually related!"

Fillis winked at Remy, and Remy laughed and began to relax a little. Fillis wasn't just kind—she seemed like the type of person who knew what to say to put people at ease. She wouldn't say anything to embarrass Remy.

"I want you to know that I'm so happy to welcome you to our family here. Lots of people 'round here call me Second Mama, 'cause they ain't had their own mamas around for a long, long time. And I'm here to take care of 'em 'til they can go be at peace with their other families again."

"That's very kind of you," Remy said. It was a comfort to know that Avery had someone to take care of him when she couldn't be around.

"And I know it ain't the same as comin' from your own mama, but I want you to know I think you're such a wonderful girl. I only just met ya, but I feel like I know you already. You're a special young lady, Remy." Fillis glanced over at Avery. "You caught this one's eye straight away, and not just 'cause you're pretty, neither! He told me all 'bout how kind you were to him and to everybody you meet."

"Aye, that's Remy, all right," Avery said, smiling proudly.

Fillis was sure to look Remy in the eye when she spoke again. "You're such a strong woman, Remy. I know you've been treated with cruelty, yet you still turn 'round and treat people with kindness. I know that ain't easy."

Remy nodded. That was an enormous compliment coming from someone like Fillis. She had spent her life as a slave, and yet she loved so many Confederate soldiers with all of her incredible heart. That must have taken tremendous inner strength.

"And this one," Fillis said, gesturing at Jesse and smiling fondly. "I love him like he was my own little boy. I've been his honorary mama for more years than I can count. I'll never f'get, he was a nervous wreck on his first day on the job. He was so scared he's gonna get fired that he didn't even tell Lucy he had a job yet!"

Jesse chuckled and nodded. Remy knew that Jesse told Lucy *everything*, so he must have really been worried. She smiled softly, remembering the drop-dead sexy yet incredibly nervous guy who walked into the tour company that day. She had liked him immediately.

"He came and told me how nice that manager lady was and that she took good care of 'im, makin' 'im feel welcome and tellin' him he was gonna do just fine. Might seem a simple thing, but you don't forget somebody who done a kindness to your child."

Remy smiled warmly at Fillis, who was everything a mother should be. Proud, strong, supportive. Loving. Remy already found herself tempted to call her Second Mama. For a moment, she forgot to feel self-conscious about her family's dirty laundry and simply felt at peace. Remy could only hope she made others feel this good when she spoke to them.

"Thank you so much, Fillis," Remy said, knowing her words couldn't possibly express the gratitude she felt.

"Like I said, I know it ain't the same as your own mama sayin' it, but for what it's worth, I'm proud of the wonderful woman you've made of yourself."

"I'm proud of you, too," Avery said, looking at her affectionately. He reached over and touched her cheek. It always felt like he was rubbing an ice cube on her face when he did that, but she loved it anyway. It was his way of telling her how much he wished he could touch her.

"I think that was always the hardest part for Jesse," Fillis observed. "Not being able to touch Lucy."

Remy nodded slowly. There was so much she wanted to say, so many feelings she'd kept bottled up for so long. She'd never had close friends before, only casual acquaintances in high school and college, so there had never been anyone to confide in before. Now, here in this brief moment of silence, she could feel the love and support from Avery, Fillis, Jesse, Lucy, and Theresa. It really did feel like she had a family now, and she felt braver about opening up about her feelings.

"That's the thing. It's not just Avery," Remy began softly. She looked at Avery, then looked down, avoiding anyone's gaze. "But it's like…no one touches me. I don't exactly come from a touchy-feely family. Even as a child, my parents never gave me much affection. And now, I live by myself and all and, you know, aside from the occasional handshake or when I take a tourist's hand to help them up the hill or something, I don't have any physical contact with anyone. Sometimes I really miss that."

"I never thought about that," Jesse said quietly. "When I was dead for so long, nobody could touch me, neither, but I didn't miss it all that much because I couldn't feel anything anyway. Like bein' hungry, I guess. You don't really miss food when you're a ghost, 'cause you can't eat and you don't feel hungry. But when you're alive, you need food and water, and you need companionship."

Remy tentatively looked up at Jesse and nodded. She couldn't help but feel like an unlovable, pathetic loser after confessing her thoughts out loud, but Jesse made it clear that he understood. She was grateful for his words.

Lucy stood up and walked over to where Remy sat. She held out her hands for Remy to take. Remy laughed a little self-consciously, but took Lucy's hands and allowed her to pull her up to a standing position.

Lucy looked into Remy's eyes and said, "I really do think of you as family. I love you like a sister. I hope you know that."

Lucy wrapped her arms around Remy in a warm embrace. Remy closed her eyes as she felt Lucy's warm body envelop hers. The last thing she wanted was pity, but it felt good to have some human contact.

"I think of you as a sister, too, girl," Theresa said, jumping up so she could join them. She wrapped her arms around both Remy and Lucy in a warm group hug.

Remy laughed, but she held on to the two women for as long as she reasonably could. She'd worked hard her whole life to put her past behind her, to forget her upbringing and to start a new life for herself, but inside sometimes she was still the little girl who craved love and affection. She swallowed hard, afraid that if she started crying she'd never stop.

"Thanks, guys," Remy said, loosening her grip a little. "I know it's so stupid…"

"It's not stupid," Theresa said with uncharacteristic solemnness. "I come from a super touchy-feely family, and they make me nuts sometimes, but I never realized how much I took them for granted." Then she brightened a bit and said, "You can hug me whenever you want, sis!"

"Me, too!" Lucy said, pulling Remy in for another hug.

Theresa leaned in and murmured in Remy's ear, "And you know damn well that Avery would love to touch every inch of your body if he only had the chance!"

All three women laughed together, and any awkwardness Remy felt evaporated. It was like she was laughing with her sisters. They didn't make her feel like a charity case. They made her feel loved.

Remy took a step back from Lucy and Theresa and was about to sit back down when she saw that Jesse had stood up and was walking toward her.

"Hey, do I get a hug?" Jesse asked.

Remy laughed. "Of course."

"Actually, I want two hugs. This one is from me," Jesse said, opening his arms and wrapping them around her. The feel of his big, strong body against hers reminded her of how long it had been since any man had touched her. The hug was warm and firm, the kind that was appropriate from a platonic male friend. He pulled away, glanced over at Avery, and then back at Remy. "And this one's from Avery."

With that, he pulled her in for another hug. It was still firm, but gentler. Remy closed her eyes and imagined that it was Avery finally holding her.

Avery walked over and whispered in her ear, "*Adhraim thú,* Remy."

Remy smiled, remembering the phrase. *I adore you.*

Jesse gently rubbed her back as he held her. Remy squeezed her eyes tight, wishing with all her heart that Avery could hold her in his arms and never let go. Of course, she was acutely aware that Jesse was the one touching her, but being lovingly held by a dear friend who cared deeply about her was wonderful in its own right. And how thoughtful, how like Jesse, to think of such a sweet gesture.

Remy pulled back from Jesse and smiled. "Thank you, Jesse." She looked over at Lucy, who was holding her hand over her heart and looking at Jesse adoringly. "And thanks for letting me borrow your boyfriend."

Lucy laughed and nodded.

"Ugh! Okay, enough fussing over me!" Remy sat down on the ground, and the others followed suit. "So Fillis, do you know why you're still here after all this time? What's keeping you here?"

Lucy and Theresa both folded their arms at looked at Fillis, making her laugh.

"Oh, lordy, don't you start, too!"

"What?" Remy asked.

"Them two been after me 'bout that, too," Fillis said, looking at Theresa and Lucy like they were her own stubborn yet lovable daughters.

"I've been telling her she should let Theresa counsel her, or at least she could talk with me about it," Lucy said. "After all, I helped Joel cross over *and* I even helped him and Jesse become friends first. I am a miracle worker!"

Fillis and Jesse laughed heartily.

"Well, I cain't argue with that. No, ma'am. You done the impossible."

Lucy smiled proudly, but still looked concerned for Fillis. "You've done so much to help the others. Why won't you let us help you?"

Fillis waved Lucy off, dismissing her own troubles.

"Fillis," Lucy said gently. "I know how much you must miss her. I know we could help you go home to her if you only let us."

Remy eyed Fillis curiously. Did she have a daughter like Avery?

"I done told you, I don't want you fussin' over me!" Fillis said kindly but firmly.

"Oh, I see. It's okay to fuss over us, but we're not allowed to return the favor?" Remy crossed her arms just as Theresa and Lucy had, so now all three of them were staring her down.

Fillis laughed, looking at the women with affection. She looked over at the guys. "Jesse! They's gangin' up on me!"

"Yep," Jesse said, offering no further assistance.

"Who are you missing, Fillis?" Remy asked, and Fillis looked over at her with fondness. But she didn't answer right away.

"A woman who was very dear to me," Fillis said wearily.

"You don't have to tell me if you don't want to," Remy said. "But it seems only fair, since you know all about my life."

Fillis laughed and shook her head. She looked over at Avery. "Oh, she's good."

"I know it!" Avery said. "I look into those beautiful blue eyes of hers and I'm under her command."

Remy laughed and looked adoringly at Avery and sighed. He was so wonderful.

"Long and painful story told short," Fillis said with a sad smile, "Back on the plantation in Virginia, me and the master's wife were in love. She was my secret lover for more than thirty years. Spent most of my lifetime with her, but I lost her when her husband found out. I had to run away. Got as far as Gettysburg when I fell sick and died."

It took Remy a moment to process Fillis's words. Fillis was a *lesbian*! It was strange how she never thought about gay people in the 1860s. Naturally, there had been homosexuals around since the beginning of time, but only recently had it become a more common and accepted thing. Not accepted enough, but certainly better than it had been for a long time.

"Helene is waiting for you, Fillis. You know that, right?" Lucy said softly. Jesse reached over and squeezed Lucy's hand, looking sorrowful. He knew what it was like to be in love, and he must have known how painful it was for Fillis to be separated from her soulmate.

"Yes, I know that," Fillis said.

"We can help you go home to her, Fillis," Lucy said. "I know it!"

"I told you, I don't want none of y'all fussin' over me!"

"But Fillis, I know Theresa and I can help you, if you just let—"

"Lucy!" Fillis shouted. Oddly, she wasn't angry even though she was yelling. Fillis laughed and shook her head, looking at Lucy with her usual motherly love. "Don't you understand, child? I can *go* any time I want. Whatever issues I had that kept me here, well I worked 'em out long ago. But I cain't go. Not while my boys need me."

Everyone stared at Fillis and the truth dawned on them all.

Lucy's eyes opened wide. She glanced over at Jesse, who looked equally shocked. "You stay for them," she whispered, as the magnitude of her sacrifice sunk in.

Fillis snapped her head in a nod. "Now. That's enough of that!"

Remy, Lucy, and Theresa looked at each other in astonishment. A silent understanding passed among them.

They were going to help Fillis go home to Helene.

Chapter 15

After the comfort that Fillis and the rest of Remy's surrogate family had provided, she was more determined than ever to help Ellis. She was thrilled to find him in the usual spot at Culp's Hill on Monday evening.

As usual, he glowered at her when she approached. "I was afraid you'd come back."

"No, you were hoping I'd be back. Otherwise, you wouldn't be here," Remy said, calling his bluff.

"Don't flatter yourself, ya whore. I'd have been here anyway."

"You know, I'm pretty patient, but I'm not a saint. There's only so much abuse I'm gonna take until I finally just give up on you," Remy informed him. She wasn't even angry. He'd said much worse to her before, and "whore" was his generic, knee-jerk insult. However, she was tired of playing games with him. He wanted and *needed* her help and companionship, and they both knew it. It was best for both of them if they quit wasting time.

Ellis glanced up at her, his expression unreadable.

"You and I both know you're lonely. You don't have anybody and until recently, neither did I. I want to help you and be your friend, but I deserve better than to be called a whore."

Ellis looked away and, after a moment, he mumbled, "You're right. Sorry."

Remy was shocked that he had apologized. That was the biggest breakthrough with him yet.

"Why were you alone?" he asked.

Remy let out a sigh. "I want to tell you, but I'm afraid you might throw it back in my face."

He shrugged slightly and nodded. They both knew he was capable of cutting people down by saying the cruelest thing he could think of. Telling him any of her secrets was a risk as it provided him with ammunition.

Remy watched him for a moment. He looked sad and lonely. Devoid of any hope. Finally, she said, "My parents neglected me for most of my life. They were sorry I was born and had no problem saying so."

The glimpse of compassion on Ellis's face was gone as quickly as it came, but it was there. And it was real.

Ellis put his head down and said bluntly, "Yeah, we all got our problems. My mother touched me in ways you ain't supposed to touch a kid."

Shockwaves coursed through Remy's body at his startling confession. "My God, I'm so sorry," she whispered.

"I don't want your pity!" Ellis roared, probably regretting what he'd told her.

"Well, too bad!" Remy shot back, even though she understood completely how he felt. She hated being pitied, too. "You were just a child. You didn't deserve that, and I'm really sorry that happened to you. No wonder you hate women so much. We're not all like that, you know."

"Wish I could believe that," he mumbled, glaring in her direction. At least now she understood more why he found it so hard to trust her or anyone else.

"You don't have to tell me the rest, but I get the feeling there's more," Remy said.

Ellis nodded. As always, he took his time in responding, and Remy patiently waited. "Yeah. There's more. Never had nobody who cared 'bout me my whole life. Nobody. Then I found a girl. I loved her, and she loved me. Or least I thought she did. She turned out to be a slut just like all women. Sorry," he said, mumbling an apology to Remy that didn't seem quite as sincere as the last time. "Turns out she was whoring around with some other guy. Wrote and told me all 'bout how she was sorry but she met somebody else. Happened while I was off and fightin'. Got her letter the day before the Gettysburg battle."

Remy's heart ached as she listened to Ellis's story. Each word he uttered was drenched in pain. She imagined how she would feel in his situation. If Avery were alive and he cheated on her just when she thought she'd found someone who actually cared for her. It would have been devastating. She remembered Ellis telling her about what he'd done to those men in the Railroad Cut. *I was havin' a real bad day that day. Real bad. And killin' folks has a way of makin' you feel better, ya know?* She knew being dumped by a woman was certainly no excuse for murder, but at least she understood what was going on his head and heart during that awful day.

"Every day I was in camp I thought about her. What our life would be like if I made it back home alive. I was gonna ask her to marry me if I got back. Jane. That was her name. She was a small girl. Brown eyes. Really long brown hair. She looked so much like—"

"Lucy," Remy finished for him, finally understanding his irrational fury at her friend.

"Yeah," Ellis nodded grimly. "When I first saw Lucy...my God, I couldn't believe the resemblance. If I still had a beatin' heart it woulda stopped. And every time I see her fawnin' all over that man of hers, I keep picturing Jane spreadin' her legs for some other guy like the cheap slut she was."

"Ellis, I can't even begin to imagine how painful that was for you."

"No pity, goddammit!" Ellis yelled.

Remy nodded. Ellis knew she cared about him, and that would have to be enough. He couldn't handle her expressing sympathy out loud.

"Good thing your boyfriend is dead. Least you know for sure he ain't stickin' his dick in other women."

Remy grimaced. She was no prude, but she really wished Ellis wouldn't be so vulgar. She rather enjoyed being around gentlemen like Jesse and Avery, who would never speak like that in front of a lady.

"He would never do that, Ellis. Even if he was alive."

"You're an idiot if you think that," Ellis said. "You better watch out. You trust him too much. You trust everybody too much."

Remy could hardly blame him for not wanting to trust anyone ever again. She'd be jaded, too, if she'd been through what he had suffered.

"I know it's painful for you to be around Lucy, and that it brings up terrible memories, but it's not fair to take it out on her. She's a wonderful person who wouldn't hurt anyone if her life depended on it. And she's my friend. Please don't hurt her anymore."

Ellis looked into Remy's pleading eyes.

"I'll try," he grumbled. "Can't get near her anyhow with your boyfriend standin' watch."

Remy smiled at the thought of Avery standing guard to protect her and Lucy. She remembered how furious he was when Jesse told him that Ellis had been harassing her, too. *He wouldn't be too thrilled if he knew where I was right now,* she thought.

"Will you consider coming to the counseling group?" Remy asked.

"No fucking way."

"Ellis," Remy said gently, "don't you want to cross over?"

Ellis shook his head.

"Why not? Why would you want to stay here like this? Is there somebody here on earth you don't want to leave?"

"No. I got nobody. Never had anybody in life, and I don't got nobody now."

"You have me."

Ellis snorted at that, but didn't argue.

Remy let the issue drop for now. Knowing Ellis, he would tell her eventually, but he needed time.

"I have to go for now. Tomorrow I want to go see Avery, but Wednesday I'll come back to be with you."

Remy got up and looked down at him. She couldn't help but wish for some form of acknowledgment for her efforts. And for putting up with him.

Ellis lifted his head and looked at her. It wasn't often that she got a good look at his face under that big black hat. His dark eyes had softened somewhat, and he didn't look quite so creepy anymore.

"Okay, Remy. See ya then."

*****

As always, Remy relished Avery's sweet smile and look of eager anticipation when he saw her approach at Little Round Top. She had spoken to him briefly during the earlier tours during the day, but she'd been busy with talkative tourists. This time in the evening was just for the two of them.

"Hello, beautiful," Avery said.

"Hello, handsome," she responded with a smile.

"Sit down, darling. You must be exhausted."

"I am," Remy said wearily. It had been a good day but a busy one. At least the weather was cooling down a bit as it was early fall. Being out in the heat all day really wore her out.

Remy let out a sigh. As much as she loved talking with Avery, she wasn't particularly looking forward to this conversation. She despised keeping secrets from him, and she figured she owed it to him to tell him about her friendship with Ellis.

"You all right?" Avery asked with concern.

"Yes. It's just that... Okay, if I tell you something, will you promise not to be mad at me?"

Avery looked perplexed and a little worried. "Okay. I'll try."

"Lately, I've been talking a lot with someone."

"You met someone else," Avery said, a look of devastation crossing his face.

"No!" Remy cried. "God, no, Avery. Of course not!"

"Oh," Avery said, looking incredibly relieved.

"Avery, darling, you're the only man in my life. Romantically, anyway. It's just...I've been talking a lot with Ellis George lately, and we've kind of become friends."

"Remy!" Avery cried. He didn't seem angry. He looked terrified for her safety. "Why would you go anywhere near that horrible man?"

"I know it's hard to understand. I didn't tell you at first because I didn't want you to worry, but I don't want to have any secrets between us. The guy is all alone, and I know exactly what that feels like."

Avery nodded sorrowfully. "I don't like you goin' anywhere near that guy. With us both bein' spirits, I don't have any way of protecting you from him!"

"I don't need protecting from him, Avery," Remy said, feeling incredibly touched by his concern. "He's a sad, lonely man who had a terrible family like I did."

"You shouldn't trust him, Remy!"

"He said the same thing about you," Remy said. She instantly regretted it as she realized that was hardly helping her case.

"Why would he say something like that?" Avery said, his eyes flashing in anger.

"Because he's been hurt very badly. He also thinks Lucy and Jesse will cheat on each other and split up."

Avery actually laughed at that and shook his head. "Then he doesn't know them too well, does he?"

Remy chuckled, too. The idea of Lucy and Jesse breaking up *was* laughable. She had never seen two people more in love. Jesse came back from the dead to be with her, for heaven's sake. The two were inseparable and would be together forever, in this life and beyond.

"I don't blame him for not trusting anybody. He's been hurt too many times by too many people. He told me some very personal things that I can't tell anyone, not even you. But believe me, Avery." Remy gazed into Avery's eyes, wanting to be sure he understood what she was saying. "He's been through hell, and I just want to help him find peace."

"Please be careful, Remy," Avery said, his face full of fear and concern.

"I will."

"You have such a good heart, Remy," Avery said, regarding her with affection instead of anger at her confession. Remy felt calm and at peace with Avery. He understood her so well.

"Thank you for understanding, Avery. I should have known you would."

Avery gazed down at her and smiled. He looked thoughtful for a moment. Nervous, even.

"Remy," Avery began slowly.

"What?" Remy asked with concern.

"I just…I just want to tell you…that I love you."

Remy was stunned. She knew Avery had strong feelings for her, and she shouldn't have been surprised by his words, but she was. Remy dragged her gaze away from his and drew in a breath. She didn't know what to do or how to respond. The silence was too much. *Say something, you idiot. Say something!*

"I-I…Avery…I…" she faltered.

"Hey," Avery said, his voice gentle but firm. "Look at me."

Remy turned to face him.

"Darling, I'm not lookin' for you to say it back. I'm not pressuring you. I just wanted you to know how I feel about you."

Remy nodded, but was still so overwhelmed she couldn't speak. She drew in a shaky breath, but still no words came.

Avery looked concerned and bewildered by her responsible. "Remy… Please…don't… Don't be upset…"

Guilt tore through her when she saw his baffled expression.

"Oh, Avery, of course I'm not upset. I-I'm s-sorry. I'm sorry, it's just that…" Remy looked into his gentle, loving eyes and whispered, "No one's ever said that to me before."

Avery's expression relaxed into one of understanding and compassion. He nodded.

"I-I mean…not even my parents…ever said…." Remy said in a shaky voice.

"It's all right, my love. Remy, you don't have to say anything at all. All I want is for you to let me love you. Can you do that?"

Remy nodded, quickly wiping away the tears from her eyes. She struggled to get hold of herself.

"Avery, I know it's a horribly inadequate thing to say to something so beautiful, but thank you."

Avery nodded and touched her cheek like he always did when he wanted to express his emotions for her. His smile was kind and gentle, and she knew her response was enough for him. At least for now.

She stood up. "I'll-I'll see you tomorrow, okay?"

Avery stood up, too, and nodded. He looked worried and a bit confused, but he let her go.

Remy desperately needed to talk to someone, and she knew exactly who she needed right now. As she drove away from Little Round Top, she put her phone in the car dock and hit speed dial.

"Hey, Remy!" Lucy answered cheerfully. "What's up?"

"I'm having kind of a personal crisis," Remy said with a nervous laugh. "Can you meet with me somewhere? Are you busy?"

"Of course I'm not too busy for you. We can meet for a drink or— Oh, sorry. Sorry!" Lucy said, obviously remembering that Remy didn't drink.

"No, it's fine," Remy said, chuckling. "I can drink a virgin something or other. Let's meet at O'Malley's. Might as well be surrounded by all things Irish considering who I need to talk to you about."

Lucy was waiting for her at a table for two by the time Remy arrived. Her warm smile put Remy at ease immediately, and she was grateful to have such a wonderful friend to lean on. And if anyone could understand what she was going through, it was Lucy.

The server came and took their orders, a fuzzy navel for Lucy and a virgin strawberry daiquiri for Remy.

"Now," Lucy said. "What's going on?"

"Avery told me he loved me," Remy said simply.

"Awww," Lucy said, putting her hand over her heart.

Remy laughed softly. "I know. It's so sweet, but ugh. It totally freaked me out."

"Well, it's a big deal. I can understand that." Lucy didn't look all that surprised, which made Remy feel slightly less crazy.

"Really?"

"Of course."

"It's just that…nobody's *ever* said that to me before," Remy told her.

"Oh, Remy, I'm so sorry. Sometimes I forget how terrible your family really is," Lucy said with a touch of anger in her voice.

"It just shocked me. I knew we cared about each other, but…" Remy said in amazement. The news was finally sinking in. Avery *loved* her.

Lucy smiled. "You're the only one who's surprised. We all knew he loved you, Remy."

"Really?" Remy asked incredulously.

"Oh, yeah. That day Jesse introduced you to him? He was *already* in love with you. Before you even knew he existed."

"How is that even possible?"

"Avery has been absolutely crazy for you since the day you first helped him. When he had just come back from vanishing for so many years and he was lost and terrified. He's seen you helping all the tourists and knew how kind and smart and charming you are. Fillis helped him, too, and told him how Jesse came back. That's how Avery and Jesse became friends. Avery found out that Jesse loved a living woman while he was dead, too. He talked to Jesse about it because he knew he would understand."

"That's amazing," Remy said in a whisper. "He fell in love with me, and I had no idea…"

"I know," Lucy said. "Isn't it wonderful?"

Remy nodded. The server brought their drinks, and Remy sipped hers absently for a few moments.

"Oh, poor Avery," Remy moaned, covering her face with her hands. "I was such an idiot when he told me. I-I didn't even know what to do!"

"I'm sure he understands."

"I think so, too," Remy said with a sigh. "Because he's sweet and perfect. He *loves* me. Now what do I do?"

"What do you mean, Remy? How do you feel? Do you love him, too?"

Remy took her time answering. When she finally spoke, she said, "And what if I do love him? He's dead. What if…" Her voice shook as she struggled to finish her thought. "What if he's the love of my life and he has to go away forever?"

Lucy's soft brown eyes were filled with empathy and compassion. She let out a long sigh. "Then Jesse has a *huge* 'I told you so' coming. I was worried this might happen if he introduced Avery to you. I knew how much Avery loved you, and he's a wonderful man. I knew there was a good chance you'd fall for him, too."

Remy nodded and smiled sadly. "He is wonderful."

"I know. And I understand everything you're going through. It's an amazing feeling to have an incredible man tell you he loves you, but I understand the fear and uncertainty that comes with loving a ghost." Lucy's voice quaked with emotion. "You never know when he might cross over, and you don't have any idea of how you'll be able to go on if that happens."

Tears spilled from Lucy's eyes. She wiped her tears and pulled herself together, still eager to help Remy through her struggle.

Lucy reached over and squeezed Remy's hand, and the warmth of her touch was soothing. "I was in denial for a long time about my feelings for Jesse. I didn't want to admit to myself that I was in love with him, because he was dead, and I thought there was no chance for us to be together. At the time, I had absolutely no idea he felt the same way about me. Did I ever tell you about the time I first told him I loved him?"

"No," Remy responded, eager to hear the tale.

Lucy laughed. "Well, Joel and Jesse and I became close friends, and I just couldn't help falling for Jesse. And you know how shy I am—I wasn't planning on ever telling him how I felt. Then Theresa got me drunk."

"Oh, no," Remy said, laughing.

"Well, to be fair, I asked her to take me out. I needed a few drinks because, well…that was the day Jesse, Joel, and I went to Devil's Den and…"

"And that's when you felt Jesse's death," Remy said gently. "Oh, Lucy that must have been so awful."

"It was," Lucy said, swallowing hard and grimacing at the memory. "It was terrifying, and the pain was indescribable. When it was over, I remember Jesse looking down at me where I was lying on one of the rocks. He was so upset, so worried about me. I know he blamed himself for what happened to me. Still does," Lucy said sadly. "It really wasn't his fault. Anyway, I remember looking up at him and realizing what I had just gone through was how he died. And I just couldn't…I couldn't bear the thought of his suffering like that."

Remy nodded. She couldn't help picturing Avery being shot to death on Little Round Top. She drew in a breath.

"Anyway," Lucy said, shaking off the terrible memory. "I came home and slept for a few hours first. I swear, I'd never been so exhausted in my life! And then when Theresa came home—we were still roommates then—I was like, girl, we need to *talk*!"

Remy laughed and nodded. "Kinda like how I dragged you here."

"You didn't drag me, but yes," Lucy said with her usual sweet smile. "So I told her about what happened at Devil's Den. Good God, was she pissed."

"Why?"

"Well, at the time, neither one of us had any idea there was such a thing as battlefield sympathy pains, but Joel and Jesse knew."

"Really?" Remy asked. "But then why—"

"That's why Jesse still blames himself. Look, you have to understand it's an extremely rare phenomenon. Even spirits like Jesse who have been around here since the year 1863 have only seen it a handful of times. It just…they just didn't think of it. Jesse would never, ever put me at risk on purpose."

"No," Remy said confidently. "He wouldn't." *Poor Jesse,* she thought. He loved Lucy with all his heart, and he must have been devastated to see her suffering, especially if he thought it was his fault.

"So I spilled my guts to Theresa, getting drunker by the second. I felt like an idiot for falling in love with a ghost, but Theresa reminded me that Jesse wasn't just a spirit. He was an incredibly wonderful man, and she understood completely why I loved him so much. So, when we left the bar, Joel and Jesse were out on the street. Oh, God, Remy. I saw Jesse standing there and I just couldn't take it anymore. I started crying, and I just blurted out that I loved him."

"Awww, that is so sad and so sweet at the same time," Remy said.

"Yeah," Lucy said with a laugh. "I was so humiliated the next morning when I woke up and realized what I had done. I didn't know how I would ever be able to face Jesse again. But I did."

"And he said it back," Remy said happily.

"Yes," Lucy said, affectionately remembering that special day. "I was stunned."

"I know the feeling."

"Yeah, I'm sure you do. You know I understand better than anybody what you're going through. It's okay to love him, Remy."

Remy took a deep breath and said, "I do love him. I love him so much."

Lucy smiled and nodded. "It's up to you what you want to do. But I just can't stop thinking about how happy Avery would be if you told him how you feel about him. When Jesse was still, you know, like Avery, we didn't know what would happen or how long he would be around and, well, I was glad we said we loved each other while we had the chance."

"What if he crosses over?" Remy whispers, tears forming in her eyes.

"Then you'll still have your family here to help you through it," Lucy said, squeezing Remy's hand.

Chapter 16

Remy's emotions were churning so hard the next day she felt physically ill. She didn't want to love Avery, but she did. There was a strong chance that her relationship with him would end in heartache and disaster, and the idea of him crossing over and leaving her behind was agonizing. Lucy still teared up at the mere thought of losing Jesse every time she spoke of the day he had almost crossed over.

And Remy would never, ever get over Avery O'Rorke if he crossed over. She was sure of it. She would love him for the rest of her life, even if he disappeared forever.

When the tour group stopped at Little Round Top, Remy didn't even get off the bus. She was a complete emotional wreck, and she just couldn't go see Avery. She needed time.

"Jesse," Remy pleaded. "Go see Avery. Tell him… Oh, God, I don't even know what you should tell him."

"It's okay, Remy," Jesse said. "I'll take good care of him."

Remy let out a breath and nodded. She was grateful that the driver got off the bus to stretch his legs, giving her some time alone. She looked out the window, trying to catch a glimpse of Avery through the woods, but the trees were too thick. She felt horrible for not going to see him, but she was desperately trying to figure out what she should do. Continuing to see Avery would just make it worse when he eventually had to leave her.

Remy put on a brave face for the rest of the tour, but it wasn't easy. She tried to distract herself when they got to the Gettysburg Visitor's Center, but it proved to be impossible. This had been a quiet, reserved group of people who didn't ask many questions.

Remy couldn't help but walk straight over to the wall of photos of Civil War soldiers. Her heart jumped violently when she looked down at Avery's picture. She stared into those beautiful, soulful eyes of his and had a sudden, desperate urge to go see him. She berated herself for refusing to see him that morning, and she cringed again when she recalled how she'd reacted when he told her he loved her. She imagined how she'd feel if she'd been brave enough to say *I love you*, only to have Avery act upset instead of being happy. She would have been devastated. A bolt of fear shot through her. *What if he crossed over before she had the chance to tell him how she felt?* Though she knew there was no reason to think Avery would suddenly make it to the other side now after all this time, the idea still terrified her. She would never, ever forgive herself if he had to leave without her telling him that she loved him.

The wait to see him was excruciating. Remy literally white-knuckled the bus seat in front of her as they headed to Little Round Top that afternoon.

"You all right?" Jesse asked, alarmed.

"I have to see him," Remy whispered.

Jesse nodded, looking relieved. The moment the bus stopped, Jesse jerked his head toward where they both knew Avery would be waiting and said, "Go. I got this."

Remy nodded, and raced off the bus, leaving Jesse to handle the tourists. She lifted the skirts of her Jennie Wade costume so she could run faster.

"Avery!" Remy called as she ran.

Avery stood up, his face awash in hope and anticipation when he heard her voice. Then he looked a little worried when he saw her running toward him, as if he was afraid something was wrong.

"Avery!" Remy cried again, panting, face flushed as she reached him. She took a few seconds to catch her breath, then she looked up into those beautiful eyes of his and said quietly, "I love you, too."

Avery smiled broadly, gazing down at her with joy and wonder. "Remy, me darling…thank ye for telling me."

"I'm so sorry it took me so long. I just…I-I-"

"You don't owe me any explanation, my love," Avery said tenderly, filling Remy's heart with warmth. She didn't have to explain because Avery knew her so well. He understood this was all new to her, and he was content to give her all the space she needed, even when it caused him pain. But she didn't want space anymore. All she wanted was to be with him for however long they had to be together.

"I'll come sit with you tonight. As soon as I get off work," Remy said with a smile.

"Sounds wonderful," Avery said.

Remy looked into his eyes again, reveling in the happiness she saw in them. At least now, whatever happened, Avery knew that she loved him.

"I better go help Jesse. I kind of abandoned him with the tour group the second the bus stopped."

Avery laughed and said, "Okay, go do what you gotta do."

Remy ran off to help with the tourists, who were a lot more inquisitive than the morning group. She happily took family photos for them, answered questions, and showed them where to get the best view from the top of the hill.

At one point, Jesse walked past her as he guided some of the tour members toward the popular 44th New York Infantry monument, which was near where Avery always hung out.

Jesse grinned knowingly as he glanced toward Avery in the distance. "What did you say to that boy to put such a smile on his face?"

Remy bit her lip and smiled, knowing she didn't have to answer. Jesse knew.

Once Jesse showed the tourists how to climb up the monument, he stayed on the ground, talking to Avery. It made Remy so happy to watch them together, talking and laughing. Remy knew Avery had told him what she said, just as she had confided in Lucy when Avery first professed his love. Avery looked so happy and excited that she could hardly believe she'd been the one to make him feel that way.

After work, she raced home and quickly ate a peanut butter and jelly sandwich for dinner. It was all she could afford to eat until her next paycheck hit, and she was far more interested in seeing Avery than in food right now. She quickly changed her clothes and put on a simple blue dress that she knew would bring out her eyes. She also grabbed a jacket since the air was getting chilly now, especially in the evening.

Remy arrived quietly, and Avery didn't see her at first. Her heart clutched when she saw him sitting alone on the hill, looking out across the battlefield probably not far from where he had died. Tenderness overwhelmed her.

Avery stood when he heard her approach. He looked down at her dress and then back up at her face, taking all of her in. He seemed pleased by what he saw.

Remy gazed into his eyes and asked, "Will you say it to me again?"

Avery smiled. "I love you, Remy."

"I love you, too, Avery."

Avery gestured to her to sit down, and she did. He sat as close to her as possible. She longed to rest her head on his shoulder and let him wrap his arms around her.

"*Tá grá agam duit,*" Avery said. "That's 'I love you' in Irish."

"Really?" Remy asked, her eyes lighting up. "Teach me how to say it."

Avery smiled and repeated the phrase slowly and phonetically. "Tah graw agam ditch."

"Tah graw agam ditch," Remy repeated slowly. "Tah graw agam ditch." Then she said it faster and more naturally, "*Tá grá agam duit,* Avery!"

"Well done! You've got it!" Avery said proudly. "My God, it does sound even sexier in Irish."

"Told ya," Remy said. "But in your case, it's not just the language. You've also got a wonderful, deep, *manly* voice."

"Well, I'm glad you think so. It's one of the few things I have to offer ya. *Tá grá agam duit, a chuisle.*"

"A keesh-la. What does that mean?" Remy asked.

"*A chuisle* is like 'my darling' or 'my love.' Literally, it means 'my pulse.' That's a perfect name for you. I don't have a pulse anymore, so you can be mine." Avery looked into her eyes in a way that made her want to swoon and whispered softly, "You can be mine."

Remy swallowed hard. "Avery, do you think you could come back? The way Jesse did?"

"I don't know. I just don't know."

"I mean, when Jesse's time came, he was given a choice. It was up to him if he wanted to go or if…"

"I know," Avery said, looking worried. "But when my time comes, I might not get that choice. According to Fillis and everybody else, Jesse is the only one who came back."

"He might have been the only one with a reason to come back," Remy said. She thought of Ellis and wondered why he wanted to stay if he had no one to live for.

"Well, now that I know you love me, I have good reason to come back."

"Oh, Avery," Remy said. "I want to touch you so much."

"That alone would be reason enough to come back from the dead," Avery said, a look of desire in his eyes.

"You know, ever since the day I first met you, I've had this fantasy about you."

"Really?" Avery asked, fascinated. "What is it?"

"Well, I just always imagined how wonderful it would be to have you pick me up in your arms and carry me to the bedroom," Remy confessed a bit shyly.

Avery moaned. It was a low, sexy sound that told her exactly how he felt about her fantasy. He sounded like he would make it come true right now if he could.

"Oh, God, I would love to do that."

Remy drew in a breath and looked intently into his eyes. A tingling desire stirred between her legs. If he could touch her there, he would know how aroused he made her just by his words and that look of passion in his eyes.

"I would pick you up and hold you close, and then I'd lay you down on the bed." Avery told her seductively.

"Then what would you do?" Remy asked, breathlessly.

"Anything you wanted," Avery said in his deliciously masculine voice that sounded even more deep and sensual than usual.

Remy let out a soft, rueful sigh and said, "I'm so inexperienced I wouldn't even know what to ask for."

"Remy," Avery asked her gently. "Have you even been with a man?"

"Technically, I guess the answer is yes. Though he was more of a boy than a man. It was after prom."

Avery furrowed his brow. "Prom. What's prom?"

Remy smiled. "It's a like a fancy ball, but for high schoolers. I was seventeen at the time. You get all dressed up and go to the dance with a guy, and lots of people lose their virginity afterwards. Ugh, I feel like such a cliché. It was in the back of his pickup truck."

"Oh, darling, you deserve so much better," Avery said sadly.

"That was the only time I've had sex," Remy admitted. "It was a pretty miserable experience. All I really remember was that it hurt. A lot."

"He hurt you?" Avery asked, his expression darkening.

"No, no. Not on purpose anyway. He was nice enough, but neither one of us really knew what we were doing. It usually hurts a girl the first time."

Avery nodded grimly. "Yes. I didn't enjoy hurting my wife on our wedding night, that's for sure."

Remy let out a sigh of longing as she thought about how much better it would have been if Avery had been her first. He would have been so sweet, so gentle.

"Well, it's not like I've got so much experience either," Avery admitted. "I've only been with one woman, and we didn't do much, that's for sure."

"We could have learned together," Remy said, her voice tinged with sadness.

Avery nodded. His brow furrowed for a moment.

"What?"

"I think I've got an idea. Come with me," Avery said, standing up.

Remy stood up and followed him. He led her across the street and past where she had parked her car.

"Where are we going?" Remy asked.

Avery didn't answer. He kept walking, looking around for

something. He nodded to himself when he saw whatever it was he was looking for. He led her to a secluded spot in the woods, hidden from view.

He gestured for Remy to sit under the tree, and he sat down close to her.

"Okay," Avery began, looking a bit unsure of how to express what he wanted to say. "Remy, I want you to know how much I love you, how much I desire you. How much I *want* you."

Remy nodded, a tingle of excitement rippling through her. This was the first time a man had expressed sexual desire for her, and it was thrilling.

"I still have a sex drive, though not as strong as when I was alive. I guess that's good since there's nothing I could do about it anyway."

"That's true," Remy said, feeling guilty that she hadn't thought too much about the fact that Avery might be feeling sexually frustrated.

"But I want you to know that I've never wanted to please a woman more than I want to please you. Oh, Remy," Avery said. Now he did sound frustrated. "I want so much to satisfy you and your needs, and it makes me crazy that I can't."

"I understand, Avery. It's not your fault. I still love you even though we can't be, you know, intimate together."

"That's just it, Remy," Avery said, his eyes wide with intensity and desire. "Maybe we can. There's a way…you don't have to do it if you don't want to. If it makes you uncomfortable, but…Remy. I want you to lie down."

Remy looked at him, confused.

"It's all right. Just lie down. Please?"

Remy nodded. "Okay." She lay down on the ground and looked up at him. He lay down on his side beside her, positioning his face close to hers. It was so easy to imagine what he would look like if he were on top of her. Inside her.

Avery glanced down at her hands, then down the rest of her body, and then back up at her face.

"You're still able to feel pleasure even though I can't," he said.

Remy suddenly realized what he was going to ask her to do.

"A-Avery," she said, her face flushing with embarrassment. "I-I can't…"

"I don't want you to do anything that makes you uncomfortable. I just…oh, my love, I just want to take care of you. I can't touch you myself, but you can, you know…as if it were me."

Remy nodded, anxiety welling up in her. She couldn't actually do this in front of him…could she?

"*A chuisle*," he began, and she felt her resolve weakening.

"That's not fair," Remy said with a moan. "You know I can't resist you when you speak Irish."

Avery grinned a knowing, commanding smile that made the wetness pool between her legs.

"*Tánn tú go hálainn*, my love," Avery said seductively. "My darling, let me take care of you. I want so much to make you feel good."

Remy looked into his eyes, finding him impossible to resist. So many emotions stirred inside her. Bashfulness, anxiety, and intense desire. When she looked into his eyes, she knew desire was going to win out.

"Avery," she said softly.

"Yes, *a chuisle*?" he said, leaning closer to her. He looked concerned now, like he feared that he might have upset her.

She locked eyes with him, feeling connected to his soul and even to his body. "I'm so wet," she whispered.

Avery's eyes flashed with excitement and desire. He understood that her admission of arousal was her way of telling him she was willing to go along with what he wanted to do.

"Put your fingers between your legs, Remy," Avery said huskily. "Touch yourself and imagine it's me."

Remy nodded, nervous and excited. She looked around to make sure no one was around even though she knew they were alone in the forest. Hesitantly, she slid her hands down to the bottom of her dress and Avery's eyes followed her movement. She opened her mouth to plead with him not to watch, but then changed her mind. He clearly loved what he was seeing, and she wanted to please him, too. She pulled her dress up and slid her right hand into her panties.

A soft moan escaped Avery's throat. He gazed into her eyes and said, "It's me touching you, Remy."

Remy nodded and began to move her fingers over her clit. She knew her expression betrayed her pleasure because Avery's eyes opened slightly wider as he watched her.

"That's it, *a chuisle*," he murmured in her ear. Remy closed her eyes and listened to his deep, sexy voice. "We're finally going to make love, Remy."

"Yes," she whispered, her pleasure growing as she circled her clit with her fingers.

Avery paused a moment, and then asked her, "Have you ever touched yourself while thinking of me?"

Remy's entire body tensed at his highly personal question. She felt her face get hot, and she knew her deep blush had already given her away. She squeezed her eyes shut tighter and nodded. Avery was her lover, or would be if it were at all possible, and she knew she shouldn't be embarrassed, but she was.

"Oh, my darling, please don't be ashamed. I'm sorry. I couldn't help but ask. I think that's the sexiest thing in the world, Remy. To think that a beautiful woman like you would pleasure herself while thinking of me."

Remy's body relaxed slightly. She still didn't open her eyes, and she stopped touching herself. She didn't want to look at him.

"Remy," Avery said tenderly, and Remy knew exactly what his expression looked like even with her eyes closed. He had that worried look on his face because he knew he'd upset her. "If I were alive, I wouldn't be able to keep my hands off myself while thinkin' of you. I would stroke myself over and over again thinkin' of makin' love to you. I'd rub meself raw, I would!"

Remy laughed, eyes still closed. She felt better.

"But then again, if I were alive, I might be lucky enough to have the real thing, wouldn't I? We would make love all the time. Oh, I'd carry you to bed, all right. I'd kiss you all over your beautiful, naked body. I'd kiss your breasts," he said, the huskiness back in his voice. "I'd stop to lick your nipples…"

Remy drew in a soft breath. Eyes still closed, she began rubbing her clit again.

"I would take my time with you, touch and stroke your body while I kiss your soft lips."

Remy let out a cry of pleasure.

"What do you want me to do?" Avery murmured.

Remy opened her eyes and looked up at him. She was glad she did, because it seemed to make Avery happy. He smiled a wonderfully seductive smile at her.

"I want you inside me. Make love to me, Avery. I want to feel all of you."

Avery nodded. Remy closed her eyes, eager to hear what he would say next. She rubbed herself faster, knowing it wouldn't be long before she found the sweet release of the tension Avery had been building inside of her since the moment they met.

"I'm on top of you, Remy," Avery said, his voice louder and more commanding.

"Oh!" Remy said, her soft cry of passion telling him to keep going.

"Open your legs for me, *a chuisle*," Avery said, drawing another pleasured cry from her lips. "I'm so goddamned hard for you. Can you feel me?"

"Yes!" Remy cried, eyes shut. She rubbed herself faster and faster, the pleasurable sensation between her legs so strong that she forgot to worry about being self-conscious. She was to the point not caring if anyone else heard or even saw her. She just needed to *come*.

"Are you close?" Avery whispered, probably already knowing the answer.

"Yes, Avery. Yes," Remy panted. She opened her eyes and saw his handsome face filled with lust and desire. He leaned in close, and the powerful, tingling sensation between her legs was so erotic that it actually felt like she was having sex with him.

"I'm *pounding* you, Remy. As hard as I can. I want you to *come, a chuisle. Tánn tú go hálainn!*" Avery said, along with more Irish words that she didn't understand, but the sexiness and pure urgency in his deep voice was enough to shove her over the edge.

"Avery!" she cried as she reached a powerful orgasm that seemed to go on forever. The vibrations shook and convulsed her entire body. Relief flooded though her as her body released all those wonderful post-orgasm hormones that left her feeling relaxed and satisfied. When it was over, it took her quite a while to catch her breath.

A moment or two of silence passed as Avery allowed her to recover. Once the aftershocks of her climax subsided, doubt and self-consciousness began to creep in. *She had just masturbated in front of Avery.* Her face flushed red. She eventually opened her eyes, but didn't turn to look at him.

"*A chuisle*," Avery said in that tender voice that never failed to melt her heart. "Look at me."

Remy turned to look into Avery's eyes, which were full of gentle understanding. He knew she was feeling vulnerable, and that there was a fine line between this experience being intimately erotic or utterly humiliating for her.

"Thank you for doing that with me," he said. "I would give anything in the world if I could touch you and satisfy you with my body, but this was the next best thing."

Remy smiled, feeling relaxed all over again. Her anxiety evaporated when she looked into the eyes of the man she loved more than anything in the world. In this wonderful moment, it really felt like they had made love. She felt closer to him than ever before.

"It felt really good," Remy admitted with a shy smile.

"I'm so glad," Avery said. "And I'll let you in on a little secret. It's always been a fantasy of mine to hear a woman scream out my name during sex. Can't tell you how many times I've fantasized about making love to you and hearing you say my name. And you did it! When you, you know," Avery looked so delighted that it made the whole experience worthwhile. That, and the fact that she'd had the most incredible, satisfying orgasm she'd ever had.

Remy bit her lip and said, "I couldn't help it."

Avery's smile widened.

"I just wish I could do something like this for you," Remy said wistfully.

"It's all right. It's different for me. I miss sex, but I don't have the same urges as you do anymore."

So I can get horny but you can't. The thought embarrassed her, and she looked away.

As always, Avery sensed her discomfort. "Remy." He waited until she looked at him before continuing. "It's not that I don't desire you, because I do. I want to make love to you more than I've ever wanted anything in my life and beyond. Being with you like this is the closest I can get. I love you so much, and I just wanted to be intimate with you in any way that I could."

"This was a wonderful idea, Avery," Remy said, realizing how much she really meant it. "Thank you for being with me like this."

Remy pulled her dress down and then sat up. He looked at her lovingly and touched her cheek. She shivered involuntarily. His touch was frigid, and the autumn night air was already chilling her.

"It's cold out, isn't it?" Avery asked with concern.

Remy nodded and pulled on her jacket.

"I wish so much I could hold you and keep you warm."

"I know," Remy said softly. She looked around at the darkening forest. "It gets dark so early now. We need to find another place to meet."

Avery nodded. "Someplace inside would be best. Can't have you freezin' out here."

"And you know, I'll have lots of ghost tours now that it's October. Gets really crowded here around Halloween. But I'll always make time for you, Avery. I promise."

"I know you will. But you must be careful not to overdo it. You work too much as it is."

Remy sighed and nodded. She hugged the jacket around herself, aching for Avery's warmth. She truly felt like they'd just had sex, and more than anything she just wanted to be held. She felt tears begin to prickle behind her eyes.

"Maybe you really can come back to life. Maybe Theresa could help counsel you. And Lucy. They've been able to help others," Remy said, a glimmer of hope surfacing within her.

"Maybe," Avery said. "Might be worth a try, but if I let them counsel me, I might be allowed to come back, but I also might…"

"I know," Remy said, swallowing hard. "I understand the risks. But darling, you can't just stay here forever. I have to be strong…like Lucy was." Remy choked back a sob. "And help you. Do what's right for you. I want you to be at peace, whether it's here with me or…"

She shook her head, unable to speak the words out loud. "But that's a worry for another day. Right now, I have you here with me."

Avery nodded, looking down at her with love and affection.

"It'll be really dark soon. I better go before I can't even see my way out of the forest."

"Right," Avery said firmly. He began to lead the way back toward the road.

When they got to her car, Remy turned to look at him. "Avery, about what we did tonight. You wouldn't tell anyone, would you?" she asked nervously.

Avery's eyes opened wide. "Of course not! I would never tell Jesse or anyone else. Our lovemaking is just between us."

Remy smiled. *Our lovemaking* was such a wonderful way to describe what they had done.

"*Tá grá agam duit, a chuisle mo chroi,*" he said to her. "*A chuisle mo chroi* means 'you are the pulse of my heart.'"

"I love when you call me *a chuisle*. And I love you, Avery." Remy said, touching his right cheek the way he often did with her. Reluctantly, she got into her car and drove home.

Chapter 17

"You all right?" Ellis asked the moment he saw Remy walking toward him at Culp's Hill. Lately, Ellis was finally becoming more at ease with talking to her. And he'd also begun to know her well enough to notice when something was wrong.

"Yes, I'm all right," Remy said with a smile.

It meant a lot to her that Ellis was worried about her. Getting someone like him to care was no easy feat. He had so much anger and hate inside him, but Remy had known all along that he had a softer side in there somewhere.

"It's nothing new," Remy said, taking her usual seat beside Ellis on the rock facing the huge tower. She watched a couple of young, excited kids racing up the steps and marveled at their energy. "Sometimes it just hits me hard knowing that Avery might actually cross over one of these days, you know?"

Ellis nodded. Remy was still careful with how much of her personal life she divulged to him, but it was no secret to him that she loved Avery.

"Most of the time I try not to think about it. I try to be happy with things the way they are."

"Which isn't so great," Ellis said in his gruff voice. "No real dates, no sex, no nothin'."

Remy suppressed a smile when she remembered the deliciously sensual experience she had recently shared with Avery. There was no way in hell she would ever reveal something like that to Ellis. He was fairly nice to her most of the time these days, but she knew someday she might piss him off, and he would have no problem in using her private confessions to humiliate her.

"Yeah, it can be tough. But the hardest thing is the uncertainty. It's terrifying to think that he might just disappear one day. Cross over without me getting to say goodbye," Remy said sadly, staring off in the distance.

After a moment or two of silence, Ellis said quietly, "Yeah, but he knows how you feel. Even if he has to leave without sayin' goodbye, 'least he knows you love him."

Remy smiled at Ellis, proud of his progress. A few months ago, he never would have said something so kind.

"Avery agreed to let Theresa and Lucy counsel him, help him work through all the stuff that's kept him stuck here all this time. We're hoping that maybe he'll be allowed to come back to life like Jesse did. But there's also a huge risk that he'll cross over," Remy said, and then added, "I'm scared."

Ellis looked up at her and nodded. "Yeah. I get it."

"Have you thought any more about letting Theresa help you, too? You wouldn't have to go to her group. Avery's not. He's just gonna talk with Theresa and Lucy and me. Maybe you could do that too, sometime."

Remy waited for Ellis to start yelling that he never wanted to let Theresa help him and that she should shut up and mind her own business. That's what he always said, no matter how many times she broached the subject. This time he stayed silent for a moment.

"I don't want to cross over," Ellis said.

"I know you don't," Remy said. Ellis had told her that many

times. "But I don't understand why. I really wish you would tell me. Don't you trust me by now?"

Ellis studied her face. "I don't know. Every single person I ever trusted in my entire life let me down. Every one. You seem different, but that don't mean anything. How do I know you're not laughin' at me behind my back with all your friends?"

"I would never do that!" Remy said. Ellis looked so broken, so scared that it made her chest ache.

"They all hate me."

"They don't hate you," Remy lied. Jesse hated him, that was for sure. She'd gently told him the truth about befriending Ellis, and he was not happy. He'd held his temper, but Remy could see it was a struggle. Ellis had hurt Lucy, and that was unforgivable as far as he was concerned. Remy avoided talking about Ellis around Jesse whenever possible. "They're just, you know, afraid of you."

Ellis nodded. Lucy was afraid of him, that was for sure, and Avery was afraid on Remy's behalf. He didn't like her hanging around Ellis because he was afraid he might hurt her. And sometimes he did. Sometimes when he was feeling especially angry or bitter, he might say something awful to Remy like "no wonder your parents didn't want you." Though she felt crushed inside, she always kept her expression neutral, refusing to give him the satisfaction of knowing he'd hurt her. It was times like those that she wondered why she put up with the guy.

Days like today reminded her of why she still came to sit with him so often. He looked like a scared little boy. He needed her, and she couldn't bear to abandon him like everyone else in his life had.

"I would never, ever laugh at you, Ellis. You really should know that by now."

Ellis looked at her curiously, but nodded. "You're pretty goddamn patient with me, I'll give you that." He paused a long while, then said, "I don't want to cross over because…"

Remy held her breath. She didn't want to move for fear of scaring him off. *Please tell me, Ellis. Then maybe I can help.*

"Because…because I don't know where I'm gonna go."

Ellis's expression of raw, primal fear stunned her. He looked at her with unadulterated terror. *My God, he thinks he's going to hell.*

Remy nodded carefully, afraid to speak in case he wanted to share more.

"I wasn't…I'm not a good man. Wasn't in life, and I ain't now. Remy, I killed those two guys in the Railroad Cut. I murdered 'em. I mean, sometimes in war you got to kill, but those men? They were beggin' for their lives, and I shot 'em both. I shot 'em." Ellis's face was full of horror and regret. So different from when he'd once bragged to her about the killings. She realized now that his bragging about their deaths was just a front. In reality, he was torn up, full of torturous guilt inside over killing them.

"That was right after you found about Jane," Remy said cautiously. "You were upset and in a rage, and that's part of why you killed those guys."

Ellis blinked as he looked at her. He seemed surprised that she understood.

"Yeah," he said. "I know it ain't no excuse, but I was really fucked up that day. Wuz like one minute I had a whole future ahead of me— I was gonna get married to her and maybe finally have a real family, and then I found out it was all over. Just like that. No reason to go back home. No one to go back home to. I didn't care who I killed or if I got killed. I think I wanted to die, too. Didn't give a shit if I caught a bullet. 'Cause I thought it would all be over." He laughed a bitter, sarcastic laugh. "Still ain't over. After all this time."

That poor man, she thought. His whole life had been filled with such pain, and so was his never-ending afterlife. That was why he'd vanished for so long, and why he was so terrified that he couldn't vanish much anymore. He was petrified that Judgment Day was at hand for him.

"You're afraid you're going to hell for killing those men," Remy said softly.

"Wouldn't you be?" Ellis roared, looking at her with such ferocity that it actually frightened her. She couldn't help but jump when he startled her, but she tried to keep her face and demeanor calm otherwise.

Remy nodded. "Maybe. I understand why you're afraid. But Ellis, you know Jesse has been around forever. He didn't vanish much while he was dead, and he's seen a lot of guys cross over. He told me it's always peaceful, wonderful. He's never seen anybody go to hell."

"They were good people. I'm not a good person."

"You made mistakes, Ellis. You're not evil."

"But there ain't no way to atone for what I done!" Ellis said.

"No, there never is. Not after all this time. But none of the other soldiers could do anything to fix what they'd done in the past, either. Anyone they'd ever hurt was dead, and they couldn't touch anyone or do anything for anybody else to make up for their sins."

Ellis considered her words. She couldn't tell if he felt better or more hopeless.

"I think you just have to forgive yourself," Remy said. "You have to find peace here before you can find peace in heaven."

Ellis stared off in the distance.

"Will you at least consider letting us counsel you?"

He didn't answer for a long time. Finally, almost imperceptibly, he nodded.

*****

Avery's first counseling session took place at Gettysburg College. It was getting too cold to meet outside, so Theresa found an empty classroom they could use to meet. They arranged the chairs in a circle so they could all face each other. Remy sat between Avery and Lucy, and Theresa sat on the other side of Avery.

"Okay, so what we're working on here is trying to figure out exactly what has kept Avery stuck here for all this time so we can get him to the point where he can cross over," Theresa said in her best gentle yet authoritative psychologist voice. She wasn't officially a psychologist yet, but she was currently working toward her Ph.D. in psychology. "Of course, we're hoping once he gets to that point, he'll be given a choice to stay. But we all know that there's no guarantee that will happen, right?" Theresa looked directly at Remy with concern.

"I understand," Remy said in a small voice. She was determined to help Avery find peace no matter what happened, but it was already harder than she had imagined. It was impossible to imagine her life without Avery. It would feel like a part of her was gone, leaving a black, empty hole in her soul.

Avery gently brushed her cheek and said tenderly, "It's all right, *a chuisle.*"

"Lucy and I have seen several people cross over. The way it usually works is the person feels an uncontrollable urge to return to where he died. So Avery, if you ever feel a compelling urge that you must go back to Little Round Top, it probably means it's your time."

Avery nodded.

"With Jesse and Joel, they both needed to go back to Devil's Den right away," Lucy gently explained. "I went with them because I knew what was happening, and I needed to be there to say goodbye to Jesse." Lucy was visibly struggling to keep her voice steady for Remy's sake, but her voice quavered and there was a threat of tears in her eyes. Remy could not to begin to imagine how Lucy must have felt that day, heading to Devil's Den and trying to prepare herself to let Jesse go. "When we got there, we saw this amazing, beautiful portal. Oh, it's so hard to explain, but it's like it was filled with light and love, and oh, Remy," Lucy grabbed her hand in both of hers and said, "Please understand that whatever happens, Avery will be happy. He'll be surrounded by comfort and peace if he…"

Remy drew in a shuddery breath and nodded, tears already spilling down her cheeks. The idea of Avery disappearing into the portal without her was excruciating, but the knowledge that he would be all right brought a sense of peace and calm to her heart. She would rather suffer the pain of grief than have him go through it.

"Joel went into the light to be with his wife and children, and when Jesse's portal opened he, well, he disappeared at first," Lucy choked back a sob. "I'm so sorry. I'm supposed to be trying to make this easier for you!"

Lucy let go of Remy's hand so she could wipe her eyes.

"It's okay, Lucy. It's better that I know what I'm facing here."

Lucy nodded. "Well, he-he disappeared, but then he said he heard a voice, and he was asked if he wanted to stay. And he stayed." Relief washed over Lucy's face at the memory. "One minute I'm crying my eyes out, and the next minute Jesse's picking me up and holding me in his arms."

Theresa smiled at Lucy, visibly touched by her story. Then she turned to Remy and said, "That's the thing with Avery—he has loved ones on both sides of the divide. He has family, a daughter in heaven, and he has you here on earth, so it's hard to know which way this is gonna go."

Avery and Remy looked into each other's eyes, and Theresa fell silent to give them a moment.

"If I happen to be nearby when it happens, when Avery feels the call to go back to Little Round Top, I can go with you if you want," Theresa told Remy, "but Lucy really shouldn't. It's much too dangerous for her to return to where Avery died."

Remy nodded. "I agree. I don't want her getting hurt."

"But Remy," Lucy said gently. "You know I'll be here for you afterward. No matter what happens."

"Thank you," Remy said, first looking at Lucy and then Theresa. Avery put his head down.

"You all right, Avery?" Remy asked him.

"I just…I feel so torn," Avery said, still staring down at the floor. Then he glanced up at Remy. "I love you so much, Remy. But I love me daughter, too. I feel terrible about leaving her…*again*…if I stay. She's waitin' for her daddy, been waitin' all this time, and I don't know what to do." Avery looked at Theresa and told her, "I know that it's guilt over my little girl, Charlotte, that's kept me here all this while."

Remy was dimly aware of Lucy putting a gentle, comforting hand on her back as she listened to Avery speak.

"Oh, Remy, you're the love of my life, and beyond…but I'm afraid I will end up leaving and I feel so awful about it. I-I-"

"Avery, don't ever feel bad about wanting to be with your daughter. You're such a wonderful father," Remy told him, her voice barely a whisper. His devotion to his precious little girl only made Remy love him more. "I have to do what's best for you, whatever that might be. With Theresa's and Lucy's help, we can help you work through your problems and help you reach your final destiny, whatever that is."

Avery looked deeply into her eyes, "I will always love you, *a chuisle*. Whatever happens."

Remy smiled and said, "I'll love you forever, darling. No matter what." She took a deep breath, gathered every ounce of strength she could muster, and turned to Theresa and nodded.

"Okay, Avery. Tell me everything," Theresa said, leaning forward.

Chapter 18

Avery continued his counseling sessions over the next few months. Remy was present most of the time, but she insisted that he go without her once in a while. She wanted to give Avery enough space to express his thoughts and feelings to Theresa privately without always having to worry about Remy. The therapy seemed to be working, as Avery seem calmer and more at peace now. He was progressing well, which was alternately exhilarating and terrifying. Remy lived in constant fear of losing Avery, and it was exhausting.

She still met with Ellis regularly, but he wasn't making as nearly as much progress as Avery. Remy knew he needed professional help—Theresa's help. He no longer yelled at her every time she mentioned the counseling idea, but instead kept saying he would think about it.

Then, at last, one day he said, "Maybe I'll try it soon."

Remy considered that to be a huge leap for him. She didn't want to push him too much, so she'd said simply, "When you're ready, you name the time and place, and I'll make it happen."

So far, he hadn't made any concrete plans to meet with Theresa and Lucy, but Remy had the feeling he would soon. Ellis was still having trouble vanishing. In fact, it was getting worse. Many times, he couldn't even make it through the night before being jolted back to consciousness. It was like a horrible case of insomnia, and she knew it scared him. He didn't understand what was happening to him, and he was afraid he might be forced to cross over soon. Ellis was still convinced he was going to hell, and it was horrible for Remy to see him so tormented.

Remy was suffering torment of her own. She'd spent the last few months in a constant state of panic that Avery could leave her at any moment. Thank God for Lucy, who understood exactly how she felt. She, too, had been working with Jesse to help him face his issues and find peace. Remy was in awe of her courage. After all, Lucy had had absolutely no way of knowing that there was even a chance that Jesse could come back. And yet she'd still done everything in her power to help him even though it had torn her up inside. Lucy might be gentle and shy, but she wasn't weak. She'd loved Jesse enough to let him go, and Remy was doing her best to follow her example. She would always put Avery's happiness above her own.

It wasn't easy. Remy was emotionally drained, utterly worn down by the constant worrying. She was also physically exhausted, as the strain of working two jobs was starting to take its toll. At least it was springtime now, and the weather was turning warm. She was able to sit outside with Avery again, which made her happy. During the winter, the tour bus didn't stop at Little Round Top because it was too cold to let the tourists wander around. She missed those daytime visits with Avery, and the thought of him being alone all day filled her with sorrow. Though spring in Gettysburg was usually mild, the last few days had been unusually and ferociously hot. The heat wave was supposed to last all week, and Remy was fairly uncomfortable in her long-sleeved Jennie Wade costume.

When the tour bus stopped at Little Round Top, the unusually active group had peppered her with questions, photo requests, and the like. At first, all she could do was wearily wave at Avery while she and Jesse tried to take care of their guests' needs. Finally, she had a moment to breathe, and she eagerly walked toward Avery.

On the way over, a sudden wave of dizziness came over her. She put her hand on a nearby tree to steady herself. Avery rushed over to her.

"What's the matter?" he asked when he reached her side.

"I'm okay, Avery. Just a little dizzy. It's so *hot*," Remy said, fanning herself with a map of Gettysburg.

"Darling, you don't look well. Why don't you sit down?"

"I'm fine, Avery," Remy said, even as another wave of dizziness struck her. She realized she needed to quit being stubborn and sit down before she passed out. She slid down to the base of the tree and drew in a few deep breaths.

"Are you sick?" Avery asked, eyes full of concern.

"No, no. I'm fine. Really."

Remy looked up at him and was slightly alarmed at his expression. *Do I look that bad?*

"Jesse!" Avery called out. Jesse turned around and saw Remy sitting on the ground with Avery crouched beside her. Avery sounded urgent, so Jesse jogged right over after a quick apology to the tourist he'd been helping.

"Have you got any water?" Avery asked him.

"Yeah, yeah. I got some on the bus," Jesse said. He looked down at Remy. "Are you all right?"

Remy waved him off. "I'm fine. Quit worrying."

"That damned outfit is too hot in this weather. It's not healthy," Avery said.

"I know," Jesse said, looking worried. "I'll be right back with some water."

Jesse ran up the hill toward the bus.

"*A chuisle*," Avery said somberly. "Love, you're working too much. You have to get yourself some rest."

"I can't," Remy said. "You know that. I have to work all the hours I can get."

"I wish so much there was something I could do," Avery said miserably. "I can't bear seein' you like this, and there isn't a goddamn thing I can do about it."

"Please don't worry, Avery. I'll be okay," Remy said, looking into his eyes. She hated making him worry, because she could imagine how helpless he felt.

Jesse came running up with a water bottle. He twisted off the top and gave the bottle to her.

"Thank ye, Jesse," Avery said, looking relieved. "Drink, love. Please."

Remy nodded and drank half the bottle with one swig. "Thank you, Jesse. That helps." Remy fanned herself again with the map. "I just feel a little dizzy, that's all. I'll be fine in a few minutes."

Both men looked at her with concern.

"Remy," Jesse said sternly. "Have you eaten anything today?"

Her silence was all the answer Avery and Jesse needed.

"Remy!" Avery cried, horrified.

"I'm *fine*, goddammit!" Remy yelled, glaring at both of them. "I've taken care of myself this long, and I don't need a man to take care of me!"

Avery blinked and moved back a little to give her some space. He didn't look hurt by her outburst. He just looked worried. Worried and weary.

Remy closed her eyes and leaned back against the tree. "I'm tired. I'm just so tired." Tears escaped down her cheeks, but she was too exhausted to wipe them away. It was all too much. Working so much tired her out, but it was her heartache over Avery that was killing her inside. She loved him so much that it scared her. Being with him made her feel like she finally had a family, but what would she do if he had to leave? It was like loving someone with a terminal disease, knowing they could die at any moment.

Remy opened her eyes to see Jesse and Avery sitting on either side of her, gazing at her with such tender concern that it made her want to weep harder.

Avery looked helplessly at Jesse and said quietly, "I just don't know what to do."

"Remy," Jesse said, taking her hand in his. "Everybody knows what a strong woman you are. Fillis was right when she said you should be so proud of everything you've accomplished all on your own, but nobody can make it by themselves. It's not about needing a man to take care of you." Jesse thought for a moment then went on. "Look at me. When I came back, I had *nothing*. Lucy had to buy me clothes, socks, and I didn't even have underwear!"

Remy laughed softly at Jesse's wide-eyed look. Avery looked relieved to see her smile.

"Theresa gave me food and a roof over my head. Sean helped me get a social security card and taught me how to drive. And *you* took a chance on an idiot cowboy who had no prior work experience."

"You're not an idiot, Jesse," Remy said, calming down a little as she looked into his eyes.

"Point is, I *never* could have made it on my own. And the great thing is, I didn't have to. And neither do you. Remy, we all love you so much and you got to let us help you! Darlin', please don't go hungry any more. You're breakin' my heart. And you're *killin'* him," he said, gesturing at Avery. "You know, so to speak."

Remy nodded, tearing up again. She turned to Avery and spoke, her voice breaking. "Oh, Avery, I'm so sorry for yelling at you."

"Don't you worry 'bout that," Avery said, moving closer to her again. "I know you're upset. I just want so much to help you."

"I just…I can't let myself need you, Avery," she said, choking a sob. "B-b-because I can't have you."

Remy covered her mouth to stifle the noise of her crying while the tears streamed down her face.

"Jesse," Avery said, his voice anguished. "Hold her. *Please.*"

Jesse looked into her eyes, imploring her to let him comfort her but unwilling to do so without her permission. Remy nodded and opened her arms.

"This is from Avery, Remy," Jesse said as he gently took her into his arms.

Remy wrapped her arms around Jesse, taking in a few deep breaths as she tried to calm herself. Of course, it wasn't the same as being held by Avery himself, but it was still a tremendous comfort. Jesse's words and his tender touch were reminders that she really wasn't alone and never would be, even if Avery had to leave her.

Jesse took a few moments, gently stroking her back to soothe her. He did a wonderful job of navigating the fine line of what was appropriate and what was not when it came to holding a woman who was not his girlfriend. His touch was more intimate than when he hugged her as himself, yet still distant enough so as not to make either one of them uncomfortable.

After Remy had stopped crying and while he was still holding her, Jesse said in his best imitation of Avery, "For the love of *jaysus*, Remy, let Jesse help you. He's a good man!"

Remy burst out laughing and released Jesse. She smiled warmly at him, and then spoke to Avery as if he'd actually been the one to say it. "You're right, Avery. He is a good man."

"So you'll let me and Lucy set an extra place at supper tonight? Before your ghost tours start?" Jesse asked.

"Yes," Remy said. "Thank you so much."

"Are you all right, *a chuisle?*" Avery said, gazing deeply into her eyes.

"Yes, I'm okay. I didn't mean to worry you. I'll be all right."

Jesse looked at the two of them sorrowfully. Remy knew he understood how badly they wanted—*needed*—to touch each other.

"When I was dead, I was able to kiss Lucy once," Jesse said.

"Really?" Remy asked.

Jesse nodded. "Yeah, I was all worked up inside at the time, emotional, you know? Lucy was…well, she was…in a lot of pain…suffering." He winced, the memory still painful for him.

"It was that time at Devil's Den," Remy said quietly.

"Yes. Yes, exactly. And God, I just wanted to make the pain stop. Do something, *anything* to take her mind off what was happening to her. So I just concentrated real hard and gathered all the strength I had, and then I leaned down and kissed her on her forehead." Jesse smiled at the memory. "I would have kissed her lips, but this was before I knew how she felt about me. She said my touch was actually *warm.*"

"That's amazin,'" Avery said, looking at him in wonder. He glanced over at Remy, a hopeful look in his eye.

"You sit here and rest a while, Remy," Jesse said. "Take your time. We ain't gonna leave without ya."

Jesse winked at her, then wandered off to give them some privacy.

Avery stared at Remy's lips, concentrating with all his might. Remy sat perfectly still, hoping against hope that it would work. She would have given anything and everything she had to be able to touch Avery just once. To feel his tender kiss.

When he was ready, he leaned over and pressed his lips to hers.

It felt like someone had rubbed ice cubes on her mouth. Disappointment flowed through her. He leaned back and looked at her hopefully. She sadly shook her head.

Avery nodded grimly. "I didn't feel anything either. I'm sorry."

"It was worth a shot," Remy said wearily. "Besides, the cold felt good on my skin."

Avery nodded. "Now why didn't I think of that sooner?"

With that, he placed his hand on her cheek like he always did.

"Ah," Remy said with relief. "That does feel good." She was so overheated by being in the hot sun that his icy touch was a relief.

He smiled, happy to be able to help for once. He touched her forehead and her other cheek.

She let out another sigh of relief. "Ah, that really helps."

"Lift up your hair," Avery instructed.

Remy did as he asked, and he placed his hand on the back of her sweaty neck. His touch cooled her immensely.

"Thank you, Avery. I feel so much better."

She saw Jesse approaching, and she realized she needed to get back to work. How she hated leaving Avery!

"Here, darlin'," Jesse said, handing her a granola bar. "Got this from somebody on the bus. Told them you weren't feelin' well and needed somethin' to eat. There's no rush, okay? Take it easy, and we'll get goin' when you're ready."

Remy nodded. "Thank you so much, Jesse."

"Any time, Remy," Jesse said, and then jogged back up toward the bus to keep the tourists occupied while they waited for her.

Remy bit gratefully into the granola bar. With minutes, she felt some of her strength returning. She realized she had been stupid and stubborn not to ask for help. She would feel a lot better after having a good meal with Jesse and Lucy tonight, and the food would give her the energy to get through the nighttime tours. She would gladly help any friend in need, and she realized she needed to stop being so damned hard on herself.

Remy took a few deep breaths. She still felt tired and emotionally drained, but a little more hopeful. She drank the rest of the water in the bottle, and then got to her feet. Avery stood up, too, then looked down at her.

"Are you feeling better?" he asked.

"Yes, much better. I'm okay now."

"And you're going to let Jesse and Lucy help you?" Avery asked, still looking worried.

"Yes, I promise."

"Good, good," he said, looking relieved.

Remy blew him a kiss and then headed up the hill to the bus.

Yes, she needed to take better care of herself. For her own sake, and for poor Avery's worried heart.

*****

Remy stopped by to see Ellis quickly on the way to Jesse's house for dinner. She hoped Ellis would understand why she had to cut her visit short tonight. Remy reminded herself that she really didn't owe the man any explanations. She was tired and hungry and needed a break. If he didn't understand that, that was his problem.

"Hey," Remy said as she walked toward him. "I'm sorry, but I really can't stay long tonight."

"Why?" he asked her somewhat suspiciously.

Remy let out a sigh. She was in no mood to argue, so she decided she wasn't going to. She would tell him why she couldn't stay and offer no excuses or further explanations.

"Because I don't have any money for food, and I won't until I get paid in two days. I'm going to Jesse's house for dinner. I nearly passed out today from hunger, and he and Lucy are going to feed me."

"I'm sorry things are so rough for ya," he said, looking like he meant it.

"Thanks," she said with a smile. Ellis could be sweet when he wanted to be. "I'll come back tomorrow and we'll sit a while, okay?"

"Yeah. Thank you, Remy. I really do appreciate what you're doing for me."

"You're welcome, Ellis," Remy said, genuinely touched. His simple statement was an outpouring of emotion coming from him. "See ya soon."

Remy headed back to her car, and then Ellis called after her. "Remy!"

"Yeah?"

"I'm ready to try now."

She ran back over to him. "You mean you want to meet with Theresa and Lucy and me? For counseling?"

"Yeah," Ellis said, a tentative smile playing on his lips.

"Great. That's great!" Remy said happily. "Where? When?"

He waved her off. "We'll work it out tomorrow. Go. Eat."

"Okay. We'll talk then!" Remy smiled warmly, feeling excited about Ellis's progress. How wonderful it would be if Ellis could find the peace in crossing over that had evaded him his whole time on earth.

*****

Remy felt much stronger and more energetic after enjoying a home-cooked meal of pot roast and mashed potatoes, courtesy of Lucy and Jesse. The only time she ever had a meal like that growing up was if she cooked it herself. Lucy was a pretty good cook, and it was cute how Jesse, ever the Texas cowboy, poured hot sauce over everything. The company was wonderful, too. She ate most of her meals alone in her kitchen, looking at the empty chair across from her and daydreaming about what it would be like to have Avery share a meal with her. Not only was he physically unable to eat, but her apartment was too far away for him to travel. How she wished she lived inside the town of Gettysburg proper! Then he could spend so much more time with her.

"Where is she meeting you?" Remy asked Lucy as she drove her into town to meet Theresa for a drink. Remy had to work ghost tours that evening anyway and had volunteered to give Lucy a ride.

"O'Malley's," Lucy responded.

"Perfect. Right near where I need to be anyway!" Remy said. "Do you need a lift back?"

"Nah, Theresa said she would drop me off. Wish you could come with us," Lucy said.

"Thanks," Remy said sincerely. It always felt good to be included in Lucy's and Theresa's plans. "Gotta work. You know how it is."

Lucy nodded sadly. "You work too much."

Remy laughed. "You sound like Avery. Thanks again for dinner. I really appreciate it."

"I know you do, Remy. It's really no trouble. I have my income and Jesse's, plus my parents are pretty well off. I mean, nothing compared to Theresa's family, but my mom and dad are pretty comfortable, and they send me money all the time. You're more than welcome for dinner any time, okay?"

Remy nodded and smiled. "Thanks, Lucy. So hey, do your parents know about Jesse?"

"Well, they know *of* him. They know I live with my boyfriend. They don't know anything about his past or anything like that. They couldn't possibly understand. They would think we were both nuts."

"Yeah," Remy said. "I can't imagine how hard that would be to explain. At least with Avery, you could show me he was a ghost. Jesse's alive now, so why would they believe a crazy story like that?"

"Exactly," Lucy said. Then she grimaced and said, "I told them his parents were killed in a car accident. I hate lying to them, but eventually they're gonna expect to meet his family."

"Oh, yeah, good point."

Remy was happy to find a great spot on the street to park, and they both got out of the car.

"Heyyy, there's my bitches!" came a familiar, cheerful voice.

Remy laughed, honored to be called one of Theresa's bitches. It was a term of endearment coming from her.

"Okay, good. Since I have you both together," Remy began cautiously.

"Uh-oh. I'm scared," Theresa said, taking a step back.

Remy laughed and said, "You probably should be. Ellis agreed to try counseling."

"You serious?" Theresa asked, and Remy nodded. "Damn, you're a miracle worker."

"Yeah, we'll see about that. Anyway, he agreed to meet with all three of us, but I'll understand if you don't want to come along, Lucy. I know he's been a real creep to you. To be honest, he's still a creep to me sometimes. He's just scared. And he's lonely." Remy said sadly.

"I know he is," Lucy said with sympathy, though there was still fear in her eyes. She wasn't comfortable with the guy, and Remy didn't blame her one bit.

Theresa and Lucy had been aware of Remy's friendship with Ellis for some time now. Though Remy knew they didn't completely understand it, they were still incredibly supportive of her. They trusted her judgment.

"I really do want to help if I can," Lucy said. Yes, she was scared of him, but she was tenderhearted and had a soft spot for lost souls just like Remy did.

"That's so sweet of you, Lucy. Really. That's so cool of you to give him another chance."

"I'm happy to help. But you're gonna get me in hot water with Jesse."

Remy wrinkled her nose and said, "I know. He is *not* gonna be happy to hear you're going anywhere near Ellis. And speaking of boyfriends, is Sean coming this weekend?"

"Yes, and hopefully I will be, too. I haven't seen him in two weeks, and I need to get *laid*," Theresa said bluntly.

Remy and Lucy burst out laughing.

"And least you *can* get laid," Remy grumbled.

"I know, girl," Theresa said. "It's so unfair. Damn, Remy, you just *know* Avery would be amazing in bed. He's so tall, so *big...*"

"Stop it, you're killing me!" Remy moaned.

"I know. Sorry. Sorry!" Theresa said.

"All right, I gotta run. I'll talk to Ellis and make us all a date," Remy told them. "See ya, girls!"

With that, Remy started walking toward work, her head already filling with sexual fantasies about Avery thanks to Theresa.

Chapter 19

Remy was looking forward to seeing Ellis now that he'd said he was willing to let Theresa and Lucy help him, too. She just hoped he hadn't changed his mind. His moods had a tendency to change quickly.

Ellis glowered at Remy upon her approach, and her heart sank. He hadn't looked at her like that in a long time. He was still a little grumpy sometimes, but he was rarely mean to her anymore. Sometimes he was downright friendly. Not today.

"You all right?" Remy asked.

"Fine."

"You haven't changed your mind about meeting with us, have you?"

After a long pause, he finally said, "No, I didn't change my mind. I'll meet with them two harlots. Promised I would, didn't I?"

"Ellis," Remy began gently. She waited until he looked at her before she continued speaking. "Theresa and Lucy are my friends, and they really want to help you, but you have to be nice to them."

Ellis rolled his eyes.

"I mean it!" Remy said sternly. "I understand this must be hard for you, and I know you're angry about lots of things." *And defensive,* she knew better than to add. She realized he must be feeling vulnerable and afraid at the prospect of sharing his personal problems with relative strangers. "Look, I can deal with your insults about me, but you have to promise not to hurt my friends."

"Fine. I promise," Ellis said testily.

"Please," Remy begged, anxiety welling up in her stomach. It would be just like him to get angry and lash out at Theresa and Lucy, saying horrible things he couldn't take back. "I'm trusting you."

Ellis whipped his head and said furiously, "And I'm trusting *you!*"

It had been a long time since she felt afraid of him, but the angry look in his eyes scared her.

"Ellis, I know it's hard for you to trust anyone, but I hope you know you really can trust me. I'm your friend, and I just want to help you," Remy said tenderly, doing her best to understand why he was so angry. *He's scared,* she told herself. *Be patient with him. He needs you.*

His expression softened, and the sorrowful look in his eyes stunned her. He looked so lost, so alone.

"Where do you want to meet with us? Pick a place where you'll be comfortable. Just not on a battlefield."

Ellis nodded slowly. "Somewhere outta the main part of town. Not in front of everybody on the street."

"Of course not, Ellis. We'll go somewhere private where we can all talk."

"How 'bout the Railroad Depot. The one that's across the street from that Lincoln Diner. Behind the depot so nobody'll be around to hear us. Saturday. Six o'clock at night."

Remy nodded, knowing just the place he was talking about. It was on the bus tour, but the bus didn't stop there. She and Jesse just explained the history of the Railroad Depot building as they drove by.

"Yeah, that should work. That building is a museum now, but it'll be closed then, and nobody should be around. Good idea!"

Ellis smiled and nodded.

*****

Theresa, Lucy, and Remy met up in Lincoln Square, which was just a short walk from where they were to meet Ellis. They wouldn't be alone, however. Once Jesse found out what they were up to, he made sure Sean and Avery were aware of the situation. Jesse stood with the women now, eyes narrowed. As Remy had predicted, he was not happy that Lucy would be in close proximity with Ellis. In fact, Jesse didn't want any of them to have anything to do with the guy, but he knew better than to try to talk them out of it.

Avery showed up next, looking worried. He stood next to Jesse, and they both looked mad. Remy stifled a giggle. They were kind of cute, the way they stood there ready to draw their proverbial swords to protect their women from Ellis.

Remy's eyes opened wide as she saw a tall, incredibly handsome man walking toward them. She knew right away it must be Sean. Remy turned to Lucy and mouthed, *Oh, my God.*

Lucy mouthed back, *I know, right?*

"I saw that, little lady," Jesse said with a wry smirk. Lucy smiled and blew him a kiss.

Theresa had not exaggerated when she had described her sexy boyfriend. Sean was a Staff Sergeant in the Air Force, and the guy was *huge*, with bulging muscles everywhere. He was dressed head to toe in camouflage and looked incredibly handsome. Theresa got a running start and literally *leapt* onto him, locking her legs around his waist. Sean laughed heartily as he wrapped his arms around her. He seemed amused but not the least bit surprised at how she had greeted him.

Yeah, Remy thought. *She's definitely getting laid tonight. She probably pounces on him like that in bed, too.*

Theresa pressed her lips to his, and he eagerly kissed her back. It was obvious how much they missed each other when he was stuck on base and couldn't make it home for the weekend. It made Remy smile to see her so happy with him. Theresa finally disentangled herself from him and got back on her feet.

"Come meet Remy!" Theresa said, pulling him by the shirt.

Sean walked toward Remy with a friendly smile. He was so gorgeous that Remy felt a little shy in his presence.

"So nice to finally meet you!" Remy said warmly.

"Nice to meet you, too!" Sean said, bowing slightly instead of shaking her hand. She found it odd at first, but then she recalled Theresa telling her that he had lost several fingers in the line of duty and was self-conscious about his hands.

Remy drew in a deep breath, feeling nervous about her friends meeting with Ellis. "Thank you so much for your help with Ellis, guys," she said to Theresa and Lucy.

"We're glad to do it, Rem. I'm just happy he finally agreed to let us help him," Theresa said.

"Me too, but," Remy said. "I just hope he behaves himself. He was in an especially bad mood yesterday. I know he's nervous about talking about all his personal stuff…and-and…Theresa, I want to tell you… Look, I swear to God I didn't tell him, but he knows…well, he knows what your ex-boyfriend tried to do to you."

Theresa went slightly pale, then nodded.

"You know, since he's a ghost, he can go wherever he wants, so he sees and hears lots of stuff."

"Tell me about it," Lucy muttered.

"He has such a bad temper, and he can get really defensive sometimes. He lashes out when he's mad, and I can just see him saying something horrible like…like you deserved to be raped or something." Remy winced, hating to have to say those awful words out loud, but she wanted to be sure Theresa was prepared for anything.

"If he does, I swear to God," Sean said, his voice nearly a growl. His muscles tensed, and he looked pretty scary.

"Easy, tiger," Theresa said to him, then she turned to Remy. "It's okay. It's part of the psychiatry gig. You can't expect to work with stable patients all the time. At least in this case, the patient is dead so there's only so much damage he can do. The worst he can do is say hurtful stuff, and in the end, it's just words. It was good you warned me, though. It'll be easier to keep my composure if I'm expecting him to say something like that." Theresa nodded, thinking. "Yeah, I know his type. He'll probably feel the need to test me a few times to see if I'll break."

"Yes, that's exactly what he does!" Remy said, marveling at Theresa's professionalism. She was going be a great psychiatrist. "God, I just hope this isn't a horrible mistake. He just…he's so lonely, and he needs help."

"I know, Rem, and it's real swell of ya to want to help," Theresa said, punching her gently on the cheek. Remy laughed and felt slightly better. "We're gonna do everything we can to help him. I promise. Just think how amazing it would be if we could actually help him cross over. He's had a rough life *and* afterlife, and he deserves to finally find peace."

"Exactly," Remy said. "Thank you."

Lucy looked a little nervous.

"You okay?" Remy asked her.

"Yeah, it's just that Ellis knows some personal stuff about me, and I guess I'm kind of afraid that he'll use it against me if he gets mad," Lucy said.

"Darlin', you *don't* have to do this," Jesse said, eyes blazing.

"He's right, Lucy," Remy said firmly. "I mean it. The guy's been horrible to you, and I wouldn't blame you one bit if you didn't want anything to do with him."

"No, it's okay," Lucy said, nodding with determination. "I know he's had a really hard time of it. Sometimes it's the meanest, angriest people who are suffering the most. He's obviously in terrible pain and I want to do what I can to help him."

Remy smiled at Lucy with admiration. Ellis clearly knew something about her that she didn't want to be public knowledge, and it just might be once they were done with his session. Even though Lucy was the soft, sensitive type whose feelings were easily hurt, she was plowing forward anyway. That was the definition of bravery as far as Remy was concerned.

Theresa pulled out her cell phone from her pocket and glanced at the time. "Okay, it's almost six. He should be along any minute." She turned and faced Sean, Jesse, and Avery. "Listen, you boys need to behave. You can be nearby if you insist, but you can't be listening in on Ellis's private session. He's not gonna be an easy patient, but then neither were you as I recall." She looked directly at Sean, who smiled at her with affection and admiration. Theresa had fallen in love with him while counseling him for his struggles with PTSD.

Remy took a deep breath, nervous but excited to help Ellis. She surveyed this wonderful group of friends, all here because they were doing her a favor. She felt like she was part of a family for the first time, and she felt good about paying it forward with Ellis. She wasn't alone anymore, and he shouldn't be either.

Theresa put her hands on her hips, still addressing the men. "I mean it! If you get in his face, you'll scare him off. So *please*, none of you step in unless we ask for help, okay?" She spoke firmly, but Remy could see the affection in her eyes for all three men. They were all wonderful boyfriends who just wanted to protect the women they loved.

Avery, Jesse, and Sean all nodded rather grimly. They respected the strength and independence of the women, but it would be a struggle for them to stand back and watch Ellis hurt them if he got out of hand.

Theresa began walking down the street toward the Railroad Depot building, and Remy and Lucy fell into step behind her. As promised, the boys lagged behind, keeping a respectable distance.

"Good thing they can't touch Ellis, because they are out for *blood*," Theresa observed.

"Yeah, they are," Lucy said. "It's kind of sweet."

"It really is," Remy said with a smile. She loved how everyone treated Avery like a person, not as a spirit. To them, he was just one of the guys.

The three women walked behind the building of the Railroad Depot to the empty parking lot. Remy looked around, and there was still no sign of Ellis. Disappointment rippled through her as she realized it was entirely possible that Ellis was going to stand them up.

Lucy suddenly let out an agonized shriek, shattering the silence. She dropped to the ground on all fours, then rolled onto her back, moaning in pain.

"Lucy!" Remy cried, dropping to her knees beside her. "What happened?"

"I don't know," Lucy said in a weak voice. "I don't know." She closed her eyes and cried out again.

Jesse's shoes pounded the pavement as he rounded the corner to the parking lot. He dashed to her side, with Sean and Avery close on his heels. He dropped to his knees beside her, a look of sheer panic on his face as he looked at Lucy writhing in pain on the ground. He looked up at Remy and Theresa and asked in a voice filled with terror, "What happened to her?"

FOREVER, DARLING

"I don't know, Jesse," Theresa said, trying to keep her voice steady for Jesse's sake. Remy could see it was a struggle for her. "She just dropped to the ground."

"Lucy," Jesse said, leaning down and looking into her eyes. "Darling, what happened?"

"I-I don't know," Lucy croaked out. "But something's really wrong…with my l-leg…it's my leg…"

Jesse yanked up her skirt and inspected her legs. "Where? Where does it hurt?"

"My l-left leg. Around the knee."

Jesse carefully inspected her leg. When he touched her knee, she screamed in agony.

"I'm sorry, I'm sorry, my love!" Jesse said grimacing. "I just had to see." Jesse looked up at Sean and Avery, panicked. "I don't see anything wrong!"

Jesse sat back on his haunches, and Remy could see he was searching for any possible explanation for Lucy's suffering. Then he groaned and said, "No, no this can't be happening. It's not supposed to be happening here! We're not on a battlefield!"

"You think she might be feeling battle pains?" Theresa asked, eyes wide.

"Yes," Jesse said, eyes filled with sorrow. "This is just what happened at Devil's Den. Sudden, horrible pain with no physical injuries… Godammit, I don't understand! We're nowhere near a battlefield!"

Realization suddenly slammed into Remy with sickening clarity. She didn't want to tell Jesse what was happening to Lucy, but she knew she had no choice.

"Jesse," Remy said, her eyes filling with tears. "The building."

Jesse slowly raised his eyes up to the Railroad Depot building. Remy watched in horror as the truth dawned on him.

Jesse closed his eyes. "Oh, my God."

215

"What?" Lucy managed to say though heavy, panting breaths.

Jesse and Remy exchanged sorrowful looks.

"Tell me!" Lucy shrieked.

Jesse leaned down and slid his arm underneath Lucy so he could cradle her.

"Darling," Jesse said as gently as possible. "The railroad building was used as a hospital during the war…it's where…it's where they used to do amputations to the soldiers."

Lucy closed her eyes and began sobbing. She nodded through her tears. "That must be what's h-h-appening to me. Oh, Jesse, it hurts so much."

"I know, my love, I know," Jesse said, holding her close to his chest, his face awash in anguish and grief over her suffering.

"Th-that's how Ellis died." Remy said, struggling to choke out the words. "His leg was amputated."

"That *son-of-a-bitch* set her up," Theresa said, her voice quaking with rage. "He told us to meet right here at this time."

Ellis could be mean, but Remy could hardly believe he was capable of something as horrific as this. "May-maybe he didn't know. Maybe he didn't know Lucy was sensitive to—"

"He knew," Jesse said, gritting his teeth. "He loves to taunt me about Devil's Den, tellin' me it was my fault she suffered through my death."

Still on her knees, Remy covered her face with her hands. *This is my fault. I did this to her. I put her in danger. She's being tortured because of me.*

Remy uncovered her eyes and saw Lucy was frighteningly pale. She let out a moan, then closed her eyes and fell completely limp in Jesse's arms.

"Lucy!" Jesse yelled. "Lucy!" He desperately shook her, trying to revive her.

"Let me see her!" Sean roared. He rushed over and carefully but firmly pulled Lucy from Jesse's arms.

Jesse looked up, scared and bewildered.

"It's all right, Jesse," Theresa said in a soothing voice. "He has medical training. From the military."

Jesse nodded numbly. Theresa held out her hands, and Jesse allowed her to drag him to a standing position. Remy knew she had to pull herself together to help Lucy and Jesse get through this nightmare. She shakily got to her feet, and both she and Theresa stood on either side of Jesse and wrapped their arms around him.

It's gonna be okay, Jesse," Remy reassured him. "It'll be over soon, and she'll be okay."

Jesse's grief-stricken look was almost more than Remy could bear. "Why does she have to be so sensitive," Jesse moaned. "Why couldn't it be me? *Why couldn't it be me?*"

"I know you'd bear it for her if you could, cowboy," Theresa said gently, pulling him close and squeezing him.

Sean held Lucy in his arms while he examined her. She was still unconscious, which was scary. He leaned in to listen to her breathing, then grabbed her wrist and counted her pulse.

He looked up at Jesse. "She's breathing fine. Her pulse is a little off, but that's to be expected." Next, he pried open her eyelids and examined her eyes. He nodded, then he gently pulled up her skirt to examine her knee. "Physically, she seems to be fine. Doesn't seem to be any physical trauma, and her vitals are good."

Jesse nodded, looking slightly relieved. He gazed down at Lucy's unconscious form. "We gotta wake her up!"

"I'm not so sure, Jess," Sean said, looking worried.

"Whut?"

"She seems to be all right at the moment, physically. Seems more merciful to let her stay out for the moment. At least she's not suffering now," Sean said, looking down at Lucy with sadness. "Poor, sweet girl."

Jesse nodded. "Is there any risk to lettin' her stay unconscious?"

"I don't think so, but I can't swear to it," Sean said truthfully. "Maybe let her go just a few minutes then we'll try to revive her."

Jesse nodded, his expression agonized as he looked down at the love of his life.

"You can hold her if you want, Jesse," Sean said softly.

Jesse nodded, then sat down beside him. Sean gently placed Lucy in Jesse's arms.

"My rose," Jesse said, stroking her cheek. "My beautiful rose."

Remy looked up to see Avery standing sadly off to the side. He must have known there was nothing he could do, so he stayed out of the way.

He locked eyes with Remy and said, "She'll be all right soon, Remy."

She was still terrified for Lucy, but Avery's kind expression comforted her. It was entirely possible that all her friends would hate her after this, but Avery would never leave her. At least, he wouldn't leave her unless he crossed over and had no choice.

Lucy began moaning again.

"Lucy! Lucy, darlin'…" Jesse said, as he stroked her cheek. He studied her face, desperate to know that she was all right.

Lucy opened her eyes and looked up at him and said weakly, "Jesse."

"It's all right, love. I'm here. I'm right here. Does it still hurt?"

Lucy nodded. "Yes, yes, Jesse, it hurts so much." Her eyes welled up with tears again. "Jesse, I can't do this…I-I can't… It hurts." She broke down in sobs of agony again.

Remy could Jesse's heart ripping in half right in front of her.

Jesse looked up at Sean. "Isn't there anything we can do? There must be something we can do to stop this!"

Sean's expression was mournful. He shook his head. "If it were something physical, maybe there would be something, but this?" He looked as frustrated and helpless as Jesse did. Remy knew they certainly didn't cover this type of emergency in the military.

"Jesse," Avery said as he crouched down beside him. "Let's try to get her away from here. Maybe getting her away from the building will stop the reaction."

Jesse glanced down at his beloved Lucy, who was still sobbing in his arms. "But it hurts her worse if I touch her," he said, looking down at her knee. He had touched her there when she first collapsed, and she had screamed in agony.

Avery gazed sorrowfully down at Lucy. He looked back up at Jesse. "I know Jesse, but we've got to do something. We can't let her go on like this."

Jesse nodded, but still hesitated, his face ashen. He was terrified of causing Lucy even more suffering.

"Jesse," Avery said firmly. "This isn't your death this time. We have no idea how long it took Ellis to die. It's our only hope of helping her."

"You're right," Jesse said with determination. He started to get up while still holding Lucy. Sean came forward immediately and gripped Jesse in his strong arms, helping him to his feet.

Jesse gripped Lucy under her legs so he could carry her, and she let out an ungodly shriek of sheer agony.

"Lucy," Jesse moaned.

"Stay strong, Jesse!" Avery commanded. "Get her out of here!"

Jesse nodded and broke into a near run with Lucy in his arms, trying his best not to jostle her any more than he absolutely had to. Lucy's sobs became whimpers, which were somehow worse than her screams. It was like she was losing the strength to cry out anymore.

Sean, Avery, Remy, and Theresa ran alongside Jesse as he carried Lucy away from the Railroad Depot building. Lucy lifted her head after they got several yards away from the parking lot where she had collapsed.

"Jesse!" Lucy cried, her eyes wide and she looked up at him. "It stopped! It doesn't hurt anymore!"

"Oh, thank God," Jesse said, his eyes filled with utter relief and gratitude. "Thank God, thank God!"

*****

Relief flooded through Lucy. As soon as Jesse got her away from the building, the pain stopped abruptly. She wrapped her arms around Jesse's neck, feeling too weak to even cry anymore. Lucy took in a few deep breaths, telling herself, *It's over, it's over, it's all over.*

Jesse carried her a little farther away just to be sure. He spotted a bench in a nearby park and carried her over to it, gently laying her down. Jesse sat with her, cradling her head and shoulders in his arms while the rest of her body was stretched out on the bench.

"Lucy, Lucy," Jesse moaned as he gazed down at her. "Are you all right?"

Lucy nodded. She wanted to reassure him that she was all right, and that she couldn't have gotten through this horror without him, but she felt too weak to speak.

"It don't hurt anymore?" Jesse asked, his eyes pleading.

"No," Lucy managed to say. "No, it doesn't hurt at all anymore."

Sean crouched down next to her, gazing at her with concern. Lucy looked around at all of her friends, watching her with worried expressions. Normally, she was uncomfortable with people fussing over her, but right now she found it soothing to be literally surrounded by her friends. Jesse was holding her in his arms, and Sean was right by her side. Remy and Theresa were at the foot of the bench, and Avery stood just behind it. Ellis had done such a horrific, cruel thing to her, but Lucy felt like she had a wall of love and protection surrounding her. It felt like a balm to her wounded body and soul, knowing there were still good people left in the world.

"Lucy," Sean said gently as he knelt beside her where she lay on the bench. "I'm gonna check your pulse, okay?"

Lucy nodded. Sean picked up her hand and put his forefinger and middle finger on her wrist and counted the beats. She remembered Theresa saying it was a good thing that he hadn't lost his trigger fingers in that terrorist attack in Afghanistan, or his military career would have been over. Sean looked up at Jesse and nodded, indicating that her pulse was good.

Next, Sean looked deeply into her eyes, examining them. *He has such pretty eyes,* Lucy thought. They were a lovely shade of hazel, and he had long, dark eyelashes. She didn't know what he was looking for, but he seemed satisfied with what he saw.

"Is it okay if I take a look at your knee?" Sean asked. He knew Lucy was painfully shy, and any kind of medical examination from a male might be uncomfortable for her. She didn't mind at all, though. She adored Sean and trusted him completely.

"Of course. Thank you, Sean," she said softly.

"Left one?" Sean asked, and she nodded.

He carefully rolled up her skirt only as far as he had to in an effort to protect her modesty. He pressed on the front of her knee. "Does that hurt?" Lucy shook her head. Next, Sean slipped two fingers behind her knee and pressed down. He looked up at her questioningly, and she shook her head. "Good, good. You still look a little pale. You don't feel like you're gonna faint again, do you?"

"Did I faint?" Lucy asked in astonishment. She had no memory of it.

Sean nodded grimly. "Yeah. You blacked out for little bit there.

Jesse was holding you so you didn't hit the ground."

Lucy looked up at Jesse gratefully and he stroked her cheek.

Sean placed his hand on Lucy's forehead. "Good, you don't feel feverish. You seem to be okay overall." He glanced at Jesse, then back at Lucy. "Just keep an eye out for anything unusual. The last thing we want to do is ignore any real medical symptoms because we just assume it's related to, you know, what happened. I mean, God forbid you have a blood clot in your leg or something. Keep an eye out for any soreness, heat around the area, redness, that kind of thing."

"Okay, I will," Lucy said. "Thank you, Sean."

He nodded. "You bet. Right now I think you need rest more than anything. You look exhausted."

Jesse nodded. "Yeah, that's how she was after Devil's Den, too. She was so tired she could barely move." He let out a mournful sigh. "She had to, though. Joel died at Devil's Den, too, and we didn't want her suffering through that as well. So she had to get up and somehow make it all the way to her car."

Sean nodded sympathetically. Jesse was obviously still torn up over what had happened to Lucy that horrible day. "You don't have to go anywhere any time soon. Just rest."

Lucy nodded weakly.

*****

Avery stood quietly next to Remy, watching her try not to fall apart. She couldn't, at least not now. Right now her focus needed to be on Lucy. Remy stared at her lying there on the bench, looking pale and drawn. She couldn't even begin to imagine the agony of feeling your leg being amputated, the sensation of cold, sharp steel slicing through muscle and bone.

And Jesse. He looked devastated, destroyed.

And it was all Remy's fault.

She put a hand over her mouth, doing her best to stifle her sobs as tears ran down her face. The tiniest noise escaped her throat, and Jesse looked up at her.

Jesse looked heartbroken to see Remy so distraught. "Come now, Remy. None of that."

Remy finally took her hand off her mouth and allowed the dam to burst. "J-J-Jesse, I'm so sorry. I'm so sorry. This is all my fault!" Remy broke down in wails of sorrow and regret. She couldn't believe how utterly stupid she had been to trust that horrible man.

Avery did his best to comfort her, but she could barely hear his words over the sound of her own sobbing. Jesse looked at her helplessly, like he wanted to get up and hug her, but he couldn't bear to let go of Lucy.

Sean still had his back to Remy, where he had been kneeling in front of Lucy. Remy could see how much Sean cared about Lucy, and Remy was nervous about what might happen when he turned around. She feared he would be furious with her.

Finally, Sean stood up and turned around. He somehow looked even bigger than he had earlier when she first met him. He stared right at Remy.

Sean had a grim expression on his face. He was angry all right. He took a forceful step toward Remy, who gasped and stumbled backward in fear. Avery was between them in a flash, staring Sean down as if he would punch him if he took one more step toward her. Remy almost believed he could do it.

Sean looked at Avery, then at Remy. He blinked, looking confused for a moment. Then he held up his hands, and Remy couldn't help but stare at his missing fingers.

"Sorry. Sorry! I can be pretty intense sometimes," Sean said, his expression softening as he looked at Remy. She realized he was angry that Lucy had gotten hurt, but he wasn't angry with her.

"Remy, I-I want you to know," he said, struggling with what he had to say. "I—well, my best friend was killed right in front of me, and for a really long time I blamed myself. Finally, I came to understand that when somebody's hell-bent on destruction, sometimes there's nothing you can do." Sean put his hands on Remy's shoulders. His expression and his touch were gentle now, so she wasn't afraid. Sean looked her in the eye and said firmly, "Ellis did this to Lucy, and he *alone* is responsible for his actions. This is *not your fault*, understand?"

Remy nodded, tearing up again. Sean gazed into her eyes for another moment, then let go of her shoulders. Avery caught his eye and nodded gratefully at him, and Sean returned the gesture.

"Of course it's not your fault, Remy," Lucy said quietly. "There's no way you could have known he was capable of something like this. Please don't cry."

Remy nodded, wiping her tears and trying to calm herself.

Theresa wrapped her arms around Remy's shoulders. "Honey, we all know how sensitive Lucy is, and we've always done our best to keep her safe, keep her off the battlefields. There's no way you or anyone else could have known this would happen." She sighed bitterly. "I admit there was a certain evil genius to what he did. He can't touch anyone or anything, but he figured out how to hurt us anyway."

Remy nodded, a sense of betrayal and anger brewing. *How could he have done something like this? After everything I've tried to do to help him?*

"Theresa's right," Lucy said weakly. "Please don't blame yourself. Nobody thinks this is your fault, so you shouldn't either."

Remy looked around and was overwhelmed by the looks of love and support from all of her friends. *So this is what it's like to have a family.*

"Shhh," Jesse said tenderly. "You need to rest, Lucy. Please just rest now."

Lucy nodded. She closed her eyes, and in no time she was asleep in his arms.

Chapter 20

Jesse gazed down at Lucy, who was sleeping in his lap. Sean sat on the ground next to Lucy with Theresa on his other side. Avery sat close to Remy, doing his best to keep her from tearing up again. Everyone was emotionally exhausted from fear and worry over what had happened to Lucy. It was the calm after the storm, with nothing left to do but figure out what to do next.

"That fucking *bastard*," Jesse said through clenched teeth. Remy had *never* heard Jesse curse before, especially when there were ladies present. Remy couldn't imagine the pain and anger he was feeling. He looked at Remy and said, "I hate him for makin' you cry and *goddamn him for what he did to Lucy.*" His body tensed even more as he looked over at Sean. "I just don't know how to protect the girls from him. 'Til now, I never thought he could physically harm them."

"I know," Sean said, looking at Lucy as she slept. "I never could've imagined something like this could happen."

"There's got to be *something* we can do to stop him," Jesse said, struggling to keep his voice low so he wouldn't wake Lucy. "He's so goddamn slippery, he can go wherever he wants!"

"Aye," Avery said grimly. "Hard to keep him away from Remy and Lucy at the same time."

Remy couldn't help but think of all the times she had gone to see Ellis willingly. It seemed impossible that she needed protection from him, but there was no denying the horror she had seen today. The man was dangerous.

"I know!" Jesse exclaimed in a hoarse whisper, trying to yell without yelling. "We could do an exorcism! That's the only way I know of to get rid of a ghost."

Sean looked intrigued by the idea, but Avery wasn't so sure. "I don't think we could do it," Avery said wearily. "Like ye said, he's a slippery one. Not like he haunts one particular place. Soon as we got started, he'd run off."

"True," Sean said. "And I admit pretty much all I know about exorcisms is from the movies and stuff, but you need a priest to do that, right? And before they'll even attempt it, they need lots of evidence of demonic possession."

"That's true," Avery said. "And that's the other thing. Ellis is a horrible person, but I don't think he's possessed by the devil."

"I guess not," Jesse grumbled. He looked down at Lucy. "Once she graduates in the spring, we can get the hell out of Gettysburg, but we're pretty stuck until she finishes school."

Remy's heart ached at the idea of Lucy and Jesse moving away, but she knew it was for the best. It was too dangerous for her to be surrounded by battlefields and other sites where soldiers suffered and died. If she stayed around, it was only a matter of time until this happened to her again.

"I just gotta stay with her when she's working late. He knows when she's working, and God knows what he'll do to her late at night when she's closin' up the restaurant," Jesse said, his voice full of fear and anguish.

"I can take the weekend shift when I'm in town, Jesse," Sean volunteered. "You let me know when she's working, and I'm there."

"Thanks, Sean," Jesse said, sounding relieved. "That would be great."

"It's true that Ellis can go wherever he likes," Avery said, determination in his voice. "But so can I. I'll keep an eye on Remy and Lucy as best I can. Theresa, I know you're out of harm's way where you live because he can't go that far, but I know you volunteer at the Gettysburg hospital. You've never seen him 'round there, have you?"

Theresa shook her head. "Not so far, no. And I never, ever walk to my car alone. I have a security guard walk me out every night." Her voice trembled a little, and Sean wrapped his arm around her. Remy knew that Theresa had been heading home from the hospital the night her ex-boyfriend attacked her. She had been especially vigilant ever since.

"I guess all we can do is keep watch so that bastard doesn't get anywhere near the girls," Jesse said angrily. "I just wish there was something more we could do."

Lucy stirred in Jesse's arms. She opened her eyes and looked up at him.

"How are you feeling?" Jesse asked, stroking her hair.

"Better," Lucy said with a smile.

"Your color looks better," Sean said, looking pleased with her progress.

Lucy started to sit up, and Jesse gently helped her. She took a deep breath, then looked around at her friends.

"How long was I asleep?" she asked.

"About an hour or so," Jesse told her.

Lucy blushed and said shyly, "You all didn't have to wait around here for me."

"We wanted to, Lucy," Avery said with affection. "We wanted to make sure you were all right."

"Thank you, guys," Lucy said with a sweet smile. She stood up, and Jesse put his hand on her back to steady her. Sean and Theresa got up, too, to see if there was anything they could do to help. Lucy was a little wobbly, but was all right otherwise.

Remy and Theresa both looked at Lucy sorrowfully.

"Come here, you two," Lucy said, opening her arms to both of them. The three women went to her, and they shared a warm hug. Remy was relieved that none of her friends blamed her for what had happened. In that moment, it felt like a shared traumatic experience that they would all get through together.

When she finished hugging her best friends, Lucy said to Jesse, "We should walk Remy back to her car to make sure she gets there safely."

"Avery and I will take care of Remy," Sean said firmly. "You guys just go home and get some rest."

"Thanks, Sean," Lucy said, standing on her tiptoes to hug him. She looked so tiny in his arms.

Lucy walked over to Jesse, and he put his arm around her. "Do you want me to carry you?"

She laughed softly. "No, I'm fine, Jesse." She kissed him gently, then he guided her toward the car.

*****

The moment Lucy collapsed to the ground, Ellis realized he'd committed an unspeakably horrific act of malice toward an innocent woman.

Now he sat alone, invisible at Culp's Hill, wishing with all his heart that he could undo the damage and pain he had caused.

At first, he really had wanted to meet with Theresa and Lucy, hoping they could help him face his demons. But that was before he heard the three women laughing at him the other day. Theresa and

Lucy had seemed genuinely concerned about him, but then they had all dissolved into giggles at his expense. He couldn't hear what they were saying, but it didn't matter. Remy was laughing at him with her friends behind his back, just like he had feared.

After that, all of his fear and paranoia came flooding back as his thoughts spun out of control. He could hardly vanish at all anymore, so he'd spent the last few nights wandering the dark streets of Gettysburg, consumed with the pain of his past and drowning in the shame of knowing his personal problems had become public knowledge. Had Remy told everyone how his mother had touched him? The humiliation of it was too much to bear. His mother's betrayal, Jane's betrayal. Everything was mashed together in his brain in a mess of trauma and heartache, and he was lost in the eternal blackness of his bleak existence.

Ellis couldn't get the image of Lucy having sex with Jesse out of his head. She looked so damn much like Jane. Images of Lucy on her back with Jesse fucking her on the bar melded with images of Jane fucking some other guy. Probably lots of other men.

He had thought that hurting Lucy would feel like getting revenge on Jane, but it hadn't. As Ellis watched Lucy suffer, he realized it would have been horrible even watching Jane suffer like that. Even that whore didn't deserve that kind of physical torture. Besides, Lucy wasn't Jane. Lucy loved Jesse with all her heart, and she was faithful to him. He was sure of it. She was a sweet, gentle girl who was kind to everyone. He realized what a coward he'd been to hurt her.

And Jesse. His suffering had been nearly as bad as hers. Maybe worse. Ellis had been nearby, invisible, watching the whole nightmare unfold. Avery was the only one who could have seen him, but he was too preoccupied with helping his friends to notice him. As Ellis witnessed Jesse's devastation, he realized how much Jesse truly loved Lucy. The way he kept saying that he wished it were him suffering instead. Ellis realized that Jesse truly meant that he would bear the pain for her if only he could.

Worst of all, he had finally broken Remy. Nothing he had ever said or done directly to her had seemed to faze the brave, strong-willed girl. No. The way to crush her heart was to hurt someone she cared about. He pictured Remy's beautiful face with those sweet blue eyes. He knew he would never forget the sight of her sobbing, blaming herself for Lucy's suffering.

The highlight of his existence was when Remy came to visit him. He had such tender feelings for her. Feelings he had no idea how to express. And now she was lost to him forever. He knew he deserved to lose her, to suffer the empty void her absence would bring. Ellis only wished he had some way of making Lucy and Remy understand how sorry he was for hurting them. And that he would give his immortal soul if he could only take it back.

How he despised himself. For torturing an innocent girl in front of the man who loved her more than life itself. For betraying Remy. For killing those men in the Railroad Cut, who may have had women back home who loved them as much as Lucy loved Jesse.

Ellis couldn't believe how badly he had hurt Lucy, how he had unfairly blamed her for another's woman's betrayal of him. Ellis had always thought of Lucy as some kind of cheap slut for having sex with Jesse at the bar, but now he allowed himself to see the real story. She had been enjoying a sexual adventure with the man she loved and, knowing how shy and reserved she was, it was a brave thing for Lucy to do. She wasn't some cheap harlot who was cheating on her man. She was with Jesse, the love of her life. Ellis remembered the rest of the encounter he had witnessed that day. The way Jesse had gathered Lucy into his arms, tenderly lifting her up off the bar and setting her on her feet. Then he had wrapped his arms around her and had told her, "You *are* my fantasy." He treated her with tenderness, and Ellis knew he probably took her home and held her in his arms when they got back to their own bed.

A sharp stab of guilt pierced Ellis's heart. He was a monster for taunting Lucy about that night, destroying a private, precious memory of hers and using it for ammunition. Any woman would have felt violated by such an intrusion, but it must have been even more painful for sweet, shy Lucy. It must be excruciating for her to know that Ellis had watched her having sex.

Ellis ached to tell Lucy how sorry he was for all the horrific things he had done to her. Even after he had taunted her mercilessly, she was still kind enough to want to help him. And what had he done? Set a cruel trap for her, leading her to agony like an innocent, trusting lamb to the slaughter.

Oh, Lucy, I'm so sorry. How he ached to say those words to her. Ellis knew Jesse wouldn't allow him anywhere near her, and who could blame him? Ellis decided he would at least try to speak to Lucy long enough to tell her how sorry he was for hurting her.

Ellis knew he was unspeakably evil and utterly beyond redemption. If he weren't already dead, he would have killed himself. He knew that this waking nightmare of an existence was his penance for being a horrible human being, in life and in death. He could barely vanish to escape the pain of his memories. He was haunted day and night by his past sins. He no longer feared eternal damnation, for he knew it was what he deserved.

*****

Remy saw Jesse standing outside on the patio of the tavern, keeping watch while Lucy cleaned up the outdoor tables.

"Everything okay?" Remy asked as she and Avery walked up to them on the street. Remy didn't have a ghost tour that night, so she and Avery wanted to stop by and make sure Ellis wasn't bothering Lucy.

"Yeah," Jesse said, his face grim. "No sign of him yet."

"If he's smart, he'll stay away. I wouldn't want to mess with you!" Remy said with a smile. Jesse's face relaxed into a smile, too, and he looked more like his usual, sweet self.

Lucy gasped suddenly, and Jesse whipped his head around to see what was wrong with her. He followed her gaze and, sure enough, the dreaded, black-hatted man was walking down the street heading right toward the tavern.

Jesse began to charge forward, but Lucy said firmly, "*No*, Jesse." He turned to see that Lucy had a look of strong determination on her face. "*I* want to talk to him."

Jesse looked into her eyes, then slowly nodded. Remy could see it was tearing him up inside not to go charging after Ellis and protect Lucy from him, but he respected her wishes. She had the right to confront her attacker if that was what she wanted.

Remy watched with pride as Lucy's shock at seeing Ellis turned to anger and strong resolution. She was done being his victim.

Jesse tensed as Lucy strode right up to Ellis where he stood at the railing that separated the restaurant's outdoor tables from the street. She stared him straight in the eye and spoke in a strong, unwavering voice.

"I want to make something perfectly clear. I *no longer care* that you saw Jesse and I having sex in the bar here," she said, gesturing toward the inside of Meade's Tavern.

Remy and Avery exchanged shocked looks. Clearly, neither Lucy nor Jesse had let either of them in on that little secret.

"I will *not* let you tarnish that wonderful memory of being with the man I love." Lucy leaned in close to Ellis and stared him down. "You're just jealous because all you could do was stand by and eat your heart out while we had sex right in front of you. You're jealous because you could never make a woman scream out your name in passion and *pleasure* the way Jesse makes me cry out his name every…single…time…he makes love to me."

Jesse's jaw dropped, his eyes wide, watching Lucy with pure fascination.

"He's not only an incredible lover, but he's more of a man than you could ever hope to be," Lucy went on, her voice only getting stronger the more she spoke. "Only a *sniveling coward* would play a horrific trick on someone like you did to me. And that's what you are. You're a coward and a bully, and *I…am…not…afraid…of you.*"

Ellis stared at Lucy for a moment, his face expressionless. Then he simply disappeared.

Lucy let out a long breath, then turned on her heel. She smiled at Jesse, Remy, and Avery, looking satisfied, peaceful.

"I'm gonna go finish up inside," she said brightly, then walked into the restaurant.

Jesse, Remy, and Avery all looked at each other, wide-eyed.

Remy grinned at Jesse and punched him on the shoulder. "Way to go, lover boy!"

A slow, proud smile spread across Jesse's face. He was far too much of a gentleman to have bragged that he'd had sex with Lucy in the bar, but he wasn't sorry the secret was out. He was also clearly proud of Lucy for standing up to Ellis. He glanced at the tavern where she had just disappeared.

"That's my *girl!*"

*****

Though Remy was thrilled that Lucy had told Ellis off the way she did, she couldn't believe the guy had the nerve to come to the tavern to harass her. Remy kept turning over the events in her mind. She had spent months patiently helping Ellis with his troubles, all the while ignoring his rude comments about her, until he finally agreed to submit to some therapy. Over time his mean comments had become fewer and farther between, until he was fairly civil most of the time. She couldn't understand what had made him suddenly turn on her.

The more she thought about it, the angrier she got. Remy couldn't get the image of Lucy's suffering out of her head, and she knew she would never forget the sound of her agonized screams. How could he do such a thing to her? How could *anyone* do a thing like that?

Remy was agitated all day and found it hard to put on her happy tourist face. She managed to be nice, however, reasoning that her guests didn't deserve to be on the receiving end of her bad mood.

"What's wrong, *a chuisle*?" Avery asked the moment she headed toward him during the afternoon tour at Little Round Top.

Remy sighed. She should have known better than to think she could hide anything from him.

"I just keep thinking about Ellis, and…I *have* to know why he did what he did. I deserve some answers," Remy said.

"What are you plannin' to do?" Avery asked, looking worried.

"I'm going to confront him after work today," Remy said firmly. She hadn't even realized what she wanted to do until the words came out of her mouth.

"Remy, I wish you wouldn't do that," Avery said.

"I have to, Avery. He owes me a goddamned explanation!"

"Aye, that he does," Avery said. "But that doesn't mean you'll get one. And God knows what he'll do."

"He can't hurt me, Avery," Remy said reassuringly.

"That's what I used to think," Avery said mournfully. "We all know better now."

"I have to do this, Avery. Lucy confronted him, and I need to do the same. I really do."

"Be careful, love," Avery said, gazing at her sadly.

"I will. Please try not to worry," Remy said with a soft smile. She blew him a kiss and headed out to find her guests.

Remy went to Culp's Hill after her day tours ended and around the same time she used to visit Ellis. *All that time wasted. I was an idiot to think there was any hope for him.* She thought of how much pain he had caused Lucy and Jesse, and her anger flared up again. Thinking of how worried Avery must be feeling pushed her over to the boiling point. *That son of a bitch has one hell of a lot of explaining to do.*

Her heart sank when she arrived at Culp's Hill only to find he wasn't there. At least, that was what she thought at first. She gasped slightly when Ellis appeared out of thin air. Good thing there weren't any tourists around.

"Remy!" Ellis exclaimed as he saw her. He looked happy to see her, which angered her even further.

Remy stalked toward where he stood among the usual rocks.

Eyes blazing, she spat out, "Why, Ellis? For my own good, I need to know *why* you would plan such a vicious attack on the only people on the planet who actually wanted to help you?"

"Oh, Remy, I'm so sorry," Ellis said, his brown eyes sad and mournful. The man actually did seem genuinely remorseful, but only a damned fool would believe him. And that was what she had been. *A damned fool.*

"Why?" Remy asked again. "Why would you do such a horrible thing to Lucy? And to me?"

"I-I know it's no excuse—there is no excuse—I just…I heard you all laughing at me and I just fucking *snapped*. I'm so sorry, Remy. I wish to God I could take it back!" Ellis's eyes pleaded with her to believe him.

"What? What are you talking about? I never laughed at you!"

Remy shouted, more confused than ever.

"I heard you talking about me with Theresa and Lucy on the street. Y-y-you told them I finally agreed to counseling."

"Yes!" Remy said, blue eyes blazing. "Which they *graciously* agreed to even though you treat everybody like dirt!"

"Th-then you all started l-l-aughing at me. I couldn't hear what you said, but you laughed at me." Ellis looked haunted by his own words, like he realized that his argument was insane. The idea that having someone laugh at you behind your back should be punishable by physical torture.

Remy racked her brains, trying to remember what they had been talking about on the street that day. She suddenly remembered. Yes, at first they had been talking about Ellis, but soon they were giggling about how hard up for sex Theresa was with her hunky boyfriend out of town.

"We weren't laughing at you!" Remy screamed, furious at the notion that some idiotic misunderstanding had resulted in Lucy experiencing the agony of Ellis's gruesome, violent death. "We were talking about something else when we were laughing! *I would never do that to you! I would never have betrayed you!*" Remy's entire body was trembling, and she was too angry to cry.

Ellis let her words sink in. He had an awful time trusting anyone, but she could see that he believed her now. She hadn't betrayed him, but he had utterly double-crossed her.

"I-I thought…I thought you might have told them all how my mother…how s-she…how s-she—"

"My God, Ellis," Remy said, her voice a whisper. "How could you think I would ever do such a thing?"

Ellis stared at her dully and said as if in a trance, "I don't know."

"I know you had a horrible childhood," Remy said, her voice quaking. "So did I! But I try to make the world a better place instead of trying to destroy everyone around me. I wouldn't ever to do somebody else what was done to me. I would never betray or abandon *anyone!*"

"I know you wouldn't," Ellis said, looking deeply into her eyes. There was a depth of sadness in his face, like he had fallen into a bottomless pit of desperation from which there was no return. Remy felt pity well up in her, which was terrifying. *NO!* She wanted to scream. She felt like she really was dealing with a demon. Someone so tricky he could make you believe anything.

"Oh, Remy, I'm so sorry," Ellis said. He sank to his knees and looked down at the ground. "I was there. I-I saw it happen…I heard her screams…." He looked up into her eyes again, and she saw the raw anguish in his soul. "And I remember the pain…oh, my God, the pain….and I made her feel it…Lucy probably never hurt anyone in her whole life…and she's small…God, she's so small…."

Remy nodded, tears welling up when she remembered how tiny Lucy had looked in Jesse's arms as she lay there, pale and limp.

"I'm so sorry," Ellis whispered, and Remy could feel deep in her heart that he meant it. Somehow, she just *knew.* He wasn't evil, and he wasn't lying. He was a shell of a man who was worn down by life and his eternal death.

"Remy, sweet girl, I'm so sorry," he whispered.

Still on his knees, Ellis looked down at the ground. And disappeared.

Remy turned and began to walk away. She was shaking, her footsteps unsteady as she headed to her car.

"Remy," came a deep voice behind her.

Remy gasped and whirled around.

"Oh, darlin', I didn't mean to frighten ye!" Avery said, eyes wide.

"Avery!" Remy said, her shoulders slumping with relief.

"I couldn't let ye go it alone. I've been worryin' about ye all day.

Are ye all right?" Avery asked, touching her cheek. The familiar coolness of his touch calmed her.

"Yes. Yes, I'm okay. Thank you for coming to check on me." Remy said gratefully. Oh, how wonderful it was to be *loved*. She thought for a moment, then glanced over at where Ellis had disappeared. "I couldn't see you, but he must have been able to."

Avery nodded. "He knew I was here."

Remy stared at where Ellis had been, then back at Avery. "Is he still here?"

Avery nodded. "Yes."

"I better go," Remy said, wanting to get out of there. "I love you, Avery. I'll see you tomorrow."

"I love you, too, *a chuisle*."

Chapter 21

Several weeks went by, and no one had seen or heard from Ellis. Remy wondered where he was hiding, since he couldn't vanish much anymore. She felt stupid, not to mention disloyal to her dearest friends, for worrying about him. Still, she found she couldn't help it. He had seemed so agonized the last time she had seen him that day at Culp's Hill when he told her how sorry he was. Remy couldn't imagine the bleakness, the endless midnight of his existence, from which he had no escape.

They had a quiet tour group today, so Remy was able to sit with Avery at Little Round Top while the tourists explored the hilltop. A grandfatherly type of man from her group grinned knowingly when he saw Remy sitting with her handsome soldier.

"Hey, now, I didn't know Jennie Wade had a suitor!" the old man said with a friendly wink.

"Ah, but she did!" Remy informed him with a friendly smile. "Jack Skelly, a corporal in the 87th Pennsylvania. He died just a few weeks before she did, though she died before she got the news." Remy lowered her voice, then said, "But don't give away the ending to the other tourists. You're not supposed to find that out until a later stop!"

The man laughed, eyes twinkling, and seemed utterly charmed by her. He exchanged a warm smile with Avery as he went on his way to explore.

Remy smiled at Avery and said, "And what a handsome suitor you are, Avery."

"Why, thank ye, miss," Avery said.

Remy let out a sigh. He looked at her with concern, so she figured she might as well confess what was on her mind. "It's so stupid of me, but I can't help worrying about Ellis."

Avery's expression darkened. "He been botherin' you?"

"No, no. I mean, I'm worried *about* him. I know I shouldn't be. After what he did to Lucy, I shouldn't give a damn what happens to him. But I do. He was such a mess the last time I saw him."

Avery nodded. "That he was."

Remy looked up to see Jesse standing nearby. He didn't look happy. "I-I'm sorry, Jesse. I'm not defending what he did or anything," Remy said.

"I know you're not," Jesse said wearily. "And I didn't mean to listen in on what you were sayin'."

"It's okay," Remy said. It wasn't like she and Avery could have a personal conversation with so many tourists around anyway.

"Maybe he finally crossed over," Avery offered hopefully, looking at Jesse and Remy.

"It's possible, but I doubt it," Remy said. "He was a wreck the last time I saw him."

"Good," Jesse said bitterly.

"I know I should hate him for what he did, Jesse," Remy said, looking at him sorrowfully. "But I think he really is sorry for what he did. Not that it makes up for anything. Not even close. But he was watching that day, and he was horrified at what Lucy went through."

"Why?" Jesse said, voice rising. "He's the one who did it to her!"

"Yes, he did. And it was despicable of him," Remy said, picturing

Lucy lying on the ground, writhing in pain. "But I think he'd give anything to take it back."

Jesse's rage continued to rise. Remy could see his muscles tense and his fists clench, and she found herself wishing Jesse could punch Ellis right in the face. Truth was, it would have made both men feel better. Ellis wanted to do penance for his horrible deed, but he couldn't.

"He's always been terrified to cross over," Remy said softly. "He's afraid he's going to hell."

"*I hope he does go to hell!*" Jesse said menacingly, struggling not to lose his temper and make a public scene. "Christ, Remy. How can you possibly defend him?"

Remy had never seen Jesse so mad, and it hurt that he was angry at her. But she knew he had every right to be furious with her. She *was* crazy to defend Ellis, and both he and Lucy deserved so much better.

"Jesse, I can't imagine how hard this is for you," Avery said, his eyes full of empathy. "But please don't yell at her."

Jesse's face softened just a bit as he looked at Avery.

"Remy understands Ellis on a level that none of us could ever do. Her family was terrible to her, so she knows what he went through in life and now in death. She understands what that kind of abusive home life does to a person."

Jesse looked at Remy sorrowfully. He was such a gentle soul, and didn't want to see her suffer, no matter how angry he was.

Avery looked at Remy with love and affection. "Just like Lucy feels the physical pain of soldiers, I believe Remy can feel other's emotional pain. She just…understands."

Remy gazed into Avery's eyes, amazed at how well he understood her. He knew her so well, and their connection ran so deep. They were soulmates in the most literal sense of the word. She didn't even know how she would be able to breathe if he crossed over and left her behind.

Tearing her gaze from Avery, she turned to Jesse and said softly, "I'm so sorry, Jesse."

"Hey," Jesse said firmly. "It's like Sean said, you didn't do it. Ellis did. It's okay, Remy."

Jesse's hard expression was back, and she knew it wasn't really okay. He was angry that Remy felt sorry for Ellis, but he didn't hate her for it. They were still friends. Remy knew she'd better quit talking about Ellis with Jesse around. It was the least she could do to keep from traumatizing Jesse further. God knows he had suffered enough.

It wasn't until many weeks later that she finally caught sight of Ellis. It was at Culp's Hill in the middle of the day during one of the tours. Jesse was preoccupied, racing one of the kids from the tour up those millions of stairs to get to the top of the huge metal lookout tower. Remy's legs hurt just watching them.

She turned and saw Ellis, quietly standing among the rocks and looking at her. God knows how many times he'd been there during her tours lately, but she couldn't see him if he chose to be invisible.

Remy walked over to Ellis and stood in front of him. He looked haunted, sorrowful, but there was also a glint of hope in his eye.

"How's Avery?" Ellis asked. "Is he making any progress with his counseling?"

Remy sighed wearily. The fear of losing Avery seemed to crush her more and more each day. "Not really. Sometimes I'm afraid I'm holding him back." Even as she spoke the words, she had no idea why she was confiding in Ellis of all people. It was strange, but for some reason she felt he would understand. "Maybe he really just wants to be with his daughter and his worrying about me is keeping him stuck here. It's probably me and my selfishness."

Ellis laughed so loudly that it made Remy jump. He looked at her fondly. "You don't even know how to be selfish. You can trust me—I'm an expert on the subject." He fell silent for a moment, and then said, "That day I hurt Lucy…Jesse kept sayin' over and over, 'I wish it was me, why can't this happen to me instead of her.' You'd do that for Avery. If you had to let go of 'im, let him cross over, I think it'd hurt you just as bad as havin' your leg torn off your body. But you'd do it anyway. You'd do it for him."

Remy's eyes welled up with tears. "I would. If it would make him happy, I would let him go."

Ellis nodded sadly. "I wish I could bring him back to you, Remy. I'd give up my own soul if I could make that happen."

Remy stared at him, feeling the truth behind his words. *He would really do it, too.*

"Why can't you just stay the hell away from her?" Jesse snarled angrily as he charged toward them.

"Jesse!" Ellis said, looking strangely relieved to see him. "Jesse, I want to tell you I'm so sorry for hurting that sweet girl of yours. Lucy didn't deserve that. She's an angel and—"

"Yes! She is!" Jesse snapped, eyes blazing. He leaned in close to Ellis's face and said in a low, threatening voice, "And you better pray to God you don't need my forgiveness to get into heaven, 'cause you ain't never gonna get it. You can burn in hell for all I care." Jesse stared at him coldly, then walked away.

"You're right. Lucy didn't deserve to suffer like that," Remy said softly to Ellis. "But neither did you."

That tiny sliver of hope was back in Ellis's eyes.

Remy gathered her skirt and rushed over to calm Jesse.

*****

Remy had dinner with Lucy and Jesse that night at Jesse's insistence. She was afraid he would be furious with her, but he seemed more worried than anything else. He didn't like Remy being anywhere near Ellis, fearing that his sorrow was just an act to set some kind of trap for her.

As always, the dinner Lucy had prepared was delicious. Spaghetti and meatballs with garlic bread. Remy probably ate more in one meal at their place than she would in a week of small frozen dinners in her apartment. It was such a relief to have a full stomach for once!

Remy and Jesse had explained their encounter with Ellis as best they could, trying not to upset Lucy. She did her best to stay calm, but it was clear that Lucy was nearly as angry as Jesse was.

"I'm not ready to forgive him, that's for damn sure!" Lucy said, and Jesse nodded his approval. "It was just so awful…and he went through the same thing, so he *knew* what he was doing to me. I mean, God…the *pain*…you just can't imagine how horrible it was."

"No, I can't," Remy said in a small voice, feeling like a wretched, ungrateful person for feeling sorry for Ellis when he had viciously harmed her best friend.

Lucy glanced over at Jesse, who looked devastated just thinking about what happened. Lucy clenched her teeth. "And I *hate* him for putting Jesse through that. He still blames himself for what happened to me at Devil's Den. He shouldn't, but he does. And it's like he had to go through it all over again."

Lucy looked into his eyes and squeezed his hand.

"I know," Remy said. "I don't know what I would do if I had to stand back and watch Avery suffer like that." The mere thought of someone torturing Avery made her sick to her stomach. "I'm so sorry, Lucy."

Lucy gave her a reassuring smile. "It's not your fault, Remy. And I'm not mad at you. I won't say I understand why you feel sorry for him, because I don't. But I'll be damned if I let that awful man mess up our friendship, so don't stress about it, okay?"

"Exactly," Jesse said, nodding. "I don't know why you care what happens to him, but you do. I'm mad at him, not you, got it?"

Remy nodded gratefully at him.

"Well, one thing's for sure," Lucy said, looking at Remy. "If you don't help him, nobody will."

Exactly right, thought Remy.

Chapter 22

This has been such a nice place to work, Lucy thought as she swept up the restaurant's dining room, *but I'm not going to miss these late nights.* Excitement fluttered in her stomach when she thought about the future. She would be graduating soon, and she hoped she'd find a teaching job in the fall. It would be wonderful to be around children all day, teaching them new things and getting them excited about learning. She smiled softly to herself as she finished her work.

"Well, hello my lovely rose," came Jesse's deep voice from the back of the room.

Lucy smile widened when she saw her favorite person in the whole world. "What are you doing here so late?"

Jesse hardly ever came by the restaurant this late at night anymore since Ellis had stopped bothering her, though Avery still checked on her frequently just in case.

"I missed you," Jesse said with a grin.

"And you couldn't wait a half hour until I got done with work?" Lucy said with a laugh. She put down her broom and went over to wrap her arms around him. He was just so damned irresistible.

Jesse pressed his lips to hers in a sweet kiss. She brushed back the hair from his forehead and looked down at his outfit. He was wearing his work clothes—his usual gray wool pants, white shirt, and suspenders.

"Having you dressed like this and visiting me here reminds me of when we first met," Lucy said fondly. "I loved having you here, but I was so nervous around you!"

"I was nervous, too," Jesse said. "You were so beautiful and so sweet, I just couldn't take my eyes off you. Still can't."

Lucy kissed him again, and then said, "Well, I better finish up. Shouldn't take me too long."

"Okay, darlin," Jesse said, then he released her. "Oh, wait. There was just one thing I wanted to ask you."

Then he got down on one knee.

Lucy stared down at him with astonishment.

"Lucy, I love you with all my heart. I've been in love with you since the first moment I laid eyes on you," Jesse said as he lovingly looked up at her.

She looked down into those precious, blue-gray eyes of his and was utterly overwhelmed with love for him. He took a ring from his pocket and held it up to her.

He gazed at her for a moment, then said, "Lucy Ann Westbrook, will you be my wife?"

Lucy gasped. She could hardly believe what was happening. She had always known she would spend the rest of her life with him. Having him by her side felt like a miracle every single day, but somehow she hadn't given much thought to making it official.

She stared down at the ring. "H-how did you…"

Jesse grinned. "Put in some overtime at work while you was workin' late so I could get it for you. I know it's not much."

Lucy looked down at the gold ring with its tiny diamond. She couldn't imagine how hard he must have worked to afford it. The ring was sweet and humble, just like Jesse. Lucy could not imagine a more beautiful piece of jewelry. She was stunned, overwhelmed, and doing her best not to burst into tears.

"Lucy?" Jesse said, looking a little worried. She realized she hadn't given him an answer yet.

"Oh, Jesse," Lucy said, her voice trembling with emotion. "*Of course* I'll be your wife!"

Jesse grinned that boyish grin of his that still made her heart pound. Tears spilled from her eyes, and Jesse had to hold her left hand steady so he could slip the ring on her finger.

"Jesse!" Lucy cried. He stood up and she threw her arms around him. He hugged her so tightly that he lifted her off the ground.

He finally released her, looked into her eyes for a moment, then kissed her.

"I love you so much, my rose."

"I love you, too," Lucy said.

Jesse suddenly took a step back from her, a mischievous grin on his face.

"What are you up to, cowboy?" Lucy asked suspiciously.

Jesse drew in a deep breath, and then shouted, "She said *YES!*"

The door to the restaurant kitchen burst open, and out came Theresa, Sean, Remy, and Avery.

"Sean!" Theresa yelled. "Quick, open this!" With that, she thrust a bottle of champagne into her boyfriend's hands.

Sean laughed, then popped open the bottle. Theresa grabbed it from him and raced toward Lucy, squealing. She grabbed Lucy in a forceful embrace, spilling champagne on her.

"Sorry, babe! Got champagne in your hair!"

Lucy laughed and said happily, "I don't care!"

Remy ran over, too, and the three embraced each other, laughing.

"You planned all this?" Lucy asked Jesse.

He nodded proudly. "Craig and Mandy and all your coworkers

left already so we could have a private party."

Lucy sighed happily. Jesse had planned the *perfect* proposal. A public proposal would have made her uncomfortable and would have been all wrong for her. This way, he'd popped the question in private, but she still got to celebrate with her friends.

"I want to be the first to make a toast!" Remy said. Theresa ducked behind the bar and started pouring champagne. At first, Remy just grabbed an empty glass.

"Wait, give it here," Theresa said, gesturing at the glass. Remy handed it over, and Theresa filled it with soda water for her.

"Thanks," Remy said, happily accepting the glass. She waited until everyone else—except Avery, of course—had a glass of champagne. She took a deep breath and looked at Lucy and Jesse. "Okay, here goes. I'll never forget when Jesse Spenser first came to work for the Blue and Gray Touring Company, because I developed a *mad* crush on him pretty much the moment I met him."

Lucy gasped. She covered her mouth, giggling. She looked at Jesse, who looked equally surprised. Jesse glanced at Avery, who chuckled and nodded, making it clear that this was not news to him.

"Then, I met Lucy," Remy said, and everyone laughed knowingly. "And it wasn't just that Jesse was taken. I took one look at the two of them, and I knew she had his heart forever. When I saw them together, I just knew that they had that amazing, everlasting kind of love. And this was before I knew the incredible tale of how Jesse managed to cheat death to be with her." Remy's voice shook a little when she said that part, and everyone in the room knew why. Their looks of empathy and understanding threatened to overwhelm her, so she knew that she'd better wrap it up. She raised her glass and said, "To Lucy and Jesse, and to their happy ever after."

"Hear, hear!" Theresa shouted, and they all toasted the happy couple.

Remy walked over to Lucy and Jesse, looking slightly abashed when she glanced at Jesse.

"I can't believe it!" Jesse said. "You liked me first, then you threw me off for the Irish guy!"

Remy laughed, and Lucy's heart swelled with affection for Jesse. It was the perfect thing for him to say to ease any discomfort Remy might have felt over her confession.

"What can I say?" Remy said, looking at Avery with fondness. Then she turned to Lucy and said, "I'm sorry, but I *have* to know." Remy glanced around at the room, then back at her friend. "Where?"

"Where what?" Lucy asked.

"Where did you two, you know…"

Lucy groaned and hid her face in Jesse's shoulder. Jesse laughed, and stroked her hair. When Lucy lifted her head, she saw that *everyone* was looking at her, waiting for her answer.

Lucy slowly walked over to the bartop near where Theresa had just been pouring drinks. She put her hand on the section of the bar where she and Jesse had made love, then turned around. Flushing a deep red, she laughed, letting her friends know that it was all right to tease her about it.

Theresa starting applauding, and the others joined in. "All right, *Luce!*"

Jesse walked over and put his arm around Lucy, laughing. "I'm sorry, honey."

"No, you're not," Lucy said with a smile.

Jesse shrugged guiltily. "Well, I'm a *little* sorry."

"Got started on the honeymoon a little early, did ya, Jesse?" Sean teased, then fist-bumped him. "Okay, now *I* want to make a toast."

"Be nice," Jesse warned Sean, waggling a finger at him, then glancing at Lucy. Jesse seemed to appreciate that Lucy had a sense of humor about discussing their sex life, but he didn't want the teasing to make her too uncomfortable.

Sean raised his glass and said, "To the most wonderful couple I have ever known. Jesse, I know you're gonna be chasing Lucy around furniture even when you're old and gray. To a long and happy life together. Cheers!"

Lucy laughed along with everyone else as they clinked glasses. She reveled in the warmth and happiness of being with her loved ones.

Jesse put his glass down, and as soon as Lucy put hers on the table, he grabbed her and dipped her down low, kissing her. When he put her back on her feet, she looked over to see Theresa and Sean kissing as well.

Avery and Remy stood off to the side, their grief at not being able to touch each other palpable.

Lucy walked over and looked at the both of them sorrowfully. "I understand," she said softly. "God knows I understand. We just have to keep praying for another miracle."

Remy nodded, then said, "Oh, Lucy, please don't worry about us. This is your night. I'm so happy for you both!"

Lucy could see the joy in her dear friend's eyes. Remy was happiest when others were happy.

Remy hugged Lucy warmly, then Avery blew her a kiss.

"Congratulations," Avery said with a smile. "Your joy is our joy."

*****

Lucy and Jesse had asked Fillis to meet them at a quiet spot on the grounds of Gettysburg College. They wanted to tell her the happy news, and they also had a few other important things they wanted to discuss with her. Theresa, Remy, and Avery were there as well. For support. They all loved Second Mama, and they wanted what was best for her. It would be almost like an intervention of sorts, and Lucy hoped it went well.

"Well, well, the gang's all here!" Fillis said as she walked up to them. She looked slightly worried at first, but visibly relaxed when she saw all their happy faces. She looked lovingly at all her adopted children, reserving her fondest look for Jesse, who had been her baby for longer than any of them. Much, much longer.

Fillis sat down next to Jesse and said, "Now. What's this all about?"

"We have some good news to share," Lucy said, holding up her left hand and showing off her ring.

Fillis's eyes opened wide. "Oh, my land!" She stared down at the ring, then looked from Lucy to Jesse. "Will you look at that? My baby's getting married!"

"Yes, Second Mama," Jesse said, his face glowing with happiness. "I sure am."

"Jesse, my God. Could you ever have imagined?" Fillis looked at him in wonder. "Oh, I remember settin' with him when he was still dead. He was so heartbroken over you, Lucy. Thinkin' he could never be with you. He never even imagined you could love him back!"

"'Til I got drunk and told him how I felt," Lucy said with a laugh.

Fillis laughed, too. "Yes. He came and told me and says, 'She loves me, Second Mama. She loves me!' I ain't never seen him happier. Well, 'til just now."

Jesse put his arm around Lucy, and they both smiled at Fillis. It felt good to see her so happy.

"But you know, Second Mama," Jesse said gently, pulling away from Lucy a bit and focusing on Fillis. "Lucy's family lives in Maryland and, well, when we get married, we're planning on moving down there."

"I understand," Fillis said, with sadness in her eyes.

Fillis wasn't the only one who looked sorrowful. Lucy saw Remy's pained look when she heard the news about her and Jesse moving away. Lucy felt awful. It hadn't even occurred to her how this would affect Remy. Besides Theresa and Sean, Lucy and Jesse were her only family. Lucy made a mental note to talk with her, to reassure her that Maryland was just a short car ride away, and that they would still see her as much as possible.

"We're hopin' she can get a teachin' job around there, and I'll be so glad to get her away from Gettysburg. It's gettin' more dangerous for her 'round these battlegrounds every day and I just can't stand the thought of her gettin' hurt again," Jesse said, looked devastated just thinking of what had happened to Lucy.

"Amen to that!" Fillis said, looking equally worried. "I understand, child. I want you to get on with your life. Your *life,* Jesse! I still cain't believe it!"

"I don't know how you do it, Second Mama," Theresa said. "You've loved and lost so many of the soldiers around here. All those guys you loved as your own, only to have them always leave you to cross over."

"That's the way it should be," Fillis said, though the heartbreak was written all over her face. First she'd had to lose the children from the plantation she'd lived on. Helene's two sons and her daughter, whom Fillis loved as her own. Then after she'd died, she'd loved and nurtured so many others, only to have them cross over and leave her behind. It was too much grief for any mother to bear.

"We still want to help you cross over and be at peace," Lucy said gently. "Fillis, I think it's time."

Fillis opened her mouth, ready to dismiss the idea, but Lucy held firm.

"Just hear me out!" Lucy insisted. "I was able to find some information on the Bellflower plantation online. And I found some information on Helene."

Fillis stared at Lucy, as everything around them went still and quiet. She nodded slowly. Lucy could see the fear in the old woman's eyes. Fear that Lucy would tell her that something horrible became of the woman she loved after Fillis ran away from her home.

"The Master didn't kill her, Fillis. In fact, he only lived for a few more years after you died."

"Oh, thank the sweet lord! Dear God, I just hope he didn't beat her…or hurt her none." Fillis said, her voice shaking with anxiety and grief. Her love for the master's wife was as strong now as it had been one hundred and fifty years ago.

"I don't think he did, Fillis. I've read up on the history of the plantation , and there's no record of any harm coming to her," Lucy said, thankful that she didn't have to break the woman's heart. "Did you know that the plantation is still open?"

"It is? How's that possible? After all this time!" Fillis said in wonder.

"It's an historical landmark now. A place where tourists can visit. You know those gardens that Helene used to take care of? They're still there! The place is known for their amazing flowers, and people come from all over to see them!" Lucy said excitedly.

"You mean they's people walkin' all over through her gardens?" Fillis asked.

Lucy nodded slowly, fearing she might have upset the poor woman. She exchanged a concerned look with Jesse.

"My God, she would've loved that," Fillis said softly.

"Really?" Lucy asked hopefully.

"Oh, my, *yes!* Them flowers were her pride and joy. To think…they's people walking around admirin' her lovely gardens. Oh, she'd be tickled pink!"

Lucy smiled, then picked up her tablet device and unlocked the screen. "I have some pictures online of the gardens as they are now. Would you like to see them?"

"Oh, Lucy, I would love that," Fillis said, her face filled with emotion. Lucy couldn't imagine all the memories she had locked away in her heart. Precious memories of the woman she had loved for almost two centuries.

Lucy pulled up the website of the Bellflower plantation and showed Fillis the photo gallery of the lush gardens. The photographs were like something from a fairytale. All those vibrant colors of flowers, the green of the trees, and there was a tranquil lake and a lovely, romantic bridge that covered the water. It was so breathtaking that it made it frighteningly easy to forget the horrors of slavery that lurked behind all that beauty.

"My God, it's just as I remember," Fillis said softly.

"Fillis," Lucy said gently, trying not to break the spell that Fillis was under. "Someone painted a portrait of Helene. Would you like to see a picture of it?"

Fillis looked up at Lucy, eyes filled with hope. "Very much," she whispered.

Lucy nodded, then scrolled through the website's photo gallery. She found the portrait, then put the tablet in front of Fillis so she could see.

Fillis let out a choked sob when she saw the portrait of Helene. The woman had a lovely, kind face. Her hair was brown and her eyes a soft gray, a lot like Avery's eyes. Lucy thought she was beautiful. She found herself drawn to the woman in the photo, as anyone loved so dearly by Fillis was precious to her as well. Lucy knew in her heart that it was time the two were reunited in a place where they would never, ever be torn apart again.

"Fillis," Lucy said softly. "We want you to cross over to be with her. You've done your maternal duty long enough, and it's time for you to go home."

Fillis looked up at Lucy uncertainly, but for the first time, she didn't protest immediately at the thought.

Remy got up and moved closer to Fillis. "Second Mama, we've been talking to Mary over at Farnsworth. I know you're good friends with her, and you know how she cares for all the guests who stay at the inn, watching over them. She said she's more than happy to take care of the soldiers after you're gone."

Fillis sat still, taking in Remy's words. She looked at Helene's picture again and said quietly, "I miss her so much."

Jesse spoke up softly, saying, "Promise me you'll at least think about going home to her."

After a moment of silent reflection, Fillis nodded.

Chapter 23

The next evening, Remy went to visit with Ellis at Culp's Hill. This time he was visible, and she wondered if he'd been waiting for her. His eyes lit up when he saw her, the look of hope in his eyes beautiful and heartbreaking at the same time. Empathy overwhelmed her, and she hoped she wasn't a fool for opening her heart to him again.

"I'm so happy to see you, Remy. How are you doing?"

"I'm okay," Remy answered. She smiled and added, "Lucy and Jesse got engaged last night."

Remy was surprised at the warmth in Ellis's smile. "That's nice. I'm really happy for them."

"Me too, but," Remy hesitated.

"What's wrong?" Ellis asked, looking concerned.

"They're gonna move to Maryland where Lucy's family lives. I'm happy they're getting married, but I don't want them to go," Remy said, feeling a heavy sadness in her heart.

"Maryland's not so far away," Ellis said in a soothing voice. "Hell, lots of us guys marched through there on the way to Gettysburg. And nowadays? It's nothin' by car. You'll still see 'em all the time, Remy."

Remy smiled gratefully and nodded. Ellis was much kinder nowadays and hadn't said a single nasty word since that horrible day when Lucy felt his death. They sat in silence for a while as they often did.

Finally, Ellis asked, "Do you think I do need Lucy's forgiveness to cross over? Or Jesse's?"

"No, I don't. I think you need to forgive yourself. Theresa and Lucy always told me that's what really keeps ghosts stuck here. They don't make it to heaven until they believe they're worthy of it."

Ellis scoffed. "I ain't worthy. Never was, never will be. I don't belong in heaven with all them good people. Besides, spirits around here, they got family waitin' on 'em in heaven. Not me. There's nobody for me there. Nobody I want to see, and nobody who wants to see me."

Remy didn't know what to say to comfort Ellis. He was right. He had no loved ones waiting for him on the other side. *How sad for him,* she thought.

"It doesn't matter. I don't deserve salvation."

"Of course you do, Ellis."

"*No, I don't!*" Ellis yelled. He looked at her sadly. "I'm sorry, Remy. I didn't mean to holler at you. But I'm not worthy. I'm a terrible person. I'm a murderer. And even in death, I managed to hurt people. I don't want to be saved."

"I want you to be saved. What about what I want?" Remy asked him.

Ellis looked into her eyes and said, "I wish I could give you everything you want. I wish I could make Avery alive again so he could love you and protect you the way you deserve. I wish I could make sure that you were never hungry or cold or lonely ever again."

"That's so sweet of you, Ellis," Remy told him, nearly choking up with emotion at his kindness. After a moment, she said, "But that's not all I want. I want you to be happy and at peace. That's what *you* deserve. You've made mistakes, but you've also had a very hard life.

You're not a terrible person, Ellis. You're my *friend.*"

"I'm so sorry I ever doubted you. And I would give anything, *anything* if I could take back what I did to Lucy. Don't you think what I did to her was unforgivable?" Ellis asked plaintively.

"To Jesse, it is," Remy admitted. Jesse was a kind and gentle soul, but hurting Lucy was the one cardinal sin he probably couldn't ever forgive. "But you don't need his forgiveness."

Ellis looked weary and hopeless, and Remy wished she could hold him in her arms and somehow make him feel worthy of love.

"I'm going to give you a homework assignment, Ellis, for you to work on after I leave. Will you promise to do it?"

Ellis looked at her quizzically. He lifted his ghost hands. "What can I possibly do?"

"Promise me," Remy said firmly, but with a smile.

Ellis returned the smile and said, "I promise."

Wow, Remy thought. There was a time not so long ago that he would have screamed at her for far less.

"Ellis," Remy said in a soft, soothing voice. "I want you to think back to the little boy you were when your mother abused you. Can you do that?"

Ellis nodded slowly.

"I want you to talk to the boy you once were. I want you to tell that precious child that what happened to him was not his fault. His mother did awful, confusing, scary things to that sweet, innocent little boy. Things he didn't understand. Things he still doesn't understand. I want you to tell that beautiful little boy that he deserved a mother who loved and protected him. One who cherished him and held him in her arms the way a mother is supposed to do."

Ellis's look of pain and anguish hurt Remy so badly that she nearly didn't go on. *Keep going,* she told herself. *It hurts him, but he has to face it to heal him. Like when Jesse had to pick up Lucy and carry her away from the building. At first it hurt her, but then it healed her.*

"Then I want you to think back to the young man you were at war. I want you to talk to him, too. Tell him he didn't deserve to be betrayed by somebody he loved while he was fighting so far away from home. Tell him it was okay to be angry, but it wasn't okay to kill those men. Tell him that he did a horrible thing, but then gently remind him that he can't change it. Tell that young man he's not unforgivable. He's not unlovable. Ask him to tell those men and their wives and their children that he's sorry for hurting them. They're all in heaven, Ellis, and they can hear what's in your heart. Ask their forgiveness. Then ask God for forgiveness. And then, Ellis, ask yourself for forgiveness."

Ellis closed his eyes and hung his head. His shoulders trembled in a tearless sob.

Please God, bring him home to you, Remy though. *End his suffering. Bring him peace.*

"I won't give up on you, Ellis. Don't give up on yourself."

Ellis nodded, eyes closed.

Remy quietly got up and left before he opened his eyes again.

*****

Over the next few weeks, Remy continued to visit with Ellis. Sometimes she would give him different affirmations to work on, and sometimes they would just sit quietly together. But the overall theme of their visits was the same. Worthiness and forgiveness. The change was subtle, but Ellis did seem calmer and more at peace now.

Avery, meanwhile, never seemed to make any progress. He was still stuck halfway between life and death, between Remy and his daughter, Charlotte. Remy, too, seemed perpetually trapped between the emotions of hope that he could come back and despair that she would lose him forever.

It was a warm Saturday afternoon and Remy, Avery, Jesse, and Lucy were walking down the street after visiting with Fillis when Ellis came running toward them. Jesse's eyes blazed, and he stepped forward, as if to stop him from getting near Lucy or Remy. Ellis ignored Jesse, looking past him like he wasn't there.

"Remy!" Ellis said, eyes wide. "I have to…I'm supposed to go to Culp's Hill *right now!*"

"Really?" Remy asked, her heart swelling with hope for him. "That must mean it's your time!"

"Y-yes, I think so," Ellis's voice dropped to a whisper, and his face was filled with horror. "Oh, Remy, I'm so scared."

"It's all right, Ellis. You're not going to hell," Remy reassured him, but she knew her face probably betrayed her own fears. She was hardly an expert on the afterlife, and it was certainly possible that Ellis wouldn't make it to heaven.

"I have to go. *Now.*" Ellis turned as if he were being physically shoved toward his final destination.

"I'll go with you!" Remy said, rushing to catch up to him.

"So will I," Lucy said. She turned to follow them, but Jesse grabbed her arm so hard that she cried out in pain.

"Lucy, no!" Jesse's eyes were wide with fear. "You can't go there. It's a battlefield."

Ellis managed to stop running and turned around.

"It's all right, Jesse," Lucy said in a calm but firm voice. "He didn't die at Culp's Hill. He died near the railroad building."

"Who cares? Lots of other soldiers died there! What if you knew one of 'em? And why do you even care about that guy? He practically tried to kill you!" Jesse cried, sounding more panicked than angry.

Remy knew Jesse was right to be scared when she heard the determination in Lucy's voice. Lucy was sensitive and shy, but she was much stronger than people gave her credit for. There was no talking her out of something once her mind was made up.

"Jesse, he's terrified," Lucy said, her eyes filled with compassion. "And I want to be there to support him. And Remy."

"Please, Lucy," Jesse begged, looking nearly as terrified as Ellis. Lucy hesitated just a moment. After all, Jesse was her Kryptonite.

"I'll be all right." Lucy turned to Ellis and Remy and said, "Let's go."

Jesse let out an anguished moan.

Ellis stared at Lucy in wonder and said, "My God, you're so *brave.*"

"You're damn right she is," Jesse said, glaring at Ellis. "You should never confuse kindness with weakness."

Ellis nodded, then turned and headed toward Culp's Hill.

The five of them walked briskly toward the battlefield, with Remy doing her best to reassure Ellis that everything would be all right. Avery fell into step next to Jesse, trying to keep him calm and assure him that Lucy would be all right.

They got to Culp's Hill, and everything was quiet. Ellis glanced around, looking bewildered and petrified.

"Wh-what do I do? What happens now?" Ellis asked.

"I don't know," Remy said, wishing she knew what to tell him.

"All you have to do is wait, Ellis," Lucy told him. "When the time comes, you'll—"

Suddenly, a large, blindingly bright portal appeared near the rocks where Ellis and Remy always sat and talked.

Ellis staggered back from the portal, visibly terrified for his immortal soul.

"Remy!" Ellis pleaded in terror, as if there was anything she could do to stop the will of God, whatever that might be.

Remy rushed to his side and stood next to him as they both stared at the portal. A blond-haired, blue-eyed man with a mischievous smile stepped out of the portal.

"Who is that?" Remy whispered.

Ellis rapidly shook his head. "I-I don't know."

The blond man turned and winked at Lucy. "Hey, sweetheart."

"Joel!" Lucy cried joyfully.

Ellis whipped his head around and looked at Lucy.

"This is my friend, Joel," Lucy told Ellis with a reassuring smile. "And he's from *heaven*."

Ellis slowly turned his head and looked at Joel and the portal behind him. Remy watched as an otherworldly expression of peace came over Ellis's face. He was going home to heaven. In watching his tranquil face, it seemed like he was halfway there already.

"Ellis, my name is Joel Casey, and I'm here to take you home." Joel smiled warmly at Ellis.

Ellis nodded, the look of peace growing even stronger somehow.

"You can have a few minutes to say goodbye to your friends," Joel told him. Then added gently, "You can touch them now."

Ellis turned and walked straight toward Lucy. Jesse took a step forward, but Remy reached up and grabbed him by the shoulder.

"It's okay, Jesse," Remy told him.

Jesse stared at Ellis, ready to rush over and scoop Lucy up in his arms if need be.

Ellis looked tenderly at Lucy and said, "Lucy, I am so sorry for hurting you."

"I forgive you," Lucy whispered.

He bowed his head to her and said, "Thank you." He looked up at her again and told her, "I'm so sorry for all those horrible things I said to you. You're a lady, and you deserve to be treated like one."

Jesse visibly tensed as Ellis reached for Lucy's hand. He kissed it gently, then looked fondly down at her engagement ring. He looked into her eyes and said, "You're going to be the most beautiful bride."

Lucy's eyes lit up, and she smiled like she always did when anyone spoke of her marrying Jesse.

Ellis turned to face Remy. She relished the incredible calmness and quiet joy on his face. That haunted look had vanished, and she knew his days and nights of suffering were over.

"Remy, I don't even have the words..." Ellis began.

"You don't have to say anything, Ellis. I am just so happy for you!" Remy's bright blue eyes lit up with joy. She would miss him, but she would sleep better at night knowing he was safe in heaven. Safe and loved and whole again.

"I should tell you that I lied to you before," Ellis said with a grin full of mischief. "You actually have *great* tits."

Remy burst into laughter. "Thank you. I think."

"Oh, Remy. I'm so much in love with you."

Ellis had said the words so casually that they didn't register in Remy's brain at first. "Wh- what?" Remy said, staring at him.

"I think that's probably why I flipped out so bad." Ellis looked over at Lucy apologetically. "Not that it's *any* excuse for what I did, but I was falling in love with you and, well, the last time I fell in love it didn't turn out so well. So when I thought you betrayed me, I just snapped."

Ellis looked at her so adoringly that Remy couldn't believe how oblivious she had been to his feelings for her. Had she known, she wouldn't have gone on and on about how much she loved Avery. She would never have twisted the knife in Ellis's heart on purpose.

"No one in my life or in my death has ever been so kind and so unbelievably *patient* with me. I don't know how you did it! But you stuck with me. You *saved* me."

"You saved yourself," Remy said, still trying to recover from the shock of his profession of love for her. "I just reminded you that you were worth saving."

"Remy," Ellis said, looking her directly in the eye. He grabbed hold of her shoulders, and she gasped in surprise that he could touch her. "I know that Avery is the man you love." Ellis looked up at Avery with a smile and said, "You're all she ever talks about, man."

Avery stared at him, stunned. He couldn't get over Ellis's confession either.

Ellis gazed into Remy's eyes again and said firmly, "I know how much you love him. Remy, I swear, when I get to the other side, if there is *any way* that Avery can come back to life to be with you, *I will find it,* you hear me?"

Remy nodded, eyes filling with hopeful tears.

Ellis wrapped his arms around her and held her tight. "I'm not giving up on you and Avery, so don't you give up, you hear?"

"Yes," she whispered.

Ellis pulled away from her, looking at her one last time.

"Thank you for everything, Remy. Goodbye, sweet girl."

With that, Ellis walked over to the portal and reached for Joel's outstretched hand. Just before Joel pulled him to the other side, he looked at Jesse and shouted, "And by the way, *screw you, Secesh!*"

Jesse laughed heartily, then flipped him the middle finger.

"Some things never change," Lucy said, looking at Joel and Jesse fondly.

The portal vanished, taking Ellis and Joel with it.

Avery looked at Remy and held up his hands questioningly.

"A-Avery, I swear, I had no idea that he…" Remy tried to explain.

Avery laughed that deep, sexy laugh that Remy loved. "I know, me darlin'. I could tell by the look on your face when he told you. I'm just jealous that he got to touch you."

Remy smiled fondly and said, "It was nice to hug him."

"Lucy, *please* let me take you home now," Jesse pleaded with her. He was still, understandably, a nervous wreck having her standing on a battlefield.

"Yes, yes, we can go now," Lucy said. She dashed over to Remy and threw her arms around her first, though. "Great job, Remy. He's at peace now."

"Yes," Remy said, breathing out a sigh of relief.

Jesse walked over and put his arm around Lucy, then guided her away toward the main road.

Remy turned to Avery and asked, "Do you think Ellis can help us from where he is now?"

"I don't know, *a chuisle*. I just don't know."

Chapter 24

It was a few weeks later, the day of Lucy's graduation ceremony, and Jesse was about to meet Lucy's family for the first time. He was a nervous wreck. Lucy had told him that her mother was kind, if a bit high maintenance. Her family was fairly well off, and Mrs. Westbook apparently enjoyed the finer things in life, such as designer clothes, handbags, and jewelry. Jesse couldn't help but be self-conscious about the ring he had gotten for Lucy. Her mother probably wouldn't approve of the simple ring with such a small stone, but it was all he could afford. Lucy told Jesse that, though her father complained about her mother's spending habits, he loved her dearly and seemed to genuinely enjoy indulging her.

Jesse was dressed in a suit and tie that he had bought from a local thrift store. He wiped his sweaty palms on his dress pants as he made his way across the lush lawn of Gettysburg College where Lucy's graduation would take place and where he would meet his future in-laws. His heart leapt when he saw Lucy dressed in her cap and gown. She looked so beautiful and he was so proud of her for all her hard work at school. How was it possible that a woman so smart and so lovely could have fallen for a guy like him?

"Jesse!" she happily called to him when she saw his approach.

Her mother and father turned to look at him, as did her older brother and younger sister. Jesse's throat went dry as he shakily walked toward them.

Jesse glanced at her family, then back at Lucy. She smiled reassuringly at him, then said, "Mom, Dad, this is Jesse Spenser." He relaxed slightly when he heard the love and pride in her voice when she spoke his name. "My fiancé."

Jesse couldn't help but grin, as that was the first time he'd heard her say the word "fiancé" out loud.

"Nice to meet you, Jesse," her father said, extending his hand to shake Jesse's.

Jesse firmly shook the man's hand and said, "Sir." He bowed slightly to her mother and said, "Ma'am."

Jesse's mother had been scrutinizing him pretty carefully, but she smiled softly when he called her Ma'am. He knew his Southern charm was one of his strengths.

"So nice to meet you finally. I'm Caroline, and this is my husband, Kurt. And our son, David, and daughter Alison."

David, an older man who had Lucy's brown eyes but was much taller than her, stuck out his hand and pumped Jesse's eagerly. "Nice to meet ya."

"Hi, Jesse," Alison, Lucy's high-school-aged sister, said shyly. She had her father's blue eyes and seemed to have some of Lucy's natural shyness.

"Nice to meet ya, miss," Jesse said with a smile.

Alison blushed. *Oh, yeah. She's Lucy's sister, all right.*

"I'm sorry to leave you all, but I better get going. They're going to start soon," Lucy said. She put her arms around Jesse and kissed him. "I'll see you soon, okay?"

Lucy looked worried that she was leaving him alone with her family, but he grinned at her and said, "Okay, darlin'. I'll be cheerin' for ya!"

The second Lucy was out of earshot, David snarled at Jesse, "What is wrong with you? Asking Lucy to marry you before her own family has even *met* you!"

Jesse stared at him, having no idea what to say. The silence was horrifying.

David burst out laughing, then punched Jesse on the shoulder. "Sorry man, I just hadda bust your balls. Welcome to the family!"

Jesse laughed heartily. David chuckled warmly, and just like that, the ice was broken.

"David, for heaven's sake," Caroline said. She turned to Jesse and said, "I admit I am a little concerned about Lucy getting married so young and to someone we just met, but she's got a good head on her shoulders. If she says you're the one, then you're the one. Welcome to the family, honey." With a smile filled with warmth and affection, she opened her arms, expensive bracelets jangling. Jesse eagerly hugged her back. She was nice, but she seemed unsure of him.

"Well! We better get to our seats," Caroline said.

Jesse sat next to David and was able to talk to him for a while. The guy was friendly and had a great sense of humor. Jesse found he rather liked his future brother-in-law. Alison was shy, but sweet, just like her sister. Lucy's mother still seemed wary, but who could blame her? Jesse understood that she just wanted what was best for her daughter, and she needed time to get to know him.

Jesse flipped through the graduation program and swelled with pride when he saw Lucy's name. She was graduating with honors with a Master's Degree in Education.

Lucy looked incredibly beautiful when she crossed the stage to accept her diploma. Jesse could not take his eyes off her. He heard Lucy's mother mutter, "Well, the boy's in love, that's for sure."

Jesse turned to her and said, "Yes, Mrs. Westbrook, I am in love. And I'm going to spend the rest of my life making sure your daughter never wants for anything."

Caroline's face broke into a lovely, sweet smile that looked so much like Lucy's. She looked relieved, and Jesse realized how much she just needed reassurance that her precious little girl would be happy. She wrapped her arms around Jesse and squeezed him tight.

"Thank you, honey."

The Westbrooks took everyone out to dinner after the ceremony, and it was the perfect way for the family to get to know Jesse better. Lucy's father seemed pleased at the gentlemanly way Jesse treated his daughter, and her mother seemed equally charmed. There were also times when Caroline looked at Jesse with a hint of sadness, and Jesse remembered Lucy telling him how upset she was to find out that he had no family of his own. Caroline reminded Jesse a bit of Fillis— like she wanted to adopt him as her own.

"So, I have some exciting news to share!" Lucy said, eyes sparkling. Jesse nodded and proudly put his arm around her.

Kurt and Caroline Westbrook looked slightly horrified.

Lucy giggled. "I'm not pregnant, Mom."

Caroline laughed, too, then nodded. "Not that a baby wouldn't be great news. Just not, you know, yet."

"I got a job!"

"Yeah?" David asked. "Way to go, kiddo!"

Lucy squealed. "Oh, I'm so excited. I found a job at a school only about fifteen miles from your place in Rockville. I'm gonna be teaching third grade!"

Caroline smiled happily, and reached across the table to grab her daughter's hand. "That's wonderful, Lucy. Congratulations! And third grade. Such a fun age!"

"I know," Lucy said dreamily. "I can't wait."

Jesse gazed lovingly at her. She was smart and so kind. Those were some lucky kids to have a wonderful teacher like her.

"So, Jesse and I have been talking and, well, we want to be married by then."

"By September?" Caroline asked. "*This* September?"

"Yes. We want to be married before I start working and settle into an apartment near the school. Jesse is looking for work around there now."

"But how can you plan a wedding by then?" Caroline asked.

Lucy and Jesse exchanged worried looks. "Well, that's the thing. We don't really need an actual wedding. We could just go to the courthouse and—"

"What?" Caroline shrieked.

"Caroline," Kurt said, looking uncomfortable with her making a scene.

"Sorry," Lucy's mother said. "I just—don't you want a wedding with a gown and a cake and a reception?"

"I'm sorry, Mrs. Westbrook," Jesse said, looking down. "I-I just… I can't afford to give her none of that. I wish I could. God knows she deserves all that and more but—"

"Oh, honey," Caroline said, her face filled with empathy for her precious, orphaned future son-in-law. "Of course I don't expect you to be able to provide that. You both are so young, and you're just starting out. We'll pay for it all!"

Kurt's eyes opened wide, but when he looked into his wife's pleading face, he softened. Yes, Caroline had him wrapped around her finger every bit as much as Lucy had Jesse wrapped around hers. Kurt drew in a deep breath and nodded.

Caroline squealed. "Yay! But we're still gonna need more time than September! I've got to hire a caterer and talk to the church and get a cake and—"

"Mom," Lucy said. "Don't get carried away."

"Oh, and you can get designer gowns for the girls, and maybe we can get that banquet hall over at Smith Avenue and—"

"Mom…"

"And we gotta find a really nice place for the rehearsal dinner and—"

"Mom…"

"And then we've got to—"

"*Mom!*"

Caroline looked at her daughter like she had forgotten Lucy was there. "What?"

Lucy gazed lovingly at Jesse, then looked back at her mother. "I just want to be married to him. By September. That's all I want."

Caroline looked at her daughter and smiled. Lucy was happy, and her mother knew that was all that mattered.

"Okay, sweetheart. Pick a date late in August, and I'll make it happen."

Lucy nodded and snuggled up next to Jesse.

*****

At long last, Fillis decided it was time for her to go. She met with Theresa and with Mary, the spirit guardian of the Farnsworth House, on how best to care for her soldiers after she was gone. Fillis spoke at length about each of her adopted children, explaining every quirk and every special need. This one had doubts about his actions in the war, that one struggled with his past relationship with his father, and that one had two children die of illness after he left for war and still blamed himself.

Fillis was emotional when speaking of her boys, and several times she nearly changed her mind about leaving. Mary reassured her that she would keep careful watch over them and would always be there for them, day and night. Theresa would still be in Gettysburg for a while, as she was still in school pursuing her psychology degree, and she would continue to counsel any soldier who asked for help.

"We'll take care of them, Second Mama," Theresa reassured her. "And you know that Lucy will care for Jesse."

Fillis nodded and smiled softly. Jesse had always been her favorite soldier, one of the few who had been with her all the way back to 1863. She knew she never had to worry about him. Not with Lucy around.

Fillis's portal had actually opened for the first time nearly forty years earlier. After decades of struggling with her private issues—mainly her guilt at having an affair with a man's wife and with wrestling with the homosexuality that she had once believed was sinful—she was finally at peace with herself. She came to understand that her love for Helene was a blessed thing, and something to be celebrated. Once she felt worthy, she was invited to heaven.

She declined. She refused to go until all her soldiers were taken care of. Finally reassured that they would be well cared for, she made the decision to go home to God. And to Helene.

Fillis took her time saying her goodbyes to all of her soldiers. When it was time to leave, there was quite the crowd gathered. She had passed away under a tree in a field not far from where the battles had taken place, succumbing to her illness. That was where the portal had opened the first time.

"I'm gonna miss you so much, Second Mama," Jesse said, struggling to keep his composure.

Lucy wrapped her arms around him. It was painful for her to see Jesse hurting, but they both knew they had to be strong for Fillis. If Jesse broke down, she would never go to her reward.

"I'll always be watchin' over you, ya hear?" Fillis said, anguish in her eyes. Lucy could see the pain of losing hundreds of her children in her eyes, and now she was losing her favorite. However, there would be no more pain, no more loss where she was going.

"Yes, I know," Jesse said. "I love you, Second Mama. Thank you for always takin' such good care of me."

"I love you, too, Jesse," Fillis said. She reached out and touched his face, but her hand went right through. Lucy could feel her aching to touch her child.

Jesse drew in a sudden breath as the portal opened. Theresa, Remy, Avery, and lots of soldiers who had gathered to see their mama off on her final journey all turned to see it. Many of them had seen people cross over, but it was easy to tell which ones hadn't. Some of the soldiers stared, slack-jawed at the sight of the blindingly white portal.

Fillis walked over and stood in front of it. Her eyes lit up with love and recognition.

"My God," she whispered. "You're just as beautiful as I remember."

Tears fell from Lucy's cheeks, and she hugged Jesse tighter. "She's going to be so happy now," she whispered to him. "Happy and at peace. Now and forever."

Jesse nodded. "That's what she deserves."

The look of grief on his face was more than Lucy could bear. She hoped she hadn't made a mistake by helping Fillis to cross over. She felt like she had sent Jesse's mother away.

"I don't know if I could've moved so far away, knowin' she was still here. I know it's for the best," he said, his voice quavering.

Lucy gently stroked his back as they watched Fillis. They couldn't see Helene, but they all knew she was there.

Fillis turned around and looked at the throngs of loved ones gathered to say their final goodbyes to their mother. She blew kisses all around, then her eyes rested on Jesse.

Fillis ran over to him, and then opened her arms. Jesse gasped with understanding, then pulled her close into an embrace.

Lucy pressed her hand to her mouth to stifle her sob as she watched the love of her life finally get to hug his second mother.

"I'm so proud of you, boy. So proud!"

Fillis finally let him go.

"I'll see you on the other side, Second Mama. You be sure to keep Joel in line!"

Fillis's eyes were filled with peace, love, and happiness. Not only would she be reunited with Helene, but with all of her children she'd lost along the way.

"I goin' do my best!"

With that, she walked over to her portal. A delicate, feminine hand reached out and pulled her into the light.

Chapter 25

It was several months later when Avery felt the call to return to Little Round Top in the middle of the night. He had been wandering the streets around two o'clock in the morning. It was increasingly harder for him to vanish anymore, and the nights were long and lonely. He longed for the warmth of Remy's companionship and the light of her beautiful smile. She was always out of reach during the night since her apartment was too far for him to travel, but now she was even farther away. She had left for Maryland earlier in the day to help Lucy prepare for her upcoming wedding that weekend.

Avery had been aimlessly wandering down the empty streets when he felt the urgent pull to go to Little Round Top. He almost never went there at night because there was no reason to. He spent a lot of time there during the day so Remy would always know where to find him. Now he turned on his heel and headed straight for the battlefield where he had died.

It was his time. He knew it in his heart. Avery felt an all-encompassing sensation of joy at the thought of seeing his beloved daughter again.

Charlotte, Charlotte, my little girl!

Avery felt the urge to run to Little Round Top, to rush to see his baby girl again.

Remy.

Avery pictured her lovely face and sweet smile. Grief tore through him at the thought of leaving without being able to say good-bye to her. He pictured her returning after the wedding, desperately searching for him to no avail.

No! A chuisle, mo chuisle... *Please, no. I can't go without telling her that I love her one more time!* Avery's heart cried out for her, but he knew he had no choice. There was no way to fight the supernatural strength and power of the call to cross over. He had to go.

Avery got to Little Round Top, and there was nothing but dead silence. He looked around for any sign of what was to come. As he gazed from atop the huge hill at the wide expanse of dark sky and battlefields below, a blinding white portal appeared right in front of him.

Avery stared in awe as a pretty young woman who looked to be in her twenties stepped out of the portal. She had his gray eyes. She smiled softly and looked like an angel.

"Hi, Daddy!" she chirped happily.

Avery was too overcome to speak at first. Finally, he found his voice. "Charlotte, me girl...Charlotte..."

Charlotte gazed lovingly at her father. Avery felt the decades of grieving for her fade away, replaced with sheer joy.

"Jaysus, look at you. You're all grown up!" Avery exclaimed as he stared at his beloved daughter.

"I actually lived until I was sixty-two years old, but I didn't want to show up lookin' older than me father!" Charlotte laughed, a delicately feminine, tinkling sound.

"My God, how I've missed you," Avery said, his voice almost a whisper. "Oh, me sweet girl, I'm sorry. I'm so sorry! I never should have left you..."

"Daddy, it's not your fault you died," she said, looking at him with adoration. It was like Avery could physically feel pure love radiating from her.

"I shouldn't have joined up to fight. You grew up without a father!" Avery gazed sorrowfully at the beautiful young woman his daughter had become. He grieved for the loss of missing her childhood, her young womanhood. Her whole life.

"I grew up knowin' I had a father who loved me very, very much. Mama told me all about you, talked about you all the time. And I was old enough to remember you, Daddy. I remember our walks to town. I remember our talks together."

"Oh, Ch-Charlotte," Avery moaned, finally breaking down with emotion. "My *baby!*"

"I'm still your baby," Charlotte said soothingly. "I love you, and I'm so happy to see you, but it's not my turn to be with you yet."

Avery looked at her, but was still too emotional to speak.

"I know what's in your heart, Daddy. I know you're hurting because you feel like you're bein' disloyal to me by wantin' to stay, but you're not. A certain wild-eyed black-hatted man kept insistin' to me that the only way you'll be able to let go of the past is if I come back and see you!"

Ellis.

"He's mighty persistent, I'll give 'im that. He knew what a debt he owed Remy, and he wouldn't rest 'til he settled it. Wouldn't let go 'til I was allowed to come see you. And I'm sure glad he did," Charlotte said, her soft gray eyes sparkling with happiness. She looked into Avery's eyes and said, "Daddy, I'm happy. I had a long and wonderful life. I had four sons. I lost one when he was just a little boy, but it's all right because we're together now. You have beautiful grandchildren, Daddy. *I* have beautiful grandchildren," she said with her lovely, tinkling laugh. "I'm at peace where I am now. I'm not goin' anywhere, so I'll be here when you're ready to join me. But you're not ready, are ye?"

"I don't know," Avery said, still conflicted. How could he look Charlotte in the eye and tell her he was leaving her again?

"I think Remy is such a wonderful lady," Charlotte said, and Avery could feel his daughter's love for Remy, too. "She has such a good, pure heart. She loves you so much."

"I love her, too."

"I know you do. I kinda like the idea of her as me stepmother," she said, a twinkle in her eye.

That thought made Avery smile. The idea of he, Remy, and Charlotte as a family, even if separated temporarily by death.

"*Be happy,* Daddy. I know you want to stay with Remy. It doesn't mean you love me any less. All I want is for you to be as happy as I am."

"What do I do?" Avery asked.

"Decide," Charlotte told him.

"I want to stay with Remy," Avery whispered.

Charlotte shrugged her shoulders and giggled. "Then it's done!"

"Just like that?" Avery asked.

"Well, just one more thing," Charlotte said with a smile. She opened her arms.

Avery gasped.

"Well, you can't stay behind without a proper hug, now can ye?" Charlotte said.

Avery opened his arms and walked toward her, afraid to hope that was she was saying was true. *Could he really touch her?*

Avery let out a choked cry when he wrapped his arms around her and felt the warmth and softness of her body. He held her close, sobbing uncontrollably.

"Charlotte, Charlotte," Avery cried as he held her in his arms. "My baby, my little girl."

"It's all right, Daddy. I'm here. I love you so very much,"

Charlotte said in a soothing voice.

Charlotte held him close until he finally stopped weeping.

She looked him in the eyes, love still radiating from her whole being. "I love you, Daddy. It's all right to miss me, but you don't have to grieve for me anymore. I'm not lost. I'm home. And your home is with Remy until it's time for us all to be together again."

Avery nodded as a sense of peace and calm settled over him.

Charlotte was right. His home was with Remy.

*****

As a bride, Lucy was about as low-maintenance as they come. She had one demand and one demand only for her wedding day; she wanted to marry Jesse. As long as they were husband and wife by the end of the day, she wasn't about to fret over anything else. She had said that the flowers could wilt or the wedding cake could collapse and it would all be fine with her.

That being said, she was an excited, happy bride who gushed over every aspect of the wedding that her mother had meticulously planned. Lucy exclaimed that the church looked beautiful, the flowers were exquisite, and she loved how her hair and makeup had turned out. The wedding vendors adored her and seemed to go out of their way to cater to her needs since she was so gracious and appreciative of everything they did.

"Oh, Lucy, you look so beautiful!" Remy gushed.

Lucy did look lovely in her elegant gown with her brown hair falling in soft curls at her shoulders. She was excited and so much in love that it enhanced her natural beauty.

"So do you, Remy," Lucy said, admiring the way Remy looked in her blue bridesmaid dress. "That dress brings out your eyes like you wouldn't believe. I only wish Avery could see you. We'll be sure to show him lots of pictures."

Remy nodded and smiled.

Theresa came bustling in, looking incredible in her blue bridesmaid dress as well. The dress also brought out the color in her light blue eyes, and it seemed to make her strawberry-blonde hair look a darker red. She looked amazing, and Remy knew Sean would be thrilled when he got a look at her.

"Girl, your cowboy cleans up *good.* He looks so adorable. Wait 'til you see him!" Theresa said, her eyes sparkling with affection. Jesse was wonderful, and it was impossible not to love him.

"Is he nervous?" Lucy asked.

"No, not at all. He's just really, really excited. It's so cute!" Theresa gushed.

"I'm a nervous wreck," Lucy admitted. "Not about marrying him! I just mean, all those people…"

"I know, Lucy," Remy said sympathetically. Lucy was one of the few brides who didn't really enjoy being the center of attention. "I know crowds aren't really your thing."

"You can say that again," Lucy said nervously.

Remy faced Lucy and gently fussed with her hair until her brown curls fell just right onto her shoulders. She looked into Lucy's eyes and said, "Just focus on Jesse when you walk down the aisle. Just look at him, waiting for you at the front of the church. I promise, you'll forget about everybody else."

Lucy smiled softly. "You're right. All I have to do is look at him, and I'll be just fine." She let out a soft, happy sigh and looked calmer already.

*****

Jesse could hardly wait to see his lovely bride walking down the aisle. He stood at the front of the church with Sean and Lucy's brother, David, at his side. He hadn't seen Lucy since yesterday. They had decided to spend the night apart so he wouldn't see her until she was all gussied up in her gown.

His stomach fluttered with excitement when Lucy's little cousin walked down the aisle, tossing rose petals as she went. The sweet little girl giggled when Jesse winked at her. Jesse was overwhelmed with joy at being surrounded by Lucy's extended family, who had welcomed him with open arms since he got into town yesterday. Lucy's parents had come to like and trust him over the last few months, and must have spread their goodwill to all the aunts, uncles, and cousins because everyone had been quite kind to him. It was wonderful to have such a loving new family.

Lucy's little sister, a junior bridesmaid, walked shyly down the aisle. Jesse was sure to meet her eye and give her an encouraging smile, which seemed to calm her. He felt a surge of protectiveness toward her, like she was his own little sister.

Remy looked lovely as she walked down the aisle, her sweet smile lighting the way. Jesse knew that underneath her pretty, soft exterior beat the heart of a warrior. She was such a strong lady. She'd been through hell and back with her family, Ellis, and with loving a man she feared she could lose at any moment. Jesse was proud to call her his friend.

Theresa walked down the aisle next, looking as beautiful and fiery as ever. Her eyes opened wide as she caught sight of Sean, who looked resplendent in his military dress blues. Theresa had a serious weakness for men in uniform, especially *her* man in uniform, and Jesse was pretty sure she hadn't seen him all decked out like this before.

Oh, yeah, Jesse thought. *He's gettin' laid big time tonight.*

The music swelled as Lucy made her entrance on the arm of her father.

Jesse was overwhelmed at the sight of her. Lucy's pretty brown hair fell in soft curls at her shoulders, and she looked dainty and delicate in her white gown. Her wedding dress had some ruffles underneath, but it wasn't a crazy-big dress like those hoop skirts from back when Jesse was alive the first time. The off-the-shoulder gown was perfect for her small frame, and with her wedding veil flowing down her back, she looked like an angel.

My God, that gorgeous, incredible woman is about to become my wife.

Lucy glanced out at all the people watching her, and Jesse could see how nervous she was. *My poor rose.* Her shyness was part of the reason she had wanted a small wedding to begin with. He knew she also wanted to make her mother happy, but she was truly uncomfortable being stared at by so many people.

Jesse suddenly gasped loudly. He waited a second until most of the heads turned his way, then he put his hand over his heart and staggered backward dramatically, as if stunned by her beauty. His tactic worked, and people in the congregation chuckled at his antics, drawing some of the attention away from Lucy.

Lucy locked eyes with Jesse and smiled with gratitude. He watched her lovely face relax as she looked into his eyes.

That's right, darlin'. Pretend it's just you and me. Forget all these people. It's just you and me right now.

Jesse gazed lovingly into her sweet brown eyes when she reached the front of the church. He eagerly took her hand as her father gave her away, but not before looking into Kurt's eyes, which were welling with tears. A silent understanding passed between them, with Jesse nonverbally pledging to love and care for his precious child.

Lucy eagerly grasped Jesse's hand and squeezed it tight. She was on the verge of tears for most of the ceremony. She managed to hold it together until it came time for the vows.

"I-I, L-Lucy Westbrook…" she began. "T-take you, J-Jesse…"

Tears spilled down her cheeks as she struggled to gain control of her emotions. Theresa quickly handed Lucy some tissues, and she dabbed at her eyes. Lucy's breath came in gasps as she tried to stifle her sobs.

"I'm sorry, Jesse," she whispered, still dabbing her eyes. "I just keep thinking of how close I came to losing you. I can't believe we made it this far!"

"It's all right, my beautiful rose. Take your time," Jesse murmured lovingly as he stroked her cheek. As long as these were tears of joy, she could cry all she wanted.

Lucy took few more deep breaths, still overcome with emotion. She glanced nervously out at the congregation, which had fallen completely silent. She blushed deeply and lowered her head.

It was such a beautiful moment that Jesse hated for Lucy to feel embarrassed. He took a deep breath and said in a voice loud enough for the congregation to hear, "Darlin', this is the happiest moment of my life. Feel free to drag it out as long as you like!"

All their gathered friends and family members laughed, reassured that nothing was wrong. Those who knew Lucy best wouldn't be surprised at how emotional she was.

Lucy smiled gratefully at Jesse and seemed a bit calmer. Jesse nodded at the minister to continue the ceremony.

Jesse stroked Lucy's cheek and looked deeply into her eyes, which helped to steady her. She was able to get through her vows this time.

When the minister told Jesse to kiss his bride, Jesse whispered to her, "I promise I will never take a single kiss for granted."

Jesse tenderly kissed his new wife, and the congregation burst into happy applause.

After the ceremony, Lucy and Jesse took their time greeting their friends and family in the receiving line. Next up were the pictures taken with members of the bridal party. Though it was wonderful being with Lucy's family, Jesse couldn't help feeling sad that there were no members of the Spenser family there for his special day. His parents had died so long ago, and his closest friends were spirits. And even many of his ghost friends had crossed over. Jesse was excited and happy about his new life with Lucy, but he couldn't help but grieve for all the loved ones he had lost along the way.

The last photographs to be taken were of just the bride and the groom, so Lucy and Jesse sent everyone else off to the reception. They would join the party as soon as they were done. It was wonderful to have a few moments alone with Lucy. Jesse happily kissed and held his new bride, and was aware of the photographer taking candid shots as he did so. Those were sure to be some of the best pictures, the ones where Jesse and Lucy naturally expressed their love for each other, rather than being posed for photographs.

*****

Once the pictures were done, the photographer headed to the reception in his own car, and the limo waited in the parking lot for Lucy and Jesse. It was rather nice to have a few precious moments alone on their wedding day. Jesse took Lucy by the hand and carefully helped her step out of the front of the church so she wouldn't trip over her dress.

Jesse stopped dead in his tracks when they got outside of the church. Lucy was alarmed at his stunned expression, then followed his gaze. She gasped at what she saw.

There, standing outside the church waiting for them, was a large group of people. Every single one of them was dead, their images transparent and glowing with light and love and joy. The men and women stood in two lines on either side of the bride and groom.

"Hey, sweetheart!" Joel said happily, his blue eyes shining brighter and happier than ever before.

Next to Joel stood a stunningly beautiful woman with honey-blonde hair and blue-green eyes. She smiled warmly, radiating love and happiness.

"Emma?" Lucy whispered. She knew this must be Joel's wife. Lucy would have known her anywhere from Joel's description of her. He loved her so deeply and had talked of her often when he was still an earthbound spirit.

"Yes!" Emma said. "Oh, Lucy. Thank you so much for bringing Joel home to me."

"I'm so glad I could help!" Lucy said, filled with happiness at seeing Joel and Emma together. Emma was even more beautiful than Joel had described.

Emma ran her eyes over Lucy's wedding gown, then looked back up at her face. "Lucy, you look *so beautiful!*"

"So do you!" Lucy said, eyes wide. Emma laughed, an ethereal, angelic sound.

"You look so lovely, Lucy," Joel said, blue eyes twinkling. He looked at Jesse and said, "You're damn lucky she lowered her standards and agreed to marry you, Secesh."

"Don't I know it!" Jesse said with a smile.

Lucy looked down the line at all the people gathered. Her heart swelled when she saw Adam and Elijah standing side by side, looking happy and in love. They had both fought for Maryland in the Civil War, one for the North and one for the South. Theresa and Lucy had helped counsel Adam to cross over so he could finally be home with Elijah.

"Daaaamn, you are lookin' *fine,* Lucy!" Teddy Frederick exclaimed. Teddy had died in battle at the tender age of nineteen, but he looked like he was barely sixteen years old. Theresa had also helped him cross over, but not before the kid had developed a massive crush on Lucy.

"Teddy, it's so good to see you!" Lucy cried.

"Teddy," Jesse said mock sternly. "So we meet again…"

The kid had been full of spunk as a spirit. His last act on earth before crossing over was to grab Lucy and kiss her passionately. It had been his first…and last…kiss.

"Tell ya one thing," Teddy said, eyes sparkling mischievously. "You better treat her right or I'll haunt you to hell and back again!"

Jesse chuckled. "Fair enough."

Jesse gasped as he stared down at the end of the line of people.

"Lucy," he whispered. "It's my mama…"

Jesse took Lucy's arm and walked her down to the end of the line. She looked into the older lady's soft, blue-gray eyes. They looked just like Jesse's.

She gazed at Jesse with tender love and affection. "My son," she said softly. Then she looked at Lucy fondly and said, "And now I have a daughter."

Sarah Spenser smiled warmly, and Lucy could feel the love emanating from her. Lucy's eyes spilled over with tears. She turned to see that Fillis was standing right next to Jesse's mother.

"Our baby is finally married," Fillis said to Sarah.

Sarah laughed happily. "Isn't it wonderful?"

Lucy and Jesse turned together to gaze at their loved ones who had gone before them. The love and support they felt from the spirits overwhelmed them.

After a moment, the spirits disappeared, but Lucy could still feel their presence. Their love.

Jesse wrapped his arms around Lucy and held her tight.

*****

After the bridal party was introduced and Theresa and Sean gave their toasts, Lucy shyly made it through her first dance with Jesse in front of everyone. The song was "True" by Ryan Cabrera. Jesse had always said he thought of Lucy every time he had heard it, even before Lucy knew he existed. It was their song, and it was lovely. Lucy enjoyed dancing with Jesse, but she looked forward to being able to dance with him when others were out on the floor, too, so she wouldn't have to feel so self-conscious.

As Lucy stepped off the dance floor, she looked over at Remy. She was smiling, but there was sadness behind her eyes. Lucy knew Remy was happy for her, but she also knew it must be painful for her to be around so many happy couples when she felt her own future with Avery was so uncertain. Lucy knew it was time to cheer Remy up. Just before dinner was served, she walked over to speak with her privately.

"Hey, Remy," Lucy said, as she looked down where Remy sat. "I need you to do something for me."

"Anything!" Remy said, eager to be a helpful bridesmaid.

"I hate seeing you alone at my wedding, and there's somebody I'd like you to meet."

Remy's face fell. Lucy could see she had no interest in anyone but Avery.

"Please?" Lucy asked. "I just want you to be able to dance with somebody at my wedding. I'm the bride, so you can't say no."

"Really?" Remy asked wearily. "You're playing the bride card?"

"Well, yeah. When else am I gonna play it?" Lucy said with a smile. She held out her hand, and Remy grudgingly accepted it.

"Fine, fine," Remy said, plastering a smile on her face, planning on being polite for Lucy's sake.

Lucy practically dragged Remy out of the ballroom.

"Where are we going?" Remy asked.

Lucy pulled her out into the hallway and back toward the bridal room where they had all primped their hair and makeup before being introduced at the reception.

"He's in here," Lucy said, flinging open the door to the bridal room.

Remy froze where she stood.

Chapter 26

Remy stared at the tall man who stood toward the back of the bridal room. She felt like all the air had been sucked out of her lungs.

Avery.

Dressed in a suit and tie and not in his gray Confederate uniform.

Avery.

More than a hundred miles away from Gettysburg.

"He came back yesterday," Lucy gently explained to Remy. She turned to look at Lucy, whose face was alight with joy. "He managed to find Jesse before he left for Maryland, so Jesse brought him here. Oh, Remy, it was *killing* me not to tell you sooner, but he wanted to get all cleaned up for you. That, and he insisted on not disrupting the wedding and wanted to wait until after the ceremony to tell you."

Lucy put a gentle hand on Remy's back to steady her. Good thing, because Remy truly felt like she might faint. She looked over at Avery's handsome smiling face.

"Is…is it true?" *Oh, dear God, please don't let this be a dream. Please, I can't bear to wake up and find this isn't real.*

"She doesn't believe us, Avery," Lucy said with a happy laugh. "I guess we better prove it to her."

Lucy walked toward Avery, her wedding gown rustling. She held up her hand to him the same way she had when they were trying to prove to Remy that Avery was a ghost. Avery grinned at Lucy, then slapped her hand hard in a high-five.

It made noise when he touched her, Remy thought as she stood there, trembling.

"Ow!" Lucy said with a giggle.

"Sorry, me sweet girl!" Avery said. He grabbed Lucy's hand and kissed it, making an exaggerated smacking sound with his mouth on her hand.

"Oh, my God!" Remy cried, putting her hand over her mouth.

Lucy rushed to her side and said, "It's true, Remy. He's alive, and he's here to stay. Now it's your turn to touch him!"

Lucy squealed with excitement, then gathered her skirts and rushed out of the room, shutting the door behind her to give them some privacy.

Remy stared at Avery, afraid to move at first. If she tried to touch him and her hand went right through him, she knew her heart would never recover.

"Come to me, darling," Avery said, opening his arms. "I need to hold you."

Remy walked over to him on rubbery legs, feeling like she could collapse at any moment. She stood right before him, still afraid that this was all a dream.

He's breathing. I can hear him breathing.

She carefully reached up and touched his shoulder and made solid contact with his strong, muscular build.

"Avery!" Remy cried as she threw her arms around him. He was so big that she couldn't reach all the way around his back. He wrapped his strong arms around her and held her tight as if he would never let go.

"Remy, Remy," Avery murmured in her ear as he held her, rubbing her back.

Remy closed her eyes and let the sensation of his touch overwhelm her, body and soul. They held each other for a moment, then Avery pulled back slightly so he could look at her.

Avery gazed deeply into her eyes and said, "My God, how I love you, Remy."

He tenderly cupped her face in his hands and pressed his lips to hers. She let out a soft moan and felt her knees buckle slightly beneath her. His mouth still on hers, Avery put his arm around her back and gripped her tight. Remy ran her fingers through his soft hair as they kissed.

Avery forced himself to come up for air, then gazed down at her. "You all right? You look a bit pale."

"Y-yes. I'm okay," Remy said softly. He smiled down at her, then lifted his right hand and gently touched her cheek the way he often had as a ghost. She braced herself for the chill out of sheer habit, but his hand was warm. She let out a soft, happy sigh. "Avery...how?"

Avery's face broke into the most wonderful, happy smile. "Oh, Remy," Avery said, his voice breaking with emotion. "I saw me daughter!"

Remy's eyes opened wide. "You saw Charlotte?"

"Yes. She came to see me at Little Round Top. Stepped out of the portal, straight from heaven. Oh, Remy, she looked so beautiful. She was all grown up! And happy. She looked so happy!"

Tears fell from Avery's eyes, and Remy tenderly wiped them away with the back of her hand. "She pretty much told me to quit my nonsense and go be happy already!"

Remy laughed, reveling in the look of joy on Avery's face. She had never seen him look so peaceful.

Avery ran his fingers through Remy's hair. "Oh, she thinks the world of you, Remy."

"Really?" Remy asked, thrilled that someone so dear to Avery approved of her.

"Oh, yes. Said she'd love to have you as a stepmother!"

Remy put her hand over her heart and said, "Oh, I'm so honored."

Avery smiled. "She said she knows how much you love me, and she knew what was in my heart. Charlotte knew I wanted to stay, but she knew I couldn't do it without her blessin'. Remy, it was Ellis who sent her to me."

Remy gasped.

"It's all because of you. If you hadn't been so kind to him, I might not be standin' here with me arms around you right now."

She pictured the look of determination on Ellis's face when he pledged to find a way to bring Avery home to her. *My God, he actually did it.*

"Be-before she left…" Avery struggled to go on, his tears flowing again. "I got to hold her. I got to hold me little girl again!" He broke down sobbing, and Remy pulled him close to her.

"Oh, Avery, I'm so glad." Remy held him close until he was calm again. She rested her head on his chest as he stroked her hair. And that was when she heard it.

His heartbeat. Remy pressed her ear to his chest and listened.

When she lifted her head, Avery said, "*A chuisle.*"

My pulse.

*****

Remy and Avery eventually emerged from the bridal room and joined the reception. Lucy politely excused herself from the group of relatives she had been visiting with and rushed over to Remy.

"You okay?" Lucy asked Remy.

"Oh, my God!" Remy exclaimed and threw her arms around Lucy. They hugged each other and laughed, both trying not to cry.

"It was making me *crazy* not to tell you before the wedding!" Lucy said. "I about fainted when I saw him arrive with Jesse yesterday."

Remy punched Lucy on the shoulder. "And you kept sayin' we were gonna have to show Avery pictures of me in my dress when we got back."

Lucy giggled. "I know, and I'm such a terrible liar. I was afraid I was gonna blow the whole thing."

Avery tenderly stroked Remy's face. "I was goin' crazy, too. Believe me. I just couldn't bear to disrupt their weddin' day any more than I already have. I thought it best to wait at least 'til after they were safely married off! I was at the wedding, though. Hidin' in the back." Avery smiled at Lucy. "Such a lovely ceremony. You looked so beautiful, Lucy, but I confess I could hardly take me eyes off Remy. I wanted to charge right up that aisle, I did!"

Remy laughed and put her arm around Avery.

"Your attention please!" boomed the DJ from the dance floor.

"It can't be time to cut the cake already!" Lucy exclaimed.

"The groom has requested another special dance with his lovely bride!" the man said into the microphone. Sure enough, Jesse was standing on the dance floor, grinning at her.

"Oh, Jesse," Lucy whined. "What did you do?"

Jesse looked irresistibly handsome in his tuxedo as he extended his hand to her, and Lucy found that boyish grin of his irresistible as always. She pasted a smile on her face and headed to the dance floor. *I thought the dancing all by ourselves part was over,* she grumbled inwardly.

"I'm gonna kill you, Spenser," Lucy said, smiling through gritted teeth.

"This is a special song dedicated to Lucy by her new husband," the DJ said.

Jesse held up his arm dramatically, and Lucy put her hand in his, ready to dance to whatever song he had selected.

Lucy laughed heartily when the song began to play. It was "The Yellow Rose of Texas," an upbeat song that held special meaning to both of them. Those closest to the couple knew that Jesse called Lucy his honorary Yellow Rose of Texas, and anyone who had heard Jesse speak could tell he was from the Southern state.

Jesse grinned at Lucy and, as always, she felt swept away in his arms. It wasn't so long ago that they had danced to this song on the Gettysburg College lawn, only then they had danced without being able to touch each other. Now, as Jesse eagerly spun her around the dance floor, she found it easy to forget that anyone else was watching. Her face was flushed with happiness, and the way she freely danced with Jesse was truly a testament to the strength of her love for him. Only Jesse could make her forget her inhibitions and truly dance as if no one was watching. In that moment, it was just Lucy dancing with Jesse, her soulmate and the love of her life. At the end of the song, Jesse dipped her down low to a loud round of applause.

Jesse pulled her to her feet and kissed her.

"I love you, Jesse."

"I love you, too, my beautiful rose."

"Jesse, may I please have the next dance?" Lucy's mother Caroline asked as she walked toward the two of them.

"Why, Ma'am, I'd be delighted!" Jesse said, bowing to her. Caroline laughed, finding his charms as irresistible as Lucy did. Jesse took her hand and led her to the dance floor as Lucy watched proudly.

"Since Jesse is busy dancin' with another woman, may I dance with you?" came a deep male voice just behind Lucy.

She turned to see Avery offering his hand.

"Oh, Avery, I would love that," Lucy said, happily taking his hand. How strange and wonderful it was to be able to touch her dear friend!

As they danced together, Lucy saw Remy watching, her pretty blue eyes lit up with happiness. Next to her new husband, Avery's return to life was the most beautiful wedding gift Lucy could have asked for. When the dance ended, Avery tenderly kissed Lucy's cheek and returned to Remy's side.

Caroline and Jesse walked up to Lucy after they were done with their sweet dance together. Caroline looked at Jesse, her eyes full of concern.

"Jesse, I want to ask you something. And, honestly, it's okay if you say no. I promise I won't be offended. But, I was just thinking, with your family situation and all," Caroline said, her eyes full of empathy for her son-in-law, "that maybe, you know, instead of Ma'am... you might want to call me...*Mom.*"

Lucy put her hand over her heart. She watched Jesse visibly struggle with his emotions. He still grieved for his mother, lost to him so long ago, but Caroline had no way of knowing that he'd recently lost another dear mother figure when Fillis crossed over.

"I believe," Jesse said, swallowing hard. "I believe I'd like that." He nodded, looking at Lucy's mother gratefully.

"Come here, you sweet boy!" Caroline cried, pulling Jesse close. She hugged him warmly like he was her own child. When she finally let go of him, she patted his cheek with affection before heading off toward Lucy's father.

Lucy looked into Jesse's eyes, and he smiled at her. "I've had three wonderful women wantin' to be my mama. How lucky can a guy git?"

*****

Avery slow danced with Remy to a soft, romantic song. Holding her in his arms was like a dream come true. She felt soft and delicate, and she looked incredibly beautiful in her blue bridesmaid gown. Her eyes were always lovely, but now they seemed a richer, brighter blue, both set off by her dress and by the love and happiness in her eyes. Avery had never felt more joy.

Or more excited. Dancing with her, he felt like a nervous and horny teenager touching a girl for the first time. It had been a long time since he had touched a woman, and Avery had never felt this way about anyone before. Before he met Remy, he hadn't even known he was capable of loving anyone so deeply, so passionately, and now that he was back in his physical body, his sexual urges had returned with a vengeance. He ached to make love to Remy, but he didn't want to rush her.

Remy gazed up into Avery's eyes and smiled. He had never dreamed that any woman would ever look at him the way she did. He bent down and pressed his lips to hers, and she eagerly kissed him back. He knew she must've felt how hard he was for her since she was pressed so close to him.

"Mmmm," Remy moaned seductively in his ear, making him imagine all the things he could do to her in bed to make her moan even more. "Oh, Avery, I can't wait to get you alone."

"Really?" Avery asked hopefully, his cock getting stiffer by the moment. *Don't push her*, he reminded himself. *Follow her lead.*

"Of course," Remy said. "Lucy told me that Jesse and Sean packed some of their clothes and stuff for you, and she made sure they put your bag in my hotel room. You should have everything you need."

Avery nodded, waiting for her to continue.

"And all I need is you," Remy said, trailing her finger across his chin.

"Only if you're ready," Avery said. "I don't want to rush you, *a chuisle*."

Remy pressed her lips to his and said, "We've had to wait long enough, don't you think? Avery, I want you to make love to me. *As soon as possible.*"

Avery grinned like a schoolboy. He'd never had a woman initiate sex before, and it was sexy as hell.

"Do you think Lucy and Jesse would mind if we ducked out early?" he asked her.

"I think of all people, they would understand," Remy said with a smile.

Remy pulled Avery by the hand, and they rushed over to where Jesse and Lucy were standing together.

*****

"Lucy, I hope you don't mind, but…um…Avery and I are going to head out now if that's okay," Remy said.

Jesse raised an eyebrow and grinned at Avery, knowing damn well what they were rushing off to do. Remy blushed deeply, and Lucy shot an annoyed look at Jesse. Lucy knew exactly how Remy felt. People had been making uncomfortable comments all day about her upcoming wedding night, and Lucy hated it. Lucy smiled at Remy and focused on making her friend more comfortable.

"Of course we don't mind," Lucy said gently. "I know you want to spend every second together right now."

Remy nodded gratefully.

"Your joy is our joy," Lucy said happily. She engulfed Remy in a hug, and then did the same with Avery.

Lucy watched as the two headed off to start their new life together, then she pulled Jesse into her arms and began slow dancing with him.

*****

Though Remy was excited about being with Avery, she couldn't help but feel a little nervous. They had waited so long, and yet it all seemed to be happening so fast. She'd been so overwhelmed with emotion at discovering Avery was alive, that she hadn't had time to mentally and emotionally prepare herself to be intimate with him.

"Wow, this is amazing!" Avery said, looking around at the hotel room. "Of course anything *different* is amazing to me right now."

"I guess it is! You've been looking at the same scenery for years and years," Remy said, thinking of how strange and new everything must be for him. *And he's probably every bit as nervous as I am.*

"You look so handsome, Avery," Remy said, looking him up and down. "Where did you get this suit?"

"Borrowed it from Sean."

"I know how you feel. Mrs. Westbrook paid for my dress, not to mention this hotel room. I never could have afforded to be in the wedding otherwise." A sudden, horrible thought suddenly occurred to Remy. "My God, Avery, we don't have a dime between us, do we? And it's not like you can get a job right now. How will we—"

"It's all right, Remy," Avery said, wrapping his arms around her. He'd had about twenty-four more hours to think of such things than she had, and this thought had obviously occurred to him before. "We'll be all right. We're gonna have to lean on our friends a bit to get by until I can get on my feet. Sean has connections to get me the proper paperwork, just like he did with Jesse. He can get me a social security card and get me square with the law. It'll take a bit, but we'll survive, my love."

Remy nodded. "You're right. You're back. You're *alive.* As long as we're together, we can handle anything."

"That's me girl," Avery said with a smile.

Remy looked at him nervously, unsure of what to do next. Avery picked up on her anxiety like always did. He lifted her chin gently and kissed her. Remy calmed immediately, his touch already familiar. She was getting used to his body, but she already knew his heart and soul. Avery's kisses became more urgent, as did Remy's desire for him.

Avery kissed her mouth, then down her neck.

"Oh, Avery," Remy moaned. She hated to interrupt this intimate moment with practical details but better now than later. She needed to tell Avery that she was already on the pill due to pain and other complications with her menstrual cycle. "Darling, just so you know, we don't need to use anything to keep me from getting pregnant. I—"

"I know," Avery said, eyes twinkling. "Lucy told me that you already take birth control pills to help with your female troubles. Poor girl blushed somethin' fierce when talkin' about sex with me, but I'm glad she told me."

Remy laughed. "Now, where were we. Ah, yes, you were kissing my neck and driving me crazy."

"Mmmm," Avery said, pressing his lips on the sensitive skin on her neck. "Like this?"

"Yes," Remy whispered. Avery ran his hands over the front of her dress, and she felt her nipples harden at his touch. She could hardly wait to have him touch her bare skin. She began unbuttoning his shirt, but struggled with his necktie. "I've never taken off a man's tie before. I don't know how!"

"I'm not sure meself! I've never worn such a fancy getup before. Lucy tied it on for me," Avery said.

It made Remy smile to think of Lucy taking time out of her busy wedding day to take care of Avery. Remy and Avery worked together, laughing, and eventually freed him from his tie. She eagerly pulled off his shirt and ran her hands over his broad, bare chest.

"You're so strong, Avery," Remy said, impressed by how muscular he was.

Avery seemed pleased by the compliment. He bent down and kissed her again, reaching around her back with his left hand. She expected him to unzip her dress, but he had something else in mind. He slid his right arm under her legs and scooped her up in his arms.

He smiled proudly at her.

Remy let out a happy sigh. "You remembered."

"Of course I remembered!" Avery said. "I haven't been able to stop thinking of it since you mentioned it. I just never thought I'd get the chance to do it!"

Remy happily threw her arms around his neck as he carried her to the bed. He gently laid her down, then reached around her back. She lifted her body so he could unzip her dress and slide it off. Avery kissed her neck again, then moved his mouth to just above her breasts. Remy reached around and unsnapped her bra for him, and he eagerly slid it off.

"My God, you're a beautiful woman," Avery said. He kissed her right breast, and she arched her back and moaned.

Remy fumbled with his belt and managed to get it off. He took off his pants and underwear, then slid off her panties.

"Oh, Avery," Remy said, desperate to feel him inside her.

Avery positioned himself on top of her and she breathlessly waited for him to take her. "Avery, I need you so much," Remy said, kissing him and pulling him closer.

"Open your legs for me, Remy," Avery murmured, the same way he had all those months ago in the forest when she had pleasured herself as he watched.

"Oh, Avery," she said dreamily. "I'll do anything you say."

Avery laughed his deep, sexy laugh. "Just let me inside your beautiful body. That's all I ask." He hesitated a moment as he looked down at her. "I'm a bit afraid of hurting you."

Remy gazed up at him. "It shouldn't hurt my second time, right?" She couldn't help remembering the pain of her first sexual experience. She felt her body tighten a bit.

"I don't know," Avery said, eyes full of concern. "I hope not. I'll be gentle, just in case."

Remy nodded. She closed her eyes and parted her legs. Avery gently eased himself inside her. She felt the walls of her vagina stretch to accommodate his size, but it wasn't painful. It was a tingling, pleasurable sensation.

"Oh, Avery," Remy moaned, as she opened her legs wider.

"Are you all right?" Avery asked.

"Yes," Remy cried. "Yes, oh, yes, Avery. Keep going…it feels so good. Avery, you're so *big.*"

Avery carefully slid the rest of the way inside her. He let out a groan and she let out a soft cry of pleasure.

"Avery, Avery," Remy cried.

"God, I love the way you say my name, me darling," Avery breathed in her ear.

Avery began to move harder and faster inside her. Remy dug her nails into his shoulders as she kept crying out his name. She opened her eyes to find him watching her as he made love to her.

"*A chuisle,*" he said in that wonderfully masculine voice that always turned her on. Now, with him pounding into her, the sound of his voice intensified the pleasured sensations between her legs.

"Avery!"

Avery thrust in and out of her, faster and faster, his groans getting louder. She wanted him to climax, for him to experience that deepest pleasure, and yet she was desperate for her own release. Avery slowed down his thrusting, then gently pulled out of her.

"What's wrong?" Remy asked, worried that he wasn't experiencing as much pleasure as she was.

"Nothing's wrong," Avery said with a gentle, reassuring smile. "I've just got to make sure I take good care of my girl."

Avery lay down beside her, gazing into her eyes. He trailed his fingers up her thigh and then teased the entrance between her legs. Then he slipped two fingers inside her and gently began rubbing her clit with his thumb. Remy gasped.

"Do you like that?" Avery asked in a husky voice.

"God, *yes!*" Remy turned to look at him, pleading with her eyes. She was *desperate* for release. She hadn't touched herself in a long time, and she had never been touched like this by a man before. Especially not one as handsome and sexy as Avery. "Keep doing it. Keep touching me, Avery," she pleaded, knowing it would be unbearable if he stopped. "Make me *come!*"

Avery made that deep, growling noise that she remembered from the day in the forest, that sexy, manly sound that meant he was incredibly turned on. He rubbed her faster, giving her the most intense pleasure she had ever known. He circled her clit over and over, and the tingling sensations grew stronger and stronger until she could hardly bear it.

"Avery, Avery!" Remy cried, gripping his shoulder with her hand as she held on for dear life. She threw her head back and cried out as she reached orgasm, still gripping his shoulder as the waves of rippling pleasure vibrated throughout her whole body.

When her climax finally subsided, she lay back on the pillow, her eyes closed. Avery nuzzled up close to her and put his arm around her neck.

"Oh, Remy," he murmured. "You look so beautiful when you're having an orgasm."

Remy bit her lip shyly, then opened her eyes. She felt a little self-conscious, but she wasn't sorry he had watched. It was wonderfully intimate, and she loved being so close with him, sharing her most private moments with him.

"That was amazing, Avery. It feels so much better when you do it," she said, blushing a little. She wanted to give him as much pleasure as he had given her, so she parted her legs again. "I need to feel you inside me again."

*****

Avery groaned as he slid back inside of Remy. Her beautiful body was delightfully tight, due to her lack of sexual experience. She had attributed the sensation to his size, and he was hardly about to argue. *Avery, you're so big.* She made him feel so strong and masculine when she said things like that. And the way she cried out his name! She made him feel like an incredible lover, and he'd never felt prouder in his life.

"Avery, oh, God, Avery," Remy moaned as he moved inside her again. He gazed down at her as she arched her back, moaning and crying out his name. She looked like she was in *ecstasy.* Avery could hardly believe that he was the one doing this to her.

"Oh, Remy, you're so beautiful. You're so lovely," Avery said as he pounded her harder. The harder he thrust, the more she cried out for more. He felt himself getting close to orgasm, but he couldn't help but wonder if he could give Remy another one first. She was gripping his shoulders again like she had when she was close to climaxing when he fingered her, and her pleasured cries kept growing louder. It was painfully difficult to delay his own gratification, but he wanted to please Remy more than anything in the world.

Avery suddenly pulled out of her. Before she could say anything, he slid down between her legs and began stroking her clit with his tongue.

"Avery!" Remy screamed. "Oh, G-God...Avery!"

She's screaming. I'm making her scream my name.

"Avery, Oh God, oh God," With one final cry of passion, Remy's body spasmed with another orgasm. Avery stroked her until she stopped screaming and started panting, trying to catch her breath.

Avery plunged back into her, pounding her over and over again until he finally found his release. He grunted out loud as he emptied himself inside her. "Ah, Remy!" he cried. His whole body shuddered with the strength of his orgasm, the pleasure beyond anything he had ever experienced. Avery buried his head in her shoulder, and she reached around and ran her fingers through his hair.

Avery rolled off her, looking over at her in wonder.

"Avery, that was *amazing*," Remy said, her pretty blue eyes full of love for him. He had never seen her look so *satisfied*.

Sex with Remy had far surpassed his wildest fantasies. She made love like she did everything else—with great passion. It was wonderful the way she wasn't shy in expressing her pleasure during sex. Avery looked into her eyes knowing he had found in her everything that had been missing in his life the first time around.

Remy gasped and sat up, looking at him with concern. "Look what I did to you! I'm so sorry!"

Avery glanced at his shoulders that were full of scratches from her nails. On his right shoulder, she'd actually drawn blood.

"Are ye kiddin'? These scratches are badges of honor! Means I've done somethin' right." Avery pulled her in for a kiss, and then said, "I'm half hopin' somebody'll ask me where I got 'em!"

Remy laughed happily and wrapped her arms around him. "Oh, Avery, you are one incredible lover." She let a deep, happy, and exhausted sigh.

Avery stroked her hair and said, "I love you, Remy. You can't know how much."

Chapter 27

Theresa wrapped her arms around Sean as they swayed together on the dance floor. To say that she found her boyfriend desirable in his military dress blues was a vast understatement. He looked unbelievably sexy in his crisp, blue uniform, with a white turndown collared shirt and a double Windsor necktie. Theresa moaned as she ran her hands across the fabric.

"Have I told you how incredibly sexy you look in this uniform, Sean?" Theresa murmured seductively.

"You might have mentioned it several hundred times," Sean said with a grin. Theresa knew how proud he was of his military career, and she knew it pleased him that she found him so irresistible in his military garb.

Theresa's lips found his, and she kissed him with more intensity than was probably appropriate on a public dance floor at a wedding. "Oh, Sean," she moaned in his ear. "You're making me *crazy*."

"I'm not doing anything," Sean said, knowing damn well how turned on she was by him and enjoying every moment. "Watch out, or you'll get drool all over my uniform."

Theresa laughed and kissed him again, harder and longer. "I can't help it. You just look so damned...*heroic*...in this outfit. You know

I've never seen you actually wear it in person before. The only time I've ever seen you in it was in the official photo when you got your Airman's medal…for *bravery.*"

Theresa could never understand why some women had a thing for bad boys. Not her. She had a serious hero complex. There was nothing sexier than a strong, brave, good guy. And that was Sean all over.

"I can't wait any more, Sean." Theresa told him, eyes flashing.

"What do you mean?" he asked her warily.

"I need to have you. *Now.*"

"You can't be serious," Sean asked, eyes wide. He was fairly used to Theresa's wild eccentricities, but sneaking off to have sex at her best friend's wedding was crazy even for her.

"I mean it. You're my *hero,* Sean," Theresa said seductively, nuzzling his neck. "And I need you to rescue me from my sexual frustration."

"What frustration? We did it last night after the rehearsal dinner at the hotel. And you didn't sound frustrated then, the way you were screaming my name." Sean said with amusement.

"I know, but you weren't wearing *this,*" Theresa said tugging on his uniform.

"I wasn't wearin' anything!"

"I can't help it, Sean," Theresa said, and now the frustration was clear in her voice. "I need you to take me, *hard,* while you're wearing your dress blues. I can't wait until tonight."

Sean looked into her pleading eyes, and she knew his resolve was weakening. She could also feel the bulge between his legs growing larger by the moment.

"Baby, you know this is my fantasy," Theresa said, running her finger across his lips.

Sean nodded. He knew. He frequently made love to her while

wearing his dog tags around his neck because it drove her wild with desire. He'd also once taken her up against the wall with his camo fatigue pants around his ankles. Theresa always came hardest when he was wearing some kind of military gear.

Sean looked nervously around. "Okay, but we have to be quick. And you *can't scream*. I mean it! If Lucy found out what we were up to at her wedding—"

Theresa's eyes lit it. "I promise. Let's go!"

With that, she grabbed Sean's hand and pulled him off the dance floor and dragged him off to the bridal room.

The bridal room door didn't lock, so Sean put a chair up against the doorknob to keep anyone from coming in. Theresa sat down on a table and looked at him hungrily.

"Come to me, baby," Theresa said, reaching for him. Sean pushed her down on the table, then he reached under her dress and pulled down her panties. "Oh, Sean, Oh God, Sean."

Theresa kept her eyes open as she watched him unbuckle the pants of that delicious uniform. She didn't want to miss one moment of her heroic staff-sergeant boyfriend as he made passionate if quick love to her in that gorgeous getup.

"You know there's certain code of conduct I'm supposed to maintain in this uniform—"

"Take me, Sean!" Theresa pleaded.

Sean climbed up on the table, his pants down but still dressed otherwise. He opened her legs and flung her right foot over his shoulder. She opened her mouth to cry out but he reminded her, "*Don't scream*, baby."

"I'll try," Theresa panted. He rammed himself inside her, and she pressed her lips together to stifle the cry that ached to escape from her mouth. She whimpered with pleasure as he thrust in and out of her, making the table squeak underneath her.

"God, you feel good, baby," Sean said in a husky voice. He glanced a bit nervously toward the door. They both knew this had to be a quickie if they were going to get away with it. Sean reached between her legs and began gently stroking her clit to get her there faster.

"S-Sean, Sean, Oh, God, Sean," Theresa was so aroused and the strokes of his finger were so perfect that she knew it wouldn't take long for her to reach orgasm. "Oh, Sean…I'm *coming*…I'm *coming*!"

"I know baby, but you can't scream!" Sean said.

Theresa opened her mouth to do just that, and Sean pressed his mouth over hers to stifle her cries of passion. She felt his lips tremble with laughter as he tried to shut her up with his kiss. Her orgasm slammed into her with wave after wave after wave of intense, blissful pleasure. She gripped his shoulders, and the feel of the rough crispness of his uniform only intensified her climax. When her body finally stopped spasming and she lay back on the table, Sean finally took his mouth off hers.

Sean kept thrusting in and out of her, chasing his own orgasm. He gripped the heel of her stiletto, which was still over his right shoulder. "These shoes are so goddamned sexy."

"Next time I'll wear the shoes and nothing else," Theresa said, still gasping for breath.

Sean moaned, and apparently that image was enough to push him over the edge as he emptied himself inside her. Theresa felt the strong vibrations of his orgasm ripple through her body. He lay on top of her for a moment, gasping for breath, then shifted off her a bit so she could breathe without his full weight on her.

He looked down and her and asked, "Feel better now?"

"God bless America," Theresa moaned, making him laugh. "Thank you for servicing me, Sergeant.

"My pleasure. *Believe me.*"

Theresa looked at him adoringly. "I love you so much, Sean."

"I love you, too. You're crazy, but I wouldn't have you any other way."

Sean slid his arm underneath her and pulled her close, holding her as best as he could on the hard wood of the table. He kissed her tenderly, and she ran her fingers through his hair.

*****

Lucy narrowed her eyes when she saw Theresa walk back into the ballroom, straightening her hair and her dress. She knew *exactly* what her friend had been up to.

"I cannot *believe* her!" Lucy exclaimed.

"Whut?" Jesse asked, following her gaze.

Lucy lifted her skirts and stalked over to Theresa with Jesse close on her heels. Sean headed over to the bar, leaving Theresa alone for the moment.

"Oh, hey, Lu—"

"You had sex at my wedding!" Lucy said.

Jesse's eyes opened wide, while Theresa feigned innocence. "What?" she asked.

"Don't *what* me. I used to live with you. You know how many times I've seen you stagger out of your bedroom after a night with Sean lookin' like you can barely walk? I know your after-sex look, and that is it!" Lucy said, gesturing at her friend.

"We didn't have sex at the wedding. It was at the reception!"

Jesse laughed out loud, then put his hand over his mouth, not wanted to upset Lucy any more.

"It was the dress blues. I couldn't help it!" Theresa said, pleading with her eyes for Lucy to understand.

Lucy couldn't stay mad for one second longer. She never could hold a grudge, especially with her best friend. She burst out laughing, and Jesse joined in and so did Theresa.

"God, you're a slut," Lucy teased.

"I know, right? I'm sorry," Theresa told her.

Sean came walking up holding a beer and a glass of wine. He handed the wine to Theresa, then looked at Lucy.

"What?" Sean asked, perplexed by Lucy's accusatory stare.

Lucy put her hands on her hips. Sean looked at Theresa questioningly, eyes wide.

"She didn't tell me. I guessed," Lucy told him.

"Oh," Sean said, looking appropriately guilty. He put his beer down on a nearby table. "I'm sorry, Lucy. We didn't mean to be disrespectful on your big day."

Lucy looked into Sean's sweet, sorrowful eyes. He was such a good man, and he loved and cherished Theresa the way she deserved.

"I know. And you do look handsome in your uniform," Lucy said with a smile. She slid her arm around his waist and rested her head on his shoulder. Sean grinned and slipped his arm around her, eagerly hugging her back.

"She started it!" Sean said, looking at Theresa.

"I don't doubt it!" Lucy said.

Jesse raised his eyebrow and nodded at Sean, clearly approving of his amorous activities.

"I saw that, Spenser!" Lucy chided.

"Hey, you let Remy off the hook. I saw her sneak away with Avery," Theresa said with a sly grin. Lucy nodded happily.

"She's such a sweet girl," Sean said. "I'm so glad she has him in her life for good now. She's been through such hell, and she really deserves some stability in her life."

Lucy turned to Theresa, "You didn't tell Remy yet, did you?"

Theresa smiled and shook her head. "No, not yet. I don't want to overwhelm her. She's got enough to celebrate for today."

Lucy nodded. She stood on her tiptoes to kiss Sean on the cheek, then went over to cuddle up next to her new husband. Sean and Theresa headed back out to the dance floor.

"Seems like everyone is having sex on my wedding day but me." Lucy said to Jesse.

"Don't you worry, my rose," Jesse said, nuzzling her neck. "I can't wait to ravish you once we get to that bridal suite. You've been lookin' so sweet and innocent in your white dress all day. Makes me want to do some not-so-innocent things to you."

"That sounds *wonderful*," Lucy said, wishing they could rush off right now like Remy and Avery had done.

Chapter 28

Jesse swiped the key card for the hotel room and opened the door for Lucy. She was about to walk into the room when he stopped her.

"Wait! Ain't I supposed to carry you over the threshold?" Jesse asked.

"I don't know," Lucy said. "Isn't that just for when you get home?"

"Better safe than sorry," Jesse said, eyes twinkling. "Don't want bad luck."

Jesse scooped up his giggling bride in his arms and carried her into the hotel room. The first thing she did was kick off her high-heeled shoes while she was still off her feet.

"Finally! Those things *hurt!*"

Jesse kissed her, then gently set her down. She glanced around the fancy hotel room.

"Wow, this is such a nice ro—" She stopped short when she caught sight of a vase filled with yellow roses. "Oh, Jesse."

Lucy walked over and gazed at the flowers, then bent down to breathe in the scent. She looked up and saw Jesse smiling at her.

"You're always so thoughtful. Thank you," Lucy said, truly touched by the gesture.

"Well, I figger this time you didn't have to pay for 'em yourself!"

Lucy smiled, remembering when Jesse was still dead and had lamented that he couldn't bring her flowers. She had bought yellow roses for herself and showed them to him, saying they really were from him since he would have gotten them for her if it had been humanly possible. Then she had taken out the card that came with the roses and asked what he would have written on it if he could have.

Lucy lifted her wedding gown and walked over to her purse and pulled out her wallet. She took out a small card and handed it to him.

Jesse smiled as he read the words. *To my beautiful rose, All my love, Jesse.* "You kept it!"

Lucy nodded. "I wrote it down, but they were your words. Of course I kept it."

"How you feelin', baby?" he asked.

"Tired. Happy, but tired," Lucy said.

"Darlin', I'll understand if you're too tired to—"

"No way!" Lucy protested, then said in a sultry voice, "You promised to ravish me."

She leaned back against the wall and looked at him expectantly. He grinned. "That I did, that I did."

Jesse looked at her with desire and walked toward her. She drew in a deep breath, already excited, anticipating his touch. He pressed his mouth to hers, and she ran her fingers through his hair as she eagerly kissed him back.

"Oh, Lucy, I've been waitin' for this all day," Jesse said, kissing down her neck and down toward her breasts, which were plumped up thanks to the bodice of her gown.

"Me, too," Lucy said. "Jesse, you look so handsome in that tux."

"Darlin', I wanna make love to you while you're still wearin' your gown," Jesse murmured in her ear.

"Fine with me," Lucy said breathlessly, suddenly no longer tired.

Jesse pressed his mouth to hers and kissed her deeply, passionately. She loved the way his body felt against hers. "Oh, Jesse, we've never done it up against the wall before." The desire in her voice made it clear that she was up to try something new.

"Oh, God, Lucy," Jesse said, gripping her shoulders and pushing her hard against the wall.

"Yes, Jesse, *yes*," Lucy moaned. They'd had sex on the floor once, and she remembered how good it had felt, how deeply Jesse had been able to penetrate her in that position. She could hardly wait for him to spread her legs and ram inside her against the wall.

Jesse lifted his head and looked into her eyes. "I feel kinda bad, though."

"Why?" Lucy asked, perplexed.

"I dunno. I mean, I feel like I ought to be sweeter with you, ya know. For our first time as man and wife?" He looked at her questioningly, wanting so much to do the right thing for her.

"We've got plenty of time for sweet, my darling. I want you to take me against the wall. In my wedding dress. *Now*," Lucy said, breathing heavily with anticipation.

Jesse grinned and said, "I like the way you think."

He pressed his mouth against hers again and began fumbling with her gown, trying to get through all the ruffles and lace. After several moments, he chuckled. "I can't *find* you!"

Lucy laughed, too. "Well, don't give up!"

"Never," Jesse said, sounding determined. He dropped to his knees and lifted her dress that way. Lucy rested her head on the wall and waited. She could no longer see Jesse under all that fluff, but she could feel him.

First, she felt his hands on her panties as he pulled them off. Then, he slipped his forefinger and middle finger inside her.

"Oh, Jesse." He stroked her with his fingers for a short while, then she felt his tongue swipe across her clit. "Oh, Jesse!" Lucy cried louder, as she closed her eyes and surrendered to the kind of intense pleasure every bride should experience on her wedding night.

Jesse flipped her dress up higher so she could finally see him as he pleasured her. Lucy looked down and watched as he gently picked up her leg and draped it over his shoulder, opening her up wider.

"Oh!" Lucy cried, as he continued to stroke her with his tongue. "Oh, Jesse, oh, Jesse....don't stop...please don't stop...Oh, Jesse.....*don't stop!*"

Lucy always pleaded with him not to stop when she was close to coming. Jesse was fully aware of this, and usually took that as his cue to go faster. He flicked his tongue more rapidly, making her scream even more. "Jesse! Jesse!" She let out one last cry of ecstasy as a powerful orgasm claimed her. She threw her head back against the wall as her body shattered into paroxysms of sheer bliss. Finally, she stopped crying out and gasped to catch her breath.

Jesse stood up, and she threw her arms around his neck. "Oh, Jesse...oh, God, you're so damn good."

Lucy reached for his belt and pulled it off as quickly as she could. She unbuttoned his pants and pushed them down along with his underwear. He was rock hard and looked even bigger than normal, which was truly impressive. Then she waited for him to make the next move.

Jesse grabbed her leg and flung it over his shoulder. He seemed concerned that he had been too rough with her, because he glanced up at her face. Lucy leaned back against the wall, ready for him to take her. Without hesitation, he rammed himself into her.

"Jesse! Oh, God, *yes!*"

He pounded her hard against the wall, all the while looking down at her dress. Lucy loved seeing how aroused he was by having sex with her in her wedding gown. It never occurred to her that it would be such a turn-on, but she thoroughly enjoyed watching Jesse's pleasure. He had satisfied her so completely, and she wanted nothing less for him.

"Lucy, Lucy, my darlin'," Jesse moaned as he thrust in and out of her. Lucy still found that Texas accent of his sexy as hell, and she loved when he spoke during sex.

"Oh, Jesse, you feel so good," Lucy cried, her arms wrapped around his neck as she held on for dear life. She loved feeling him so deeply inside her. Lucy felt his cock tighten within her, and she knew he was close. Sure enough, he let out one final groan and came hard, gripping her shoulders so tightly that it hurt a bit.

Jesse took a moment or two to catch his breath, then gently eased out of her, carefully putting her leg back down on the floor. He gazed into her eyes and affectionately stroked her hair. Lucy let out a happy sigh. So far, they'd had sex on the floor, in the car, and on top of a bar, and no matter where they were or what crazy position they might experiment with, Jesse was always tender and affectionate afterward. *Always.* He always kissed her softly, told her that he loved her, and held her in his arms. He made her feel valued, cherished. Adored.

"Thank you for marrying me," Jesse said tenderly as he looked into her eyes.

"Thank you for asking," Lucy said with a smile.

Jesse looked at her now fairly disheveled wedding gown. He had ravished her all right, and she'd loved every thrilling moment of it.

"You look so beautiful in that dress, and I know I'll never forget the way you looked today," Jesse said to her. "But that thing *cannot* be comfortable!"

Lucy laughed. "No, not really."

"Then let's get you out of it," Jesse said, taking her by the hand and leading her to the bed. She sat on the bed, and Jesse straddled her from behind and got to work on unbuttoning the dozens of buttons on the back of her dress. He stopped every few buttons to plant tender kisses on her back as he went. When he got all the buttons undone, he helped her step out of her dress and slipped her nightgown over her head.

After brushing their teeth, they climbed into bed together, happy but utterly exhausted. They snuggled up close, warm and comfortable in bed.

"I love you, Jesse."

"I love you, too, my beautiful rose. And I'll love you forever, darling."

Chapter 29

Remy woke up the next morning, still wrapped in Avery's arms. It took her a moment to remember where she was and what was going on. Her face broke into a huge smile as the memories of yesterday came flooding back. Avery was *alive*. They had finally made love. And now he was holding her close.

She sat up in bed and looked down at Avery, who was gazing up at her with those beautiful gray eyes she adored.

"Good morning, me love," he said in a voice that seemed even deeper this early in the morning.

"Good morning. Did you sleep well?" she asked.

"I certainly did. Don't think I ever slept so soundly in my life." He thought for a moment, then asked, "I don't snore, do I?"

Remy giggled and shook her head. "Are you hungry?"

Avery looked guilty when he said, "I really am."

"Don't worry. They've got free breakfast at the hotel. After that, well, we'll figure something out."

Avery nodded. "Do you want to get a shower first?"

"No, you go ahead. Do you, you know, know how?" she asked.

"Yes, but only because Jesse showed me how everything works."

"Good," Remy said with a smile. She leaned down and pressed her lips to his.

"Hmmm. Who needs food? If I get to wake up to your kisses every day, that's all I care about," Avery said.

"I promise to kiss you every single morning for the rest of our lives," Remy told him.

Avery looked as if he might tear up. "How wonderful," he said softly.

He got up, and Remy admired his chest as he headed toward the shower. He had slept in camouflage pants, so she figured they probably belonged to Sean.

If I can manage to scrape together a few bucks, I can at least take Avery to a thrift store so he can pick out some clothes of his own, Remy thought.

Remy washed her face and brushed her teeth at the sink that was outside the bathroom as Avery took his shower. She glanced at the television and was about to turn on the news when she spied an envelope on the floor near the door. It said REMY on it.

Anxiety welled up in her. What on earth could that possibly be? She hated checking the mail at home because it was usually nothing but bills; therefore she had a negative association with anything addressed to her. It was never good news.

Her hands shook a little as she opened the envelope. It was a handwritten letter. Remy skimmed to the bottom and relaxed when she saw that it was from Theresa. Another piece of paper fell from the envelope and fluttered to the ground. Remy gasped when she picked it up. It was a check made out to Remy Waters for five thousand dollars.

Dearest Remy,

I was going to tell you this in person, but seeing as you currently have an extremely sexy Irish man in your bed, I figured it might be best to write you a letter...

I can't begin to tell you how happy I am that Avery is back among the living and that you two can finally begin to build what I know is going to be a wonderful life together. Rest assured, Sean is already working on getting Avery's documents together. His friend is going to have quite the side business going with all these soldiers coming back from the dead!

I also want to tell you how much I admire you for everything you have accomplished in your life already with absolutely no help from your family. I could never have made it this far in my schooling and in my life without the generous support, both emotional and financial, from my family. You've done so much all on your own, but I want you to know that you never have to be alone ever again. You have a big family now. Jesse and Sean are your brothers, and Lucy and I are your sisters. Avery is your best friend and now your lover (and girl, I want DETAILS!!!) We all have your back, girl, now and forever.

I've been talking to my dad about you lately, and he was very touched by your story. He is just as amazed as I am by your strength, courage, and incredible kindness in spite of all the obstacles life has thrown at you. He is a man of strong Christian faith, and believes in helping others. I told him the way you helped Ellis and believed in him when no one else did (leaving out the fact that the dude was dead, of course). As I knew he would, my father wanted to do something to ease your burdens and reward you for the kindness you have shown to others. That's why he made the decision to pay off the rest of your college loan. I know you have a hard time accepting help, but I assure you there's no stopping my father when his mind is made up. The man is LOADED, so please don't worry about the money. They paid for my college, just as Lucy's parents paid for most of her schooling. There's no reason why you should have to shoulder the heavy debt of your education alone, not when you have family now.

Remy, please understand that you are no charity case. You have earned this money, through every kind word you've ever said, every smile you've given to a stranger, and every person whose life you've touched with your tender grace. You came from nothing, had nothing, and yet somehow you always found you had something to give to others. Please, please, let others help you now. The check is to help get you started on your new life with Avery. The man is HUGE (and I did I mention sexy?) and you're gonna need the money if you're gonna keep that guy fed!

Love ya, honey,

Theresa Hetty
P.S. The college loan is a done deal, but I know I can't force you to cash that check. All I can say is — please accept our help. If you can't do it for yourself, do it for Avery.

Remy had read the letter four times and was weeping by the time Avery got out of the shower.

"Remy, my God, what happened?" Avery said, fastening a towel around his waist and rushing to her side. He looked horrified at the sight of her crying.

She looked up at him, eyes full of tears but she was smiling. "It looks like your coming back to life wasn't the only miracle."

Avery's face relaxed a bit when he realized Remy was all right. She handed him the check first.

"*Jaysus*," Avery said as he saw the amount.

Then she handed him the letter, watching him as he read it. He smiled at the first line about the sexy Irish man. She watched his eyes as he scanned the letter. "My God, Remy…"

"I know!" Remy said, wiping her eyes.

Avery finished reading the letter and looked at her, stunned. Then he said, "She's right, ye know. About your kindness. The way you just want to take care of everyone around you. Even when ye don't have enough to eat and you barely have the strength to go on, you still want to help everybody." He smiled fondly at her. "There are so many things that I love about you, *a chuisle*, but your kindness is what I love above all. First time ye saw me, you could see I was lost, a total mess, and ye came runnin' up to me, wantin' to help."

Remy stood up and grabbed a tissue from the nightstand and wiped her eyes. She walked over to Avery and he stood up.

She looked up and into his eyes and said, "Oh, Avery. Theresa's right. We're going to have the most wonderful life together."

Avery bent down and kissed her softly and tenderly. Remy kissed back with forceful passion, making him stagger backward a bit.

"Avery, you were *amazing* last night…but I need *more*."

Remy reached around his waist and yanked the towel right off him. He chuckled warmly.

"*Tá grá agam duit*, Avery," Remy said.

"I love you, too, *a chuisle*," Avery said with a smile.

Epilogue

Remy and Avery were married in a quiet ceremony at the courthouse just as soon as he received the proper paperwork to make him legal in the eyes of the system. Remy didn't even bother to tell her family that she was getting married. Lucy, Jesse, Theresa, and Sean were in attendance and provided all the familial love and support the couple needed.

Avery found work at a grocery store during the day and took a few college classes at night. It turned out that he had quite a head for business. He and Remy were able to secure a business loan and opened a quaint bed and breakfast in the Colonial Williamsburg area in Virginia.

Remy and Avery befriended all the ghosts who haunted the area, and Remy loved running her own ghost tours. The spirits were happy to give a good scare to the guests who were seeking a thrill, and always backed off from those who were a bit too timid. Remy was like a sister or even a mother figure to the spirits, much the way Fillis had been to all of her adopted children. She did her best to bring peace to the spirits and helped them to cross over whenever possible. Those who were still earthbound were more than happy to stand guard over the bed and breakfast during the several times in the year when it was closed to the public, allowing Avery and Remy the chance to travel like they had always dreamed.

They remained in close contact with Lucy, Jesse, Theresa, and Sean, and managed to make friends all over the country and the world as they traveled.

It was important that Theresa and Sean marry as well, so she could live with him on whatever military base where he was stationed. Sean had begun writing about his struggles with PTSD and planned on writing a book in the hopes of helping other soldiers. When he eventually retired from active military duty, he wanted to travel around and give talks to soldiers, hoping to break the stigma of the debilitating disease. Theresa graduated from school and began a career counseling soldiers, specializing in those who suffered with PTSD and those who were victims of sexual assault in the military, both male and female. After her graduation, Theresa married Sean in an elaborate military ceremony on base paid for by her parents. Remy was thrilled to finally be able to meet her generous benefactor, Theresa's father. She had written him many letters, telling him of her success and how she was putting her college degree to good use. Remy asked him to dance at the wedding, and he happily agreed. He was one of the kindest, most charming gentlemen she had ever met. As for Theresa, it wasn't easy, but she managed to make it all the way through the wedding ceremony and reception before having sex with her new husband.

It was the first time Lucy had ever seen Jesse cry.

She greeted him at the door when he came home from work one day and wrapped her arms around him.

"Hi, darlin'," Jesse said, kissing his wife.

"You know, I've been thinking," she began.

"Oh, no, should I be worried?" Jesse asked, a twinkle in his eye.

"You know how I have lots of special names for you like darling, my love, my cowboy, Rebel-of-My-Heart…"

Jesse chuckled and said, "I believe that last one's my favorite."

Lucy smiled. "I think I have another one for you."

"'Zat right? And what might that be?"

Softly, she said, "How about…Daddy?"

Jesse stared at her for a moment, processing the information. Then he looked at her plaintively, silently pleading with her to tell him it was true. It had always been his dream to have children, a dream he had thought was lost to him when he had died so young in the war.

Lucy gently stroked his face and said, "You're gonna be a father, Jesse."

He glanced down at her stomach, then back up to her face. "Lucy," he whispered.

She pulled him into her arms and held him close. When she released him, she saw that his eyes were filled with tears.

"Thank you, my darling," Jesse said, letting his tears spill down his cheeks.

Lucy laughed gently and said, "Well, I had help, you know." She took his hand and placed it on her belly.

Jesse nodded. "*Our* baby."

"Yes," Lucy said, pulling him into her arms again.

As soon as the ultrasound revealed they were having a daughter, Jesse began referring to the baby as his little Rosebud. He read lots of parenting books and spoke to Lucy's belly so much that she swore the child would be born with a Southern accent. They pored over baby name books together but had trouble coming up with a name that sounded just right for their child.

Then one day, after spending the day shopping with her mother, the answer finally came to Lucy.

"Jesse, I think I know what we should name the baby," Lucy said as she sat on the couch next to him.

"Yeah?"

"Sarah Fillis."

Jesse's eyes opened wide. "Both my mamas!"

"Yes," Lucy said, putting her arm around him and snuggling up next to him. "I just keep thinking how lucky I am that my family is close by and can be a part of our baby's life. This way yours can be, too."

"Yeah...yeah! That's her name!" he said, smiling and rubbing Lucy's growing belly.

When Sarah Fillis finally arrived, Jesse pronounced her the second most beautiful girl he'd ever seen. She had his blue-gray eyes and soft, brown hair. The hospital was overrun by Westbrooks clamoring to see the new baby, but Jesse and Lucy finally had a moment alone in the hospital at the end of the day.

Lucy held Sarah, who was sleeping in her arms, as Jesse leaned down and pressed his head down to cuddle up next to his wife and daughter. He closed his eyes, savoring the moment. When he lifted his head, his eyes were wet.

"Lucy, it's like you're makin' every dream I ever had come true, one by one."

She smiled up at him, and he kissed her softly.

"I love you, Jesse."

"I love you, too, darlin'."

Join my mailing list at
http://wannabepride.com/blog/?page_id=3466
and be the first to hear about my new book releases.
Sign up now and I'll send you **TWO free books**!

The importance of online reviews for an author **cannot be overstated**! I hope you will take just a few seconds of your time to leave a review on Goodreads or whichever online store/venue you purchased Forever, Darling. I would be so grateful if you could rate the book from 1 – 5 stars, and then leave a quick review that can be as short as one or two sentences.

Heartfelt thanks to you!

I would love to hear from you! You can contact me in any or all of the following ways:
Email
   lindafausnet@gmail.com
Facebook
   www.facebook.com/lindafausnet (author page)
Twitter
   @LindaFausnet

ATTENTION ROMANCE NOVEL FANS!
I hope you'll join our romance novel fan club on Facebook - **Romance Novel Addicts Anonymous** - Here you can profess your love for all things romance in the privacy of a closed Facebook group!

Acknowledgments

Thanks to my beta readers and editors, Joanna Hughes and Katriena Knights. Thanks also to proofreaders Dan Kalwa and Erick Boeder. Thanks to Chuck DeKett for his beautiful cover design. Thanks as always for the support of my parents Cecelia Wasiljov and Bernard Wasiljov, and my sister and webmaster Zann Wasiljov, and my best friend Lisa Winders. Thanks to my beloved husband and real-life romantic hero, Bill, and my beautiful children Celia and Noah. Thanks also to the terrific tour guides, shopkeepers, and restaurant workers in Gettysburg. I am a frequent visitor to the town and they are always wonderfully knowledgeable and hospitable. If you ever in the area, be sure to take in an historic tour and a ghost tour! You also may want to visit O'Rorke's tavern. The place is Avery's namesake and the inspiration for Meade's Tavern.

35797641R00209

Made in the USA
Lexington, KY
07 April 2019